PACK RIVALS PART TWO

AN OMEGAVERSE ROMANCE

THE ROCKVIEW OMEGAVERSE

HANNAH HAZE

Hannah Haze x

Front covered designed by EVE Graphic Design LLC

Edited by Buckley's Books

Created with Vellum

FOREWORD

Human beings are flawed. We all make mistakes. Writing a book where the characters have to amend for those mistakes has been a lot of fun. Writing a character who has a heart big enough to forgive even better. Time for a happy ending folks! Enjoy!

If you do spot any typos in this book, please drop me a line so I can make it right: hannahhazewrites@gmail.com (Or just drop me an email anyway. I love to chat!).

You can find a guide to my omegaverse at the end of this book. If you're new to omegaverse, you may want to take a look.

This book is a sweeter 'why choose' (reverse harem) omegaverse with one female omega character and six (yes six!) alpha males. There are scenes of violence and abduction in this book as well as a parent who is terminally ill. The female main character has been in an emotionally abusive relationship in the past. For more detailed content warnings, please visit my website.

PROLOGUE

ngel

Ten years ago

Time stops.

Freezes.

Ceases.

So does the beat of my heart.

The breath in my lungs.

The sparking of my nerves.

Time stops and when it starts once more, nothing is the same.

My mind takes several long minutes to start churning again, to compute what I'm seeing.

Like my brain doesn't want to believe. Like it can't. Like it's trying to reject the very truth presented before my eyes.

Because it can't be true, can it?

Not my girl? Celia.

Not my brother? Axel.

Not together.

But it is true.

It's plain to see.

They're outside the door of his apartment.

He's kissing her.

My brother is kissing my girl.

She balances on the tips of her toes, lips moving against his, palms resting on his chest. His hand is tight on her elbow, his mouth pressed to hers.

The truth of it is there. Plain as day. Plain for everyone to see. Everyone, including me.

My heart cracks. Right down the middle. The pain so intense, I huddle over my knees and try not to hurl.

The two people I love the most in the world. Behind my back. Betraying me.

How? How could they do it?

I dry heave right there on the sidewalk outside his apartment block, and as the last violent retch wracks through my body, the pain ceases. In its place rampages rage; red hot and raw.

I jolt upright, tipping my head back to peer up at the balcony that runs around the apartment doors.

They're a pace apart now. Axel's talking to her. I can't see his face or hers.

She takes a step towards him and he takes one away. She laughs, and he shakes his head. Then she's spinning around and walking away. I watch her disappear into the stairwell, observe as Axel watches her go, his hand scraping through the dark hair on his head.

Does he feel any guilt? Any shame? Any reproach?

Does he feel anything at all?

No. He doesn't.

It's always been this way.

Always the same.

He could never stand for me to have anything of my own. He could never bear for me to have something he didn't. He could never let that be. He always had to take it. He always had to break it.

I shouldn't even be surprised.

I hear the click of her heels on the stairs, and I step into the shadows, my fists tight balls, my nails cutting deep into my palms. I watch her trot along the pathway, hips swaying, and climb into her car.

Her figure once had my blood pumping; now it runs cold in my veins.

Fuck, I liked that girl a lot.

Fuck, I thought she was the one.

Fuck, how could I get this so wrong?

I laugh bitterly to myself as she melts into the shadows.

Because there's cruel irony to this.

It's why I'm here after all.

To discuss it with my good old brother.

I shake my head and step back out into the lamplight. Axel's door is closed now.

But I don't give a shit.

I still have a word or two to say to my elder brother.

I climb the stairs slowly, each footstep growing heavier and heavier, weightier and weightier, as the anger inside me grows bolder and bolder, hotter and hotter until it's steaming through my veins.

I'm going to fucking kill him.

I'm going to hurt him like he's hurt me.

The image of them hangs in front of my eyes. Taunting me as I climb the stairs.

Other images too. Of them twined together, of him rutting her hard, of her taking his knot.

Of them laughing. Laughing at me.

Shit!

Shit!

I pause at the top of the staircase, gazing along the row of apartment doors. He shares this one with Nate. We talked about getting a place together. All of us, once Silver leaves the army. That's not going to happen anymore.

A lot of our plans are no longer going to happen.

My feet carry me past the other doors and soon I'm standing outside number 16. The numbers spin and it seems like another man entirely lifts his hand and pounds on the door.

I swallow. My mouth is dry and I feel like I'm choking on my own fucking tonsils, every breath sharp in my constricted throat.

More footsteps. This time heavy.

They stop on the other side of the door.

There's a moment, a moment as he reaches out to take the handle, that I could turn around, that I could leave, that I could pretend I never saw a thing. Because this is the moment, this is the moment everything changes. Once he's opened that door, there is no going back.

But my feet won't budge. They are rooted to the ground, determined to see this through, determined to unleash my anger on the man who has shattered all my dreams.

The door swings back. Axel stands in the dark hallway.

He knows. He knows as soon as he sees my face.

His brow furrows. His shoulders tense.

He's ready for the blow, but he's prepared to preempt the damn thing anyway.

"It's not what you think, Angel," he says.

And it's something about those words, those words in particular, that has me erupting like a fucking volcano.

Does he think I'm stupid? Does he think I'm blind? Does he think I didn't see it all?

I slam my fist into his jaw, and though I hear my knuckles crunch, though I perceive my skin split, I don't feel anything. Nothing at all.

Axel stumbles backwards.

"Jesus Christ," he mumbles. "Will you just stop, Angel? Will you just stop for one minute and talk to me?"

"I saw you," I say quietly, coming for him again. "I saw you together."

I swing at him a second time. But this time he ducks and my arm flies through empty air. He barrels into me, forcing himself right up into my space so I can't swing for him again.

"No," he says.

I find the front of his shirt, gripping it in my hands. I slam him into the wall. But he's just as big as me, just as strong, and he pushes right back, jamming me into the wall on the opposite side of the hall.

"You had to take her," I yell into his face. "You had to take her from me. You couldn't let me have this, could you?"

I push him and he pushes right back. We tussle in the hallway, stumbling through the open door and out onto the balcony.

"I don't want her," he yells.

"Of course, you fucking don't, but you had to take her anyway."

I stamp on his toe and kick at his leg and he jabs me in

the ribs, the force of it ricocheting all the way through my bones.

"You're being fucking ridiculous," he spits.

And the rage magnifies tenfold.

Ridiculous? *Ridiculous*?

"You know what's fucking *ridiculous*, brother?" I snarl into his face. "If you'd waited, if you'd been patient, you could have had her. I wanted to make her ours. Our pack omega."

"Then what the fuck does it matter?" he snaps back.

"You went behind my back." I shove him hard. He stumbles away from me and now I have the space to launch at him. I punch his face and his head, his chest and his gut.

There're more footsteps, running, then halting, and then Nate in the doorway.

"What the fuck's going on?" he yells.

"Stay out of this," I snap.

But the distraction has given Axel the upper hand. He wrestles his arm around my neck, jamming me into a headlock. He squeezes.

"You're a fucking idiot," he tells me. "A fucking idiot."

"Stop it," Nate says, trying to pull Axel off me. "Stop this. What the fuck is going on?"

Axel's arms go limp and Nate crowbars us apart.

My brother spits on the ground. Sweat skids down his face. The night is hot and steamy, the air heavy. My own sweat drips into my eyes. I blink it away, grinding my molars together.

"He's being a fucking idiot," Axel mutters again, and I run at him, run at him hard, run at him with ten tons of anger.

I slam into his body, and he stumbles backward. One

step, two steps, and then he's losing his footing, his feet slipping from under him.

Time stops again.

Axel hangs in the air.

Horror slaps across his face.

And then he's falling, falling over the balcony railing, falling through the air.

"Axel," I scream, lurching forward.

But it's too late.

I can't reach him.

My hand swipes through empty air a second time.

My brother falls.

And everything changes forever.

1

Connor

I'VE BEEN SENT to track down Nate and bring him home.

I'm the only one who ever can.

That's because Axel, Mrs. Finch and all the others assume I have to drag him kicking and screaming from one of the strip clubs, gambling dens, or maybe some illegal fight scene.

They're wrong.

To some degree anyway. I'm sure he thundered his way through all those joints, like a tornado of destruction leaving a path of floating bank notes, busted noses and broken hearts.

However, like every fucking tornado, eventually he'll blow himself out. Even a force of nature like Nate has limited funds and limited energy.

Eventually, all that rage will burn itself out and he'll be nursing his wounds.

If I leave it long enough, give him time to cycle through his rampage, there's only one place I'll find him.

I slam my fist on the horn and yell a string of abuse at the car meandering along in front of me. The grandad driving seems to be incapable of finding the accelerator. As soon as I can, I swerve into the oncoming traffic and overtake the stupid fucker, giving him the finger and a murderous glare as I do.

Every fucking minute is precious. Every second wasted a fucking failure.

"Call Nate," I tell the car's interior computer system.

"Calling Nate," the computer tells me and, for the tenth time already, I hear the call connect straight through to voicemail.

I'm going to smack him around the head for that.

Usually, I have unending amounts of patience for my packmate. Today, I have none.

I skid to a screeching halt outside *Nanny Moo's most marvelous ice cream parlor* and leap out, sprinting towards the brightly painted diner. The colors are hideous enough to give me a fucking migraine and the big cartoon cow dressed in a bonnet and frilly dress, a collection of farmyard friends gathered round her legs, has always creeped me the fuck out. It's the smile and the big teeth.

I have no fucking idea why Nate likes this place so much.

I slam open the door, some ditzy tune playing as I step through into the parlor, so fucking pink it looks like a candy floss exploded in here. The place is choc-a-block with children and their parents tucking into tall glasses of ice cream sundaes. Scores of tiny voices squeak and squeal and I flinch, scanning the place for Nate.

Immediately, I spot where he's lurking. That's because there's a ring of empty tables around him, everyone keeping the fuck out of the scary-looking man's way.

He's dressed all in black like he's auditioning for the part of Lucifer, and he's leaning back in his chair, his boots resting on the table top. Red liquid, I hope the kids mistake for ketchup, oozes down the leather and a large mountain of ice cream sits in front of him. It's untouched and melting as Nate stares at the ceiling.

I walk towards him, aware of the way parents wrap a protective arm around their kids and nervous eyes flick between us.

I don't give a fuck what these people think of us.

There's only one thing I give a fuck about right now.

"Nate," I bark, and his eyes drag away from the fan rotating above his head and meander towards me. They are brimming with anger and hurt, rejection and guilt.

Nate's always been good at putting on an act, hiding all that vulnerable shit that lurks deep inside him. At Nanny fucking Moo's, it always comes flooding to the surface.

It's like this place is both his kryptonite and his salvation.

"If you've come to drag me away, Connor, I'm–"

Usually, I'd flop down into the seat beside him, tug that ice cream towards me and gently, gently, nudge him towards home.

I haven't got time for all that mollycoddling shit today.

Bea is missing and the sooner we find her, the better.

"Nate," I cut through his words, "Nate, listen to me, man." He can hear the seriousness in my tone and he lifts his eyebrows. "Bea's gone."

He hammers his fist down on the spoon in front of him,

making it leap into the air and a woman sitting a few tables away yelps.

"I know she is, Connor."

"No." I shake my head firmly, making it clear that's not it. "She's missing." Nate cocks his head, the tendons in his neck popping out like steel wires. "Someone's taken her."

He swings his feet off the table and they meet the ground with a thump. The lady yelps a second time.

"Is this some kind of fucked up way you and Axel have–"

I glare at him, leaning down on the table, my eyes flaring with anger. "You think I'd kid around about something like this, Nate?"

He flicks his tongue against the ring in his lip, studying my face.

"Shit," he mutters. "Shit."

Then he's up on his feet, the spoon clattering to the floor along with his chair.

He slams a wad of notes on the table and then he's halfway out the door, pausing in the doorway to look back at me.

"Are you coming or not, motherfucker?" he calls.

I roll my eyes, hearing several small kids ask their moms what a motherfucker is, as I weave my way through the tables and step out into the street. The sky is heavy with gray clouds and I can smell the storm coming, rolling in from the ocean.

Nate paces as he waits for me to catch up, his switch-blade spinning in his right hand.

"Tell me," he says as I unlock the car and we both dive inside.

"Her cousin rang Axel. Said she dropped Bea off at the clinic–"

Nate wheels off a long string of expletives. I wait for him to finish, then continue.

"The cousin went back a few hours later to deliver Bea's phone, and she'd gone. No one could – or would," I add darkly, squeezing the steering wheel between my fingers so that I can see my white knuckles through the straining skin, "tell her where Bea was."

Nate fidgets in his seat, flicking the blade of his knife in and out.

"So we going there? To the clinic?"

"Axel and Angel are already on their way. I came to pick you up."

Nate's fingers freeze; the blade pauses halfway in and halfway out of its handle.

"Axel *and* Angel?"

I nod.

"What the fuck?" he growls.

I nod again. I can't get my head around it either. The two brothers have hardly said a civil word to each other – have hardly looked in each other's direction without fists flying – for nearly ten years. Yet, who was the first motherfucker Axel called when he heard Bea had been taken? Not me. Not Nate. Not even Mrs. fucking Finch.

No. He'd called his brother Angel.

"Are you fucking with me?" Nate growls, giving me a look that would have most people shaking in their boots.

"No, I'm not."

We're both quiet for a moment, watching as fat raindrops begin to hit the windscreen and slide down the glass. The wipers switch on, creaking back and forth, and the beat has my heart pumping faster.

"Who took her?" Nate asks finally.

"We don't know."

"You haven't looked into it yet," Nate says, with a disapproving tone.

I snap my head round. "I was looking for your sorry ass, you dickwad."

Nate slides the nail of his thumb along the blade of his knife, the metal singing when his nail flicks against the point. "I'm going to kill them. I'm going to slice every single one of their fingers off their hands, and then I'm going to twist this knife in their gut and watch the motherfucker bleed out, slowly and painfully and—"

"Get in line!" I swing the car left, racing down the side streets and avoiding the gridlocked city roads.

Nate's eyes flick up and down the street. "Where are we going?"

"Back to the apartment."

He tugs on the door handle. "Nope. I'm going to that clinic, Connor. I'm going to wring every neck until someone tells me where she is."

Which is exactly why Axel ordered me to take him to the apartment. We need to find Bea and getting our asses arrested for busting up a load of medics will only hinder our aim. Nate can't be trusted to control his fists. Axel, he's always had a way of making people talk without ever having to swing his arm. It's his persona. It's enough to encourage tongues to wag. Throw his brother into the mix and they'll be wagging like a puppy's tail.

"Axel's orders. Head to the apartment." Nate sinks into his seat. He may be a fucking maniac, but when it comes to Axel, he does what he's told. "We're meeting Silver and Hardy there."

Nate chuckles bitterly. "This is fucked up. Are you telling me we're working with Pack Boston now?"

"You want to get the girl back or not?"

"Do I want those fuckers to steal her from right under our noses?"

"We'll worry about that later. We need to focus on finding her first." The steering wheel groans under my tightening grip. "Who knows what the fuck they're doing to her?!"

We're silent again, the wipers cutting through the downpour now, the rain hammering on the car's roof.

The omega was on the verge of heat when we left her. If some alpha – if some pack of alphas – laid their hands on her, God knows what they could be doing to her right now. The thought has bile racing up my throat and I'm surprised the wheel doesn't snap in half in my hands.

"You're right," Nate mutters, and I swing my gaze to him again. It's not often Nate tells me that. It doesn't last; next minute he's yelling at me, "Put your fucking foot down, Grandma."

I slam my foot down harder on the accelerator, screeching through the water racing down the street, and thundering down into the basement parking lot two minutes later.

Nate doesn't bother with the elevator. He blasts straight through into the stairwell and sprints up the stairs. I hesitate for a moment, then chase after him.

There's no way we can stand about patiently waiting as the elevator lifts us the twenty stories.

When we reach the top, we're both panting, our brows swimming with sweat.

Silver and Hardy are waiting outside the door, Silver with his face buried in a laptop, Hardy cracking his knuckles.

"What the fuck happened?" Hardy asks, alarm flashing across his face. "Did they find her? Is she all right?"

I shake my head. "We haven't heard anything. You?"

Silver doesn't look up from his screen, but mutters, "Nothing."

"We shouldn't have let those assholes go alone," Hardy says, resuming his cracking. "They're probably wrestling somewhere in the middle of the city and not focused on getting our girl back."

I swear he's about twenty pounds heavier and several inches taller than the last time I looked at him properly. The man is a giant.

"They'll be fine," Silver says, tapping keys. "Remember how it used to be between them?"

We're all silent, thinking. Silver glances up from his laptop.

"That was a long time ago," I say. "A lot has happened between them since then."

"Yeah," Silver says, meeting my eye.

I unlock the apartment door and we all stumble through. None of us sit, even Silver who's still cradling his laptop, although Nate stalks off towards his room muttering something about weapons.

"He hasn't changed," Silver says, watching him go.

"I doubt any of us have," I mutter. That's been half the problem over the years. We're all as stubborn as each other. "Have you found anything?" I ask, watching his brown eyes track back and forth across the screen.

"I've got my boys working on this. All of them. I've pulled them off all other jobs."

"Good." I like the sound of that. At least one person is thinking with their head screwed on. "Then I'm going to make some calls. Find out if anyone's talking about this on my networks."

Silver looks up from his laptop once more. "Who do you think took her?"

I sweep my hand through my light hair, trying to ignore the wave of panic that crashes through my body. Because honestly, I don't know and that makes this fucking complicated. It's also the reason, I know, why Axel made that call to his brother. It's going to need all of us, working together like we used to, to find her. "Honestly, Silver," I say, realizing I haven't called him that in years, "it could be any number of people."

"Yeah," Silver says, his gaze falling back to the laptop in disappointment. "It could."

2

xel

WE BLAST into the hospital together. Looking like the Grim Reaper and the Devil side by side.

Axel and Angel Stormgate.

It's been a long time since we've been seen together like this. And every pair of eyes in the hospital foyer swivels our way. Swivels our way with alarm.

The security guards glance at each nervously, obviously wondering what the hell they should do about us.

Because it's been a *really* long time since we've been seen together like this. Clearly on the warpath, and this time not heading towards each other.

We had a reputation back in the day. One for trouble and chaos. I expect there were several sighs of relief when our relationship busted up like it did. We could do far less damage apart than we ever could together.

I don't linger to see if the security guards are going to try to turf us out. Instead, I march straight for the elevator and smack the button, Angel right by my side all the way.

As we wait for the elevator to arrive, the foyer deathly silent like everyone's afraid to utter a single word, a shiver of disgust meanders down my spine.

I fucking hate this place. Always have done as far back as I can remember. As kids, we were dragged here multiple times by our mom to get a cheek stitched up, a shoulder reset, a broken arm cast up.

It was no surprise. The two of us spent our entire childhood falling out of trees, tumbling into rivers, and beating the shit out of each other. It was our favorite pastime. The majority of the scars littering my body are down to Angel's hand and no one else's.

I glance at my brother now. So like me. His eyes, his build, his coloring. Only his jaw is different and the tilt of his cheekbones. He's more like our mom. I'm more like our dad.

Maybe that's the other reason I always hated the fucker. He was always a mama's boy. Her favorite. Her baby. Ten months younger than me and yet those months seemed to make all the difference. It was always 'look after your brother' and 'you're the oldest, Axel'.

Angel grimaces as we ride the elevator up to the omega clinic. I understand why. It's the other reason I can't stand this place and the last time we'd spent in each other's company in what could pass as a civilized manner.

The door of the elevator slides open and Angel stumbles back slightly.

It's the stench. Stale omega scents, mixed with sterilizing solutions and floral candles. It makes me want to vomit. No omega belongs here. Especially for a goddamn heat. What was she thinking?

The smell catches in the back of my throat and brings back a flood of unwelcome memories. Of walking through these doors together with my brother, our mom pinned between us, demanding the doctors tell us what the fuck was wrong with her. Praying they'd find a way to fix her. Not that they could. Not that they did. And she's been withering away in front of our eyes ever since.

"I hate this place," Angel mumbles, his fingers twitching like he wants to reach for his gun and blast this place apart.

There's a serious chance that we will.

A couple of omegas sit in the plush waiting room, and they look up from their phones and magazines and whimper.

"Get the fuck out of here," I tell them and when neither of them move, I add in a bark, "Now."

They both jump to their feet and scurry to the elevator, eyes trained to the ground like good little omegas.

If I wasn't so fucking angry, I'd find it amusing.

Once the elevator door clicks shut behind us, I yell out into the empty waiting room, "You have to the count of five to get your sorry ass out here and then we start shooting. One ..."

We can hear someone scrambling down the corridor and Angel's eyes flick to mine.

"Two." I yell, nodding at him. "Three."

He thunders through the door.

"Four."

The door flies open and Angel drags out a medic by the scruff of his collar.

"Five," I say, folding my arms across my chest.

Angel shoves the man in front of me and he stumbles

down onto his knees before peering up into my eyes with fear.

"Where is she?" I say calmly because that always scares fuckers like these shitless.

"I-I-I don't know who you mean?"

I bend down so my face is hovering right in front of his.

The man gasps and shrinks away.

"You do," I say. "Because her cousin was in here less than an hour ago asking the same thing. So unless you want to confess to me that more than one omega has gone missing from your clinic, I suggest you start talking."

"I'm just an orderly," the man mumbles. "I don't know anything about what goes on around here."

"So who's in charge, then?" Angel asks, coming to stand next to me.

"Dr. Hannah." His eyes flick between the two of us as we glare at him. Angel growls. The man flinches and adds, quickly, "And Dr.," he swallows, "Machin."

"You know that name?" I ask Angel. He shakes his head. He wasn't here when we brought our mother in and, back then, Dr. Hannah had been a junior. The older doctors have since retired.

"Where are they?"

"I don't know."

I take a step towards him and he scuttles backwards on his backside. "What do you mean, you don't know?"

"They left. They didn't stay."

"I think …" Angel gestures in the orderly's direction.

"Dean," the man mumbles.

"I think, Dean, you had better start from the beginning, for all our sakes."

"I haven't done anything wrong," he whimpers, watching

with wide eyes as Angel reaches inside his jacket and adjusts his gun in his holster.

"We'll be the judge of that," I snap. "What happened?"

"An omega came in for her heat. She's new and I don't–"

"We know who she is," Angel snarls.

The man gulps. "Omegas coming here for their heats is a new thing. There have only been a couple so far and Dr. Hannah and Dr. Machin have been overseeing their care directly."

"Where did they take her?"

"To the heat room." He points down the corridor. "It's out the back. I'm not permitted to go out there. But then the cousin arrived with the omega's phone, making a scene, so I went down to the heat room to tell the doctors and ..."

"And?" I say, feeling the hairs on my skin stand on end and my blood boil.

"It was empty. There was no one there. I bleeped Dr. Hannah, but I have had no reply."

"Surely you saw them go?" Angel says, his voice laced with skepticism. "I don't believe you're being upfront with us." He turns to me. "Do you, Axel?"

"Ax-ax-ax-el? You're Axel York?" His eyes grow even wider in horror.

"I am." I stare at the man. "You're telling us you didn't hear or see a thing? That they just sneaked an omega in heat out of this clinic?"

"We've been dishing out contraception injections all day. I swear I had no idea they were gone."

"Let's take a look." Angel jerks his head towards the door.

"Get up," I grab the orderly by the elbow and drag him to his feet, "and show us."

As we march him down the corridor, I try not to look

into the other rooms, not wanting any more bad memories to haunt me today.

"Is there anyone else here?" Angel asks, also keeping his eyes locked ahead.

"The receptionist Miriam and the nurse Fiona. They both locked themselves in the supply closet when they heard you yelling. I wasn't quick enough," he mumbles.

"You need to be nicer to your colleagues," I tell him, squeezing his arm, "Then they won't hang you out to dry."

He doesn't answer me, simply stares at his shoes and I reckon Dean is an A-class jerk to his work mates. Maybe this little visit from Angel and I will encourage him to buck up his ideas.

We reach the end of the corridor, and a pair of double doors greet us. A darkened, misted-up window is set in both telling us the lights are out in the room beyond.

I push against the doors and they don't move.

"They're locked."

The orderly nods. "To keep the omega inside safe while undergoing their heat."

I snort. "Then open it."

"I don't have the code."

I slam my weight against the doors and again they don't budge.

"They're reinforced," the orderly says, "again for protection."

I smirk at the man, then glance at my brother.

Together, we launch at the entrance, our shoulders hitting the heavy doors in sync. It takes us two more whacks before we slam straight through into the darkened room.

The scent of the omega hits me immediately.

I gasp clutching at my throat like I've been poisoned,

poisoned by the sweetest, most delicious scent I've ever smelled.

My eyes roll around in their sockets, and my knees wobble. Angel clutches onto the doorframe like his legs are about to give way.

The orderly seizes his chance and scuttles down the corridor.

"Come here motherfucker," Angel yells.

But I shake my head, trying my best to breathe through my nose. "We don't need him any more."

"She was in here," Angel says, like that isn't the most goddamn obvious thing ever. The room reeks of her heat-sweetened scent. I want to lick every surface for a scrap of a taste of it. I want to roll my body around in it.

I want to find my omega. *Now.*

"Let's search the room. See if they left behind any clues."

Angel pulls the neck of his t-shirt up over his nose and we stalk around the room. There're no obvious signs of a struggle. There's a bed, a chaise couch and several clinical-looking machines. It's been designed by someone to resemble a nest, but it's a fucking awful attempt. It's too bare, too clinical, too sterile. It makes me want to vomit thinking she'd want to spend her heat here. Alone. Without us.

It makes me want to vomit, knowing it was our dumbass stupid actions that drove her to it.

"I found her bag," Angel says from the other side of the bed. It's still made up, the sheets pristine and unmoved. It's clear they didn't stay here long. Whoever took our omega and her doctors, they did it soon after she arrived. I peer at my watch. Nearly two fucking hours ago. This isn't good. Number one rule when it comes to an abduction: the more time passed, the less likely you are to find the victim. Find them and find them alive.

"Her clothes are here too," Angel says more quietly, holding an oversized t-shirt up to his nose.

"She wasn't wearing that earlier today," I say with irritation, wanting to snatch the shirt from his hand and bury my face into it.

"She was wearing it here, asshole. I can tell."

I grind my teeth, letting the insult slide.

We have to put our animosity to one side – for the time being anyway – if we're to find our girl. Silver is nearly as good at tracking people down as Connor is. If we can get them to work together – while keeping a lid on Nate and Hardy – we have a chance of bringing her home.

"How the fuck did they get her out with no one seeing?" I mumble, peering up at the ceiling, half expecting to find a ceiling tile missing.

"If the other members of staff were occupied, they may not have noticed."

I shake my head. "An omega in heat ..."

I don't need to say anything else. The noises she'd be making, the scent she'd be giving off. No one would miss her. Besides which, all those visiting omegas lining up for their contraception shots would have their hackles raised sky-high by the presence of another omega in heat.

"There must be another way out of the room," Angel mumbles and as he says it, both our eyes land back on the bed and its oversized headboard.

In the next moment, he's pushing and I'm pulling and we've shifted the thing out the way.

There, right behind, sits a door, open, and beyond a flight of stairs.

"Shit!" Angel mutters, racing through the doorway and down the steps.

It's clear our omega was taken this way; her scent spirals down the never-ending number of steps like a trail of mind-altering breadcrumbs. The effect is freaking dizzying. Twice, I have to halt, gripping the rail and getting my shit together. Angel's no better.

Then my foot slips in something sticky on the ground and I know for sure it's the omega's slick. Glistening like a puddle of ecstasy on the stone steps.

"Shit," I mutter, forcing myself to move, forcing myself not to turn around, drop to my knees and lick that mess up. "Shit, shit. Shit!"

Finally, we reach the bottom of the staircase, finding ourselves in a small and dank underground parking lot.

It's dimly lit and it's empty. Two rubber tracks mark the ground where someone has thumped their foot to the pedal and sped away.

"Shit!" I say again, slamming my fist into the wall. "She's gone, Angel."

He's calmer than me and I don't know how he can be.

"We knew she would be, Axel."

I stalk towards him, grab a handful of his shirt and slam him into the wall. "You sure you don't know where she is, motherfucker?"

"Would I be here with you right now if I did?" he snarls back into my face.

I want to slam my fist right into his smart mouth this time. But I can't afford to waste the time.

Besides, it's my fault. My fault she's missing. My fault she's been taken. If anyone should be getting his ass tanned, it's me.

A growl rumbles in Angel's chest and then his eyes flick up above my head.

"There's a camera," he says.

I peer over my shoulder.

He's right. There's a security camera pointing right our way, pointing right at the spot where the getaway car must have been parked.

"You think they're watching us?" Angel growls again.

"Perhaps," I say, letting go of my brother and turning slowly to glare up face-on into the lens of the camera. "But I'm guessing Silver can hack his way into that camera and find the footage."

I stand up on my tiptoes and, continuing to glare up into the camera, rip it from the ceiling.

3

Bea

My eyes flick open.

Immediately, before the mist lifts in my mind and I register where I am, I know something is wrong.

The smell. The temperature. The hardness at my back.

A pain pierces my gut and sweat coats my brow.

The room is bright and white.

The stench sterile.

I shift, trying to turn and curl up. I want to hug my stomach, a groan ripping noisily from my throat.

My arms and legs catch as I twist. I'm bound. I twist my head. Bound to a hard couch.

Panic swirls in my stomach and I try to remember.

Where am I? *Who* am I?

I tip my head backwards and find a strip of bare lighting shining down on my head. I peer towards my toes and spy a door. Apart from that this square room is empty. Nothing on the walls or the floors. No other furniture.

My body, I realize, is wrapped in a flimsy hospital gown that's rough against my hot skin.

Panic squirms in my stomach and a sob bubbles in my throat. I swallow both down hard, close my eyes and try to think.

I'm Bea. A beta from Naw Creek. Engaged to Karl Simpson.

The pain in my stomach swells and I'm soaking wet between my thighs.

No, that isn't right.

I'm not a beta.

I no longer live in Naw Creek.

And I sure as hell am not going to be marrying Karl Simpson.

I snap open my eyes.

The clinic.

My head hurts as I strain to arrange my thoughts logically in my head.

I went to the clinic for my heat because ...

That sob bursts free of my throat and pain sears through my heart this time.

But then what happened?

I remember the clinic.

I remember ... changing into this gown.

I remember ... taking a glass of water.

And then ... nothing.

After that, nothing at all.

Blankness until only a moment ago when I woke up here.

This isn't the heat room in the clinic.

But maybe there's no need to panic, right? Maybe this is

perfectly normal for a heat? Maybe I passed out from the pain and they had to bring me here and ... what? Tie me to a couch?

Yep, that doesn't seem right.

When I peer down at my arm, I can see a catheter in the crook of my elbow, a tube leading up to a bag hanging on a trolley.

Drugs, right? Except the liquid in the tube is a dark red. Blood. Mine or someone else's?

I consider calling out for someone. I consider demanding answers. Then again maybe I don't want to come face to face with whoever brought me here.

Turns out I don't get a choice in the matter.

The door clicks open.

A tall man in a white coat strolls through, the lower half of his mouth is covered in a surgical mask but he's familiar nonetheless. It takes me a few minutes to decipher where I know him from. But then the scent of nutmeg hits my nose and I remember.

The doctor. The doctor from the clinic.

"Where am I?" I ask, my voice sore and croaky.

He ignores my question, absorbed in the clipboard he carries in his hands. When he looks up from the pages of scribbles, his eyes are hard.

"What did you take?"

I blink at him. "Where am I? Who are you?" I struggle against my restraints. "Why am I tied to the bed?" Fear trickles down my spine.

He doesn't answer my questions. "You took something didn't you?"

I don't understand what the hell he's going on about. "I took painkillers for the pain and–"

He huffs like I'm an irritating child who won't behave.

"We'll find out eventually, we'll work it out, but it would make all our lives a lot easier if you just told me."

I frown. Is the man mad? My voice shakes when I speak again. "I don't know what you're talking about."

"Little beta, you took something. Something that triggered your change. Something pretty damn effective. I want to know what it was."

I stare at him, my mouth falling open.

"You think I took something? To change myself into an omega?" Is he crazy? Insane? "Why the hell would I do that? I was perfectly happy as I was!"

Well, not strictly true but I certainly never had a desire to become an omega.

"Don't lie to me," the doctor says, his voice and face twisting ugly.

"I'm not. I never wanted to be an omega, and I certainly didn't take anything to turn myself into one." Fear gives way to anger. This man has no idea what a mess my life has been these last few weeks; how everything I knew and understood got thrown upside down in one vicious hurricane of chaos. I thought I knew who I was. I thought I knew the path my life was destined to take. And in an instant, everything changed. I wouldn't wish that on my worst enemy. (Okay, again, perhaps not strictly true, but still.) "Is that why I'm here?" I ask him.

The man lets his clipboard drop to his side. "Yes, and you're going to remain here until we get some answers – one way or another." He smirks. "We've given you some medication to lessen the effects of your heat and some strong painkillers–"

"They're not working," I grit out through my teeth.

"You're in heat. What do you expect? Not even the strongest painkillers will knock out the pain completely.

But," he drums his fingers against the clipboard, "if you don't start cooperating, we can reduce both types of medication and let you experience the full effects of your heat."

I grimace, clutching my stomach. "There's nothing to tell."

"Little betas like you," the man hisses, "don't magically morph into omegas just like that." He snaps his fingers and then marches from the room.

What the hell?

I've hardly caught my breath when the door clicks open again and this time Dr. Hannah enters. Immediately, I can tell how nervous she is. Her eyes flit about the room as she walks in tight footsteps towards me.

"Dr. Hannah," I gasp. "I'm so glad to see you."

Whatever the hell is going on, I'm sure she will help me. She's an omega. Trusted by all the omegas in the city to deliver their healthcare. I'm guessing she has no idea what that other man is up to.

"How are you feeling?" she asks me in a clipped tone. She looks much paler than usual, gray shadows under her brown eyes.

"Feeling?" I ask, exasperated. "I don't know where the hell I am and I'm restrained to the bed."

"Just a precaution so you wouldn't be harmed while we transported you," the doctor says, resting her fingers against my wrist and counting my pulse. "And you're perfectly safe. We're at a more secure clinic for your safety."

She does that smile thing, although she struggles to make it last on her lips.

"That man–"

"Keen to understand what's going on. He can be a little impatient."

I don't feel reassured. Not one bit. I don't like the way her hands shake or the nervous way her eyes flick about the room. I don't trust her, I sure as hell don't trust the man who was just in here threatening me and I don't trust this place.

"Undo these restraints," I tell her.

"You may find that they are helpful if you begin to experience–"

I smile back at her. The same sickly sweet expression she just offered me. "I'll be fine. Please undo them. I've been known to hyperventilate when secured in this way. My last boyfriend would attest to that. The one time he tried tying me to the bed, I had a full on panic attack that lasted two days. In fact, I feel like ... oh god ... I can't breathe ... oh no ..."

The doctor glares at me and unsnaps the restraints. Her fingers are rough and her fingernails scrape against my skin but at least I'm free.

I take an exaggerated gasp of oxygen. "Oh, thank god. Oh," I rest my hand against my chest and sigh. "Now I'd like to call my cousin."

"No, I'm afraid we can't allow that."

"Then I'd like to leave."

The doctor doesn't meet my eye as she fiddles with the bag of blood hanging on the trolley. Now I look more closely, I'm pretty sure it's my blood flowing out of my arm and into the bag.

"That won't be possible either."

"Excuse me?"

"It would be entirely irresponsible of us to release a lone omega in the midst of their heat."

"So I'm a prisoner here?" I ask.

"No, you booked in for your heat and we are here to care for you."

"That's not what your colleague just said and why am I

hooked up to this blood bag?" I pull on the tube causing pain to spike in my arm.

"Please do not interfere with the equipment," the doctor says, gaze flicking to the door.

"Why not it's my body and–"

"We are here to take care of you," she says quickly, then sprints to the door before I can say more. "If you need anything, there's a buzzer." The door locks with a loud thud behind her.

I stare at the door for several minutes, my heart racing.

What is going on?

My head pounds, my belly aches and my skin is on fire. I'm struggling to understand if I interpreted those encounters correctly. Did I imagine the first doctor, his hostility and his threats? And as for Dr. Hannah ...

I don't think I misinterpreted anything.

This place makes my skin crawl.

It's bare and cold and smells all wrong.

I've seen the photos of omega nests. I have a pile of cushions and comforters waiting in our apartment – things my aunt ordered for me in preparation of a forthcoming heat. They seem like heaven right now. All I want to do is curl up among the layer of softness and be ...

I gulp.

Rutted? Knotted? Fucked until I can barely stand?

A whimper escapes my throat.

Yes, all those things.

None of which are possible in this clinic.

If it was a real one. A legit one. Surely it would be a hell of a lot more comfortable. Surely I'd be drowning in layers of cushions and mattresses.

Surely, they wouldn't be pumping blood out of my arm.

Something is seriously fishy about this place and everything in my body screams at me to get the hell out.

I peer down at the catheter in my arm and then back towards the locked door.

I was a prisoner – an unwitting one – all those years living with Karl.

No way in hell I'm being one again. Not without a fight anyway.

Gritting my teeth and closing my eyes, I grip the tube in my arm between my fingers and yank it from my arm.

The pain is so intense for a moment my vision whites and my hearing blares noise. My head swims and I force air down into my lungs, willing myself not to faint.

Spots dance across my eyes when I open them, but at least I'm still with it. A trail of blood runs down my arm and I lift the crook of my elbow to my mouth and suck on the wound hoping that will help stem the bleeding.

One problem solved. Now the next. The door. A much bigger problem.

I hobble as best I can to the doorway, pausing once to hunch over and force my head between my knees, waiting for the dizziness to pass.

When I reach the door, I find it bolted as predicted. I give it a rattle for good measure anyway. Even if I had a hair grip, I wouldn't know how to pick the lock besides which it seems electronic.

I stare around the room, searching for some tool that might help me.

There's only the bed with the unbuckled restraints, the blood, the tube and the trolley.

My shoulders slump. I'm stuck here. Stuck here while they will do god knows what to me.

I remember snippets of conversations now. There had

been so much information I'd had to absorb all at once. Learning about suppressants and heats, knots and scents. At times it had been overwhelming. And then there was all the politics, understanding how the world of alphas and omegas works, learning it was totally different to how I had imagined.

But in between, I remember now, talk about betas who wanted to become omegas. About the experiments taking place to make it possible.

I peer over to my bag of blood. I think of the blurry words of the first doctor, insisting I must have taken something.

Am I guinea pig here? An experiment?

My head spins all the faster.

No one knows where I am. No one will even know I'm missing until Courtney wonders why I haven't come home. And that won't be for another four days.

No one is coming to rescue me. I need to escape.

My eyes land on the buzzer and I formulate a plan.

My heart thumps, as well as everything between my legs. Whatever they gave me to lessen the effects of my heat are wearing off. My skin feels like a furnace, sweat slides down my neck and the pain in my gut is building.

I pray there isn't a hidden camera in this room as I steady my breathing and take a hold of the buzzer.

I'll have one chance. One chance and one chance only.

I jam my thumb down hard on the buzzer before I can chicken out. Hopefully Dr. Hannah will answer and not the other man. But either way, I'm ready.

I hobble to the door, wishing my heart wasn't beating so

damn loud, and wait. I hear footsteps in the corridor and then a shadow against the misted-out glass. Several loud beeps sound as someone inputs the code and the lock clunks open. The door handle turns. The door swings open.

I launch myself forward, gripping the needle that had been in my arm between my fingers, and stab.

4

Hardy

Our phones all ping simultaneously, and we peer at each other bemused before pulling our devices out of our pockets.

Someone has created a group chat – me, Silver, Connor, Nate and both the Stormgate brothers.

"What the fuck?" I mutter.

That someone was Axel.

"Have we dived into some alternative reality here?" Nate mutters, and I snort. The kid could always make me laugh. I glance up from my phone at him. Not that he's a kid anymore.

Our phones ping a second time. This time with a message. Two names for us to check out.

I'm out the door in the next moment, yelling at Silver to send me the addresses when he has them.

I'm at the stairwell when I realize Nate's right behind me.

"I don't need any help," I tell him.

"Coming all the same," Nate says.

I hesitate, debating whether to argue the toss. I don't need some asshole from Pack York breathing down my neck. But one thing I remember about Nate, I could never get him to back down. I'm not going to try now. I can't afford to waste the precious seconds.

We jog down the steps, our legs moving faster and faster, neither of us wants to be beaten by the other, neither wants to hit the ground floor last.

When we crash through the doorway three minutes later, we're breathing hard.

"Where's the car?" Nate asks.

"There." I point out the front where I left the car in an illegal zone.

Nate mutters something about clamping, but I'm pretty sure I could rip the clamp off with my bare hands the mood I'm in.

A mood for destruction.

Our phones beep a third time as we climb into the truck and I swerve out into the traffic, this time with two addresses.

"We'll hit the male first," I tell him. Nate nods, the glint in his eye murderous.

"Put the address into the sat nav," I tell him.

"Sat navs are for pussies," Nate says, pulling out his knife from his pocket, the same one he's had for years.

"I don't know where the fuck I'm going without it."

"I'll navigate."

"Jesus fucking Christ. You can't navigate to save your Goddamn life."

Nate's face turns even darker than it was. "That was your fault."

"It wasn't. You were in charge of the map. I was in charge of equipment."

"You took the wrong turn."

"Because you told me to fucking take it." I shake my head. "Ten hours!" I remind him. "Ten hours we were lost out there in those woods."

A smile creeps over Nate's face. "It was fucking wild, though, right? Remember we ate a frog, we got so hungry."

"You ate the fucking frog!"

I think about it for a second. Yeah, maybe it was wild. However, I'm not admitting it to this asshole.

"Just tell me where to go."

He delivers his directions in clear, perfunctory instructions. The asshole's trying to make a point. I don't give a shit though because it means we're pulling up outside a house within fifteen minutes.

"This it?" I ask, squinting towards the blurry outline of the numbers pinned above the door.

"You can't read that number, Grandpa?" Nate asks, opening his door.

"Yeah, I can read it," I mumble. "Is it the right one?"

"Number one hundred and fifty-five."

"Doesn't look like anyone's home," I say, examining the blank windows and empty driveway.

"Let's see," Nate says, jumping out of the truck and sprinting up to the door.

I curse and follow after him.

For such a big dude, he moves fucking fast.

Nate pounds on the door and we wait, counting to ten in our heads. It's silent inside. No footsteps. No doors creaking open.

Nate glances at me, then slams his shoulder against the door. It groans, and he does it again, this time the lock snapping and the door splintering. It swings back to reveal a bare hallway.

I peer over my shoulder. Someone will probably call this in – two alphas breaking and entering – but with any luck we'll be gone by then.

"I'll search upstairs, you downstairs," I say. This time Nate doesn't argue; he sets off down the corridor dashing through the first door.

I head upstairs. The scent lingering in the air is one of an alpha. It stops me in my tracks. Nutmeg? I know this scent from somewhere. I squeeze the bridge of my nose between my finger and thumb, thinking.

The break-in. The fucking break-in.

I charge through the bedrooms. This man obviously lives alone. No woman's clothes or children's toys in sight. Certainly no family pictures hanging on the walls.

Although, there's a sweet aroma hanging in the air. Faint. An omega has been here. Not ours – I'd recognize her scent anywhere. But this man has a girlfriend. The other doctor?

I stomp out to the landing and hang over the bannister.

"Find anything?" I yell down.

Nate slinks out into the corridor.

"No," he says, that darkness returning to his eyes.

I curse under my breath and jog out to the truck.

There's still the other doctor's place.

Her house is smaller, which surprises me considering she's the physician for all the wealthy omegas in the city.

The front lawn is neatly kept with bright flowers growing in the bed. Inside it's empty again but the house couldn't be more different from that alpha's. There are pillows and blankets thrown over every available surface as well as teddy bears perched on shelves and warm paintings on the wall. No sign of an alpha living here or any kids and no trace of that nutmeg scent.

In fact, there are hardly any scents at all and a fine layer of dust over everything as if nobody's been home for a while.

"You think they're together?" I ask, rubbing my head in confusion as I find Nate in the woman's kitchen. What do these bastards want with Bea?

"Nah," Nate says. "Pretty single I reckon." Nate's gaze flicks around the kitchen, lingering on the long list of tasks stuck to the fridge door. He snatches it off and plunges it into his pocket. "You think our girl was snatched by someone like the Snakebites? And these doctors got caught up in whatever went down?"

"I recognize his scent," I say, meeting Nate's green eyes. "The doctor's."

"You do?" Nate's voice grows so low it vibrates in his chest.

"Same dude who broke into her apartment."

Nate thinks about this for a moment. "So it isn't the Snakebites."

"Unless they're under their pay."

"Wanna take a ride down to their place now? Bang a few heads together?" That murderous glint sparks in Nate's eyes.

Fuck, it's tempting. It's the kind of thing the two of us used to do. We were the hotheads of our gang. Reacting with our fists before engaging with our brains. Together we caused chaos, ripping up the city together, leaving a trail of destruction.

It was freaking brilliant. The thing that tore me up the most when our group was ripped apart, was losing my partner in crime.

However, I'm older now, if none the wiser. Pulling that kind of shit landed me in a heap of trouble. I'm more disciplined these days. Mostly thanks to Silver.

"No man," I say, motioning my head towards the door. "Not until we know where she is. Not until we know it was them." Nate's shoulders sag in disappointment. There's a bruise on his cheek I'm pretty sure I gave him. "Then we'll make them wish they were never born."

Nate's face brightens. "I've always wanted to feed someone their own testicles, you know," he says more brightly as we jump back into the truck.

Fuck, yeah, I'd forgotten how twisted this fucker can be.

"You want to play with some other dude's balls, man, you go right ahead. Ain't no homophobic bullshit in this pack."

Nate shakes his head. "Not my thing. I'm all about the pussy."

Clearly, we're both thinking about one pussy in particular.

The roads are clearer now, and we speed through the city, the sun growing low in the sky and reflecting off the windows and shop fronts as we pass by.

Nate whistles a tune I vaguely remember.

"What is that?" I ask, tapping my fingers on the steering wheel.

"Bon Jovi."

I chuckle. "Oh man, you were obsessed with those guys."

"Best band in the world."

"Wouldn't stop playing their songs. Drove Angel fucking crazy."

"Yeah," Nate says with a grin.

"Didn't you try to learn it on the guitar?" I laugh louder. "You were fucking awful."

Nate flicks his tongue against his lip ring. "Hands are too fucking big, aren't they?" He holds them up. "Come in handy for certain things though. Certainly never had any complaints with the ladies." He winks at me.

"That's down to Connor, not the size of your fucking fingers. He made us all watch back-to-back YouTube videos on perfecting our fingering techniques." I swing the car left and floor the accelerator, seeing our tower in the distance. "Remember, we had that tally going on. How many girls we could get off."

"I've still got mine," Nate says, and I don't doubt it.

I drum my fingers on the steering wheel, humming that song myself. Then I glance over at Nate, his eyes glazed as he peers through the windscreen.

"I'm sorry, man, about what I said this morning, out there at the omega's place. It was a shitty thing to say." I shake my head, shame and guilt riding through my body. It was a low blow, a fucking low and dirty blow. "I didn't fucking mean it. Sometimes my tongue engages before my brain."

Nate doesn't look my way. "Don't sweat it man." His leg jigs up and down. "I thought it was funny." He turns to look at me. "Things can get a bit serious, you know, with just Axel and Connor."

I think it's his way of saying he missed me and I realize that, who have I been kidding, I missed him too.

5

Silver

AXEL SLAMS a mangled security camera into my hand.

"This is all we found," he says gruffly.

I stare down at it, my forehead wrinkling in confusion, until Angel fills me in on what the two of them learned at the clinic. Not a lot.

Usually, I'm calm as a penguin in an igloo in these types of situations. But it's never been my omega, my girl, at risk, and it's fucking impossible to stay anything resembling an ounce of calm.

My heart hammers in my chest, and every alpha fiber in my body is screaming at me to get out there and tear down the entire fucking city until I find her.

Problem is, we don't even know if she's in the city. She could be half way across the fucking ocean now for all we know.

"Can you hack into the system?" Axel asks me. It's a hell of a long time since we've worked together. It's an even longer time since he spoke to me in such an earnest tone.

"I already have my boys on it, but now we have a clearer idea of what we're looking for. A basement parking lot." I type out a message to my team. "We just have to hope it was linked up to the main system and not some separate surveillance."

"This is fucked up," Nate says, prowling around like a caged animal. "Why was there a hidden exit? And what the fuck do they want with our girl?"

No one wants to answer that question. No one wants to think about it.

The alpha inside me screams all the louder. He wants to rip apart the world. I close my eyes and breathe, letting that wildness spiral through me.

"It depends who took her," Connor says quietly.

My phone buzzes and every one of us is alert in an instant.

"Yes," I grunt, pressing my phone onto speaker.

"We've found the footage, Sir." I sigh so loudly in relief, I think the fucking building must shake. "Sending it over to you now."

"Good," I say, opening it up on my laptop as soon as it pings into my inbox.

I increase the size and twist the screen around so that everyone can see.

The footage is grainy and the parking lot dark, but we see a black SUV with darkened windows waiting by the stairwell in the lot.

For several seconds nothing happens, and Nate bounces on his toes in irritation.

Then the stairwell door crashes open and we see three

people. One tall and large, another smaller, and the third one slumped between them.

"That's her," Hardy announces like any one of us would have failed to recognize our girl.

"She looks like she's out cold," Connor mumbles, as the other two figures bundle her into the back of the car and slam the doors. We watch as the two figures climb into the front seats.

"A man and a woman," I say.

"Dr. Hannah and Dr. Machin," Axel says with a growl. "What the fuck are they doing?"

"He's an alpha," Angel spits out, "maybe he's planning to claim her for himself."

I shake my head. That doesn't seem right to me.

On screen, the car lights flick on and then the car skids away. I freeze the frame as the rear of the car comes into view.

It's blurry but I can read it.

"We have a registration number," I tell the others.

It's not an address, but it's one step closer.

"How's that going to help?" Nate mumbles.

I smirk at him, then jump back on the phone to my team. I already have them sifting through any piece of information about the two doctors that I can; now I'm going to have them hacking into the city's CCTV system and tracking down this goddamn car.

"You think you'll find the location?" Axel asks.

"Damn sure," I say, with a nod. "Time to get suited up, boys. Where's your equipment, Axel?"

I've never been inside Pack York's apartment before. The bust up between the two brothers happened long before either of our packs made our money and established our homes.

I thought the place would be tacky as hell. Full of all the latest gadgets and photos of topless girls pinned to every wall. That's how Axel's room had been back in the day. Nate's too. I guess things have changed. There's not one titty in sight. In fact the decor is pretty darn tasteful, if a little stark. This place is missing one thing. Just like our own. An omega. With their penchant for everything soft and snuggly.

My heart wrenches with that thought and I pick up my feet.

Pack York's weapon room sits behind a locked door and we wait for Axel to input the code – his mom's birthday – and the door to swing open.

We stride in, not waiting for any invitation and start loading up, adorning bullet-proof vests, and selecting our weapons of choice.

When we're done, Axel rests his hands on Nate's shoulders.

"We don't kill anyone unless we have to."

Nate snarls in his face. "They took the fucking omega."

"And our number one priority is getting her back. Revenge and retribution can come later."

The muscle under Nate's eye twitches.

Angel rests his hand on Nate's back. "The omega. That's all we focus on."

Tension swims in the room. Angel and Axel together were always a calming influence on Nate. Does that old magic still work?

Nate nods stiffly. "All right, but if anyone lays one finger on the omega–"

"You have our permission to snap those fingers off and hang them around your neck," Angel says.

Nate snorts a laugh and just like that the tension clears.

It only lasts a moment though, in the van the tension

thickens again like we're swimming in soup. Our scents are thick in the air and I swear I hear every heart thumping in this dark vehicle, the sun sunk below the horizon and the city wrapped in night.

"What do we know about the location?" Axel asks, from the driving seat.

"Not a lot. Seems to be a converted warehouse on the outskirts of the city. A lot of the space out there is unused or shut down. It would be easy to smuggle someone inside without anyone noticing."

"But that means we don't know what we're going to find inside," Hardy says.

"Isn't there CCTV footage of the place? Can't we see who's been coming and going?" Angel asks.

I shake my head.

"Nope, the footage gets wiped daily. If we hadn't tracked the car down there today, we wouldn't have tracked it at all."

"Sounds dodgy," Nate says, playing with his gun in a way that makes me freaking uncomfortable.

"Put the safety back on," I snap at him.

He looks up at me with a grin and then slowly and deliberately snaps it across.

"I don't like going in blind," Axel says, "we don't know what we might find."

"Which is why we're going to do this the proper way." I'd wanted to bring my security men along with us, but Pack York weren't having any of that. Seems they're happy to work with us to bring the omega home, but don't trust us enough not to snatch her away. I eye Nate and then Hardy. "Stick to the plan."

I run through it a third time. We're taking these fuckers by surprise. Stealth is the operative word. We don't want the omega to get hurt in any crossfire, which means we find her and get the hell out.

"What if she won't come with us?" Connor asks.

Axel mumbles under his breath. But it's a good point. One I was musing myself.

Being rescued is one thing. Being rescued by a bunch of dudes you detest another.

No one has any answers to that problem, though.

"Let's hope she will," I say. Crossing all my fingers and all my toes.

Axel circuits past the warehouse with his lights out and we take a look at the place. It's dark and I hope to god we're not too late and they've moved her on already.

He parks up a back alley and we pull our balaclavas over our heads and jog in single file back towards the building, hugging the shadows as best six large men can. There's no security patrolling outside. But I point out the cameras and we're careful to avoid their view.

The door has some electronic code system but I hold our hazing gadget to the touchpad and within a few minutes the thing has fizzled dead, an alarm along with it.

Taking a deep breath, I open the door and we step through. It's like stepping through into another world. The outside may look like a run-down warehouse but the inside has been kitted out like a clinic. Everything is white and sterile. It's also dark. It's after hours and whoever works here has gone for the day.

Not all of them though.

I'm surprised by the lax security. It makes me think whoever is organizing this shitshow, doesn't know what they're doing. Or maybe they never thought they'd be intercepted.

"It smells just like the fucking omega clinic," Axel whispers by my ear. "Minus the freaking floral candles."

I nod. Through my balaclava I can smell the omega scents as well as cleaning solutions and, what alarms me the most, alpha scents.

I motion Hardy forward. "How about Bea's scent? Can you pick it up?" There's a trace of it in the air, but my nose has never been as good as Hardy's. He's like a hunting dog.

His nostrils twitch, and his eyes swing back and forth in their sockets. Then he points towards a door.

"That way."

It's locked again, but it only takes a minute to fry the electronics and we're through into a dimly lit corridor, doors lining either side. Through some of the darkened windows we can see what looks like labs, test tubes and flasks collecting dripping chemicals, and various complicated machines resting on the countertops.

It's creepy as hell and an involuntary shudder shuffles down my spine.

"What the hell is this place?" Angel whispers.

"Fuck knows," I reply.

Hardy leads us down the corridor where it splits in two directions. He frowns.

"What?" I ask.

"Her scent crisscrosses here. She could have gone in either direction."

"Then we split up. Axel and Connor you come with me. Nate you go with Hardy and Angel."

Angel doesn't look best pleased about having a loose cannon like Nate on his team but at least he'll have Hardy to back him up. I'll be alone with just Pack York.

"Remember," I tell them, "the omega is the priority here. We grab her and we get the hell out. Anything happens, we're not waiting around for the other group. Grab the girl and go."

I look at each of them sternly. I don't think we'll have any problems. I don't expect Axel York to act the hero and save my ass. It's not like we're a close-knit group of friends here, who'll have each other's backs. Not any more anyway.

Axel, Connor and I take the left turn. The others take the right.

Down this corridor the labs give way to what look like hospital rooms. They are all pretty bare, only a bed and various clinical machines in each. We open doors and peer inside anyway, even though we know they are all empty.

"I don't like this," Connor whispers. "It's too quiet, too empty. I think we're too late."

My heart sinks. He's right. It's after hours, but this place is kitted out for a lot of people to be working. Surely someone would be here after hours.

I'm not giving up, though, not until we've searched this place ten times over, top to bottom, back to front. Not until we've checked every room, closet and cupboard.

At the end of this corridor is another locked door. I disengage the lock for a third time and we step through into absolute chaos.

An alarm blares, a red light swings around in circles and we can hear people shouting in the distance.

We glance at one another, and then we're running, all three of us, our feet pounding the ground.

There's a crowd of three people gathered outside a room. They're all dressed in white coats, and as we race towards them, they swing their faces our way. Horror and shock painted on each one.

What the hell is going on?

"Hands up," I yell, my weapon trained their way. "Hands up and up against the wall."

They back up immediately, hands waving above their heads, their faces gray with shock.

Connor positions himself in front of the four of them, the barrel of his gun directed at them all while Axel and I turn into the room.

There's a man laid out on the ground in a pool of blood; he's groaning, and another medic is bent over him administering first aid.

The medic freezes when we enter, rocking back on his heels, and I get a look at the man laid down on the floor. One of his eyes is all bloody, but nonetheless I recognize him.

The male doctor from the clinic.

Axel crouches down beside him, his face a thunderstorm of rage.

"Where's the omega?" he hisses.

The doctor moans some more. His good eye rests on Axel's face and then mine.

"Where is she?" Axel repeats. "Tell me now, if you want to keep your other eye."

The doctor whimpers. His lips quiver. He swallows, his tongue moving behind his teeth. It takes him three attempts to answer Axel.

"Gone."

Axel growls and I realize I am too.

Gone.

She was here, I don't need to be Hardy to know that. Her scent is rich in the air. Sweet and intense and so fucking delicious.

I have to shake my head just to stay the fuck focused.

"Where?" Axel says, leaning right over the fucker's face.

"D-d-d-don't know."

"What happened to your face?" I ask, the disgust clear in my voice.

He doesn't want to answer that despite our threats. I'm tempted to send a bullet into his knee caps just to make him talk.

"Someone take her?" I ask.

He shakes his head, grimacing with pain.

"We need to get him to a hospital," the medic kneeling beside him says. It isn't the female doctor from the omega clinic. It isn't Dr. Hannah. I peer out at the other medics lined against the wall. She's not there either.

"He needs to be taken to a fucking police cell," Axel snarls.

The medic cowers, shuffling back on his haunches.

I pull out my radio.

"Angel?" I bark into the mouthpiece. The line crackles, then I hear his heavy breaths. "Any luck?"

"Not yet. You?"

"We have the place where they were keeping her." I swing my gaze around the bleak-looking room. There's a bed with open restraints – which makes me want to start firing shots into knees – but nothing else. No equipment as far as I can see.

"Should we call the cops?" Connor asks, patrolling the line of medics.

"Not until we have the omega," Axel tells him.

He stands to his feet, leaving the moaning doctor to his pain. Then he walks to the line of medics.

"What's been going on here?" They shuffle on their feet nervously, eyes locked on the ground.

I'm guessing it can't be anything legitimate otherwise they'd tell us straight away.

Axel jams the butt of his gun under one guy's jaw. He is skinny and sweating profusely, his legs practically shaking. Whatever they've been doing, it's definitely bad shit. The man is terrified. Or perhaps it's simply the presence of three very pissed off and armed alphas scaring the shit out of him.

"I asked you a question," Axel says.

"Research," the man mumbles, swallowing, his Adam's apple knocking against Axel's gun.

"What kind of research?" Connor asks.

The man clamps his mouth shut and closes his eyes as if he's waiting for the bullet to his head.

What the hell?

I want to get to the bottom of this. But like I told the others, Bea is our priority here.

"Do any of you know where the omega is?"

"No, a couple of the orderlies went to fetch her back," the medic on the floor says. "She can't have got far. The place is locked down."

"And yet we got in." Axel smirks. He glances at me. "Let's keep looking. Connor, you stay here."

"They'll be coming," the man with his eyes closed says, shaking even harder now.

"Shhhh," the man next to him snarls.

"Who?" Axel snaps, "who's coming?"

But the medic doesn't have a chance to answer, because from behind us we hear the whistle of bullets.

Lots of bullets.

All flying our way.

6

ate

We sprint down a maze of corridors, twisting this way and that, her scent like an invisible string leading us on. It's like a video game. I'm waiting for the ambush.

But the place is deadly quiet.

We pass one office, lights on, computer blinking, half-drunk cup of coffee, no one there. Screens line the walls. Lots of fuzzy pictures of empty corridors.

We keep going. Keep running. Keeping finding fuck all.

Won't stop me though.

I need to find her.

My little bird.

And then she's there. Tweeting and fluttering about.

The others rush towards her. I hold up my arm, halting them. Then I raise my finger to my lips.

Shhh.

Quietly.

Don't want to spook the little thing.

"We need to get her the hell out of here," Hardy mutters.

I glare at him and he shuts his mouth.

I creep towards her. Along the corridor. Eyes locked on her, every molecule in my body alert. Tuned in to her.

She hasn't seen us yet.

She's leaning against the wall, clutching her stomach with both hands, and moaning like she needs to be fucked real hard.

There are also splatters of blood covering the front of the hospital gown she's wearing.

I don't like that.

I swallow down hard on a growl and creep forward.

Her eyes are glazed but when I whisper her name, they flick up to mine. She opens her mouth to scream.

Oh yeah, mask.

I tug it off, shaking out my hair.

Her scent gets a lot more powerful.

My knees buckle. Like they know I should be down on the floor, head between her legs.

"You!" she mutters, frowning.

Not exactly the response I was expecting.

"Yeah, it's me, little bird."

"What are you doing here?" Her eyes swim around and I can tell she's finding it hard to focus.

Looking pissed off, however, she seems to find a lot easier.

"We've come to rescue you."

"I don't need rescuing. I escaped. I'm rescuing myself." My eyebrows leap up my forehead and I hide a smile behind my hand, pretending to rub at my chin.

That's my little bird.

Still fighting.

I can hear the other two right behind me, both itching to lay their hands on the omega.

They can wait.

"You're rescuing yourself?"

"Yes, thank you very much." She flinches, grimacing as her hands grow tense against her stomach. "I didn't have a set of keys but I improvised and–"

"A set of keys?" I repeat, fucking confused, watching her pretty mouth move as the words fly over my head.

"Yes, keys, just like Courtney taught me."

Courtney the cousin.

"That's good," I say.

I don't know what she's talking about. Her heat's frying her brain.

"Wanna come with us?" I hold out my hand.

Her hot gaze swims all over my body, lingering on my mouth and my broad chest, and fuck yes, my crotch.

The blood rushes down to my pants.

"No," she says, shaking her hands.

"No?" I tilt my head. Give her the puppy dog eyes. "Little bird ..."

Angel's radio beeps.

I stiffen, then peer over my shoulder.

He holds the radio up to his ear, whispering into it as he steps away.

A shadow falls over his face.

"We need to get out!" he yells, voice full of tension, "now!"

He gives Hardy a look. Things have gone tits up.

I step closer and take the omega's elbow. She attempts to shake it off.

"I'm not coming with you!" she snaps.

Angel shakes his head in an I-told-you-so expression.

"Got no choice, little bird. The bad guys are here."

"You're the bad guys," she says, jabbing a finger into one of my pecs.

"We are," I confess, "and we're really fucking sorry. But you need to come with us. Now."

She shakes her head violently, pulling on her arm. "How do I know you aren't the ones who kidnapped me in the first place? How do I know this isn't another of your silly games?"

I swing her around to face me and lower my head so our eyes are level.

"You don't, but Bea, I'll throw you over my shoulder and drag you kicking and screaming from this place if I have to."

She opens her mouth to argue and it's then we hear the first pound of bullets.

Fuck this.

I deliver on my promise, lifting her off her feet and swinging her over my shoulder.

Her hospital gown opens at the back. I get an eyeful of her round ass. Right there on my shoulder.

Gonna bite that.

Gonna sink my teeth deep into that plump flesh.

Gonna dip my head between her thighs and–

"Nate!" Angel barks, bringing me back to the land of the living. The omega hammers her little fists against my back. Kicking her legs and narrowly missing the crown jewels.

"We got to go." He has the radio to his ear. "The others have been engaged in gunfire."

"Gunfire!" the omega yelps.

"It's okay, sweetheart. We've got you," Hardy says as he covers my front and Angel my rear.

"You think there's another way out of here?" Angel calls

from behind me. "I'm concerned the main entrance will be compromised."

Hardy jerks to the left, down a corridor we hadn't passed earlier. "Fire escape."

He crashes straight through it, sirens blaring and then we're racing through a deserted parking lot, and out towards a wire fence.

I look up at it and then down at the omega slung over my shoulder.

Yeah, I can do this.

Holding onto her with one arm, I use my other to start scaling the fence but she's squirming too much. It's impossible.

"Little bird," I warn, jumping back down to the ground.

"We need to cut through it," Hardy says and I hook out my knife and start slicing through wires. Hardy grips either side of the cut wires and tears the fence apart.

"After you," he says, when the hole is large enough to climb through. I step through, the others right behind me and then we're sprinting for the van. The omega bouncing and cursing on my shoulder all the way.

We can hear the sound of gunshots from within the building but I try not to think of that. I keep pounding one foot in front of the other until I'm leaping into the van and slamming the door behind us.

The omega lands on her back on the seats with an oof and scowls up at me.

I don't even smirk.

Instead I turn to Angel.

"Axel? Connor?"

The radio crackles against his ear but I can't make out the garbled words.

"They're coming." He jumps into the driver's seat and starts revving the engine.

"What's going on?" the omega asks, her lower lip wobbling.

"The bad guys," I say.

"The others?" she says, swinging her gaze around the van.

"Coming, sweetheart," Hardy tells her, finding a blanket and wrapping it around her shoulders.

She coos, snuggling into the material like it's made of cashmere and not some shitty rug Axel keeps in the van.

Her heat is all fucked up.

I peer through the window and my hand strays to the door handle.

"What you doing?" Hardy asks.

"Going back to join the fun," I say simply.

Angel peers over his shoulder to look at me, then makes a deliberate show of switching on the child locks.

"Motherfucker," I hiss.

But before I get a chance to find an exit through a broken window, the doors slide open and Connor and Silver barrel inside, Axel jumping into the front passenger seat.

Bullets drum against the back of the van. The omega screams and Angel slams his foot to the floor.

"Who are they?" Hardy says, covering the omega with his body even though the sounds of the bullets are fading. He looks a little too comfortable with her in his arms.

"Don't know," Silver says, "they were masked."

"Their scents?" Hardy asked.

"Masked too," Silver adds.

"Something fucked up was going down in there," Axel says from the front. "But I'm not sure what the hell it was."

"What did they want with–" Angel begins, then jams down his window. "Her scent!"

Her scent.

Juicy. Sweet. So fucking wet.

She moans underneath Hardy's body and I hook out my knife.

"Get off her, motherfucker."

He uncurls his arms and the omega scampers out.

Her face is flushed pink like candy floss, her eyes glassy and her thighs sticky with slick.

It's goddamn pornographic. It's goddamn enticing.

She peers at my knife and frowns. I flick it away and stuff it in my pocket.

"How are you feeling, sweetheart?" Axel asks from the front seat, twisting his body right around to look at her, heat swimming in his eyes.

She swallows a moan and, her little hands forming fists by her sides, closes her eyes and puffs air out of her mouth.

"Does it hurt?" Connor asks with concern.

"Want me to make it better?" I ask, licking my lips.

She cracks open an eyelid in time to see the sweep of my tongue. She squeals and slams shut her eye.

"I want to go home, please."

"We'll take you back to our apartment," Axel says. "It's closer."

"Like hell you will," Angel growls. "She's coming with us."

This again.

I grit my teeth.

"I'm not going with any of you," the omega says firmly. "I want you to take me back to the beach house."

"You're only a day into this heat, baby girl," Silver says

patiently. "You've got another two to go at least. You need us to take care of you."

"You?" she scoffs. "I wouldn't ask you six scallywags to take care of me if you were the last men on earth."

"Sweetheart," Hardy says as he tugs off his balaclava. "We just rescued you."

"I didn't ask you to," she mumbles, her forehead wrinkling, her body tensing with obvious pain. She takes a deep breath in and out. "For all I know you set all that up. Just to get me to climb into bed with you."

Silver points to a bullet lodged into his vest at his shoulder.

The omega manages a shrug.

"I told you," I say. "We're the good guys." When it comes to this situation anyway.

"You are not good guys," she says, her lower lip wobbling. "You used me. You played me. You made me fall for you and ..."

"You fell for us, huh?" Hardy says and I want to punch him square on the nose.

"Because I'm an idiot." Her whole body shakes and a film of sweat shines on her face. "Thank you for coming to help me. But I didn't ask for it and I don't want any more of it. Take me home."

Her last word trails off into a yelp of pain and she screws up her face and bends double, moaning through another stab of pain.

Her scent thickens even more. I jerk down the window and stare out at the darkness.

It stares back at me and creeps through the open window threatening to swallow me whole. My fingers itch to pull out my knife.

I peer behind the car, back in the direction we've just come. No one's following us.

I could jump out. Head back to that underground clinic. Slit a few throats.

"We'll drive you home," Axel says.

There's some murmuring from within the car.

"The lady said no," Axel says firmly, and the car is silent again.

It's like the magnitude of our fuck up has slapped us hard around the face.

Guess I shouldn't be surprised.

This little bird is different.

Not like the expensively preened usual ones.

She's not that stupid.

Risking our sorry asses to rescue her was never going to be enough.

The omega moans in agony beside me.

I could fling her onto her back, sink my tongue into her cunt and flip those moans right around.

I plunge my hand into my pants. Flick open my knife in my pocket.

I wrap my fingers around the blade and squeeze. Squeeze hard.

It's what I deserve.

What we all deserve.

The sharp metal slices through my skin.

I don't feel the pain.

The pain radiating through my chest masks it entirely.

7

Bea

I don't remember much about the journey to the beach other than the pain and the agony, and the way my body had fought me every long drawn-out minute.

My treacherous body had wanted those alphas there in the van. Had wanted to curl around their hard, strong bodies. Had wanted to lick them and breathe in their mind-tingling scents. Had wanted to open my legs and beg them to have me. All of them. Then and there. To fuck me and rut me and knot me. To fill me up. To keep me coming over and over again.

But my mind and my heart, they knew better.

And though the pain in my gut was fierce, it was nothing really. Nothing compared to the piercing agony in my heart.

Though my heat scrambled my thoughts, leaving me

struggling to remember where or who I was, one thought spun around and around in my mind.

These men had hurt me. I'd trusted them. I'd let my guard down. I'd let them into my fragile heart and they'd ripped it to shreds.

I wouldn't let them do it again. No matter how badly my body screamed for them.

At some point, when the sky was still dark, we reached the beach. I remember the sound of the crashing waves, the taste of salt on my tongue, Courtney's arms wrapped tight around my frame. And then the soft mattress of the bed. Sinking deep into layers of softness, burying under the covers. Then darkness.

I lie awake now in that same room. The sheets are damp with sweat and slick, and pain racks though my body. I bite down hard on my lip, tasting copper in my mouth. I rub furiously at my clit chasing an orgasm that won't come. Knowing if it did, it would bring me some kind of relief. Knowing instinctively that it would only be a half measure.

Only a cock deep in my pussy would relieve this incessant ache; never-ending and relentless.

I knew this would be bad.

But it's worse, so much worse, than I could have ever imagined.

I flip onto my stomach, burying my head into the pillow, my screams muffled as I thrust my fingers in and out of myself.

I consider relenting. I consider jumping in Missy and heading to the city, begging the first alpha I meet to fuck me hard.

I consider calling my alphas and pleading with them to come. I swear I can almost smell their scents in the air.

I screw my eyes up tight, as my hips lift, and images of

the six of them float through my mind, like the worst possible kind of treacherous sirens.

They are not *my* alphas.

They are not.

They never were. It was all a lie. All a silly game.

So what they rescued me? So what they pulled me away from whatever danger I'd stumbled into?

Like I told them, I have no idea if they were the cause of that danger. If it was a giant hoax, designed to humiliate me all over again.

No, I'm not going to think about those alphas. I'm going to forget all about them and when this is over, I'll find a nice respectable alpha, one I can line up for a heat and never see again.

I won't think about Axel's scent of spring rain.

I won't think of Angel's gray eyes. Or Nate's dirty ones.

I won't think of Hardy's skilled hands. Or Silver's heart-stopping smile.

And most of all I will not think of Connor Doyle.

A soft knock sounds against the door. Then Courtney's gentle voice.

"Bea? It's time for your next dose of painkillers."

I roll onto my back. The curtains are closed and so is the window. But somehow the bright sunshine of the day still stings my eyes. I would kill for the cool breeze of the ocean right now.

"Thanks, Court," I call back, trying to keep my voice natural sounding, although it's clear as day how strained it is. "Just slide them under the door."

"Are you sure I can't come in? Can't help you in any way?"

"No, no, I'm fine," I say as cheerfully as I can, biting down hard on my tattered lip as another of those waves of agony sears through my body, so painful it feels like I'm being hacked in two.

I hear a scraping sound from the other side of the door and then the packet of pills skids into the room.

"If you need anything, just call, okay, Bea?"

"Uh huh," I say, my teeth slammed down hard on my lip.

Courtney hesitates. "Are you sure I can't call those alphas, Bea? This is crazy and–"

"No," I yell out. "No, Courtney!"

She sighs and I imagine her shaking her head. "Okay, okay, I'm sorry."

When her feet pad away, I drag myself to the edge of the bed. The door seems like it's miles and miles away and I sob. The painkillers have been next to useless – not like whatever they pumped me full of at that clinic – but they have numbed the pain just a little. Enough so I don't want to throw myself through the window and drown myself in the ocean.

Oh god, that sounds so blissful. The cool waves swallowing me up and then nothing. Nothing at all. No pain, no agony, no ache.

I flop off the bed, meeting the carpeted floor with a hard thump that rattles every bone in my sore body. I straighten my arm out hoping to snatch the packet. It's too far away. With gritted teeth, I pull myself along, the carpet burning against my irritated skin, and finally my fingertips brush the packet. My first attempt to snag them only pushes them further away and I sob again. Second time, I manage to pinch the foiled plastic between my fore and middle fingers and drag the damn things towards me.

Wisely, she's only given me two. If there'd been more, I would have downed the lot.

Swallowing them dry, I curl up in a ball, the pills

scraping along my gullet. I whimper on the floor rocking myself, trying to think of the sea and the sand. Trying to imagine I'm anywhere but here. Finally the pain eases and I fall into a restless sleep.

TIME STRETCHES AND ELONGATES, every painful second lasting for hours. But finally, finally, I flick open my eyes, staring up at the same white ceiling I've been staring at for God knows how long and realize the pain and the ache, the heat and the confusion have all gone.

I roll up, sitting for the first time in days. My head swims, my body is stiff and a wave of nausea passes through me, but I feel a million, billion, trillion times better.

I sigh with more relief than I've ever felt in my life.

I was right the first time. Being an omega sucks. It sucks big time. I can't believe I have to go through these heats regularly. I need to find another doctor and a whole cargo ship's load of drugs.

I shuffle to the edge of the bed and drop my feet to the floor. I'm naked and covered in dry slick, which is frankly gross. I nearly vomit.

I glance towards the mirror hanging on the wall and flinch. Half my hair is plastered to my face and the rest is sticking up in strange angles around my head. There's also a trail of dried drool running down my chin and dried blood on my arm.

Very damn attractive.

No wonder Karl left me.

I need to take a shower. I needed to take a shower like two days ago. But first, as my stomach reminds me with an angry growl, food and water.

I find my gown hanging on the back of the door and tie it around me, then with unsteady steps, I head for the kitchen. I haven't walked in days and my legs are wobbly. Somehow though I make it.

Courtney's in there, sitting at the counter, reading a book with her earphones plugged in. I walk up right behind her, the music from her earbuds blaring, and tap her on the shoulder. She leaps three feet off her seat and lands back down with a yelp.

She tugs the earbuds from her ears and twists to look round at me, her hand on her heart.

"Jesus Christ, Bea, you scared me to death. I didn't hear you coming."

"I'm not surprised. You'll have no eardrums left if you listen to your music turned up so high."

"Sorry," she says, "I was trying to block out the sound of your cries." She frowns. "It was ... it was pretty tough to hear."

"It was pretty tough to endure."

Courtney launches forward on her seat and squeezes me tight, sniffling against my neck. My tired bones crack but I hug her back, feeling even more human for it.

When she pulls away, I notice how exhausted she looks, shadows ringing her wet eyes.

Her gaze flicks over my face and my body and then she sighs dramatically in relief. "Is it over?"

I nod. "At least I think so."

"Thank god." Courtney flops forward, her head resting on the counter.

I guess I wasn't the only one who suffered through this heat.

"Were you here the whole time?" I whisper.

She peeks up at me. "Of course, I wasn't going to leave you."

I hug her again. Then jerk back, remembering I am a gross mess. "What about your work?"

"I took some leave."

"Paid?"

Courtney shrugs in a way I know means no.

"Thank you," I tell her, hoping one day I'll be able to repay the favor.

"I was so worried about you ..." Courtney says, her eyes brimming again. My cousin always puts on this tough show, I'm not used to seeing her more vulnerable side.

"I'm okay now," I say, managing a genuine smile for the first time in days. "Although freaking starving. Is there anything to eat?" I glance towards the refrigerator. "I'm about to keel over from hunger."

"Yes." Courtney jumps down from her stool and hurries to the fridge. "There're loads. What do you fancy?" She starts pulling out dish after dish from the dimly lit interior. "Meat loaf? Lasagna? Chicken soup? Apple pie? Pancakes?"

"Did you make all this?" I ask, coming to examine all the food, my stomach rumbling even louder.

Courtney snorts. "You know I can't cook." She unwraps foil from the meatloaf and switches on the oven.

"Did you order it all then? Court, you really shouldn't have spent money on all this." Especially when she's just lost a load of her pay.

"Oh I didn't buy it," she says, absentmindedly as she slides the dish into the oven.

"Then where did it all come from?" I laugh. "The food fairy."

Courtney's cheeks blush red and she hurries back over

to her book, busying herself with turning down the corner of her page.

"Courtney?" I ask, suddenly feeling suspicious. "Where did this food come from?"

"I can't tell you," she snaps, slamming her book down on the counter. "Here, I'll make you a peanut butter and jelly sandwich while we're waiting for the meatloaf to warm up."

"Wait, wait, wait," I say, lifting my palm. "Why can't you tell me?"

"I promised him."

"Him?"

"Shit!" she says, slapping her hand over her mouth.

I try to tug it away.

"Tell me?"

She holds it firm against her mouth and shakes her head.

"Hmmm," I say, going to inspect the dishes. The pastry on the apple pie looks homemade although instead of the usual apple shape on top, there's something that looks more like a skull and crossbones. It smells divine and my stomach gurgles at the thought of consuming all that.

"It was Nate, wasn't it?"

Courtney's eyes flash above her covered mouth.

I raise an eyebrow at her.

Her shoulder sag and she nods. "He said an omega is always starving hungry after a heat and he wanted you to have something good to eat."

"But he didn't want you to tell me he brought it over?"

"No."

"Hmmmm," I say again.

I pick out a spoon from the drawer, plunge it through the crust and into the apple mixture below, then bring it up to my mouth. I wrap my lips around the spoon and moan.

"Oh jeez," I mumble. "That is so freaking good."

"You have no idea how hard it was not to eat it," Courtney says, snatching the spoon from my hand and taking a mouthful for herself. "That is so good." Her eyes roll around in their sockets.

I grab the spoon and take another chunk for myself. The second piece seems even better than the first.

"Need more." Courtney finds her own spoon from the drawer and soon we're attacking the pie like it's the last piece of food on Earth. "Fuck, I think my mouth is actually orgasming."

"Mine too," I groan.

"If his food is this good," Courtney says, "imagine how good his dick will be."

"Nope," I say, shaking my head with my mouth full. "Not going to think about that."

"You're still mad with them, huh?"

"Can you blame me?"

"No," Courtney pauses, "but they did rescue you."

"Well boo for them," I mumble. I lower my spoon. My stomach has that pleasantly full sensation I haven't felt for days. "How did they know I was in trouble? I mean, I didn't expect anybody to even realize I was in trouble for days."

"You left your phone behind. I took it to the clinic and you weren't there. No one would tell me where you were. It didn't sit right with me. I thought about calling the police. Then I decided those alphas might be more helpful."

I rest my head on my cousin's shoulder. "Thank you. Again. I owe you big time."

"You don't owe me anything. No one's stealing away my roomie without a fight." She kisses the top of my head.

"Love you Court. Although, I have to tell you," I say, picking up her book from the counter, "folding over the pages of books is sacrilegious. I may have to disown you if you don't stop."

Courtney snorts. "I like my books to be well loved and well read. They should be devoured so badly, their covers rip and their pages fall out. That is the sign of a good book." I frown. She wags her spoon at me. "None of this uptight I-can't-possibly-break-the-spine business."

"That's so wrong," I tell her. "You are a book abuser."

"Nope, it's a sign of how much I love my books. I also love you, Bea, but ..."

"But?" I say.

"You need to shower." She crinkles up her nose.

"You don't think this new look suits me?" I ask, smoothing down my wayward locks.

"You're not hipster or grunge enough to carry it off," Courtney says, "now if it were me ..."

"Okay, okay, I'm going."

I'm halfway to the door when Courtney says:

"I like that Nate dude, by the way."

Yeah, I do too. That's half the problem. If I hadn't liked them as much as I did, the betrayal wouldn't have been as devastating.

8

Silver

I SLIDE a coffee and one of those oversized donuts covered in sugar and shit towards Sampson and reclaim my seat beside Connor.

Sampson grins, and drags it towards him, lifting it to his mouth.

Connor leans in to whisper in my ear. "You know this dude from the army?" He asks as we watch Sampson demolish the thing in three mouthfuls, sugar tumbling down his chin.

Connor insisted on coming with me to this meeting. I don't know how long this temporary truce between our two packs is going to hold up, but for once I actually appreciate the presence of a second pair of intelligent ears. Finding out who was behind Bea's kidnapping is my number one priority. I smell a very big rat in all this and I won't be content until that rat is strung up by its tail.

I nod.

Once upon a time, Sampson owned the tightest set of abs in our unit but since quitting the military at roughly the same time I did, and joining the cops instead, he's let that shit slide. Not that I'm complaining. Some cops want money, girls or drugs in exchange for information. Sampson, donuts.

"What can you tell us?" I ask him, taking a sip from my own black coffee.

Sampson wipes his mouth with a paper napkin.

"You ain't going to like it, Silver. There's not much to tell."

I exchange a look with Connor. "Why's that? You have a culprit under police guard at the hospital and an entire clinic full of evidence."

Sampson brushes sugar and crumbs from the front of his shirt. He's not dressed in uniform. His shift doesn't start until later.

"The injured doctor has lawyered up tight. He's not saying one word to us."

Connor grunts in irritation. "How hard have you tried? Have you turned the screws on that motherfucker?"

"That motherfucker lost an eye. And tightening the screws looks like piddly shit in comparison. No, he's not talking."

"And the clinic?" I ask.

"Well, that is interesting." He wipes his fingers on the napkin and tosses it onto the tabletop. "There was nothing there." Connor and I stare at the man like he's talking gibberish. He laughs at us. "It had been cleared out."

"What do you mean?"

"Someone knew we were coming and did a very thorough job of clearing out any kind of evidence."

"That's not possible," Connor insists. "It was a big place."

"Yeah, with no paperwork, no equipment, no computers, nothing but a few beds and bedding."

"I assume those were swabbed for DNA and other evidence."

"They were," he says, leaning in, "but here's the interesting thing." He meets my eyes, lowering his voice. "That evidence has gone walkabout."

"What?"

"It's missing."

"What the fuck?" I growl. "How can it go missing?"

Sampson shrugs. "Very good question. Line is it accidentally got placed in the destroy pile and was incinerated."

"Fuck," Connor says, drumming his fingers on the table surface. "Fuck."

"What's your thoughts?" I ask Sampson.

"Probably the same as yours, Silver. Smells fishy as hell. We have your witness statements and when the omega has emerged from her heat cycle, we'll take hers too. It isn't enough to go on. We can charge the doctor with kidnap and assault. But tracking down the others involved? Getting to the bottom of what the hell was going on?" He shrugs. "I suspect there are higher powers involved, something bigger than this one incident."

I spin my coffee cup around in my hands, glancing down into the jet black liquid. "Yeah," I say, "I think you're right."

"Any idea who those higher powers could be?" Connor asks us both.

"Me? No," Sampson says, picking up the pot of sugar and pouring enough to rot his teeth into his drink. He stirs it with a teaspoon and drops it on the table with a clank. "How about you?"

"I have some ideas," I tell them. "Ones I'll be looking into."

"If you find anything–"

"I'll be in touch and you'll do the same."

Sampson nods.

Our culinary tastes may have deviated since we both left the unit, but Sampson's a good man. One of the few I trust outside my pack and the men working for me.

"How about the omega?" Connor asks, his voice tightening with caution.

"What about her?" Sampson asks, lifting his drink and eyeing us both with interest over the rim of his coffee cup.

If he was surprised to see me and Connor here together this morning, he did a good job of hiding it. But perhaps he reserved all his surprise for when our two packs called in this crime. Together. Usually, people are telling on us and the crap we've done to each other. I bet he choked on his donut when he learned we'd been working together.

"Is there any danger she's going to be charged for the ..." Connor points to his eye.

"The doctor has been strongly discouraged from pursuing any charges. And even if he changed his mind, it was self defense, right?"

"Hell, it was," I say.

In all honesty, the man is lucky to be alive, all those shitty medics are too. If we'd had more time, then who knows what the fuck us boys would have done to them.

"She'll be okay," Sampson says.

"You know if any charges are brought," Connor says, "we'll be finding her the best goddamn lawyers in the country."

"This one's special, is she?"

"She took the asshole's eye out, what do you think?"

Sampson smiles. "I should have known that would have been your type, Silver."

"Yeah," I say, taking a long gulp of my coffee. "She's my type."

Connor glances at me. "Mine too," he says firmly.

And I realize, we may have rescued our girl but we still have a pile of shit to sort through. Finding who was behind the kidnapping may prove to be the easiest.

I buy Sampson another donut for the road and then we head to Pack York's offices to update the others. On our way, I receive a call from one of the men I have stationed discreetly watching the beach condo where the omega has been staying with her cousin.

"Calling in for an update, Sir," he says.

I switch my cellphone to my other ear, noting the way Connor's eyes leave the road to flick to mine.

"Go ahead," I tell him.

"Apart from the one visitor delivering food parcels," Nate, "there have been no other visitors to the condo and no other suspicious activity."

"Good," I say. I'm hoping whoever kidnapped Bea won't be stupid enough to try the same thing twice, but I'm not taking any chances. "Anything else?"

"Yes, it seems she may have completed her heat."

I sit up a little straighter in my seat. "Based on what evidence?"

"She's no longer holed up in the bedroom. She's been eating and talking with her cousin."

"Right," I say, "keep up the good work."

I end the call.

"Something up?" Connor asks.

I consider keeping this new piece of news to myself. But working together hasn't been so bad, and sorting out all this mess won't happen if I'm keeping information from Pack York.

"Bea's finished her heat."

Connor is quiet for a moment, his hands tight on the steering wheel. "The thought of her going through it alone ..." he says with real pain in his voice.

"Yeah, but what could we do?" We couldn't force her to take us. There was nothing else to be done but stand back and let her endure it alone.

"We shouldn't have fucked up like we did in the first place."

"Yeah," I say, running my hand through my hair. "Yeah."

The others are waiting for us around the board table: Axel and Angel sitting on opposite sides avoiding eye contact, Hardy leaning back on the rear legs of his chair, his hands hooked behind his neck and Nate pacing by the windows.

"What did you learn?" Angel asks as I walk through the door.

"Nothing," I say, taking the seat next to the head of my pack.

"Nothing," Axel says with a frown.

I smirk at him. "Which is interesting in itself. Someone cleared out that clinic before the cops arrived and what evidence they did collect has mysteriously disappeared."

"So?" Axels say with more irritation.

"It means we're dealing with professionals," Connor tells him, "professionals with arm power and a swat team of their own."

"Snakebites?" Angel asks, and Hardy swings his chair

back to the ground with a thump as Nate takes a step towards the table.

"Could be," I say, "although it seems out of their usual realm of operation. I'm going to do more digging."

"Me too," Connor says.

I nod. "We should keep each other updated." Angel peers at me. I straighten my tie. "There's more."

"Go on," Axel says.

"Bea's finished her heat."

There's a collective intake of breath. Then Axel draws back his chair. "Then I'm going to see her."

"You think you should?" Connor asks.

"Hell, yes. I need to talk to her."

Angel stands too. "If you're going to see her, I'm coming too."

"You're not."

"Are you going to stop me?"

Hardy shakes his head and Nate snorts.

"She's pissed with us for the shit we pulled," Hardy says, "you think the two of you rocking up and demanding to see her, shoving each other out the way to get to her first, is going to help?"

"She's not going to be pissed with us anymore," Axel says, swinging his jacket off the back of his chair and sliding his arms inside. "We rescued her."

"Yeah, and she was still pissed when we did that," Nate mumbles.

"Heat hormones," Axel says with a wave of of his hand. "Now she's back in her own mind, she's going to be grateful. We risked our lives for her. Girls love that shit."

I shake my head, "It's not that simple, man," I say to the head of my pack.

But Angel seems to be listening to his big brother's bullshit and not the rest of us.

"What exactly are you hoping will happen," Connor says, "if you rock up outside her door?"

"I'm going to reaffirm our position," Axel states, "tell her how we feel about her, that we are serious about wanting her for our pack."

"Same," Angel says, "same."

"She won't like that," Hardy mumbles.

"It's clear the girl was falling for our pack," Axel says.

"She was falling for ours," Angel contradicts.

"Well, she can't have the both of us," Axel scowls at his brother, "it's about time she made her choice."

Angel nods and then before we can stop them, they're striding from the room.

Nate thumps the table in irritation and Hardy shakes his head.

"I've got a bad feeling about this," Connor mumbles.

"Yeah," I say, "so do I."

9

Bea

ONE SHOWER and one meat loaf later, I look more like my old self, even if I feel nothing like it.

Courtney and I take a mug of coffee each down to the beach, digging our toes in the fine sand and watching the waves cruise lazily into the shore. Court has the shotgun resting beside her and I have the alarm Aunt Julia gave me hanging around my wrist.

I guess I'm finally taking all the warnings about my safety seriously.

"I need to find a new job," I say, taking a sip of my coffee.

"You already have a job."

"Not one I can go back to."

"I thought you were doing well in that job. You shouldn't have to give it up just because those dudes are assholes."

"I know but," I sigh, "I don't think I could bear to see Axel every day. Or any of the others."

I wiggle my toes in the sand. Finding this job in the first place had been hard enough, and if I suspected I'd only landed it in the first place because Axel was pursuing me, everything that has happened since has only confirmed it. If I can't find anything, I'm going to have to go back to Naw Creek. I can't live on thin air, and I can't expect Courtney to keep subsidizing me.

"There's always Hooters," Courtney reminds me, "or cam work. You may as well put your amazing tits to good use."

I stare down at them. "You really think they're that good?"

Courtney snorts. "Like you don't?"

I think about it. I think about all those cruel, dismissive words from Karl. I think about how those alphas used me as part of some sick game they have going on. I dismiss all those thoughts and consider my boobs objectively. It's been a long time since I've said anything nice about myself out loud. It's been a long time since I believed it.

But this isn't some tale of Cinderella being rescued by Prince Charming. I'm going to have to rescue myself. Just like I did in that clinic – before the alphas arrived and interfered anyway.

"Yes, actually, I think they are pretty good."

Courtney smiles at me. "You're doing much better than I thought you would be. Considering everything that's happened."

"I don't have a choice, Court. I either fall apart or I keep going."

She rests her coffee on her knee. Above us gulls screech at each other in the sky and behind us, a car engine rumbles.

"What happened in that clinic, Bea? Why did they take you there?"

I take a long gulp of coffee. "I ... I don't know ... there was this one doctor who was certain I'd taken something that had turned me from a beta to an omega. He wanted me to tell him what it was. He was pretty persistent." I glance at her. "He was the one I stabbed with the needle."

Courtney lifts her palm and I high five her.

"I still can't believe Dr. Hannah was in on it."

"Me neither." Another person who's betrayed me. I'm going to have to look more carefully at who I place my trust in.

I straighten my legs and feel the cool sand against the backs of my thighs. The rumble of that engine grows louder and we turn our heads to see a black SUV trundling down the track. No flashy sports cars today, but no doubting who it is.

Courtney picks up the shotgun. "I guess it was only a matter of time before they showed up again."

"But why? They've had their fun. Their stupid bet. Can't they leave me alone now?"

We watch as the two front doors open and Axel and Angel climb out. I'm surprised to see them without their packs. I'm even more surprised to see them together. They walk towards the beach house and knock on the door.

I'm tempted to signal to Courtney that we should go hide out in the sand dunes, but then Axel's head snaps around and he spies me.

"Oh crap," I mumble as both men lumber across the sand in our direction.

I notice they're both wearing smart shoes to match their suits. I hope they end up with a shit load of sand in them. And in their socks. And between their toes too.

"Hi sweetheart," Angel says, a concerned look on his face. "How are you feeling?"

"Much better, thank you," I say as formally as I can.

The sea breeze rolling off the ocean drops in temperature about five degrees.

"Good, that's good." He nods, running his fingers through his beard.

"We're glad you're safe," Axel adds.

"I am now. So thank you for that. I appreciate it."

"We'd do anything for you, sweetheart," Axel says with a smile that makes his eyes twinkle.

"Except tell me the truth," I say.

The smile drops from his face and both men are silent while the gulls continue to squabble in the sky above us.

Perhaps a few dollops of bird shit on their suits as well as the sand?

Angel scratches his chin. "We've been looking into who took you. The police are too."

"And?"

"Nothing yet."

I stare at them both.

"How about the man Bea stabbed?" Courtney asks.

"Under arrest and still in the hospital."

"And is Bea in any trouble for hurting him?"

I snap my head around to look at my cousin. That hadn't even occurred to me. I squeak, my hands rising to my throat. Both alphas take a concerned step towards me.

"No, no," Axel says soothingly. "Not at all. She's not being charged with anything and even if she was, Pack York has the best lawyers in the city."

Angel snorts and Axel glares at him.

"I don't need your lawyers," I say. I hug my arms around my stomach. "And I'm handing in my resignation."

Axel frowns. "Why?"

"You can come work for us, sweetheart?" Angels says. "Pack Boston has always paid much better than Pack York."

"Bullshit," Axel growls.

I stare at them both. Really? This again.

"I'm grateful, really grateful, that you helped me out of that clinic. But nothing's changed here." Courtney lifts her shotgun. "You used me. You hurt me. And frankly, I've had too much of that in my lifetime. I don't want to see either one of you, or your packs, ever again."

"Bea," Axel says, frowning hard. "I risked my life to come get you. I risked my packmates' lives too. Surely you can see how sorry I am? How serious I am about you? It was a mistake. You can't keep punishing us forever. We're meant to be together. I know you feel that too."

"She's meant to be with us," Angel says, hands on his hips.

"I'm not meant to be with anyone." I swing my head from side to side. My eyes swim with tears. "You hurt me. You used me. You lied to me. And look," I point to the two of them, "nothing's changed. This ..." I screw up my face, "this rivalry. This hatred you have going on. It's destructive. I don't want to be caught up in it. I don't want to be anywhere near it!"

"We both came to get you. We can put our differences aside when it counts," Axel says, although the look on his face, like he just swallowed a live scorpion, doesn't suggest he finds the idea very palatable.

I shake my head again.

"Bea, my brother's always been shitty with words. He's always shoving his size 12 feet in his dumbass mouth but ..."

I gape at them. Angel's words trail off.

"Brother?" I whisper.

Courtney takes an involuntary step backwards.

I blink against the sunshine.

Brothers?

Holy shit.

"You're brothers?"

The two men look at each other and then back at me. They nod in unison and the expression is so alike it's almost a reflection.

How had I not seen it before?

Their eyes, their builds, the timbre of their voices, the cut of their faces. Shit even their scents are alike.

"You ... you never told me you were brothers?"

"We don't usually have to," Angel says, stiffening. "Most people know."

"But ... but ... you hate each other? How could you hate your brother?"

Angel glances to the floor and Axel shifts uncomfortably on his feet.

"I don't hate him," he mumbles.

Angel snorts.

"Not that much anyway," he adds sinisterly.

I take a step away from them.

This makes their stupid rivalry one million times worse. The way they'd fought each other, out here in front of the beach house. Hitting and pummeling each other. Drawing blood, skinning their knuckles. How could they do that to one another?

"Your poor mother," I say, and both their gazes drop uncomfortably to their sand-filled shoes.

I don't have any siblings. But I love Courtney like a sister – fierce, funny Courtney, brow pulled down in a scowl, gripping the gun. I could never dream of hurting her.

"Like I already said," I say, "I don't want to be a part of

this." I grip Courtney's arm. "I could never be with someone and watch while they tear their loved one apart." It makes my stomach twist just talking about it.

"You don't understand," Angel says, through gritted teeth. "You don't understand what he did. Not all families are the same."

"What *I* did?" Axel says, twisting towards his brother.

"I don't care what you did to him or he did to you." I fling my hands up in the air. "Do you know what Karl did to *me*? Do you?" They shake their heads. "He left me for my best friend. He left me on my wedding day. At the altar. All made up in my big fat stupid dress. For everyone to see." Tears stream down my cheeks. I can see it. All those faces staring at me with pity as I stood there alone waiting for a groom who would never come. "And what am I doing now? Am I out there plotting his demise? Have I dedicated my whole life to revenge?"

"You should do," Courtney mumbles and I give her a look.

"No, I shouldn't." I turn back to the two brothers. "I don't care what you did to each other. Because, you know what? When someone hurts you, you have two choices in life. To move on and be happy. To make something of your life. Or to simmer in your own hatred until it boils you alive. Until you're bitter and twisted." I inhale deeply. "Until it causes you to hurt the people you claim to care about."

"I do care about you," Angel says, shame in his eyes. "Bea–"

"Just go."

"But Bea–"

"Nope," Courtney declares, firing the shotgun into the air. Thick smoke billows from the barrel but she manages to stay on her feet this time. "I've been practicing," she whispers to me, before shouting over to the alphas. "Just get out of here."

The alphas look like they might start arguing again but she waves the gun at them and they slink off, climbing into the car and pulling away.

"Jeez, I wouldn't want to be in that car ride," Courtney says. "If looks could kill ..."

"Exactly," I mutter, and if I was ever in danger of wavering about these men, that danger has well and truly passed.

10

xel

THAT DIDN'T GO ACCORDING to plan.

To be honest, in the last few weeks, nothing has. Not since Bea stumbled into my life at that gas station in the middle of nowhere. Since that day everything has been different. Nothing has run smoothly. Nothing like it should.

Getting the girl should have been easy as pie.

Getting the girl back after we screwed up should have been a little more tricky, but nothing to break into a sweat about.

It seems I was wrong.

Bea isn't like girls we've dated before. She's not like any omega I've ever met.

She doesn't behave like she's damn well meant to.

And, fuck me, if that isn't half the reason I'm falling for her.

Maybe I like the sensation of whiplash. Maybe I've always liked it.

Plodding along, everything always the same, is dull, dull, dull.

I could do with a little tornado like her in my life.

Unfortunately, that's looking unlikely. Because, even facing a torrent of bullets is not enough for her to forgive me. To forgive us.

I turf Angel out of my car as quickly as possible. I should never have agreed to his stupid plan to visit Bea together. He convinced me it was important to show her a united front. I agreed through gritted teeth. But the two of us keeping a united front is like two lions in a cage agreeing not to fight.

I drive back to York Tower, taking the elevator straight up to my office and ignoring anyone who tries to talk to me.

Including Mrs. Finch as I march past her desk and slam my office door shut.

It's not enough to keep her out.

I should have locked the damn thing.

I'm standing by the window, hands in my pockets, staring glassy-eyed at the city view when she comes strolling in. She doesn't even knock.

"Bea's quit. I just received her resignation by email."

"Yeah, I know," I mumble, jiggling the loose change in my pocket.

"How do you know?"

"She told me." I peer over my shoulder at Mrs. Finch. Her mouth is twisted in an unhappy expression. "I went to see her."

Mrs. Finch snatches the glasses off her nose, letting them fall on their chain, and squints at me over the distance. "Did you do something? Did you *boys* do something?"

I swing my gaze back to the window and don't answer.

"I'm going to take that as a yes," she says and her tone reminds me of my school principal every time I did something that disappointed her. Which was, unsurprisingly, a hell of a lot.

"Is there any way things can be fixed because she was a good worker, and I found her presence to be beneficial." High praise indeed coming from my personal assistant.

"No," I say swallowing, "no I don't think there is."

"Hmmmm," Mrs. Finch says, and when I peek at her again, she looks like she'd like to send me for a life long detention. "I'm disappointed in you, Axel York. I may not agree with everything that goes on around here, or every decision you make, but you've never disappointed me before. Bea is a sweet girl."

"I don't need a lecture," I mumble.

"Lucky, because that's all I have to say on the matter. I have better things to do with my time than lecture you, Mr. York." She spins around and stomps towards the door.

My shoulders sag in relief. After the verbal bashing from Bea, I'm not sure I can take another from Mrs. Finch.

"One other thing Mr. York, your mom called."

"Right, I'll call her back."

"That's what you said yesterday. And the day before. And the day before that," Mrs. Finch snaps. "And have you?" She glowers at me.

"No."

"She wants you to go and visit. I told her your afternoon was free and you'd be there after lunch."

"You did what? I have work to be getting on with."

"Really?" she says, peering at me lingering by the window. "Looks like it."

"Call her back and tell her something came up."

"No. I find I'm very busy myself, seeing as I just lost my assistant." I groan. "Do it yourself." She reaches for the door handle. "Or even better go and actually see your mother, Axel. She sounded distressed."

Her gaze softens and I hesitate, then nod.

I glance back out towards the sea and hear the door click shut behind me.

I've been putting it off for long enough. It's about time I went to visit.

IT'S THE HOUSE – it's *mainly* the house. The old-fashioned mansion on the edge of the city with its never-ending grounds and its view of the ocean brings back too many memories. Memories that stab at my heart. Visiting brings everything I've lost over the years crashing through the very adept fences I've built and lands them well and truly front of mind.

Happy memories. Not bad ones.

Of my dad. Of my mom. Of my brother. Endless memories of my brother. Shit, we had the kind of childhood most children dream of.

A dad who loved us. A mom who doted on us. And unrestrained freedom. Fuck, the stupid adventures we had – only a handful actually resulting in hospitalization.

It was fucking glorious. And whenever I think of it, my heart aches so much I struggle for breath.

I park up in the driveway and hover outside the door.

It's most probably unlocked. Even if it's not, I still have my key. But I don't live here anymore. It's no longer my home. I can't just stroll right in. Instead, I pull down on the lever and a loud gong sounds out somewhere deep in the house.

I step back, hooking my hands in my pocket, and wait.

It takes a while, but finally I hear footsteps in the hallway and the giant door swings open.

I flip my shades off my face.

Molly.

She frowns at me.

Not the reaction I was expecting. It's been a long time since my little sister looked up at me with adoration, excitement or joy.

"Axel," she groans, "so nice of you to show your face."

Molly was meant to move out of the family house five years ago. But then dad passed and mom got sick and she never left.

"Hey Molly," I say, stepping forward and kissing her cheek. She lets me although there's no embrace, no hug. "How are you doing?"

"Do you seriously want to know, Axel? Because if you did, you might have, you know, swung by to say hi or even, god forbid, picked up the phone to check."

"I've been busy."

She rolls her eyes and rubs her hands on the apron tied around her waist. It leaves two white dusty imprints of her palms.

"What have you been doing?" I ask.

"Baking. It's my new thing. Helps with the stress and ..." she chews her lip, "other things."

I don't want to know.

She's an omega. A couple of years younger than Bea. She should be mated and settled and happy with her own family by now. Instead, she's living with our mom.

"How is she today? Is she up to seeing me?"

"Oh no, you don't." She pinches my shirt sleeve and tugs me deeper into the house. "She's perfectly well enough to see you. You're not scarpering away that quickly."

I nod, my body stiffening. Molly's eyes flick over me and she frowns at my obvious tension.

"Come on, she's just in the lounge."

Still gripping my sleeve, she pulls me along, stopping at the lounge door.

She hesitates, then turns to me. "She just got sick, Axel. She didn't turn into a monster."

"I know," I whisper, my spine so stiff it might snap. "It's just hard to see her like this."

My sister frowns even harder and jabs me in the pec.

"Oh, grow up, Axel." Then, before I can respond, she pushes open the door, sticks her head through and calls out, "Mom, look who's here. It's Axel."

"Axel?" I hear my mom say, her voice sounding frail in the vast room.

I step inside. The day is full of sunshine, but in the lounge the blinds have been pulled down against the bright light and the room sits in semi-darkness, swirls of dust spinning in the few beams that squeeze their way inside.

My mom lies out on one of the chaises, her cardigan hanging from her bony shoulders, a blanket wrapped over her legs, and a remote control resting in her lap. The giant TV is paused, a woman frozen mid-laugh on the screen.

My mom holds her hands out, beckoning me forward and I realize my goddamn feet had halted. I force them to move again.

She looks worse, so much worse than before. Her skin paper thin, her cheeks hollow, her once thick hair thinning.

I want to turn around and run.

"Axel, it's so good to see you." She smiles, more widely

than the woman on the screen. "Thank you so much for coming to visit. I know how busy you boys are."

There's not a trace of sarcasm or retribution in her tone. She's genuinely pleased to see me. At least there's one woman on the planet who isn't mad with me today.

I lean over her and let her squeeze my hands, the pressure hardly noticeable, as I kiss her cheek. Her scent has faded too. I can barely smell it.

I remember how vivid it once was. The smell of home and warm hugs and safety. A scent I will always love most.

One of the scents I will always love most. There's another that will haunt me now too. Burned fucking caramel.

My mom hangs onto my hands, soaking up my face.

"Always so handsome. So like your father."

"You mean the wrinkles?" I chuckle.

"I can't see any. But I'm sure they'd only add to the air of distinction."

I sit on the footstool next to her, and she keeps clinging onto my hands.

My sister calls from the doorway, "Can I get you guys anything to drink? Are you thirsty, Mom?"

"I'm just fine, Molly. Stop fussing."

Molly rolls her eyes and I shake my head.

"Thanks, I'm fine."

"Get him a coffee, Molly."

"I can go get myself one," I say as my sister glares at me like she's planning to throw a dagger at my face.

"No, you stay right here. I want to hear all your news. I haven't seen you in ages," my mom insists.

"Two months," Molly calls from the door. "It's been two months."

"I'm sure it hasn't been that long," I mumble.

"It has!" Molly shouts back.

"Molly, coffee," my mom says, and poking her tongue out at me, Molly slopes off. "That girl will never land a pack with manners like that." My mom tuts.

"Molly's manners are just fine."

"And she's very beautiful too, isn't she?" My mom smiles fondly. "If only she'd get out more. Maybe you could take her out, Axel, you and Angel together." I shift on my seat and my mom frowns. "Still with the silly fall out?"

I don't know what to say. She always talks as if the fall out between us wasn't so catastrophic, they had to corner off half the county.

"I'll see if she wants to come out. I doubt she'll say yes. She worries about leaving you."

"Me?" my mom huffs. "I'm perfectly fine."

We both know that's not true.

"Anyway," she says, "tell me." She tugs on my hand. I glance upwards, noticing the care she's taken to style her hair. Even though she's going nowhere. Even though she's seeing no one.

"Nothing much to tell."

"Axel Stormgate, that's not what I've heard."

I groan.

My mom might not get out these days but she still has access to a telephone. Much to my detriment, because she has her little coven of friends who supply her with an endless supply of gossip. Gossip, it sounds like, involves me this time. Not that it doesn't always.

"What have you heard?"

Her smile twitches.

She's not going to spill what she knows. She's going to see what I reveal first.

"We bought a prime piece of land by the ocean that we're going to–"

"You know I'm not interested in your wheelings and dealings." She never was when dad was alive either. She married him for love, despite what her hoity toity parents thought. He had no connections and no money. She loved him anyway and with her devotion, with her belief, he made something of himself. He bought this house.

I rub my chin. "Not much else going on. Connor bought a new piece of art for the apartment."

She sniffs and caves.

"What about the omega?"

My stomach sinks. The last thing I need is my mom getting all excited about a potential match on the horizon. Especially when I've well and truly fucked up my chances.

"What omega?" I say, stiffly.

"Don't play dumb with me, Axel. Everyone is talking about her. Your aunt sent Molly a photo. She's absolutely stunning."

"You mean Bea?"

"Bea? Is that her name?" my mom says innocently like she doesn't already know the woman's complete family tree. "What a lovely name."

"Yeah," I say, my gaze dropping to our interlaced hands.

"Oh," she says and I glance up into her silvery eyes. The whites around them are mottled and bloodshot but her irises and her pupils are as bright as ever.

"What?"

"My sources told me you are head over heels for this girl. That you were seen together at the Mackay event." She tilts her head. "Are my sources wrong?"

I manage a half smile. "Your sources are never wrong, Mom."

"But maybe you don't like her as much as my sources are making out."

"No, I like her. I like her a hell of a lot."

"But your pack, your pack don't like her?"

"No, they like her too."

"Then why the long face?" She laughs. "Is Axel Stormgate nervous about the idea of settling down because I think an omega is exactly what you need and–"

I shake my head. "It's not that." I shuffle on my seat and squeeze her hands. "I could see us being with this girl forever but ..."

"But ..."

"She won't have us."

My mom chuckles. "Don't be silly, Axel. What omega wouldn't want you and your pack?"

"This one."

"Why ever not? Is she blind? Stupid? Already bonded?"

"No, she's none of those things. She's clever and single and her eyesight is fine as far as I'm aware."

"Then what's the problem?"

"Here we go," my sister calls out, from behind me and I turn my head to see her walking across the room with a tray, a pot of coffee and a plate of cookies balancing on top. "Fresh out of the oven," she says as she places them down on a coffee table and pours out a cup of coffee.

"Are they safe?" I ask her.

"Yours might be poisoned."

"Molly!"

"I'm joking, Mom."

My mom releases my hands and I reach over for the plate. I offer one to my mom and she shakes her head.

My sister whispers in my ear, "She hasn't been eating much. In fact, it's been a battle to get her to eat anything."

"I can hear you, you know," my mom says, as Molly hands her a coffee. "I'm just not hungry these days."

I nod, and select a cookie, snapping it in half, crumbs tumbling into my lap.

Molly perches on the end of the chaise, a cup of coffee balancing on her knee.

"Axel was just telling us about this girl he likes," my sister raises her eyebrows, "but unfortunately she doesn't like him back."

Molly pretends to faint back against the couch. "How could that ever be possible?" She peeks up at me. "Perhaps because the woman has taste and a brain cell?"

"It doesn't make any sense. My boys are the most eligible alphas in the city. Women are queuing up to date them." Molly rolls her eyes and sips her coffee. "Why would this woman refuse you?"

I turn the cookie halves around in my hands.

"Because I messed up," I say quietly.

"Only to be expected," Molly says.

"How?" my mom asks.

I bite through my cookie and chew. It's surprisingly good. The last thing I ate of Molly's tasted like rabbit shit. She obviously has been practicing.

"Did you apologize?" Molly asks.

"Yes."

"Properly?"

"Of course I did."

Molly snorts.

"What?" I say.

"You're notoriously shit – sorry Mom – at apologizing, Axel. You and Angel."

I look at my mom to contradict this piece of crap but to my surprise she nods in agreement.

"I'm not bad at apologizing."

"If that were true, you and Angel would have made up a long, long time ago."

"He hasn't apologized to me."

"So what?" Molly says, placing her cup on the table. "You're both shitheads. You both hurt each other. Does it matter who apologizes first?"

"He ruined my football career!"

"Molly is right," my mom says. "I've heard both sides of the story many times–"

"So many times!" Molly groans.

"You were both to blame in this, Axel. I wish you could put it behind you."

"We've had this discussion numerous times before."

"You say you like this Bea," my mom says. "You've messed things up. You need to put them right and you're failing. Do you know why I think that probably is, Axel?"

"I have a feeling you're going to tell me."

My mom glares at me. "You've never been good at swallowing your pride and admitting when you've been in the wrong."

"I told her I messed up. I told her I'm sorry."

"Have you *shown* her?"

"Shown her?"

"Axel," my sister says, "you can tell me a million times that you're sorry you don't come and visit more often, that you don't call more often, I'll never believe you truly are. Not until you start showing up on our doorstep more often."

"Shit," I whisper, scrubbing my hand through my hair, feeling all the weight of shame I ought to.

"You've always been your father's son," my mom says, "you always wanted to be just like him and follow in his footsteps. But being a man is about taking responsibility, doing the difficult things – not just the easy ones – admitting when you are wrong and fixing yourself so it doesn't happen again."

I sit there with those words humming in my ears as my mom and my little sister sip their coffee.

I've always considered myself a man, an alpha, this big player, the top dog. People look up to me. People fear me. People respect me. Fuck, they want to be me.

But now, sitting here eating fucking cookies I realize I've been acting like a child. Playing games with people's hearts.

As the chocolate chips melt against my tongue, I realize I'm not only a child, I'm also a massive fucking asshole.

The doorbell gongs somewhere in the hallway and my mom glances towards the window.

"Ahhh, good, that'll be Angel."

11

ngel

I WAS HOPING I wouldn't see my brother again for weeks. Months. Even years.

I've spent more time with him in the last 48 hours than I have in the last decade, and while it hasn't been as terrible as it could have been, it's still been painful. Working with him, to bring Bea home, a reminder of all that we've lost.

Somehow, though, I find myself sitting out back with him on the porch, the vast patch of land that was all ours to explore when we were kids spread out in front of us. My mom, who summoned me here this morning, and my sister have both conveniently disappeared into thin air.

Usually, I've resisted every attempt to maneuver me into the same room as my big brother. Today, I'm too damn tired and deflated to try.

We're quiet. The wind whistles through the grass and

rustles the trees. In the distance the lake winks at us and right at the horizon a sliver of sea glimmers in the bright sun.

"Remember when you fell out of that tree," Axel says, lifting his arm from his lap and pointing to the large oak on the edge of the copse, its branches full to brimming with leaves, "and broke your fucking ass?"

How long has it been since he asked me something as simple as this? Since we talked about the past? It must be an entire lifetime ago.

"It wasn't my ass, it was my coccyx, and it wasn't the oak, it was the beech." I point to the red tree standing right in the center of my mom's flowers. "And I didn't fall, you pushed me."

"Nah, we were racing up to the top, and you threw a paddy because I beat you, tried to hit me, lost your grip and fell."

"It's funny how our recollection of things is always so fucking different," I mutter.

He turns his head from the view to look at me but I keep my gaze trained straight ahead.

We put our differences aside to find Bea. It was a temporary truce. One I'm not prepared to extend just because Axel here is feeling nostalgic.

"Mom was hopping mad about you flattening all her dahlias until she realized you couldn't actually sit to eat your dinner."

A chuckle breaks free of my mouth. "It was so freaking painful. I couldn't sit for like a month."

From the corner of my eye, I see him turn his head back out to the land.

Clouds pass over the face of the sun and we watch as shadows skip across the grass.

"Angel," he says. "It was ... it was good working with you again ... you and the others ... to rescue Bea. Even if it didn't work out the way I wanted."

"She's safe, man. That's the main thing." I scrape my nails through my beard and consider his words. Fuck, it's been a long time since he said anything that positive to me. It feels ... nice. "It was good working with you too."

"Made me realize how much I've missed it."

I exhale, my chest suddenly tight.

"Yeah," I say.

Axel swallows. Hesitates. It's like that phone call he made to tell me Bea was missing. I always know when he has something important to say because he always takes his merry time spitting it out.

I wonder what it'll be this time. More bargaining over Bea, over the land? A scheme to win the girl back? A discussion about what we're going to do as mom gets sicker?

"Angel." I can't take any more of his games. I can't take any more of this bullshit. Whatever he has to say, I wish he'd damn well say it. "I'm sorry." My eyes flick to him. Did I hear him right? "I'm sorry for what happened ten years ago. I'm sorry for my part in it. Most of all," he pauses, "I'm sorry I was an asshole and didn't apologize a hell of a lot sooner."

I'm quiet.

I'm still so angry at him. So fucking angry.

"You stole her from me, Ax. And you know, there was no fucking need. I was always going to share her, introduce her to the pack, make her ours. But you couldn't ... you couldn't stand that I had something you didn't."

Axel sighs like he's just as tired as I am. I see the lines around his eyes. New lines, ones that weren't there before. "It wasn't like that."

"Then how was it?" I growl.

"Celia wasn't the girl you thought she was."

Celia – this sparkly beautiful omega. She smelled like daisies. She made my head spin.

"She was playing you," he says.

"Axel–"

"No, hear me out, Angel. For once just hear me out." He stands up and walks to the rail, leaning his forearms against it. "She was seeing a string of alphas – stringing them along as well as you – ensuring she had a rich crop to pick from."

I shake my head. She wasn't like that. She was sweet. Devoted to me.

"You kissed her," I say. "I saw you kissing her. She was mine and you snatched her away."

He jerks around. "*She* kissed me, Angel. That night she came on to me. I confronted her about the rumors I'd heard – Nate had seen her out with some dudes, Connor had overheard her talking to her friends – I confronted her, and she didn't deny it. Instead, *she* came on to me. Said we could have some fun and that you never needed to find out."

I jump to my feet, my hands balling into fists. "She wouldn't have done that."

"Wouldn't she?" He sweeps his hand through the air. "If she was the woman you thought she was, then where the hell is she now? By your side? Was she there after ..." he swallows, "after the shit storm that went down? Was she there by your side helping you to pick up all the pieces?"

I stare at my brother, the sun hot on my face. "No," I say, "no, she wasn't."

She left. Said I was too much. Said my family and friends were too much. It had made me even angrier, even more furious at my brother. I'd lost her and he was to blame.

Celia moved away. A month later I learned she'd bonded with an older, wealthier pack.

"She made moves on me before," Axel says quietly, "before that night. She sent me text messages. I never responded," he adds quickly. "But I kept them. I was going to show you when the time was right ... You were so crazy in love."

"It wasn't love," I mutter, "it was ..." I swing my hand through the air in irritation. "I don't know what the fuck it was, but it wasn't love."

"She still hurt you, man."

I stare into my brother's eyes. "You hurt me more."

I feel all of that hurt now like a heavy weight on my shoulders, dragging me down down down into the earth.

"I should have told you earlier."

"I wouldn't have listened."

"I should have tried. But I was too fucking stubborn, too freaking seething about the accident."

"I'm sorry, I'm sorry too, Axel." I look away from him, blinking hard. Because it's not only the hurt, it's the guilt and the shame too. I fucked up. I hurt my brother.

"It's okay, man. It was an accident."

"But your football? I fucked up your entire life."

Axel chuckles bitterly. "I'm pretty sure I did that all by myself. But the football ... maybe it would have happened that way anyway. And I'm tired of being mad at you about it. I should have pushed that girl away. I should have told you what she was doing as soon as I knew, instead of gathering up my evidence like I was Sherlock fucking Holmes."

I shake my head.

Axel stares down at his shoes. Wet sand sticks around the soles.

"I was jealous," he says. "I wanted to shove her infidelity in your face. I was an asshole – I've been an asshole for too long – and I deserved what happened to me."

"I'm an asshole too," I say.

He peers up at me. Then he does something which surprises the fuck out of me. He steps forward and wraps his arms around me, hugging me tight, hugging me like he used to when I climbed the highest tree, or caught a fish out in the lake, or scored a touchdown in a game.

He hugs me like my big brother used to.

I close my eyes. His scent is strong in my nose and I hug my big brother right back.

"You're a dickhead," I tell him

"Takes one to know one, bro," he says and I laugh.

We walk over the lawn, The grass is long and tickles at our legs.

"Why the hell isn't this cut?" Axel says. "I thought she paid someone to do it."

"We should cut it for her."

"Yeah," he nods, "yeah, we should,"

We're heading towards the giant oak. An old tyre hangs from one of its boughs, twisting slightly in the breeze. Axel's determined that this was the tree I fell from. He wants to prove it.

"It was good having all the boys back together," I say as we walk side by side, his pace matched by mine. "I even kind of enjoyed hanging out with Nate again."

"He cooks now," Axel says.

"Nate? Cooking?" I laugh. "I wouldn't trust him not to burn down the kitchen."

"We've had a few incidents," Axel says, adjusting his shades on his nose. "Let's just say, we're on first-name terms with the dudes in the fire brigade now." I chuckle harder.

"His food is not bad though. Better than any of the pretentious shit most of the trained chefs will cook. You should come round, sample the goods."

The weight on my shoulders lifts that little bit more. My feet feel lighter. "I'd like that."

"Bring Silver and Hardy too. I missed those jerks – though don't tell Silver that."

"Silver spent six weeks after our bust up trying to persuade me to make it up with you."

"Silver? Silver did that?"

"Yeah, you used to argue like a married couple but when you weren't around he could never stop talking about you."

"I thought he hated my guts."

"He does." I grin and Axel laughs. We reach the tyre and stop. It's smaller than the picture I had in my mind. "Remember when we found the tyre out in the mud by the lake, dug it out. We told Dad we wanted to make a swing out of it and he said we could if we could bring it home ourselves. We dragged it all the way home. That thing weighed a ton, but we were determined to bring it home," I say.

My brother rests his hand on it, squeezing the worn rubber.

"I remember when Dad hung it up."

"Yeah, and you got first go."

He grins. "I was the oldest. Dad pushed us so high it nearly gave mom a heart attack." He nudges the tyre and we watch it glide through the air. "I remember him saying 'one day you'll push your own kids on this swing'."

"Yeah, he said that." I kick at the dust. "You want kids, Ax?"

"Yeah. For a long time I didn't. I didn't feel ready. But

lately I've been thinking how nice it would be to settle down with an omega and start a family."

"Bea," I say.

"Yeah, Bea." He meets my eye. "I've fallen for that one."

"Me too." I sigh and lean against the tree.

"I wasn't lying when I said I've been an asshole. I've been an asshole to Bea too. Dad was tough, but he was never an asshole, and I'm not about to be an asshole to any kid I have."

"We've got some making up to do," I say.

Because it wasn't just each other we hurt. It was our family – Dad, Mom, Molly. But worst of all it was our pack-mates – Nate, Hardy, Silver and Connor. We made them choose sides. We tore our friendship group right down the middle.

"We have."

Axel tips his head back and peers through the leaves. Then he looks back down at me and grins.

"Race you to the top," he yells, jumping up onto the nearest bough.

"Motherfucker," I yell and then I'm scrabbling up after him, chasing him just like I always did through the branches.

And for the first time in a long time things feel like they should.

12

Bea

A WEEK PASSES. If it wasn't for the beach, the ocean and the sand, I'd start to fall into despair. No one wants to hire me. My chances would be slim in the first place considering my lack of qualifications and experience. Top it up with having to explain why I left my last job after such a short time, and then having to disclose my omega designation, and there is no freaking chance.

Mysterious food packages arrive at strange times of the night. But apart from this, I don't hear from, or see anything of, either Pack York or Pack Boston. I told them to leave me alone and for once they seem to be listening.

On Tuesday, I hear from the police saying I need to go down to the station and make a statement.

I drive Missy into the city the next day, meeting my aunt's lawyer outside the run-down building. The cop on the other side of the table listens to me tell my story, politely asks me questions and scribbles down some notes, but I can tell she thinks my account is that of a crazy omega who's gotten herself all confused during her heat.

"Can you give my client an update on the case?" my lawyer asks.

The cop shakes her head, closing her notepad and placing the cap back on her pen.

Outside, the lawyer tells me not to worry and to get in touch if anything else crops up. I slump into Missy and head back to the beach thinking the case seems about as hopeless as my job search.

Over the next few days, Courtney tries to keep my spirits high, Aunt Julia takes me shopping for blankets and pillows, and Ellie comes down to the beach for a visit. But the creeping sensation that I'm never going to make enough money to survive here in the city begins to overwhelm me.

When I moan about this for the one hundredth time while eating spaghetti – another mystery food parcel – with my aunt, she drops her fork and gives me a hard stare.

"You're being over dramatic. You have options, Bea."

"No one will hire me!"

"Then why not focus on finding a pack?"

I make a face and my aunt sighs.

"I know those men hurt you but it doesn't mean they're all like that."

"Really? Because my last (actually my only) two experiences with men suggest they are exactly like that."

My aunt ignores me, picking up her fork and twizzling strings of pasta around the prongs. "I'm being asked about you at least twice daily by eligible packs – or their mothers and sisters. It's clear to me that you could have your pick and live comfortably for the rest of your days."

I make a face. "That's not what I want. I'd be bored sick."

"I can assure you, you wouldn't be," my aunt mutters.

"You mean I'd be flat on my back with my feet in the air, or pushing out yet another baby."

"That isn't what I meant," my aunt says crossly. "I've lived that life and they were the happiest years of my life."

My shoulders slump. "I'm sorry," I say, covering my aunt's hand. "I didn't mean to be rude. I'm just frustrated. I don't know how long I can keep scrounging off your and Courtney's hospitality."

"For as long as you need."

Not forever though. I can't be here forever.

I decide I need something to distract me and it seems like the ocean, the beach and running are the perfect solutions. Early next morning, I set off down the beach, the alarm wrapped around my wrist as well as a kitchen knife slid into my pocket. I'm not quite ready to carry a gun, but after my experience at the clinic I need an upgrade from keys. Especially as I no longer have my alpha shadows jogging along behind me, keeping me safe. I almost miss them. Almost; until I remember they were only using me for their silly bet.

Five hundred meters from the house, something catches my eyes in the sand. Red and half buried. When I reach it, I pause and bend down, tugging it out of its hiding place. It's a piece of garbage. It shouldn't be here. I decide I'll carry it back to the condo and place it in the recycling bin. I pick up my feet again but I haven't run ten feet more when I spy something else poking out of the sand. This time it's a beer can. I yank it out and pick up my pace again. The next thing I find is a plastic bag. Then a bottle. Then four takeaway containers. When my hands are full and I can't carry any more, I turn around and race back to the house.

When I've thrown everything away in the right trash cans, I find a trash bag and set off across the beach, determined to scour the sand for every last piece of trash that doesn't belong there.

"WOAH," Courtney cries, as she opens the front door and walks straight into a tower of trash bags. "What happened here?"

"I cleaned the beach," I call from the couch.

"You what?" she says, trying to squeeze past the tower.

"I cleaned the beach," I say, flicking through the job ads in the city paper for the fifth time that day.

"This all came from the beach? God, that's gross."

"I know. I'm going to do some more tomorrow."

"Whatever makes you happy, Bea," she says, kissing my cheek and placing a chicken pie on my lap.

I eye it suspiciously.

"It was on the doorstep."

"How is he doing this?"

Courtney peers up at the ceiling. "Drones?"

"I'd hear them."

She shrugs, then snatches it from my lap and walks towards the cooker.

THE NEXT DAY I'm back out on the beach after my run, with another trash bag. The sun is strikingly hot today, but I found a neon-pink sun visor of my aunt's in one of the closets and a pair of her oversized sunglasses. They're doing a good job of cutting out the dazzle, even if they do clash with the marigold gloves I'm wearing.

I bend down to scoop a bottle cap from the sand, and as I do a shadow falls over me. I freeze until the scent of earth finds my nose.

Silver.

"What are you doing here?" I ask him, throwing the cap into my bag and remaining hunched over, pretending to brush the sand looking for more pieces of trash.

"Came to check up on you."

"I told your packmate to stay away."

Silver being Silver he ignores this. "I know you're angry with us–" he holds up his hand when I peer up at him with a glare, "–and you have every right to be, Bea. But that doesn't mean I haven't been worrying myself sick about you. Why are you out here on the beach alone?"

I swipe the knife from my pocket and wave it in his face. "I'm fine."

"You didn't notice I was here until I was right on top of you. You were too engrossed in whatever you were doing." His forehead crinkles in puzzlement as his gaze flicks from my visor to my gloves. In the past, I'd have cringed so hard to be caught looking like I do today. But I find, actually, I don't give a damn. I'm not trying to impress this man. Not anymore. "What *are* you doing?" he asks.

"Clearing up all the rubbish from the beach."

He peers along the vast expanse of sand. "That'll take you a lifetime, sweetheart."

"I have nothing better to do."

I move past him and he marches by my side.

"Can I talk to you please, Bea?"

"No."

"Oh-kay," he says slowly, "then I'll just be keeping an eye on you from over here, making sure you're all right."

I swing my head around and waggle the knife at him again. "Oh no you don't. You played the whole we-need-to-keep-you-safe bullshit before. I'm not falling for it again."

"It wasn't bullshit. We care about you. I care about you. I don't want anything to happen to you."

"It won't."

"Omega, you were just kidnapped from the hospital."

A shudder runs down my spine. I've been trying my best not to think about that. To put it firmly out of my mind along with all the other crap.

"You know, rather than insisting on babysitting me all the time," I say to him, "teaching me how to defend myself would be pretty darn useful."

"You did a pretty good job with that doctor."

I frown. "I'm serious. Courtney's been more use to me than any of you guys. She has actually taught me stuff."

"What stuff?"

"The eye gouging."

He nods. "That's sensible stuff."

"But there must be more."

"Bea," he says, "how tall are you?"

"Five three," I say. Silver raises an eyebrow. "In heels."

"And I know you weigh practically nothing." I snort at that but he continues with the steely stare. "Eye gouging is your best line of defense. I'm not going to waste your time teaching you how to throw a dude over your shoulder, because I'm telling you now, in real situations that stuff doesn't work." My frown deepens, and he sighs. "I'm serious, sweetheart. I once knew this man; he was a champion kick-boxer. He got mugged on the street, tried to kick the dude in the head. Ended up with a bullet through his foot."

"Is this meant to make me feel better," I say. "Because I just got myself abducted, Silver, and I don't want to spend the rest of my life too scared to leave the house."

"You don't need to be. We'll be watch–"

"I don't want you to be watching. I want to know what to do!" I say with frustration.

He examines my face, his own not giving away the thoughts circulating in his mind. "Run," he says.

"Run?" I repeat.

"If you're ever in trouble, Bea. If the situation ever feels off, then you run."

"Run? What kind of advice is that?"

"Good advice. A successful soldier knows when to stay and fight, and when to get the hell out. You're fast. Nimble. Light on your feet. You could outrun a lot of people." The skin beneath his eye twitches. "You could outrun me on a good day."

I can't help grinning. "I could."

"Yeah," he mumbles, "I have a hard time keeping up with you." I grin wider and he adds quickly, "I'm a lot bigger and heavier than you."

My gaze can't help involuntarily flicking down his frame. He most definitely is.

"Okay," I concede, "running it is."

"But," he adds, and I roll my eyes like a sulky teenager, "I think it would be wise to take up my offer. If this is how you want to spend your time," he says softly, "then I'm more than happy to watch over you. Or if you'd prefer it wasn't me, I can arrange for one of my men to come watch you instead."

I exhale. "No, it's fine." Maybe I do feel a little better with him here. Although, I'm sure that must just be my stupid omega hormones because I'm still mad as hell at this man.

"However," I add, "you're not standing around and watching me work. You can help."

"Pick up trash?"

"I thought you were a soldier. Are you telling me you're scared of a bit of trash?"

He jerks out his hand, and I hook out one of the spare trash bags from the waistband of my shorts and hand it over.

"Got another one of those attractive pair of gloves, sweetheart?"

"No," I snap.

From the corner of my eyes, I watch him roll up his sleeves and get to work.

"Why don't you have anything to do?" he asks me after a while. "Don't you have that job?"

"I quit it – for obvious reasons." He nods. "And it seems no one else will hire an omega. I think they assume I'm a flight risk. That I won't stick around for long enough."

"So you're not being paid to clean the beach?"

"No, I'm not." I pause, resting my hand with the knife on my hip and letting my gaze float out to the ocean. "Although I'm beginning to think it would be my dream job."

"Cleaning the beach?" he says, prodding out what looks like a box of rubbers with the toe of his shoe.

"No, not cleaning the beach. But doing something ecological. Something with the ocean." I sigh. "Not likely to happen though. It's not like I have a degree."

Silver kicks at the box and it leaps into the air. He catches it in the bag with a satisfied grunt. "Why not?"

"Were you listening when I told you about how the job hunting is going?"

"I was a little distracted by the outfit." I frown at him. "But have you tried?"

"Tried what?"

"Applying to organizations like that? The World Ocean Federation, for example?"

"No," I mumble.

"Well ..."

I consider jabbing the smart ass with my knife, but actually it's not a bad idea. "Maybe I will."

We work for the next hour, until both our bags are full. I tie mine up and hook out the other bag I brought with me.

"You're not done?" he asks.

"Nope not yet."

"You have another bag?"

"Nope," I say, finding my water bottle where I left it on the beach and downing several long mouthfuls.

"I'll go get another one from the house," he says walking away. "Stay here. Don't go wandering off."

I roll my eyes. "The house is locked," I call after him.

"No problem," he calls back.

"And alarmed," I shout.

He shrugs his shoulders like that won't be a problem either. He really is infuriating and still as damn hot as ever.

I shake my head and concentrate on searching for more bits of plastic.

A few moments later, another shadow falls over me.

"That was quick," I say, "maybe we need to upgrade the security system if it was that easy to penetrate."

"Hi, Bea."

I jolt, dropping my bag, my visor tumbling off my head. It catches on the breeze, sailing across the sand and landing right by the feet of my former best friend. Serena.

I whip the rubber gloves off my hands and toss them to the ground.

"Serena?" I say, blinking against the light. Am I seeing things? "What are you doing here?"

"I came to see you."

I stare at her in disbelief. "You came all the way out here to see me. Why?" We haven't seen each other since the day before the wedding. She was meant to be there to help me get ready. She never showed up. Her mom said she was sick. I sent her this long voice message telling her how upset I was that she was going to miss the wedding, how it wouldn't be the same without my best friend, how I'd save her a huge slice of the wedding cake.

I had no idea she was already halfway to the airport.

I never expected to see her again.

I certainly never expected her to seek me out.

"To apologize." Her eyes flick to the handle of the knife poking out of my pocket.

Apologize? I stare at her in disbelief. "How did you find me?"

"Courtney's always been awful at keeping a secret."

"Courtney told you where I was?" I grind my back teeth together, thinking to all the ways in which I will torture Courtney when she gets home. Maybe some of this trash could end up in her bed.

"She was trying not to. She didn't think you'd want to see me."

"Yes, well, she was right."

I pick up the gloves and stomp towards the house. If I can get inside, I can lock the door.

"Bea, can we talk?" Serena asks, trotting along beside me.

"You came here to apologize. I'm not sure I want to hear it. Because," I halt, Serena nearly colliding into me as I spin around, "who is the apology for? Will it make me feel any better about ..." I choke, unable to find the words to even describe what she did to me. "Or are you only here to try to absolve some of your own guilt?"

My ex-best friend stares down at her shoes.

I notice she's more tanned than usual. Probably from the holiday in Barbados.

"I don't expect you to forgive me, Bea. But I miss you so damn much and I thought if there was only a smidgen of a chance I might be able to mend things between us it would be worth a chance."

"Mend things?" I say in disbelief. "Serena, are you still with him?"

"No, oh god, no." She shakes her head in disgust. "Bea, Karl is a mega jerk. I never realized before but spending–"

"My honeymoon!" I snap.

"Yeah," her cheeks turn pink, "spending time with him made me realize it. I'm glad you didn't marry him, Bea. You deserve so much better than him."

"I didn't deserve the two people I loved most in the world to do that to me," I say, my voice choking up as the tears begin to tumble down my cheeks.

Tears appear in Serena's eyes too and she nods her head. "I know and I'm sorry."

"Why did you do it?" I whisper.

"I was jealous."

"Jealous?" I say. "Of what?"

"You."

"Me?"

"Yes, Bea, you. You're kind and beautiful and you've always had your head screwed on right. You had this perfect little life planned out and I ... I'm going to be 30 in three years' time, and I haven't had a relationship that's lasted more than three months. I wanted what you had so badly and so ... so I stole it from you." She covers her hands and sobs into her palms, her shoulder shaking.

I hesitate for a moment, the sounds of the waves hitting the shore loud in my ears. Then I step towards her and hook my arm around her shoulder.

"My life was never perfect, Serena. It may have looked it from the outside but it wasn't. It wasn't at all and I didn't realize how unhappy I was with Karl until I finally got rid of him."

"He's such a jerk," she mumbles.

"Yes," I say, although I know it takes two to tango. I miss Serena too. But I don't know if I can ever forgive her for what she did. Not yet anyway.

"I ruined everything," Serena moans, "the best friendship I ever had." She sniffs. "For a stupid man." She sniffs again. "And everyone back home hates me. I think I'm going to have to follow your lead and move to the city." She eyes the beach house.

"It's not all it's cracked up to be," I say. "I can't find a job and no one talks to anyone here. No one even makes eye contact. And the traffic!"

"Oh God, I nearly totaled my car five times cutting through the city to get to you," Serena says with a laugh. I step away and she wipes at her face. Her mascara is a big old mess. She looks like a freaking panda. I don't think I'll tell her.

"It isn't working out here, then?" she asks. "Why don't you come back home?"

I peer out to the ocean. Is it? I love it here on the beach. But the city feels tinged with sour memories now. If I left, if I went back home, I'd miss Courtney and Aunt Julia. But at least I'd be able to find a job and I wouldn't have to worry about this constant threat to my safety every damn moment.

I'd have my heat to worry about – but hopefully that wouldn't be for a while and I could figure something out.

The sand shifts against my ankles and behind Serena I can see Silver trudging towards us. He's wearing his own pair of marigolds and is carrying a trash bag.

Serena turns to see what I'm looking at and nearly topples over in surprise, her eyes bugging in her head and her mouth falling open.

I guess I'm used to how hot these men are. I almost – almost – don't notice it anymore. But looking at him now, through Serena's eyes, I have to confess he's one of the best-looking men I've ever laid eyes on. His strong build, his shoulder length hair ruffled by the breeze and his dark eyes.

"Hi," Silver says as he comes to a stop in front of us both. Serena tucks a strand of honey blonde hair behind her ear and smiles sweetly at him. I'm extra pleased I didn't tell her about the mascara.

"Hi," she answers.

Nobody speaks and Serena gives me a look I know means 'introduce us'. I decide I'm not going to do that either.

"Thank you for coming," I tell her. "I appreciate it and I will think about what you've said."

"So you forgive me?" she asks hopefully.

I simply smile at her. I don't want to die a bitter old maid. I don't want to carry hatred around in my heart for the rest of my days. But I'm not ready to forgive her yet. The wounds in my heart are still too fresh.

Serena seems to interpret my expression as a yes though and grins back. "Good," she says. "Come home, Bea, we all miss you."

"Home?" Silver says and my eyes flick to him. He almost

looks alarmed, like me heading back to Naw creek would be the worst thing possible.

It makes me think I should give it more thought.

If I stay here, I can see how slowly these men will worm their way back into my life until I end up a plaything in their games once more.

"I'm thinking about it."

13

Bea

Silver insists on packing all the trash bags into his car and driving them to the garbage dump.

"You can't keep them here, you'll attract wild animals," he says.

I swing my head around the beach. "You mean crabs?" I ask. "Are you going to try to convince me I need to be scared of crabs now too?"

"You ever been pinched by a crab?" he asks me. I shake my head. "It hurts. A lot."

"Where were you pinched?" I ask him with suspicion.

"Never you mind," he tells me, leaning his back against the car and crossing his arms over his chest, his biceps flexing in that way that does something funny to my insides. I try hard to ignore that feeling.

"Bea," he says.

And I screw up my eyes. I'm not sure I can handle anymore half-ass apologies today.

He sighs. "I know you don't want me around right now or any of the others, but the more we look into this clinic the more concerned I am about your safety."

My eyes flick open. "What have you found out?"

"They were doing underground research on new drugs that could transform betas into omegas. There are already some on the black market but they don't work. They're basically perfume and hormone pills. This clinic was doing serious research. It's just not clear who was funding it."

"Why did they want me?"

He shakes his head. "I'm guessing there aren't a lot of omegas they can lay their hands on to do their research. Most omegas belong to–"

"Insanely rich and powerful families. Yeah, I know."

He nods. "Do you plan to do more beach cleaning?" A smile hovers on his lips.

"Yes," I say, "it's good for the soul."

"Then can I send one of my men down to watch you?"

"You didn't like getting your hands dirty, Alpha?" I tease, the words slipping out too easily. My cheeks immediately blaze.

"I enjoy getting my hands dirty," he growls, then seems to check himself. He snaps upright into that soldier stature of his. "I was under the impression you'd prefer it if I wasn't around right now."

I chew on my lip. "I'm not sure I'm ever going to want you around, Silver."

"I understand," he says, his eyes steely as if he's working hard not to give anything away.

"Why did you do it?" I whisper. "The bet?"

I swear his shoulders stiffen that little bit more.

"I can't give you a good answer to that, Bea."

"You mean you can't give me one that makes you look good?"

He pauses, then nods. "All I can say is it might appear like a stupid rivalry to you on the outside – to everyone on the outside – but here in the middle of it, there's a lot of ..." for a minute, I can imagine him in uniform, lining up on parade; not a muscle in his body moves, "a lot of hurt and heartache."

"Axel and Angel?"

"All of us."

"You need to sort it out," I say, thinking of Serena, thinking of how I know eventually I'll forgive her, even if I never let her back in my life, simply because I don't want to carry that hatred around on my shoulders forever.

He pauses once more and then nods again. "We're working on it."

My eyebrows leap up my forehead in disbelief.

"You are?"

"Yes." He hesitates. "We hurt someone important to us and we realize we don't want that to ever happen again."

I've been trying to harden my heart against these men, but, hearing his words, it softens just a tad.

"I'm glad," I say.

"Call me the next time you want to go beach cleaning."

"I'll think about it," I say and to my surprise he doesn't argue.

14

Bea

I CAN'T SLEEP that night. There's too much swirling around in my mind.

Serena. Finding a job. Silver. Home.

I toss and turn in my bed like a princess with a flipping pea under her mattress. My restless mind won't leave me alone.

In the end, I admit defeat, and in the darkness pad through to the kitchen to fetch a glass of water.

My hand is on the tap, when I hear scuffling noises from outside.

For a minute, I dismiss the noise as one of the birds that like to run across our roof. But the longer I listen, the more I'm sure it's a person outside.

I think of Silver's warning about the clinic.

My heart thumps in my chest. My blood runs icy cold.

The alarm is five paces away on the counter and the windows and doors are all locked.

The shotgun is locked in a cupboard by the door and the drawer by my hip is full of kitchen knives.

Should I call out to Courtney? Jump the intruder? Ring for help?

I lower my glass to the counter, careful not to make a noise and as I do a scent hits my nose.

Gunpowder.

Nate.

I creep as quietly to the window as I can and peer out.

He's sitting on the porch, a cool bag resting beside him and he's unloading silver foil-wrapped dishes and placing them by the back door.

I rise up on my tiptoes, leaning forward to get a closer look.

"Omega," he says, "I know you're there."

I jolt and gasp, nearly losing my balance and tumbling to the floor.

"I'm just going to leave these here," he says quietly, not turning around to look up at me through the window. "You don't have to talk to me."

He's right. I don't. But I decide I want to anyway.

Tying my gown tight around my body, I walk over to the backdoor, unlock it and step out onto the porch.

The night's air is much cooler than the stuffy air inside, and it sweeps against my face and ruffles my hair and my gown.

Nate doesn't look my way, just waits, forearms resting on his knees as he gazes out towards the ocean, the moon painting it a pale white.

I come and sit next to him on the step, and watch as the moon's reflection ripples with the water.

"Thank you for the food," I say after a while. "There's been a lot of it. You must be spending all your time cooking."

"I haven't been able to sleep."

"Me neither," I admit and he glances towards me.

"Because of us?" he asks. He looks like a puppy that got beaten. It's those eyes of his. I realize he's the one I will have trouble staying mad at most.

Perhaps I ought to run back inside and lock the door.

"Not just you," I say truthfully, "although, I suppose, your packs are a big part of it." I straighten my legs and try not to notice his eyes straying that way. "What's in the box?"

He shuffles on his backside and I swear this tough, pretty terrifying, alpha actually blushes right in front of my very eyes. He mumbles something I don't hear.

"What?" I say.

"Ljkhlhljh," he mumbles again.

"Nate," I laugh, "what's in the box?"

"Nothing," he says, lunging for it and trying to drag it away.

"Well, now I'm extra curious. Hand it over."

"No, you can open after I'm gone."

"Oh my god, what is it?"

He glares at me.

"Please?" I say, fluttering my eyelashes.

"For fuck's sake," he mutters, handing it over.

I lift it onto my lap and carefully peel back the flaps.

Nate jumps to his feet and starts to pace.

"It's really bad," he says, glimpsing my way.

I unfold the last flap but it's dark in the box and I have to shuffle around into the security light to see what's sitting in the base.

"A cake!" I squeak. "You baked me a cake."

It doesn't look like a very level cake, and the top is covered in so much pink frosting I think I'd lose a tooth if I ate it. It's also decorated with a shit ton of candy and in the center in red frosting is a wobbly heart.

"I couldn't get the heart thing in the middle to work," he says, waving his finger in my direction. "I followed a YouTube video but fuck me those pipe things–"

"Oh my God," I shriek, "I love it!"

"You haven't tried it yet," he mumbles, "probably tastes like horse shit. Never tried to bake a cake before."

I remember what Axel told me about Nate's childhood. I wonder if anyone ever baked him a birthday cake or if he ever got to help make cookies.

"Let's go try it," I say, jumping to my feet.

"Now? It's two in the morning."

"Nate, you once pushed me into a pool in a twenty thousand dollar dress."

He grins. "Shit, yeah I did."

Carefully, I carry the cake into the kitchen and rest it on the counter. I turn to open the drawer and find a knife but Nate offers me his.

I've seen it in his hands before but I've never gotten to touch it. I examine it under the light. The sharp blade glints and the handle is worn. "Is it special?" I ask.

"Who, Mack?"

"You named your knife."

He grins, flicking his lip ring with his tongue. "Just now."

I laugh.

"I like it when you laugh, little bird."

I raise an eyebrow at him and sink the knife through the mountain of icing and the sponge below. I'm not surprised to find it soft.

"I don't like that we made you sad."

"I don't like that you did too."

I hear him sigh and shuffle on his feet.

"It was a gift," he says, pointing to his knife. "From Axel's dad on my 18th birthday." I turn it over in my hands, peering at the long worn-away inscription. "He said I could use it to keep myself safe."

"Did you need to keep yourself safe?"

He manages one of those self-abasing smiles. "Always have a way of landing myself in trouble, little bird."

I cut off a triangle of cake and lift it with both hands, icing, crumbs and candy tumbling off and into the box.

I offer it to Nate and he holds out his hand.

"It looks like shit," he says and I drop the cake into his palm. He guides it up to my mouth. "You first, little bird. It's your cake." I shake my head. "Open up, Omega," he growls.

My lips part automatically, and he feeds me the cake, allowing me a bite.

"Oh my god," I say.

"Disgusting?"

"Sooooo good. Jeez Nate," I groan.

His eyes turn darker and then dirtier as he watches me chew and swallow. His scent intensifies.

I know I'm in for it.

I whimper but before I can scurry away, he pounces, pressing the rest of the cake right into my face, frosting smearing all over my nose and my chin.

"You asshole," I giggle, trying to wipe the cake off my face.

He simply chuckles back and I reach into the box, scoop a massive piece of frosting into my hand and throw it right at his face.

It smacks him on the nose.

For a long second we both stare at each other, icing dripping off his face. Then I dive for the box as he does the same, our hands scrabbling inside as we both fight to grab more cake.

I pull my hand out first, taking my opportunity at his closeness to slam a handful of cake in his face. He swears and then tries to do the same to me.

I yelp and attempt to dodge away but he grabs my arm and smears cake all over my face.

I blink away icing and lick at my lips, unable to help but laugh hard.

He grins at me. "You have a bit of cake on your face, little bird."

"Really, where?" I ask innocently.

He drags me closer and then he's kissing me, sponge and frosting melting into our mouths as his hot lips claim mine. My breath halts in my chest and then I melt into him.

His hand slides around to cup the back of my neck, smearing cake into my hair, and he pulls me in closer as his other hand comes to claim my waist.

I shouldn't be doing this. I shouldn't let him turn up with a cake and think he can kiss me. He hurt me. They all used me.

But right now, while he's kissing me, I find it really damn hard to remember why I was mad with him in the first place.

I'm too busy feeling.

He nibbles at my lips and then his mouth strays lower, along my jaw and down to my throat, nipping all the way.

"Hmmm, this cake tastes pretty good." He licks all the way up my neck, making me shudder. "Or maybe it's just you, little bird."

"Just because you made me a cake, doesn't mean I forgive you," I whimper, as the hand at my waist finds the tie of my gown.

"Let me give you something else to show you how sorry I am then." he says.

"Wh-wh-wh-what?" I whisper, as his hand slips under my gown and against my skin. His touch feels heavenly. It feels like an eternity since anyone touched me and my body rings like a bell.

He pulls back and gives me one of those wicked grins I know means trouble.

I should definitely stop things now. I should definitely send him on his way. I should definitely not lean into his touch as his hand slides over my ribs and cups my breast, squeezing ever so gently. Far more gently than I'd expect of a man like Nate. He flicks his calloused thumb over my nipple and then he lifts me up onto the counter and rolls me down flat.

God, I've been imagining this ever since I met these alphas. I couldn't stop dreaming of it all the way through my heat.

I've done a really efficient job of resisting them, of resisting all the things they could do to me, resisting all the things I could do to them. But oh jeez has it been hard! And as his mouth comes down to kiss my nipple and suck it up into his mouth, I realize I want to stop resisting for just one moment. For just once.

"I'm going home," I whisper to him. "Back to Naw Creek." He pauses, his dark eyes connecting with mine. "I'm telling you because I don't want to use you, Nate. If you want to stop ..."

He holds my gaze, his eyes swirling, not with their usual mischief but with something like a plea.

I'm not sure what he's pleading for. Permission? Forgiveness? For me to stay?

My heart pounds in my ears and my stomach swoops

with anticipation. I want him to keep touching me. I want him to keep kissing me. I don't want him to stop.

"Whether you stay or fly away, little bird, I want to show you just how damn sorry I am."

He trails a line of reverent kisses down my body, lower and lower until he reaches the apex of my legs. He nudges them apart and then he falls to his knees.

"Where I should always be when in your presence, little bird."

In my next panted breath, his mouth is right where I need it, right where I've wanted it for weeks and weeks.

Karl never liked to do this. Karl was never good at it. Karl would rather crawl through broken glass than get down on his knees for me. And yet here this alpha is doing just that.

I've always wondered if being eaten out is as amazing as other girls make out.

When Nate's tongue hits my clit, I know instantly that it is. *Oh my lord it is.*

I stuff my own fist in my mouth to stop from crying out as agonizingly slowly he swirls the tip of his wet tongue around my sensitive nub, my toes curling in pleasure, and the pulse between my legs hammering like crazy.

"So fucking delicious," he groans, the sound vibrating all the way to my core as he slides his tongue through my folds towards my hole and then back to my clit. He continues this steady stroke, around and around my clit, then down to my hole.

My skin tingles, the nerves in my body are electric and alive, and every sweep of his tongue heavenly torture.

My fingers tangle in his hair and I can't help tugging it, willing him to go harder, to give me more.

He growls, deep and low and I almost come into his mouth right then and there.

"Need more," I pant.

"Going to give you more, little bird, but I want to make you sing for me first." I curse at him but he only repeats his growls and continues those delicious sweeps of his tongue.

When the tears start to spill down my cheeks, he finally gives me more. His tongue moving more quickly, flicking against my clit and making me buck, my hips lifting from the counter.

"Yes, baby, thrust your sweet smelling pussy into my mouth. I could eat you out all fucking night and every single day."

I whimper and he kisses my cunt – properly French kisses it – sucking me up into his mouth, and making my legs shake around his head.

"Oh God!" I mutter, my fist falling from my mouth as I suck in air, dizzy with the sensations he's driving through my body. "Oh God! Oh god, oh god, oh god."

"Just like that little bird, just like that."

He pecks at my clit and the cool metal of his lip ring hits against it.

I scream out.

"Like that?" he asks.

"Hmmmm," I moan. And he does it again, knocking the metal against me over and over and over again until I lose all sense of time and place, the sensations buzzing through my body, harder and harder, until I can't breathe, I can't see, I can't hear, all I can do is feel.

I come, ecstasy crashing through my wrecked body, tears swimming down my cheeks, my body jolting and bolting with each glorious wave of pleasure, until I collapse down, washed up and wrecked and tingling all over.

He continues to lap between my legs, purring into my folds, bringing me down slowly to Earth.

When finally I can open my eyes and breathe again, he stumbles to his feet.

His face is still covered in cake, although now there's my slick and his spit making a mess of his chin.

He licks at his lips and shakes his head.

"Shit, that was no good," he mutters, frowning.

I scrabble up onto my elbows.

"Wh-wh-what?"

Did I do it wrong? Did I taste wrong? Did I squeeze his head between my thighs when I came? Was I too loud?

"Enjoyed that too much," he mumbles, still frowning, his eyes gliding down my body, my gown open like an invitation.

I feel all blissful and yet, deep in my cunt there's that ache, the one that drove me half mad throughout my heat, an ache that needs to be filled.

I'm not sure I'm ready for that though. Does that make me selfish? He just took me to heaven and back. But he makes no move to initiate that, even though I can see him straining at the front of his pants.

"Isn't that good ... that you enjoyed it?" I say. Maybe he doesn't want to sleep with me because I look a state. Dried cake stuck to my tear-stained face, my skin all flushed and hot and my hair stuck to my damp brow.

"No," he says. "It was meant to be a gift. It was meant to show you how sorry I am. I wasn't meant to enjoy it. Only you were."

He frowns harder, then before I can argue with him, he's stomping towards the door.

"Nate, your knife," I call after him.

He hesitates by the door, fingers resting on the handle. "It's yours, little bird. Just like my fucking heart."

He stomps out of the house and into the night, the door banging shut behind him.

I collapse onto the counter.

What the hell just happened?

I was stupid that's what. Stupid and far too horny.

And though that was possibly – actually easily – the best orgasm of my life; that isn't a good thing.

No more assholes. Even if they have a pair of heart-stopping eyes, a wicked tongue and a talent for cooking.

I groan. I am screwed and there is only one thing for it.

I'm going to have to go back to Naw Creek.

15

Nate

I STUMBLE out of the omega's house, out onto the beach and towards the sounds of crashing waves. My legs are like fucking jello, my heart cracking into pieces in my chest.

My little bird isn't just some little songbird, not some little garden thing. No, my little bird is a fucking phoenix. Every time she's knocked back down, she glides right back into the sky. Bright. Burning. Flaming hot.

So hot I can barely look at her. Can barely touch her.

The water comes into view, black and unmoving.

I sprint to the edge, where it laps at the sand, and fall to my knees. Then I'm scrubbing at my face, the salt stinging my eyes, the water icy cold.

I wash away the fucking cake and the taste of the omega. I don't deserve to taste her. I don't deserve the memory lodged in my head – my little phoenix writhing on the end of my tongue.

Shit. So hot. So fucking intensely hot.

Like fire itself.

I scrub at my face until everything stings, not only my eyes. Then I fall backwards and stare up at that moon.

Serene. Peaceful.

Eerily calm in the face of all the chaos crashing through me.

I could head for Smyth's bar, drink myself into oblivion. Or drive to Jem's Strip Joint, stuff a few hundreds into some girl's thong and let her grind in my lap. Or I could go down to the old gym on Lincoln's, smash my fist into a few faces.

It's always been the way to deal with the pain when it threatens to drown me. When the waters creep higher and higher, over my head, and I'm gasping for air.

Drink. Girls. Fighting.

They've always been my life rafts.

Only problem is they don't last. Soon the rafts are leaking holes and sinking along with me.

I flop down onto the sand.

For once, I'd like to wash up on dry land away from the water and its murky depths. A long fucking way away.

And for a moment, I thought I'd found that piece of salvation, between the omega's legs, driving my little phoenix high up into the air where she could spread her wings wide.

I don't deserve that.

None of us do.

Least of all me.

I lie there on my back, like a washed-up fucking deadbeat, until the first fingers of daylight crawl over the horizon.

Then I pull myself to my feet and start the long fucking walk home.

She's leaving. I'm going to have to break the news to Axel and Connor.

WHEN THE ELEVATOR doors open out onto our penthouse several hours later, I find Hardy leaning against the wall with his arms crossed over his chest.

"Shit man, what happened to you?" he says.

"Nothing."

"You look like something the fucking pussy cat dragged in."

"Something like that," I mutter, thinking of the fucking pussy I had to drag myself away from devouring mere hours ago. If Hardy knew that he'd likely try to knock my block off. Try, being the operative word.

"What you doing here?" I say.

"You haven't heard?" he says, face grimacing.

My shoulders stiffen. "What?"

"Peace talks."

I stare at him. Then snort out a blast of laughter. "What the fuck?"

Hardy shrugs his shoulders. "Don't ask me, I'm simply following instructions."

I shake my head and crash through the apartment door, colliding almost immediately with Axel and Connor.

"Ahh Nate," Axel says, the big fuck-off grin that's been glued to his face since he made good with his brother not faltering. "Thought I heard you. You ready to move out?"

"Yep," I say.

Connor eyes up my disheveled appearance. "You all right?"

"Dandy," I say with a faux smile.

I haven't slept in 24 hours, or shaved or showered – there's probably cake in my hair – but Axel doesn't seem to notice.

"Great," he says.

He steps outside and we find Silver and Angel waiting by the door too.

"Where are these 'peace talks' being held?" I whisper to Hardy.

"No fucking idea."

I watch Axel and Angel all the way down in the escalator ride and out to the car port. There the van is waiting for us. They talk to each other, chuckling away like Beavis and Butthead. As if the last ten years haven't happened.

I wonder if I stepped into a fucking alternative reality on my way home. Or maybe I'm fucking dreaming.

"What's going on?" I ask, when we're all seated in the van.

Should I tell them about the omega? About her plan to leave?

Then what, Axel and Angel will be charging around there like a pair of rhinoceri on steroids, stamping all over any chance we have to make things right with her.

I'm keeping my mouth shut.

Until I know what this is all about.

"We'll tell you when we get there," Axel says.

"I'd prefer you tell us now," Silver says firmly.

The brothers exchange glances, then twist around in their seats to face the rest of us. I'm struck by how similar the two of them are. I guess I knew it all along. Somehow I'd pushed it out of my mind. Now it's clear as day.

"We've been a pair of assholes. And it's about time we put things right."

"You suffering from a head injury?" Hardy asks. "Did your mom finally knock your heads together?"

"Something like that," Angel mutters.

Axel scratches his chin. "The omega," he says and the tension in the van ratchets up. Beside me Hardy stiffens. "We fucked things up. She's not going to forgive us until we put things right."

"What things?" Connor asks.

"Things between the six of us," Angel says. "This bull-shit happened because she ended up stuck between our two packs. And if we're honest, that's happened to too many people over the years. If we ever hope to win her back, we have to put things right between us."

"Hence the peace talks," Hardy mutters.

"You think talking can put it all right?" I say. Irritation spirals through my body. Those dark waters begging to rise.

Does Axel honestly believe everything can go back to the way it was? Can he not see the way Silver gives me a wide fucking berth, or how Connor sits in stony silence? Because things have been good with his brother for five seconds, he assumes everything can be fixed.

Like the last decade can be forgotten. Like everything in that time hasn't rotted and decayed, festered and fermented.

I reach for my knife. It's not there. The omega has it now. A warmness radiates in my chest, soothing away the pain just a fraction. I like that. If she won't have me, at least she'll have that part of me.

"You have a better solution?" Axel asks.

I snort and stare out the window into the bright under-ground car park.

Soon, the engine rumbles to life and we're speeding

through the city. It doesn't take me long to know where we're headed.

Mrs. Stormgate's.

Molly answers the door and for once I don't receive my eager greeting. Today she's stony faced and looking like she would like to whip all our asses.

She's fucking pretty. But off limits. Like a little sister to me. Anyway, even if the fear of Axel cutting off my balls wasn't enough to keep me away, the omega has ruined me for all other women.

I'm hers now. Even if she won't have me.

Molly ushers us all through to the dining room. It's laid out with all the dishes Mrs. Stormgate used to make us as kids. My mouth salivates. But I don't step in with the others. I grab Molly's wrist.

"Where is she?"

"In her bedroom."

"She's not good?"

Molly shakes her head.

"I'll go say hello."

"After," she says, pushing me towards the dining room. "Go sort out your shit and then hopefully you'll have some good news to tell her."

I groan. "You too with the talking?"

"It's what you dumbasses should have done years ago. But," she pushes her shoulder against me, trying to use all her weight to shift me, "better late than never."

I step through and she slams the door behind me.

The others have piled up their plates and Axel is actually pouring coffee for everyone.

I pinch my fucking arm, then slink down into a chair and swing my legs up onto the chair next to me. I survey the table and drag a whole plate of cookies onto my lap. Triple chocolate. Just how I like them.

"The past can't be undone," I say. I know that better than anyone. You can wish it all you fucking like. Doesn't make one damn bit of difference.

"No, it can't. But we can put it behind us."

Hardy chuckles. "You were the ones–"

"We were and if we were able to forgive each other, we're hoping you can forgive us too. Hoping you can forgive each other."

Silence.

I snap my teeth through a cookie. Everyone looks my way.

"You're serious about this?" Silver asks, perching on his chair like this is a war room and we're all fucking generals.

"Deadly," Axel says.

Angel lumbers to his feet and walks to the window. The day is overcast, dark clouds hanging in the sky and the first raindrops trickling down the pane.

"We fucked up big time all those years ago and we know the damage that caused."

"You made us choose sides," Connor says quietly. Angel peers over his shoulder at him and nods. "We weren't a pack but in some ways it felt like we were. It tore all of us in fucking half."

I place my half-eaten cookie down on the plate.

Connor's right. There's a rip down the center of my soul. And they caused it. I've lived with it all these years because what choice did I have? I couldn't lose anyone else in my life.

I toss the cookie plate onto the table and it skids across the surface.

"What happens," I say, swinging my legs off the chair and hunching over my knees, "next time?"

Axel frowns. "What do you mean, Nate?"

"Next time the two of you blow up. The next time you disagree. The next time you argue. You're telling us we should all be friends again, right?" Both brothers nod. "But will you tear us apart again?"

"It won't happen," Axel says sternly.

Hardy chuckles. "I've known the two of you since I was five years old. It's always been that way between the two of you. If it hadn't been that girl, if it hadn't been that accident, it would have been something else."

The others murmur their agreement.

"And now," Silver says, "the stakes are even higher."

"How so?" Angel asks.

"Bea."

Her name generates that warmth in my chest. My little phoenix.

"If she were to forgive us," Connor says, "she would have to choose one pack. And then what happens? You go nuclear all over again."

Axel leans back in his chair. He tips his head back and stares at the ceiling, letting a long breath rush from his mouth.

"If she chooses Pack Boston, if she chooses my brother, I'll accept her decision. I won't stand in your way." He lowers his chin and gazes around the table. "Fuck, I'll even try to be happy for you."

"Angel?" Silver asks.

Angel's staring at his brother. He nods. "Same."

"We only have your word for it," Connor points out.

"It's all we can give you."

"And how about us?" Hardy says. "Who says I'm happy to just hand her over without complaint to Pack York?"

"Because it's the only way we win her back, dickhead," Silver mutters.

I slide my tongue over my lip ring, catching a taste of my little phoenix there.

"It's too late," I say, standing.

"It's not," Axel insists.

But I hold my forefinger up to him.

"She's leaving."

The room erupts into disorder. Connor wants to know how I know that. Hardy doesn't like the idea I've been to see her. Axel doesn't believe me.

Don't give a shit.

I stroll out of the dining room.

Molly's in the hallway, playing on her phone. She glances up as I pass but doesn't say a word.

I storm up the stairs and along the hallway, pausing at her bedroom door.

I take a deep inhale, then knock.

She's sitting up in bed, cushions all around her, face made up even though she's wearing a nightgown.

"Nate," she says, her eyes brightening.

"Mrs. Stormgate, looking radiant as ever."

She rolls her eyes at me and I flop down on the bed beside her and take her hand in mine.

"Cookies were good," I tell her.

"Molly made them," she says, "I gave her my secret recipe."

"Going to give it to me?"

She smiles.

"I made a fucking cake the other day." I scratch at some dry sand stuck to the leg of my pants. "Made it for the omega."

"She certainly seems to–"

"She's leaving," I say.

"Leaving?" Mrs. Stormgate repeats. "What do you mean?"

"Going back to her hometown."

"That doesn't sound very sensible."

I shrug. "Hurt people don't do sensible things."

Mrs. Stormgate squeezes my hand. "Axel and Angel are working on fixing things."

"You think they can?"

"I think you know them better than me these days, Nate."

I sigh.

"How are the peace talks going?" she asks.

"Well, I'm up here aren't I."

Mrs. Stormgate places her other hand on top of our hands. "I know my boys can be stubborn, and, well, rather idiotic sometimes. But they have good hearts underneath it all." She pats my hand. "Give them a chance."

I glance towards the window. "I can't go through it a second time."

"You're all older now. And something tells me you others wouldn't put up with their shenanigans this time around."

I nod.

That's true.

Ten years ago, I was in awe of Axel. I thought the sun shone out of his ass. And while I still love the big guy, now I know everyone has their faults.

"It would make a dying woman very happy to see you boys reunited." I look at her and she smiles. "And maybe even settled with an omega."

And, I may have a heart of solid darkness, but how the fuck can I say no to that?

16

Bea

COURTNEY ISN'T happy about me leaving.

"You shouldn't run away," she tells me. "There's much more here than you'll ever find back in Naw Creek."

"Like what?" I ask her.

"Men!" she says, when I frown she quickly adds, "and the ocean."

"I'll miss the ocean and I'll miss you," I say, dragging her in for a hug, "But I don't plan on slipping back into my hermit ways. I'll come visit you and Aunt Julia as often as I can. But I need money. I need to afford to eat."

"You have food!" Courtney says, pointing to the half demolished cake and making me blush.

"I just need some time and space to think things through, Courtney. Without worrying about bumping into alphas and without worrying about my safety."

Courtney nods and helps me pack up Missy and then I'm off. This time I take the main roads, avoiding that gas station.

Riding through Naw Creek ten hours later, I could imagine nothing has changed at all. Mrs. Forthright is still watering her geraniums, Bob Sanders is still polishing his car, and Mindy Cooper is still turning cartwheels on her front lawn.

I could almost believe I'm still the same old Bea Carsen. A Beta. A fiancée. Soon to marry Karl Simpson. Several weeks ago, I'd almost wish that were true. Now I'm not so sure.

I pass my parents' diner and drive the last few blocks, pulling up outside their house.

I take a deep breath, plaster a smile on my face and then, before I can chicken out, I'm striding through the front door.

"Mom! Dad! Are you home?"

"Bea?" my mom calls from the kitchen. "Bea, is that you?"

She comes running down the hallway, flinging her arms around me and squeezing me so tight I can't breathe.

I laugh and squeeze her back.

"Mom. Hi."

"I didn't know you were coming home," she says, stepping away to examine me, her hands locked on my forearms as if she's expecting me to bolt. "Then again I didn't know you were leaving in the first place."

"I thought you would probably persuade me not to if I'd told you."

She smoothes hair away from my face. "Are you back permanently or is this a flying visit?"

"I ... I haven't decided yet."

"Ahhh," she says, smiling knowingly.

"What?"

"I knew it wouldn't work out in the city for you, Bea. You're not that kind of girl. You're a homebody."

"Right," I say.

"Come on," she drags me along into the kitchen. "You must be starving after that long drive. Let me rustle you up something to eat, although, " she pauses, and pokes me in the gut, "it looks like you've been eating well at least."

"I have."

I take a seat at the kitchen table and let her make me a coffee and a cheese sandwich.

"Where's dad?" I ask when she comes to sit down with me.

"At the diner."

I nod. I need to give them both an update about what's been happening in my life. I've tried to keep the details minimal in our conversations since I left home.

My mom leans her chin on her hand. "You look different, you know, sweetheart."

"Well, I probably have put on some weight, Mom, but I think–"

"No, there's some color to your cheeks too." She reaches over to squeeze my hand. "I know the whole wedding build up was stressful for you."

"The actual wedding was more stressful."

"I think it put a strain on both of you – on the relationship."

I pull a face and decide to change the subject. Maybe announcing my new designation might be a good topic of conversation after all.

"Actually, Mom," I say, lowering my sandwich, "there is something different about me."

"You're pregnant!" my mom gasps.

"No!" Why the hell does everyone keep asking me that? "No, I'm not pregnant." My mom's face drops in disappointment. Terrific. "I'm actually ... I actually came out as ..."

"A lesbian?" she asks, unconvinced by that.

"No, not that either. I'm ..." I swallow, trying my best to spit out the words. "I'm an omega."

My mom stares at me, then leans away from me and laughs.

I smile.

"Very funny," she says.

"I'm not being funny. I'm an omega."

"That's not possible, Bea. You're 26."

"Mom, you must be able to smell my scent." I'm using a ton load of blockers but I'm sure it's still discernible.

My mom's bottom lip wobbles. "I ... I assumed it was a new perfume."

I shake my head. "My scent."

"This can't be possible," she murmurs.

"No, it shouldn't. But these things always seem to happen to me." I shrug.

"This is Julia's influence, isn't it? I heard you've been meeting up with her."

"Aunt Julia doesn't have the power to turn me into an omega, Mom."

"No, but maybe she's convinced you that you are one. You left here all mixed up and confused and –"

"Mom, I am an omega. I didn't believe it myself at first, but, trust me, I'm damn certain of it now," I say, shuddering at the memory of my heat.

"No, no, you're confused. She's corrupted your mind." My mom leaps up from the table and reaches for her purse, tugging out her cellphone. "I'm calling your dad."

"Okay," I say, picking up my sandwich again. "If you want."

Thirty minutes later my dad comes sprinting into the kitchen looking flushed and concerned.

"What's happened?" he says, swinging his head from me to my mom. "What's the emergency?"

"Julia has convinced your daughter that she's ... that she's an omega."

My dad stares at my mom and then at me.

"Huh?"

"I'm an omega. I presented in the city. It seems the presence of alphas triggered it." I point to my mom, leaning against the counter with her arms crossed, glaring at me like I just confessed to robbing a bank. "Mom doesn't believe me."

"Why not?" my dad asks, turning back to my mom. "Why would Bea lie about something like this?"

"Exactly," I mumble.

"Because she's confused," my mom insists. "The big city and my wayward sister have got her all confused."

"I'm not confused. I can show you all the pills the doctors prescribed me if you want."

"You don't need to do that," my dad says.

My mom bursts into tears and rushes from the kitchen.

My dad pours himself a cup of coffee and pulls out a chair around the table.

"I thought we had a real emergency on our hands. Like the roof had caved in or you got your head caught in the railings again."

"One time," I say to him. "One time I did that."

My dad blows across his coffee and takes a long sip.

"I'm never going to let you forget it." He lowers his cup. "It's good to see you, cupcake."

"I'm not sure Mom agrees." I glance towards the doorway.

"She'll come round. It's just a shock."

"Tell me about it," I mumble.

"Why didn't you tell us earlier?"

I point towards the door and my dad nods.

"And I guess I've been coming to terms with it myself, trying to get my head around it, while dealing with all the crazy hormones and–" My dad shifts uncomfortably on his seat. "Sorry Dad."

"No, it's fine," he takes a mouthful of coffee, "go ahead."

I smile at him. "You really want to hear about my sex life?"

He gulps. "Why are you back?"

"Money," I sigh. "I couldn't find a job in the city."

"You?" my dad says. "How's that possible? No one wants to hire my wonderful daughter? Now I know you're lying."

"They don't want to hire an omega."

"Why not?"

"I don't know," I say, scratching my nails along the table top. "Because they assume I'll last five minutes before I'm whisked off by some pack of alphas. Or maybe they're just freaking bigots."

My dad frowns. "Pack of alphas?" he says.

"That's what every omega wants, apparently."

"According to..."

"Everyone I talk to."

"And what do you want?"

I sigh, and lean back in my chair. "A job. That pays money. So that I can stay in the city."

"Did Courtney kick you out?" my dad says, his frown deepening.

"No, of course she didn't, but I couldn't scrounge off her

forever. I thought if I came home for a bit, saved up some money, then I could go back and search some more. Maybe even go to college."

"College," my dad repeats.

"Yep, maybe it's a dumb idea, especially now I'm an omega and have all that stuff to contend with–"

"I think it's a great idea, Bea. You should always have gone. It broke my heart when you decided not to."

"It did?" I say. I lean forward. "You ... you never said anything."

"I should have. But your mom, she thought you were doing the right thing staying with Karl."

I make a face.

"He's back in town," my dad says. "I've been working out a way I can get under the bonnet of his truck and cut his brakes." He peers toward the doorway. "I'd better go and talk to your mom. She's probably reorganized the entire bedroom by now."

"It's okay. I'll go," I say.

When I walk into my parents' bedroom five minutes later, I'm almost hit by a flying blouse.

"It all needs sorting," my mom snaps. "All of it. I don't know why I've left it so long."

She tugs a skirt off a hanger, flings the article of clothing onto the bed and the hanger on top of a growing pile by her feet.

"Can I help?" I ask.

"No. I'm perfectly fine, thank you."

I flop down onto the bed, the mattress sagging, and begin to fold clothes.

"Left arm tucked under first," my mom says.

"I remember," I say, laying out a shirt next to me. "I'm

sorry if the news upset you, Mom, but I really am an omega."

My mom tugs at a zipper. But then her hands freeze and her shoulders sag. "I'm sorry too. It's not what I wanted for you."

"I don't think it will be so bad, Mom," I say, reaching for a sweater next. And for the first time, I actually believe those words. I'm still me. I'm still Bea. I'm in a better situation than I was three months ago. I know my own worth. Maybe I've even fallen back in love with myself. Heck, I even stabbed a guy with a needle and escaped that creepy clinic. Sure, the heats are awful. But maybe I'll find a pack, just like my aunt. Maybe I'll get my degree and land a job I actually want. I just need to start at the beginning again. "Aunt Julia is very happy."

"Julia," my mom scoffs.

"She's really lovely, Mom. She's helped me out loads."

My mom glances towards me. "She has?"

"Yes."

My mom sits down on the bed and reaches out to stroke my cheek. "I don't want to lose you, Bea, like I lost her."

"You're not going to lose me."

"You already ran off to the city. Like she did."

"That was nothing to do with my designation and everything to do with my wedding," I mumble. "Anyway, I'm going to be here for a while."

"I'm glad. I missed you, Bea."

"I missed you too." I kiss her hand. "And I think you ought to make up with Aunt Julia. She wants to make things up with you."

My mom squints at me. "Is that what she said?"

"Yes," I say.

"Then maybe I'll think about it."

She stands back up and surveys all the clothes piled up on her bed. "Talking of forgiveness..."

I cringe. Has Serena been around here too?

"Yes?"

"Karl came to see me."

I almost vomit.

"You let him in?"

"He brought flowers. Tulips. My favorite kind."

I glare at her. "Dad wants to sever his brakes."

"Your dad wasn't home," Mom says. "He wanted to know where you were. He said he wants to make things up with you."

"Only because Serena has dumped his ass."

"No, he said he realized he made a horrible mistake. That you're the love of his life and always will be. Isn't that sweet?"

"Ewww, no. Mom, Karl left me standing at the altar. He stole our honeymoon. He took Serena with him."

"Yes, but he's very sorry for all that. And he's such a sweet boy. The two of you were so cute together."

I stand up. "I'm going to take a shower." It's not just the grime and dirt of the journey I need to wash away. It's the thought of Karl too.

"Did you want me to let him know you're home? We could invite him around for dinner."

"Mom, no! Do not do that. Urgh!" I spin around and storm off to the shower. Hoping for once in my life she listens to me. Hoping shitty McShithead won't be waiting for me when I emerge out of the bathroom. Wondering if I really can spend the next six months working here in Naw Creek and avoiding my ex-fiancé.

~

MAYBE THE SHOWER gods were listening to my whinging, because the next morning, my dad knocks on my bedroom door with a cup of coffee and a concerned expression.

"There's a man waiting on the doorstep for you."

I tug the pillow from under my head and slam it over my face. "If it's Karl, tell him I've contracted leprosy and it would be very foolish of him to see me."

"It's not Karl. This man is much taller. And bigger. And he's wearing a watch I think I saw advertised once for $5,000."

I sit up bolt right. "What does he look like?"

"Fair."

"Connor?"

"Yep, that's what he said he was called."

"Oh, crap."

"Want me to tell him about the leprosy?"

"No," I yelp. "Just, I don't know, distract him or something while I get dressed." I fling back the covers, then halt. "But do not show him the photo album." My dad grins. "Dad!"

"Do we like this man?"

"I haven't decided yet. I'm kind of angry with him and his friends right now."

My dad's expression darkens. "Maybe I'll go check his brakes for him."

"No, do not leave him alone with mom," I beg.

He gives me a look I know means he's not making any promises and closes the door.

I crane my ears as I burrow through my suitcase looking for something that isn't dirty or creased to wear. Eventually I find a sundress, throw it over my head, drag a brush through my hair, a wand through my eyelashes and my toothbrush over my teeth.

I don't know why I'm making an effort. I should have stumbled out of bed in my Snoopy pajamas without a care in the world. But being back here, the reminder last night of just how badly Karl screwed me over, has put some things in perspective. Maybe one day I'll find it in my heart to forgive Karl, but certainly never, ever in one trillion, billion, million years will I take him back.

Those alphas hurt me. But their crimes in comparison seem somewhat trivial. Could I let them back into my life?

I haven't been able to forget Nate and the cake. Or Silver donning a pair of marigolds and picking up trash.

Could I?

I'm not sure.

I find Connor sitting on the sofa next to my dad, an open photo album spread over my dad's lap.

"We had to call the fire brigade," my dad says, and I know exactly which photo he's pointing at.

I race over, snatch up the album and slam it shut.

"Did he show you the pageant one too?" Connor nods and stands. "Dad!" I say, whacking his shoulder with the album.

"I thought he'd be interested," my dad says.

Connor meets my eye, opening his mouth to say something just as my mom comes bustling into the lounge with a tray of coffee and muffins. She looks incredibly flustered as she places the tray down.

"Here, refreshments. For you young folk." She stands up and smoothes her hands over her skirt, inspecting Connor with obvious admiration.

"Actually, I was hoping we might go for a stroll." He smiles at my mum. "I used to live here about fifteen years ago. I wouldn't mind a tour of the old place."

"Sure," I say, motioning towards the door.

My mom trots behind the two of us, seeing us right towards the door and watching as we stroll down the pathway and out to the sidewalk.

"Your parents seem–"

"Manic?" I ask.

"Like they care about you. You missed the tenth degree I got from your dad. He only pulled the album out once he seemed satisfied with my answers."

"Oh my god," I say, covering my face with my hands. "What did he ask you?"

"All the kinds of things I'll be asking any man who turns up wanting to see my daughter," Connor says firmly, making something in my stomach swoop.

I can't think about Connor and children. Connor and a daughter. A little girl. My ovaries might explode.

"Did you just get here?" I ask him.

"No, I arrived late last night. I've been waiting for a civilized hour to come see you." He pauses. "I wasn't sure you *would* see me."

"I'm feeling a little less angry," I admit. "But only a little." I frown at him.

"I understand."

We walk around the corner, past more houses that look just like my parents. Old Jimmy Gregor is mowing his lawn and the sprinklers in the Symms' house are on so high it looks like a Vegas fountain show.

"Are you really moving back here?"

"For the time being, yes."

"I could never stand these small towns myself," he says, eyes sliding to me.

"Why? Not exciting enough for you?"

"It always felt like I was being watched, watched and

talked about. Everyone knows your business in a place like this."

"Everyone knows your business in the city. Every magazine I read had an article about your pack."

He chuckles. "Yeah, maybe it isn't so different."

"If you've come to ask me to come back with you..."

He shakes his head and we walk past the St Luke's Church, its walls newly painted a bright white, its metal cross bright in the morning sunshine.

"You talked to Silver a couple of days ago about your dream job."

"I did ..." I say with suspicion. "You're not going to offer me another job, are you, because I can't accept it."

"No, I haven't got a job to offer you that you'd want. But," he reaches into his jacket pocket and pulls out some sheets of printed paper.

I halt, taking it from him and scanning through the text with curiosity.

"What is it?" I ask him.

"I did some research. Some of the environmental organizations have trainee programs."

I hand the pieces of paper back to him. "I'm not a graduate, remember? They won't want me."

He shakes his head, refusing to take the papers from me. "It doesn't matter; anyone can apply."

"Really?" I say, eyeing the text again.

"Really. And we'd write you a glowing reference." He grins at me. "Might even offer to make a donation if they take you on."

"Noooo," I say, shaking my head this time. Then I peer up at him and those blue, blue eyes of his. Like the ocean. My knees shake. I swallow. "You could have emailed these to me," I point out. "You didn't have to drive all the way out here."

"I don't have your email address."

"Text message."

"I'm pretty hopeless at technology."

"Connor ..."

"Okay," he says. "I wanted to see you." He shrugs and we reach the center of town with the post office, the local store and the police station. All standing neatly in a row. Opposite is the town square. The bushes neatly trimmed, flowers blooming in the straight beds.

"Has it changed much?" I ask him.

He peers at it. "Hard to remember. We moved around so much when I was a kid and all these places start to blend into one another. You, though, you, I remember." He looks down at me.

"I didn't think you did."

"Not at first but I do now. Phoebe Carsen."

My cheeks burn as my mouth falls open. He remembers?

"Nobody calls me that anymore." My teachers all called me Phoebe. Everyone else has called me Bea for as long as I can remember. I check myself. "But you could have looked up my full name. Or my mom might have told you."

"No, I remember you, *Phoebe* Carsen. I was sitting out by the field on lunch break and you came over and asked me what I was reading. I remember you had this pretty smile and eyes like nothing I'd ever seen before. We talked about my book and about the book you were reading too. I remember you used to smile at me in the corridors. I remember I was going to ask you out."

"You were?"

"But some dude on the football team beat me to it."

"Karl," I say, my heart sinking. "You really remember all that?"

"Yes."

"Hmmm," I say, not convinced this isn't another of these alphas' tricks. "What book was I reading then?"

"*Jane Eyre*. You weren't sure if you liked it."

"Mr. Rochester was an asshole."

"He was. But she forgave him in the end."

"She did." I study his eyes. The blue and the greens spinning together like the currents of the sea. "I'm not sure she should have."

"He didn't deserve her."

"He shouldn't have hurt her. He shouldn't have lied."

"No, he shouldn't have. But I think he spent the rest of his life trying to make it up to her." He steps closer so his body brushes mine. "That's what I'd do."

"You would?" I whisper, my heart thumping in my throat, my eyes lost in his, my body pulled nearer and nearer.

"Yes."

Then he leans down and kisses me. And I wonder if Jane Eyre was allowed to forgive and land the man of her dreams that means I can land an entire pack of them.

I kiss him back.

It's exactly how I imagined kissing Connor Doyle would be like. Warm and safe, yet dizzying and electric too. He holds me close, and kisses me deep, like he wants to taste every part of my mouth, like he wants to never let me go. My eyes drift shut and I forget everything around me. The rumble of the traffic, the birds singing, a distant radio. All I hear is his heartbeat. All I feel is the press of his lips and the warmth of his body.

When finally, he leans back, it takes me a moment to

open my eyes. My heart racing and every omega instinct screaming for more.

It was that damn business with the cake. It's made me an awful lot hornier.

"You know," I say, "I spent a lot of time as a teenage girl thinking about making out with you in my bedroom. Want to do that now?"

"How about your dad?"

I peer up at the clock above the town hall. "He should be heading for work about now along with my mom."

He leans in to nibble my neck and as he does a passing truck catches my eye. A familiar truck. One that used to park up every evening at the front of my house.

Karl stares back at me from the driver's seat, his eyes wide with shock. I smile as wide as I can at him and then I grab the collar of the alpha's shirt and drag him in for another kiss.

Thank you shower gods.

17

xel

AT NINE AM SHARP, I stroll into the cafe at the bottom of our tower. I left instructions with Angel and my pack to be here too. Silver's already half way through a cup of coffee which is no surprise. But the others are all late. Angel turns up with Hardy ten minutes after me, followed closely behind by Connor. He can be forgiven. He didn't roll in from his little trip to Naw Creek until the early hours of this morning.

After we'd gotten to the bottom of why the omega had left the city, it was Silver who came up with the idea about the ecological foundation. She wants a job. In the city. And this one sounded like her dream vocation. Hopefully enough to tempt her back. Much to Nate's annoyance, we voted for Connor to go and see her. He knows her hometown, plus out of all of us he won't be too pushy. I'd have a hard time not dragging her back, and Nate? Well, he's already shown his tendency for flinging the woman over his shoulder when she doesn't cooperate.

No, that's not the way we're operating anymore. Her choice, her decision.

The way Connor's bond was thrumming when he came in last night has me thinking he was successful. The way a contented smile hovers on his lip this morning confirms it.

"Things went well then," I ask, when he carries his coffee over to the table where the rest of us are waiting.

"You could say that."

Hardy glares at him. "That's all you're giving us?"

"What else do you want?" Connor asks, ripping the top off a packet of sugar and tipping the contents into his drink.

"Details, man, details."

"We spent the morning and most of the afternoon making out in her bedroom." He grins.

"I ate her pussy." I look up and Nate pulls back a chair and falls into it. He smirks at Connor.

Connor shrugs. "I'm not complaining or competing. I don't think I've spent a better five hours."

I stare at him, then flip my attention back to Nate.

"What are you talking about?"

Nate reaches for my coffee and takes a long gulp, grimacing. "That is revolting."

"Caramel shot," I explain.

"Tastes nothing like the real thing, Ax." He licks his lips.

I can't decide if I hate him or love him.

"This has to be a good sign, right?" Angel says. "Maybe we should ask Molly. Get an opinion from an omega."

"You're not telling your little sister that I ate out the omega."

"Yeah," Angel says, nose wrinkling. "Maybe I'll leave out the details."

"So why are we here?" Hardy asks. "And what's with the dress code?" We're all dressed in combat gear and suitable footwear like I instructed. Except Nate. He's in his usual ripped jeans and boots.

"Team bonding exercise."

They stare at me.

"A what?" Hardy asks.

"Team bonding exercise. Next step in trying to work things out."

"Oh man," Hardy says, leaning forward, head in hands.

"You don't want to work things out?" I ask sternly. I thought we went over this already at my mom's place. I thought we all agreed. It's time we put the past behind us and focus on making amends.

"Nah, it's good ... it's just ... it's fucking high ropes, isn't it?"

My lips twitch. I forgot this about Hardy. Big man has his Achilles' heels. One of them is heights.

"No idea," I say. "I didn't organize it. Molly did." I gesture towards the door, pointing to my little sister as she waves at us all. Behind her is one of Silver's men assigned to watch over her every time she leaves the house.

"Jesus fucking Christ," Angel mumbles. "She'll have us rolling around in fields of daisies and chanting to the wind gods."

I watch my sister as she weaves through the tables; Silver's man has his eyes locked on her. I may need a word with Silver about whether his employee is a little too eager to do his job right.

"Shit," I mumble, "I didn't think about that." I assumed she'd book us in for some survival special. That or paint-balling.

"Morning gentlemen," she says, taking a chair.

"What can I get you, Moll?" the heavy asks her and I don't like the way she smiles up at him, eyelashes fluttering. Maybe I'll need a word with her too.

My sister reels off the name of something I've never heard of but I'm certain contains a shit load of sugar and cream.

"You'll rot your teeth," Nate says.

"My teeth are perfectly fine thanks, Nathanial." She shrugs off her jacket. "So are we all ready for today's activities?"

I note the plural. "What exactly do you have planned?"

She smiles innocently at me and I know Angel's right about this.

"It better not be daisy chain making," Hardy grumbles.

"You want to mend bonds and ultimately win back the omega, right?"

"Yes," Angel and I say together.

"How about the rest of you?"

"Yes," Connor says as Silver and Hardy nod.

"Nate?" she asks.

"Yep," he says, swinging back and forth on the legs of his chair.

"So trust me on this one, okay?"

I glance at Angel who nods. Molly always found it easier to convince him to do her bidding when we were kids, but truth be told, we were both suckers for our little sister. Hence, why we ended up in her bedroom playing barbies more times than I could account for. And why my toenails were often painted a bright pink.

The bodyguard returns with Molly's monstrosity of a drink and Nate makes a gagging sound.

"Oh dear," she says, lowering her drink to the table. "I think a little Omega 101 is in order here." She eyes us with suspicion. "Can anyone name me some of the things omegas like?"

"Cock!" Hardy snaps and Angel kicks him under the table.

My sister doesn't even flinch. She has two older brothers after all. "Anything else? Anything at all?"

"A nest," Nate says.

"Yes, and what does an omega like in his or her nest?"

"Cushions, blankets, soft shit."

"Right. So you know the basics, that's a relief. But anything else?"

We all look at her blankly.

She huffs. "Security, comfort, affection, touch and," my sister lifts up her drink, "sweet things." She takes a long suck on her straw and the bodyguard's eyes turn darker. Definitely time for a reassignment.

"We knew that shit," I say, nodding with self-assurance.

"So you offered her all those things did you?"

"I made her a cake. With shit loads of sugar in it," Nate says proudly to Molly before muttering to the rest of us, "it's why she let me eat her out."

If Molly hears this additional piece of information, she ignores it.

"Good," Molly says. "Just remember the other things too. You alphas," she points a finger at us all, "can get swept up in all the sex-business. Half the men I meet are only after one thing–"

"What men?" I growl.

"–but you need to give us omegas all the other stuff too. If you want to make us happy, that is. If you want to make us purr."

She glances up at Mr. Bodyguard and smiles.

If any of these activities involve a gun, this man is in trouble.

"Are we ready to move out?" she asks.

"You're not going to tell us what we're doing?"

"Nope," she says, jumping to her feet, Mr. Bodyguard automatically matching her movements. "I wouldn't want to spoil the surprise."

I FOLLOW Molly's directions through the city, trying to work out where the hell she's taking us and what this mystery team bonding exercise is. When she instructs me to take a left and pull up into the parking lot at the mall, we all groan.

"Please tell me there's a laser tag or something in here," Hardy groans.

"No, you're going shopping."

We all groan louder still.

"Shopping is likely to tear us apart, not bring us together," I tell her.

"Then, you'll have to find a way to work through that, won't you?" She tugs her cellphone from her purse. "Now, I'm sending you all a list of items an omega would want and need in their nest. You will have to work together to buy these items and return them to me within ... hmmm ... I think I'll give you two hours." She presses her phone and ours all bleep.

"Fuck me, this list is longer than my cock," Hardy says.

"Must be fucking tiny, then," Angel says.

"Why are we doing this?" I say, glancing at the list of thirty-odd items with cynicism.

"Ax, tell me, do you have a nest set up in your penthouse?" She holds up her hand when I begin to speak. "A proper one, not something you cobbled together the last time some omega stopped by to share her heat."

I shake my head.

"Angel?" she asks.

"No, we don't."

"So, if this Bea had decided to spend her heat with one of your packs, where exactly were you going to spend it?"

"My bed," Nate says.

Molly crosses her arms. "What color are your bed sheets, Nate?"

"Black."

She raises an eyebrow like she just scored a point.

"What's wrong with black? It's my favorite color."

"Do you want your omega weeping with sorrow or joy?"

Nate grumbles something but lifts his phone to take another look at the list.

"If you're serious about wanting her back," Molly says, "you need to show her that your intentions are serious too. That you have her best interests at heart. Not your own. Show her that you care. Which means, giving these items some consideration." She pulls up a stopwatch app on the screen of her phone. "Right, your time starts ... NOW!"

"Now?" I mutter.

But I don't get to argue any further because Nate snaps open the van door and leaps out, Hardy bundling after him. Seems they are taking it seriously. Which means I'm going to too.

Before I know it all six of us are sprinting across the mall parking lot and through the main entrance. Here we skid to a stop.

"Where first?" Silver pants.

Connor holds up the list to his face. "I don't know what half this crap is."

"Then we need to be strategic about it." The others nod in agreement, even fucking Nate. "Silver, Connor, take a seat and start researching the items we're unfamiliar with. Angel, Nate, Hardy, let's head for the department store first. We can grab most of the bedding and clothing items there."

"We'll check in with you in fifteen minutes," Silver says, already scrolling through webpages. "Keep your phones on."

We leave the other two hovering by the doors and sprint through the mall towards the department store. People jump out of our way, most giving us startled looks. We look like we're on an army exercise. I'm not surprised.

"Are we under attack?" one woman asks, clutching her children to her chest.

"No, ma'am, just out shopping for our girl," I tell her and she almost swoons at my feet.

I had no idea.

At the department store entrance there's a long list of the different floors. I peer inside and it looks like a fucking maze.

"We're going to need to stick together," I say, grabbing Nate by the collar as he starts to deviate towards the lingerie on display. "That isn't on the list," I tell him.

"It should be." I glare and he mumbles under his breath.

"Floor two," Angel says, pointing to the sign, and we race to the escalator, Hardy not caring that the first one is traveling downwards and running up the thing anyway.

At the top of the stairs, we emerge into a world of furniture. About a dozen different beds crowd around us. "Where the fuck is the actual bedding?" I cry out in frustration.

"There!" Hardy yells, but when we reach the shelves he pointed at, we find towels instead.

"Get your eyes tested," Angel mutters as Hardy scowls at him.

"We should get towels anyway," Nate says. "Those big fluffy ones we can wrap her up in." We're all quiet for a moment, picturing that little image, and then Hardy grabs a handful and slings them over his shoulder.

We head back the way we came and end up next to the children's section. Angel and Hardy start on a conversation about the merits of Star Wars bedsheets over Superman and I growl at them in frustration, before spotting a salesman and ordering him to escort us to the adult bedding.

The man doesn't hang about once he's delivered us to the section and we stare at it in disbelief. There are enough sheets in here to make up every bed on the fucking Las Vegas strip.

"What the fuck," Angel says, scratching at his beard. "Fucking Molly."

"What do you think she'd like?" I ask, pulling out one sheet and then another.

"Something soft," Hardy says.

"They're all soft, asshole," I say.

"Yeah, but these ones smell funny," Hardy says, sniffing a pale cream sheet.

Next moment, we're all sniffing sheets, until we have half a dozen that aren't offensive to our noses.

"I think we should get a variety," Angel says. "She's probably going to want soft, but deep in her heat, there might also come a time when she needs ..." he swallows, "rough."

"Fuck yeah," Hardy growls.

"Okay," I say, trying to drag them back to focus. "Let's get a selection then, and head for clothing."

The fairy lights and lamps are easier to find, although we waste far too much time debating the merits of different cushions. Hardy finds a bean bag which isn't on the list but insists we buy it.

"Imagine bending her over this and fucking her from behind."

I glare at him. Paint-balling would have been so much safer.

Silver calls me as we take our collection to the cash register and explains what the other items are. I'm so distracted by the description of the various sex toys we need to find that I don't notice the giant teddy bear Nate adds to the pile. Not until everything's been paid for.

"What the fuck is that?" I ask.

"A teddy," he says, cradling the thing in his arms. The thing is almost as tall as he is and a lot rounder.

"It's ugly as fuck," Hardy says.

Nate looks at him with those murderous eyes, and Hardy holds up his hands in surrender.

"It's not for you is it, asshole," Nate says. "It's for Bea."

I stare at my packmate.

I don't think I've ever known him to buy a gift for an omega. Sure, he tips the strippers handsomely, and always buys my mom a bunch of daisies on her birthday, but that's as far as he's ever gone.

Now he's baking cakes and buying giant teddies.

"What the hell has happened to you, man?" I ask.

"Bea," he says simply.

I know what he means. If it wasn't for Bea, I wouldn't be here standing in a department store buying fluffy towels and pink cushions with my estranged younger brother.

But I realize as we ride the escalator down to the ground floor in search of Connor and Silver, that I'm actually enjoying myself. I miss this camaraderie between the six of us. I miss my brother and his unswerving focus. I miss

Silver and his careful analysis. I even miss Hardy's stupid jokes.

"Come on, boys," I say, slapping Angel on the shoulder, "let's go buy some vibrating bunnies."

Exactly two hours after we left, we're back at the van. It looks like Molly's spent the hours shopping herself; several bags litter her feet. She beckons us to pass over our goods and one by one ticks them all off the list.

"So you found the knotted dildos, then?" she says, holding a purple one up to show us all.

"Not that our omega is going to need one of those."

"Can your knot do this?" Molly asks, flicking a switch and starting up the thing's motor. It vibrates violently in her hand, buzzing furiously.

"It can do other things," Hardy says darkly.

Molly switches the thing off and throws it back in one of the bags.

"Well done. Mission successful."

We all grin madly like we just completed a Navy Seal assault course.

"So now what are you going to do with it?"

"Build a nest," I say. Wasn't that the whole point of this?

"Where?" she asks. Where? She looks at me and then glances at Angel. "You only bought one of everything. You only bought enough for one nest. So the question is: where is that nest going to be?"

And I know she's asking us a much bigger question.

Are we offering the omega a choice?

Or are we offering her all of us?

18

Bea

I HATE KETCHUP.

"Bane of my life," I mutter as I scrub at yet another tabletop where the diners have left behind a nice encrusted splodge of the stuff. "Why can't people clean up after themselves?"

"Easy there, Cupcake," my dad says coming up behind me. "You're going to scrub away most of the wood."

"I can't get it off," I mutter between gritted teeth.

"Here," he says, holding out his hand.

I toss him the dish cloth and collapse down onto one of the benches. He picks up the bottle of cleaning fluid, sprays at the stain, then gently glides his cloth over the congealed sauce, once, twice, three times until it's gone completely.

"Smart ass," I tell him.

He grins and takes the seat opposite me. The diner

closed a half hour ago, and he's been busy cleaning up the kitchen while I've been tackling out front.

"What's eating you?" my dad asks, tossing the cloth to one side.

It's only my second day back working at the diner and already the ketchup stains are getting to me.

I roll my neck. "I'm just feeling irritable."

"About?"

"Ketchup stains."

"And ..."

"Life in general."

"Life in general," my dad repeats, "sounds pretty dramatic. Life didn't seem so bad two days ago when you were locked upstairs with that mountain of a man."

"You weren't meant to know about that," I say.

"Is he your boyfriend?"

"No," I say firmly.

"Does he want to be your boyfriend?"

I drum my nails on the tabletop. "I don't know."

"But he's the reason you're feeling irritable?"

I wonder if that's true. Right now, I don't feel comfortable in my skin. I'm grumpy and skittish. If the dates weren't all wrong, I'd think I was experiencing some hardass PMS.

I wonder if it's being back home or if it's something to do with being an omega.

"You seemed pretty relaxed in his company," my dad says, "and you've been walking around like a bear with a sore head ever since he left."

Is that the problem? Lack of alphas. Just the thought of their scents, their deep voices, their strong bodies, has my shoulders relaxing and my body sinking into my seat.

Would the presence of any old alpha have my bad mood

dissipating? Or is this all about a certain group of alphas in particular?

I was half expecting another one of them to show up on my doorstep yesterday. Or at the very least a string of messages hassling me about whether I'm applying for that job, whether I'm returning to the city.

But they've been quiet. Which could mean they've forgotten me. Or could mean they're giving me my space. I have a feeling it's the latter. I hope it is.

I rest my elbow on the table and my chin in my hand.

"Do you want my advice, Cupcake?"

"It might depend on what it is. Mom was advising me to forgive Karl and get back with him two days ago."

My dad frowns. "If you even think about doing that, I'll have the doctor around in a heartbeat certifying you medically insane, because you'd have to be to take that jerk back."

"I know."

"My advice. Go back to the city, Cupcake."

"You don't want me here? I promise I'll stop taking my bad mood out on the tables."

"Of course, I want you here. But not if it makes you unhappy. Truth is, I think you've outgrown Naw Creek. I think you may have outgrown it years ago. There are more opportunities for you in the city, more chances to be who you're meant to be." I think of the ecological foundation trainee scheme. I think of those printouts perched on my desk. "I know things aren't working out for you right now, Cupcake. But I've no doubt they will. I've no doubt if you persevere you'll find a place and a life for yourself out there. Just," he pinches my chin, "don't give up. Anyone who can get up and make a speech at their wedding reception when their jerk of a fiancé has bolted, can do anything she wants."

"Urgh, that speech was horrible." I ranted and raved for thirty minutes before someone wrestled the microphone away from me along with the bottle of champagne I'd been necking.

"It wasn't. It was kick ass. I wish I'd recorded it. Could've shown it to that young man two days ago."

"Oh my God." I laugh, burying my face in my hands. "I need to destroy that photo album."

"No chance." My dad smiles. "Don't waste your time out here with us old fogies and your asshole of an ex. Get back out there, Bea, take life by the horns and ride it anywhere you want it to go." He picks up the dish cloth resting on the bench beside him, and tosses it back towards me. "Right, back to scrubbing. Let's get this place closed up and head home."

My mom greets us on the doorstep as we pull up fifteen minutes later.

"You have a parcel," she says, clutching my hand and pulling me along after her. "From the city."

"Oh?" I say, unhooking my purse from my shoulder and hanging it on the back of a chair.

A parcel the size of a shoebox sits on top of the kitchen table. My mom hovers by my side.

"Are you going to open it then? Do you think it's from that man?"

"Give her some space, Pattie," my dad tells her, placing his hands on her shoulders and pulling her back a pace or two away from me.

I examine the handwriting across the top of the parcel. It isn't Mrs. Finch's which means if it is from Connor – or any other member of his pack, a cook, for example – they sent it themselves.

I find the edge of the tape and unfurl it from the cardboard, my mom watching anxiously from the other side of the table. I wonder what she can possibly think is inside. A diamond ring. I hope not. I've had enough weddings to last me several lifetimes.

I tug away the last bit of tape and then, glancing up at my mom, fold back the tabs. Inside is packing tissue. I peel it back and underneath, nesting in more tissue, is a book.

Hardback. Its cover designed with innate gold lettering and decoration.

Jane Eyre.

I lift it up and bring it to my nose, inhaling. It smells just like books. Just like Connor.

"A book?" my mom asks, sounding incredibly disappointed.

"Yes, a book."

"Is there anything else inside the box?"

I check. "Just a note."

My mom stares at me like she's expecting me to read it to her. When I don't she huffs and turns to join my dad at the cooker.

I open the book first.

Inside, in trim black ink, Connor has written, *For Bea.*

I smile and open his note next.

> I remember that copy of *Jane Eyre* you had all those years ago was a battered, tatty looking thing. I thought it was about time you got an upgrade.

I STROKE my hands over the cover and the spine of the book. I'm not sure I'll be able to even open this book for fear of spoiling it.

I continue reading his note.

> I'm hoping by the time you receive this gift, you'll have applied for that program and will be packing ready to return to the city. If I'm honest, I'm hopeful you're returning to us. We screwed up and we're working to fix it. We're working to win you back.
>
> Maybe if we keep working hard enough – you and us – we'll all get what we want.
>
> Seems your hero Charlotte would agree. Did you know she once wrote:
>
> "I honor endurance, perseverance, industry, talent; because these are the means by which men achieve great ends and mount to lofty eminence."
>
> Keep persevering, sweetheart. Don't give up on what you want. Or what you deserve.
>
> Connor

I RUN the pad of my fingers over the words, pausing to give them thought.

I gave up on my dreams too easily before. I put them aside and let someone destroy my belief in myself.

Am I really going to let that happen again?

Or this time am I going to persevere and endure until I get what I want?

I sink into a kitchen chair, the note still in my hands.

What is it I want?

Independence. A job I love. A chance to be myself.

Yes, all those things. But also, I want strong pairs of arms to hold me, warm lips to kiss me, people who love me, people I can love in return.

I still want that white picket fence. I still want a family. Only now it's like that white fence has grown, magnified. No longer is it like a cage, encircling some little wooden house in Naw Creek. Now it circles an entire city and inside there I am with six alphas who I can't shake from my mind and my heart no matter how hard I try.

I fold the note in half and slide it inside the cover of my book.

Karl would never have encouraged me to follow my dreams. He'd never believe I was capable of pursuing them.

But these other men, they do. They believe in me and maybe it's about time I believe in myself too.

My dad insists on driving me in his truck the next day.

"I hate to break it to you, Cupcake," he tells me with his head under Missy's bonnet, "I don't think there's much more life left in the old girl."

"Don't say that," I whine.

"It's true. And I'm certainly not letting you drive alone to the city. What if she broke down?"

I don't want to leave her behind. But I also have to admit that old Missy is becoming less and less efficient. How much longer could I ride around in her anyway? Especially if I'm applying to work in an ecological organization. Nope, it's going to be buses, trains and my own pair of feet from now on, even if that means finally facing the music and purchasing a gun of my own. I've never wanted one before, but the whole kidnapping and constant threat to my safety has forced my hand.

My dad loads all my boxes once again into the cab of his truck and I go to hug my mom.

"You really do smell lovely, Bea. You must have all the alphas in the city running after you." Since meeting Connor, she's certainly changed her tune. In fact, the change seems to have come about after he told her how many properties he owned across the city. "And you will keep in touch, won't you? Let me know all your news. Especially if you meet someone."

I squeeze her tight but refuse to make any promises.

Then I'm ducking into the seat next to my dad and I'm leaving Naw Creek for a second time.

How long will I be away? I have no idea. But my shoulders feel lighter than the last time I left. My heart easier. Despite all that's come to pass, all the turmoil and heartache, I know I'm stronger now. I'm more like the Bea I should always have been.

I ask my dad to drive the back way and he rolls down the windows and pumps up Bon Jovi on his stereo. The hottest part of summer has passed and the air, though warm, is less scorching than it was when I drove down these roads weeks ago. The corn in the fields is ready for harvesting, golden and tall, and the trees we race under heavy with fruit.

As we draw closer to that infamous gas station, I twist in my seat, wanting to catch sight of it. Soon, I spy it on the edge of the horizon and then as we draw nearer, the vehicles waiting by the pumps.

One vehicle. Silvery blue.

I smile.

"Do you think we could pull in here?" I ask my dad.

"Sure, Cupcake," he says, indicating and swinging the truck off the road and next to the pumps.

Axel is there leaning against his car, arms crossed, dressed in one of those mouthwatering suits. As I open the truck door and jump down, he whips off his shades and tucks them into his pocket.

"Hey sweetheart," he says, hesitating before bending down to kiss my cheek.

"You know this man?" my dad whispers in my ear as he comes to stand next to me.

"Yes, this is Axel York."

"Axel Stormgate," he corrects and I glance at him with puzzlement as he holds out his hand for my father to shake.

"Chuck," my dad says, scrutinizing the alpha.

"Are you here by chance?" I ask with a smile hovering on my lips.

"Nope, I'm waiting for you."

"You didn't know I would be passing."

"I took a gamble," he says. I lift an eyebrow at him. "And a little bird may have told me you were packing up."

"A silver bird?" I ask, smiling. He meets my smile with one of his own. "How long have you been here exactly?"

"A while. I was hoping I could drive you the rest of the way home."

"Bea?" my dad asks.

"Okay," I say, my smile growing wider, "I'd like that."

We have some trouble fitting all my stuff into the tiny

trunk of Axel's sport's car, but dad promises to post me the last two boxes. Then he kisses me and whispers in my ear.

"You sure about this, Cupcake? I mean, he's as good looking as the last one but–"

I kiss my dad's rough cheek. "They're packmates."

My dad's jaw nearly falls to the floor and I think that is my cue to make a swift exit. I give him a wave, then climb down into the sports car and let Axel press the button that has the doors descending like an eagle tucking in its wings.

"This car is friggin' ridiculous," I mutter.

"You don't like it?" he asks.

"Well," I confess, "I've been waiting for you to take me out in it."

With a self-satisfied grin, he revs the engine and zips out of the gas station, leaving my dad standing there bewildered and me pinned back in my seat.

I laugh as we fly down the road, far too fast, and dust billows up in the air behind me.

"This is so much smoother than my dad's truck, or Missy."

"Missy?"

"My car."

"Ahh your car? Where is it?"

"She. I had to leave her behind. She needs a bit of work."

"You need a car in the city. You can borrow this one."

"Firstly, I don't need a car. Secondly, I can't borrow this. Thirdly, this car is really bad for the environment. Although," I mutter, glancing his way, "I'd love to drive her."

Axel twists his head to look at me, then swerves the car into a rest stop and slams on the brakes.

"What the hell?" I cry, but instead of explaining his actions, he presses the buttons and the doors rise. In the next second, he's out of his seat and dragging me out of mine.

"What's going on?" I ask. "Are you kicking me out of your car and abandoning me at the side of the road because I insulted your baby?"

"Nope, I'm letting you drive."

"Me?" I point to my chest.

"I don't see anyone else here, sweetheart."

"You're serious?"

"Why wouldn't I be?"

He tosses me the car keys and I catch them in my hand. Then he slides into the passenger seat, leaving me no choice but to climb into the driver's. It takes me a few minutes to pull the seat right up close to the steering wheel so I can reach the pedals, and adjust all the mirrors, triple checking them to ensure I can see anything hurtling towards us. Then I start the car and gingerly press my foot to the gas.

The car creeps forward and I immediately slam my foot on the brake. We both jerk forward.

"I don't think I can do this," I say.

"Why not?" Axel asks.

"Because this car is worth hundreds of thousands of dollars and if I crash it, or scratch it, or dent it ..."

"You won't."

"You don't know that."

"I do."

I shake my head at him.

"I have confidence in you, Bea," he says. "You won't hurt my car." I start to argue with him and he interrupts. "And anyway, even if you did, so what?"

"So what? Hundreds of thousands of dollars that's what."

"It's just a car."

"A very expensive car."

"If it makes you happy, I would like you to drive it. A car has its price limit. Your happiness is priceless." He chuckles. "Shit, that sounded cheesier than I intended. Look, Bea, if you'd rather not–"

I stare down at my hands gripping the steering wheel. Am I going to let my fear hold me back? Or am I going to persevere and endure?

I hit the gas and we fly out of the rest stop, hitting a bump in the road and both bouncing high in our seats.

"Sorry," I cry, but I don't stop.

I keep my eyes locked on the road, and the further we zoom down that empty road the more I love it. Adrenaline pumps through my veins. I'm controlling this powerful machine in my hands. It obeys my commands. The buzz is electrifying. Especially when it's accompanied by that scent of spring rain and the alpha's dazzling smile.

"You're a good driver, sweetheart," Axel says, although I'm not blind to the way he's clinging to the handle above the door.

"I'm an awful driver but thank you for being sweet." I flick my eyes from the windscreen towards that pair of silver eyes. "So what was all that about Axel Stormgate?"

"I'm taking back my surname. So is Angel."

My foot eases on the gas. "Wh-why?"

"It's part of our efforts to reconcile. No more Pack York, no more Pack Boston."

My foot falls off the gas completely and the car drifts towards the edge of the road.

"Woah, there sweetheart," Axel says, grabbing the steering wheel and guiding the car back to the center of the road.

I shake myself out of my thoughts. "Sorry." I press my foot down again. I chew on my lip. "You're reconciling?"

"Yes, we are."

"After all this time?"

"After all this time."

"But why? Why now?"

"Bea," Axel says, and my eyes leave the road to find his, "I think you know why." Do I? I stare at him blankly. He chuckles. "You."

The words hang in the car and I don't know why I would have anything to do with this.

"We were assholes to you, Bea, and it cost us our shot with you. But the truth is, we've been assholes for the last ten years. It took what happened for us to finally see the damage we were doing. We've been trying to put things back together ever since."

"Is it working?" I ask. Ten years is a long time to hate someone. To go out of your way to hurt them. To fight them at every opportunity. Can the damage they've done to each other, to everyone around them, really be repaired?

"I think so, yes. I very much want it to work." Axel leans against his window and rubs his hand over his chin. "He's my little brother and I love him. I always did, no matter what bullshit I spouted. And fuck, I missed him. I missed Hardy and Silver too. They were my best friends. It's about time we mended this shit."

My heart aches for him and I can't help but reach over and squeeze his hand. He wraps his fingers around mine so our hands are linked.

I didn't think a man like Axel Stormgate could ever be honest like that. Not after I discovered all those shady lies. I thought he was all about the front. The flashy sports car, the designer shades and the sharp suits. Underneath all that this man has a heart. One I can see has been hurt just as badly as mine.

"What happened between the two of you? Between all of you?"

This time he doesn't try to fob me off with some excuse about the story being a long one. This time he tells me everything. Some of it is ugly – a lot of it is ugly. But he doesn't try to paint himself as the good guy or Angel as the bad. It's clear they were both hurt by what happened. It's clear that they both acted poorly, spreading that hurt to the people they love most in the world.

When he's done, we sit in silence for a moment, our hands still linked, me steering the car with my left hand. We're drawing closer to the city. More buildings visible along the road, more traffic joining us.

"Now your go, sweetheart," he tells me.

"My go?"

"Yes, tell me what happened. With the ex."

So I do. I tell him everything and just like him I don't hold back. I don't only tell him about that wedding day, waiting at the altar, finding that note. I tell him about everything that came before, all those unkind words, all the times he'd put me down and belittled me. I know it makes me look like a fool but it seems some honesty is required.

"I should have left him a long long time ago."

"You should. I wish you had." He strokes his thumb over my knuckles. "I wish all that shit with my brother had never happened too. I wish we'd never fallen out like that. But then maybe I'd never have met you. I'd go through every piece of shit I have done in the last 29 years of my life, Bea, if it guaranteed I got to meet you again. At that gas station."

A lump forms in my throat and I swallow it down hard.

"Do you think you can ever forgive us for fucking things up so badly, sweetheart?"

"I don't know," I say honestly. "I'd like to. I don't always want to be the victim. At some point in my story, I'd like to be the heroine. You know, the girl who gets her happy ending."

"Happy ending." He sniggers and I snatch my hand away and whack him on the shoulder. He chuckles more loudly and the rumble in his chest has my stomach swooping, especially when he meets my eyes and I'm lost for a moment in the myriad of sparkling stars.

"Sweetheart, road," he says, and I pull my gaze away and back to the road.

The man really is too insanely good looking. And he owns a car like this! He must be irresistible to every woman (and many men) on the planet. It isn't fair for a mere mortal like me.

I screw up my eyes and glare at the traffic ahead.

"How many *happy endings* have you gotten in this car exactly?" I say.

"Pardon me?" he splutters.

"Oh, come on, this car is a babe magnet. How many happy endings? And how many," I glower at him, "blow jobs?"

"That isn't a question I'm prepared to answer."

"In other words, many."

"I haven't been counting."

"Hmmm."

"They were all a long time ago."

"I find that hard to believe."

"It's true," he says earnestly. "Fucking around with girls I didn't particularly like got old. In fact, I pretty much gave up on finding a girl I liked until you strayed into my life."

This alpha seems determined to crack the walls I've been attempting to build around my heart. That lump in my throat has me swallowing again.

In the distance, I spot another rest by, and flicking on the indicator, I swing us in behind a line of bushes and trees and cut the engine.

"That's enough driving for me. It's your turn."

"Are you sure? You looked good driving my car."

I nod. "It's been a long day and I'm tired. Also, you may not care about injuring this beauty, but I do, and the closer we get to the city the greater the chance that's going to happen."

"Whatever you want, sweetheart."

"Can I press the button?" I ask.

"Be my guest."

I jam my thumb down hard on it and the doors swing up. "I feel like a super villain." I giggle.

His gaze turns hot, sweeping down my body. "You look like a fucking super model."

We both climb out of our seats and walk towards the front of the car, meeting each other at the front of the hood. Here, he doesn't step to one side to let me pass, and I don't either. Instead, he gazes down at me and my knees wobble as I'm swallowed up by those gray eyes.

"Hi," I breathe.

"Hi," he growls and then his hands are drifting to my waist and he is spinning me around, caging me against his car.

My breath catches in my throat, and every molecule in my body begs for him to kiss me.

"I won't ever hurt you again, sweetheart," he promises, "and I'm never going to let anyone else hurt you either."

Then he lifts me up so I'm sitting on the warm hood and nudges my knees apart. He holds my gaze as he leans down and kisses my mouth. I moan. I can't help it. His scent. The proximity of his body. The tension between us. It's been building during this long journey and now it breaks like a thunder cloud as he kisses me hard and I kiss him back, my hands straying to his body. I bite on his lips showing him just how hungry I am for him, and he pulls back to look at me.

"Shit," he mumbles, then trails a line down the column of my throat. I arch into him and he finds the neckline of my top, growling as he tugs it down with his teeth and buries his face in my cleavage, his hand coming up to squeeze at my tits and pinch at my stiffening nipples.

"How many?" I pant.

"What?" he moans into my flesh.

"How many girls have you kissed like this on the hood of your car?"

"None," he says. "Only you."

I wrap my legs around him and pull him in closer, so I can feel the outline of his hard cock through his pants, pressing into me right at my core.

He tugs down my top and the cup of my bra and, freeing my tit, captures my nipple in his mouth, sucking at it and then lathering it with his tongue. His hand strays down to my thigh and he dips under the hem of my skirt and up until he finds my panties.

"Shit, shit. We can't do this," he mumbles, even as his fingers dive under the fabric and into my wet folds. "Not here, not like this."

"P-p-p-please," I beg. I've been so good, so strong, so damn sensible. I've held back. I don't want to hold back any longer. I want him inside me. I want to feel that knot the omegas all go crazy for. I want to know what it feels like. I want to know what it feels like with him.

"Baby girl," he moans, like I'm torturing him. "You have no idea how much I want this. How much I've been dreaming of it. But you deserve palaces, and rose petals, and orchestras serenading you."

I can't help but laugh. "I don't need any of that," I say. "I just need men who will love me and treat me right."

He raises his head and stares down at me. "You don't need it, Bea, you deserve it."

I nod. Yes, I do.

With a pained expression, he rolls up my top and removes his hand from my skirt.

For a moment he rests his forehead on my stomach and he inhales my scent. Then with another of those pained groans, he rolls up to standing and steps away.

"One day, sweetheart, I'm going to fuck and knot you on the hood of this car. But not today." I pout at him, and he shakes his head. "Today I'm taking you to dinner."

"Dinner?" I roll up so I'm perched on the edge of the hood. "I'm not sure I'm in the mood for some fancy restaurant–"

"Not a restaurant, home."

"Your apartment?" I think of those bedrooms with those wide, soft beds.

"No, my mom's house." He hesitates. "She's not well, and I want to be around more to help. Her and my sister, Molly."

"Sister?"

"Little sister."

"Oh." I gaze into his eyes. "Will it just be the two of us at dinner?"

"No," and I know he means both packs will be there too. "Everybody's pretty keen to see you again, sweetheart." He takes my hand and helps me to jump down from the car. "And my mom and sister too."

"At dinner?"

"At dinner. My mom's practically pulling her hair out with desperation, she's so damn keen to meet the girl we've all fallen for."

"All of you?" I ask, a little shyly.

"What do you think?"

"I think," I say, strolling around to the passenger seat, "I'm going to have to determine for myself whether that is true."

19

Bea

TWENTY MINUTES later we're gliding through a set of iron gates at the edge of the city, up a gravel driveway and pulling up in front of a large house that must have been built at the start of the 1900s. It's elegant with flowering creepers crawling over its front and its many windows winking in the light.

The large front door stands open and in front of it are Angel, Silver, Hardy, Connor and Nate as well as a small woman I recognize immediately as Axel's little sister.

She comes trotting to meet me as soon as I climb out of the car and hovers in front of me excitedly.

"Bea, this is Molly," Axel says coming round to take my hand in his. "Molly, Bea."

"Wow, you're beautiful." Molly grins. "It's so nice to meet you at last." She wrestles my hand from Axel's grip and pulls me into the house. "I've heard so much about you."

I peer around at the alphas, wondering how much she really knows.

"Molly knows everything," Angel says, coming to stand by my side.

"Yep, all their assholey actions. Don't worry I've been punishing them for you."

"Punishing them? How?"

"I told the housekeeper to take a vacation along with the gardener. These boys have been scrubbing toilets and shoveling manure. But if you want, we can sit down with a pen and paper and brainstorm some other punishments."

"She can punish me all she wants," Nate says with a wicked grin that makes me blush.

"None of that," Molly says, "we've got to go and introduce Bea to Mom. She's been asking me every minute for the last hour if you're here yet."

"Mom won't be joining us for dinner," Angel explains. "She's not up to it."

"Just as well," Molly adds, "Nate insisted on cooking."

"I like Nate's cooking," I say, peering over my shoulder to smile at him.

But I'm not given a chance to linger because Molly tugs me through the cavernous, old house. There are fireplaces in all the rooms, intricate coving around high ceilings and some of the windows are decorated with colored glass.

"She's in the lounge," Angel says, opening the door, "I told her to stay in bed but she insisted she wanted to get up to meet you."

"She really shouldn't have made the effort," I say, feeling guilty that this woman is making such an effort to meet me.

The lounge is bigger than Courtney's apartment with an

array of sofas and armchairs and large paintings hanging on the walls. The blinds have been drawn against the setting sun and an older woman, frail and thin, lies out on a chaise, covered in a mountain of blankets and propped up against pillows.

I know instantly she must be an omega, even though I catch no whiff of her scent.

"Mom," Angel says, guiding me towards her, and maneuvering a seat so I can sit beside her. "This is Bea."

"Bea," she says, her smile stretched so wide I'm concerned it might rip her fragile skin. "Well, you're a million times more beautiful than anyone had me believe."

"I've told you hundreds of times how beautiful she is," Angel mutters, starting to pull up a chair next to mine.

"Oh no, off you go. I want to talk to this young woman in peace. I want to ensure you boys have been telling me the whole truth and I don't want you hovering at her shoulder trying to edit."

"I wouldn't–"

"Angel," his mom says sternly and with a huff; he squeezes my shoulder and stands up. "I'll go get you a drink," he tells me.

"It's very nice to meet you Mrs. Stormgate," I tell her, when Angel's gone. "Your house is gorgeous."

"Isn't it? My mate found it when we first started dating and told me one day he'd earn enough money to buy it for me. He didn't have two cents to his name back then, but you know what, I never doubted him." Her smile falters a little, and she peers towards the door. "I was hoping my sons would grow up to be like their father but it seems I've failed slightly there. I'm very disappointed in them."

I stare down at my lap. Not knowing what to say. I certainly don't want a dying woman to think she failed her children. At the same time, I can't deny that their actions hurt me.

"You have two lovely sons. You should be very proud."

"Two lovely sons who I hope have learned the error of their ways. There's nothing like losing the person you love to make you see sense."

My cheeks heat so fast I'm sure Angel's mom must see them sizzle. "Love ... I'm not sure ..."

"I am," Mrs. Stormgate says, holding my gaze. "Ten years I've been trying to get these boys to mend their rift. My husband and I tried everything. Molly, my daughter, too. The stubborn goats wouldn't budge. Then you come along, and it's like everything has shifted. It takes something fundamental, something like love, to bring about such a change."

I fiddle with the hem of my skirt. "I wish it hadn't, though," I admit.

"What do you mean?"

"I wish they hadn't done what they did. I wish they hadn't lost me. I had no desire to be the catalyst in their change."

The older woman is quiet and when I look up from my hands, she is studying my face.

"You're an intelligent woman. I'm pleased. A pretty face is one thing but," she shrugs, "the number of girls they've paraded through this house with nothing but air and the desire for glittery things between their ears. I hear you have other ambitions."

"I want to work. I want to study. But," I glance to the blinds, turning red against the disappearing sun, "I want to find my pack too. I want a family. I want it all."

"Yes, of course, you do." She smiles. "I don't have long. Well, I'm sure you guessed that much. I'm sorry, Bea, that hurting you is the thing that brought my sons to their senses, but I can't be sorry for it. I can die a contented woman now. And even more so knowing my boys will be left in good hands."

"Oh I don't know ... I mean ..."

"I saw the way you looked at Angel just now. I saw the way he looked at you. It's how my husband used to look at me. How I'm sure I looked at him." Her eyes mist over as if she's remembering. "Love finds a way. It makes us better people. And it finds a way to forgive. I'm sure you can find a way to make this right."

And for the first time in days I think that maybe I can.

DINNER IS SERVED in a room that belongs in a palace. The table is so long that even the eight of us only fill one half. More old paintings hang around the walls and a silver chandelier dangles from the ceiling. Candles flicker across the tabletop and a vase of fresh daisies is arranged in the center. Around it sit every dish I may ever have dropped into conversation that I like.

"Nate's been in the kitchen all day," Molly says, leading me to a chair and taking one next to me, much to the alphas' obvious disappointment. There's a little bit of a tussle for the chair on my other side, but when Molly coughs loudly, they all step back and it's Hardy that claims the place.

"We've been doing some remedial training," Molly whispers into my ear. "They're getting there but occasionally we have some relapses." She smirks at her brother across the table who is scowling at her. "They're worse than puppies."

"What exactly does this training involve?" I ask.

"Reminding them at regular intervals that it's their

omega who should be the center of their lives and not themselves."

"I already knew that," Silver mumbles. "We didn't need you to tell us. We've been going out of our way to keep Bea safe because she's precious to us."

"Oh yeah," Molly says, the smirk falling from her lips and a serious expression lodging between her brow instead. "I heard about the thing with the clinic." She covers her hand with mine and squeezes it. "I'm so sorry."

I manage a wobbly smile, then turn towards Silver. "Is there any more news about that?"

"The police have been hopeless but we've been doing our own digging. I want to ensure the threat to your safety has gone."

My hands drop to the edge of the table and I grip it tight between my fingers and thumb. My obvious distress does something to the alphas in the room. Axel and Angel push back their chairs and leap to their feet, Hardy wraps his arm around my shoulders and Nate stabs the prongs of his fork into the tabletop.

"Okay everyone," Molly says, glancing around all of us with concern. "Take a deep breath." She inhales herself and the six men in the room do the same, although it seems to do little to dissipate the tension.

"Sorry," I say to all of them, "I just ... I didn't think there was the possibility that my safety was still under threat – not from that quarter anyway." I peer at Silver and he glances towards the other alphas. It's clear for once the man doesn't know what to do. "I'd prefer it if you were honest with me."

He nods. "Okay, the truth is we don't know. That clinic wasn't set up by some greedy doctors gone rogue, there was a bigger outfit behind it. Hence the masked men with guns who turned up to try to intercept us. At this point we don't know who they are or their intentions. Until we do, we will continue to keep a close eye on you."

"Continue?" I ask, with an arch of my eyebrow.

Silver holds my gaze. "We've had my surveillance team watching over you."

"Including in Naw Creek?"

"Including in Naw Creek."

"Thank you," I say.

The muscle in his cheek twitches and for the briefest of seconds he looks shocked, like he was expecting me to give my usual berating, not my thanks.

"You're welcome," he says.

Molly nudges me with her elbow. "Shall we eat? It's going to get cold."

I tug a creamy-looking lasagna towards me and plunge the spoon through the cheese encrusted top. "Yes, please, I'm starving."

I'm half way through my serving, when I pause and look up to Silver again. "How about Dr. Hannah? Have you found her?"

"No, and we haven't been able to talk to that other doctor again either. The cops have him under tight security." He lowers his fork. "We're working on it," he gestures to Connor, "I don't want you to worry about it."

Easier said than done, and yet knowing he is watching over me, knowing they all are, doesn't feel menacing or suffocating like it once threatened to do. Now, it feels comforting. I know with these alphas around, they'll never let anything bad happen to me. It's a pretty comforting feeling.

I tuck back into my food and when I'm done, I glance toward Nate to compliment him on his cooking and find him sitting back in his chair, his own plate untouched, watching me.

"Aren't you eating?" I ask him.

"I like watching you eat my food, little bird." I smile at him and he returns it with a far dirtier one. "I made you another cake for dessert."

"It's awful," Molly says. "The man may be able to make a half-decent savory dish, but when it comes to his baking ..." She sticks out her tongue.

"You said omegas like sweet things," Nate says sulkily.

"That doesn't mean you should have doubled the amount of sugar in the cake recipe. You'll give her diabetes." Molly leans in toward me and whispers, "It's all right I made a strawberry cheesecake for dessert."

Nate scowls at her and I worry for her safety.

"I'd love to try both," I say cheerfully, hoping to placate him.

"Or we can save the cake for later." Nate winks at me and I try, and fail, not to blush. Something I'm sure all the alphas in the room notice. Do they know about me and Nate? Do they know about me and Connor?

I decide to change the subject away from food which somehow seems far too dangerous when Nate is around.

"What else has this training involved?"

"She's had us building a nest."

My omega instincts must be strengthening because that word, the picture of these alphas building a nest, together, has me practically swooning under the table.

"You ... you built a nest?" They all nod, suddenly alert, like they're honed in on my reaction to this piece of news. "All of you together?"

"All of them together," Molly says, "and I have to say I

think they did a damn good job. If my pack makes me a nest half as good as that one I will be one very happy omega."

I listen to her transfixed, a flurry of excitement brewing in my belly.

"Do you want to see it?" Angel asks me from across the room.

And again I get the impression all six men are hanging on tenterhooks for my answer.

I feel giddy.

"Wh-wh-where is it?"

"Upstairs," Axel says, his voice deepening.

"Here?" I say in puzzlement.

Why would they build a nest here? Is it a practice one? Did they build it for Molly after all?

"Me and Angel have moved back home," Axel explains. "To be around Mom and, well," he grins at the other alphas, "these assholes couldn't live without us and followed us here."

"More like you couldn't live without us, dickhead," Hardy counters, earning him a look from Molly, "'scuse my language," he mumbles.

"You're all living here?"

"Yes."

"Together?"

"Yes."

"All of you?"

"All of us."

The giddiness overtakes me and I have to concentrate on my breathing. When I think I can speak again, I whisper, "Permanently?" My heart thumps with anticipation. I remember what Axel had told me in the car.

No more Pack York.

No more Pack Boston.

He's taken back his old surname.

And so has Angel.

"Maybe," Angel says. "It depends."

"On what?"

He pauses, looking directly into my eyes, as five other pairs of intense alpha eyes gaze my way too. "You."

"M-m-me?"

"You," Axel repeats and once again I'm struck by how alike they are. How did I not spot that they were brothers? "Did you ever wonder why you found it so hard to pick between our two packs, Bea?"

I glance towards Molly.

Why did I find it so hard? Because I'm indecisive. Greedy. Freaking horny.

No, it was because I felt this electric uncontrollable pull towards all six of these men and the thought of choosing one half and not the other had felt like asking me to rip my soul in two.

I jolt at the realization, my eyes widening as I stare back at the two brothers sitting side by side.

Deep, deep in my heart I'd always harbored this wish, this longing, this desire, to have them all, to never have to make that choice.

"You don't have to choose," Connor says as if reading my mind.

The walls around my heart crumble that much more. They'd do that? They'd do that for me?

"No," I say, shaking my head, "I'm flattered, I really am, but you can't do this just because of me. I learned that the hard way with Karl. You shouldn't compromise on who you are for another person."

"You're misunderstanding us, sweetheart," Axel says. "You couldn't choose between us because you saw something the rest of us have been stubbornly trying to ignore and deny for the last ten years. We were always meant to be a pack, Bea, one whole pack. All of us together. All seven of us."

"Seven?" I whisper.

"Me, Angel, Connor, Silver, Nate, Hardy and you, sweetheart, you."

I bite my lip. My head and my heart spinning so fast I have to grip the table again.

"Do you understand what we're saying?" Silver says. "Do you understand what we're asking?"

"Uh-huh," I manage to say.

"You feel it, little bird," Nate tells me. "I know you do."

"You should see the nest," Molly whispers to me.

"No," I say, "no, not yet."

I need to think about this. And I know if I see the nest, and it's as wonderful as Molly insists it is, I'll never be able to refuse these men. And though they may have smashed through the careful walls I've erected around my heart, that doesn't fix all the damage and the hurt.

I need to be sure that whatever I choose here, it's right for me. I'm not wasting the next few years of my life on another man, or more men, who don't deserve me.

20

Hardy

Molly stands up and pushes back her chair. "Wow, that was intense." She pulls some empty plates towards her. "I think you should all take a minute to breathe."

"I think that's a good idea," Bea says, and I have to blink away the crushing pain of disappointment that pulses through my body. She needs time to decide. To consider her options. That's all. It isn't a no. And a no, if I'm honest, is probably all we actually deserve.

I have hope though.

I can't help but have hope.

"Let's get you boys started on some washing up," Molly says.

She's been having a fine time bossing us all the hell about, something none of us would ever have considered, let alone consented to, in the past. But she's promised to help us and Axel and Angel seem convinced she can. It's worth a try, even if I think the cheeky little omega needs to be taken over someone's knee and spanked.

I glance over at Bea. I wonder if that's something our omega would be interested in. She certainly has the type of plump ass made for spanking.

Our omega. I've got to stop thinking like that.

She isn't ours.

She may never be.

"There's a dishwasher," Silver points out, as he piles about a dozen dishes in his big hands.

"Which has mysteriously broken down this evening," Molly says, with mischief. It's going to be near impossible to get her to behave once this 'helping' business is over.

We all follow Silver's example, gathering up plates, cutlery and all the leftovers. Bea stands up and tries to help, but I drag her back down into her chair.

"No," I say, "you're our guest."

She protests but nobody's hearing any of it and soon she's sitting back watching as the rest of us clear up.

Molly's reminded us numerous times that omegas like to be spoiled. And not just in the bedroom or with expensive gifts. Housework, she insists, is a major turn on.

I'm not sure I believe that last bit, not until it's only me and her left in the room, and I'm bending over the table, sweeping a cloth over the table top. Then I notice the way her scent peaks and her gaze grows hot.

I flex my biceps and her mouth makes a silent 'oh'.

Yes, there's definitely hope.

When the table is clean, I toss the cloth to one side and lean back, folding my arms over my chest in a way that makes every muscle in my arms bulge.

I grin at her.

"Are you okay, little one?"

"Yes," she says, chewing on her lip as her eyes dart to my chest, then dart away again. "It's a lot to take in, you know. A lot to think about ..." Her expression turns serious, and she swallows. "Hardy, if I don't ... if I don't decide to join this pack, do you think you'll all still stay together?"

"If you don't ..." I repeat, closing my eyes as pain sparks in my heart. I massage my chest with my palm. "Yes, I think we will. It should always have been this way. But," I open my eyes and stare into the strangely amber depths of hers, "there'll be a massive hole without you. We'll never be complete." I stare down at her face all earnest and fucking kissable and shake my head with a chuckle. "Shit, that sounded something dramatic like Connor would say. I don't want to put pressure on you."

"You really believe that," she asks, standing up from her chair.

I guess I can't blame her for finding it hard to trust us, for doubting us when we tell her something is white when we spent a hell of a lot of time telling her it was black before.

"Yeah, I do. Look." I dig into my pocket and pull out the small key ring I've been working on for her. I open my palm and show her the carving of an old-fashioned key, whittled from wood. "To go with your other one."

She takes it from my hand and runs the pad of her thumb over the smoothed wood. "A key?"

"It's representative, or some such shit," I mumble.

"Of what?"

I chuckle and glance down at the floor, at our feet, hers so small compared to my giant ones. "It's meant to represent the key to my heart. Because you already own that key, Bea." She steps closer to me and the toes of our shoes are only a few inches apart. "Plus," I say, looking up at her with a grin, "I thought it would be useful for the eye gouging."

She giggles. "Oh, I have Nate's knife for that now."

"Nate's knife?"

She nods and hooks it out of the waistband of her skirt, lifting it up to show me.

I take it from her hand and examine it, half expecting to find it's a copy. It's not. It's the real thing, all worn and well-used. "I can't believe he gave this to you." I turn it over, searching for the engraving that's long since faded. "Mr. Stormgate gave it to him. It used to cause us all kinds of grief when we were kids. The number of clubs that refused us at the door because of that thing," I shake my head, "but he refused to leave it behind." I hand it back to her. "And now he's given it to you." I chuckle. "My heart, Nate's knife, what else are you going to collect, little one?"

She shuffles forward and lifts up her hand, hesitating for a moment before she lies it flat against my chest, right above the place where my heart is pounding madly for her.

I stop breathing. I daren't move.

"This heart?" she asks, peering up at me through her long eyelashes, her lips wet.

"This heart." I close my hand over hers, pressing her palm against my ribs, wanting her to feel every beat.

She closes her eyes. I want to kiss her so badly. I'm also curious to see what this strange little omega will do next. She's so different from any I've ever met.

And I'm not at all surprised to find her surprising me again in the next minute.

She slides her hand out from under mine and when I try to catch it and drag it back, she shakes her head. Instead, she winds her fingertips down my chest, sending electricity skirting through my body, and reaches the hem of my shirt.

Here she pauses, taking a deep inhale of my scent, before sliding her hand under the fabric and back up over my chest. This time I feel her touch against my skin and I sigh with how good that feels.

When she reaches my heart, she flattens out her hand. It's warm. I want it there always.

I reach behind me and, fisting the neck of my shirt, I tug it over my head with one swift swipe.

"Wh-what are you doing?" she giggles, eyes flying open and pupils blowing wide as she takes in my bare chest.

She darts her hand away and I yank it straight back to my heart, holding it there.

"Omegas need skin-to-skin contact."

"I'm not a baby," she says, her giggle dissolving into a laugh.

"Yes, you are, baby girl," I say, tracing her jaw with my free hand, tilting it up towards me, leaning down to kiss her lips.

My heart hammers hard against her hand, hammers even harder when she moans into my mouth, hammers so hard I think my ribs might crack when I pull her in close, flush against me.

"See," I say.

"Uh huh," she mutters, sounding sweetly dazed.

Then she does it again. Whipping my fucking breath away with astonishment, when she reaches down to the hem of her own shirt and slowly lifts it over her head.

The lacy bra she's wearing underneath is enough to have all the blood in my heart running south and for a long minute I simply stare down at her tits, full, round, fucking perfect.

"Skin to skin," she says. "Is it good for alphas too?"

"You have no fucking idea how good it is for alphas," I growl.

But as I pull her flush again, she gets a good idea. I'm so hard for her now, it's impossible to miss.

"Want to carry you up to our nest so badly now, baby girl."

She whimpers, shaking in my arms. "If you take me there, I may never leave," she whispers. "And I'm–"

"Not ready for that." I nod, trying once again not to let the disappointment overtake me.

"A little more time."

"Have all the time you need, baby girl. We're not going anywhere."

She swims her hot little hands over my chest. I have to take her home. If I don't, there's a strong possibility I'll be spreading her out on the table and feasting on her.

Fuck, patience was never one of my best qualities.

I reach down for her t-shirt and carefully tug it over her head, smoothing it over those tits of hers. She arches into my touch and Jesus fucking Christ, what am I doing?

I take a hold of her arms and position her three paces away from me as I scrabble on the ground for my own shirt. I don't want to put my own back on. I like her hot little gaze all over me far too much. But I'm trying to be a better man here.

I yank it down my body, ignoring her sigh of disappointment.

Then I take her hand and lead her out to the kitchen where pots are banging and pans bashing. I poke my head around the door, leaving Bea in the hallway.

"I'm taking Bea back home."

My packmates turn to look at me and I can see the disappointment in their eyes.

Nate especially looks like he wants to gut someone. I make a mental note to avoid him for the rest of the day, especially as I must reek of the omega's sweet scent. It's only likely to provoke him.

Connor is the one to speak. "She needs time to think."

"Yeah," I say.

We only have ourselves to blame. If we hadn't fucked up, we'd be rolling around with her in our nest right now, instead of 'thinking'.

"I'll be back soon," I tell them. Nate scowls at me like he knows every dirty image floating in my mind.

I find Bea, peering at family pictures by the door and then I take her out to the garage, moving all her boxes from Axel's car to my truck. Silver comes out to help us and reminds the omega once again of all the precautions she needs to take.

"If you need to go somewhere, if you feel unsafe at any time–"

"I'll call you, I promise," she says, reaching up to grab his collar and kiss his mouth.

I lean against the truck and watch them together.

They look good and those dirty images become a fuck-load more dirty.

Yeah, I can picture how good she'll look, down on her hands and knees, suckling on my cock as Silver fucks her hard.

I'm guessing Silver receives an eyeful of that image through our bond because he leans away from the omega and peers towards me. Lust swims darkly in his eyes.

The omega looks up at my packmate and then over at me. She whimpers in that delicious way she does, and I grab her wrist and drag her towards the car.

"Maybe I could stay?" she says, appealing to us both.

Maybe I could bark at her right now? Tell her to lift up her skirt and open her legs. Maybe I could claim her and put an end to all the thinking.

Maybe. Maybe.

"Go home, think about what we had to say," Silver says stiffly, "and call us tomorrow."

She glances towards me, hoping I'll contradict my packmate.

"Get in the car, Omega. You're making this very hard for us."

She struggles against the order, but in the end she submits, opening the door and sliding into the front seat.

"Good luck," Silver says to me.

And I think I'm going to need it.

I FLICK through the radio stations and find the least sexiest music I can find. Some Bible station singing tunes about Jesus.

The omega side eyes me but doesn't complain, her thighs pressed firmly together.

The drive is still fucking excruciating. I can't stop thinking about her tits. How soft they felt under my palm. How they'd taste in my mouth.

I'm so busy thinking about them, I nearly drive straight into the back of the car in front.

I slam on the brake and we're both thrown forward.

"Sorry," I grunt. "Are you okay?"

"Uh huh," she says, tugging at her seatbelt. "Didn't you see it stop?"

I sweep my hand through my hair. "Yeah."

She scrutinizes me, noting the way I'm hunched over the wheel and squinting at the windscreen.

"Hmmm," she shifts on her seat, "see that blue sign over there, can you read it?" She points towards some blue smudge in the far distance. I doubt anyone on the fucking planet could read that.

"Yeah," I lie.

"What does it say, then?"

I squint harder, but no matter how hard I strain my eyes I can't make the blurry image focus into something readable.

"No left turn," I gamble.

"You need glasses," she says.

"I don't need glasses."

"Can you read that plate over there?"

"I don't need to read that plate over there. I can read the one twenty feet in front of me and that's the requirement by law."

She's quiet for a moment, then she says, "I really like glasses on a man," she says. "In fact, I think they're incredibly sexy."

The way she says that word has my blood pumping. "You do?" I ask, glancing at her to see if she's making fun of me.

She bites her bottom lip and nods. "It really turns me on."

"I think you're trying to manipulate me here, baby girl."

"I think I'd like to see you in a pair of glasses." She lowers her voice: "And nothing else."

Jesus fucking Christ.

I swing my gaze straight towards her and nearly crash the vehicle a second time.

She smiles all innocently, like she didn't set my cock jerking in my pants.

"Ditto, baby girl," I growl. "Ditto."

She wriggles on her seat, thighs rubbing together and I wonder if I'm ever going to make it to the beach.

"How about now?" she asks.

"Beg your pardon," I say. Can she see inside my brain? Does she know I'm imagining her leaning over to suck my cock while I drive her home?

"Why don't we go pick you up some glasses now?"

"It's late."

"There's that optician round the corner from York Tower that's open until 10pm every night." She glances at her watch. "We still have an hour."

"I should get you home."

"We should get you into some glasses."

I puff out a stream of hot air. She's flirting with me and fuck me I'm not turning that down.

I hang a right and in a matter of minutes I'm sat in a dark room with some weird creation balancing on my nose, reading out letters as the omega sits watching me and giggling.

"These weren't exactly the sexy pair of glasses I was hoping for," I mumble gruffly at the nervous optician, as he slides another lens in front of my eyes.

"We're just determining your prescription here, Sir. Then you can choose a pair from outside."

"I think this looks great," Bea sniggers and I glance away from the board of letters to give her a behave-yourself look.

Finally, the optician finds lenses that actually turn the letter from a row of smudged fuckers to crisp and clear text and I'm able to read out the smallest line.

"You're slightly short-sighted," the optician says, lifting the hideous contraption from my face. "Not too bad but I think you'll be surprised what you can actually see when you get your new glasses."

I thank him and let Bea lead me excitedly back into the front of the shop and to the racks of glasses hanging on display.

I peer at them with disgust. They don't seem much better than the stupid contraption I was just wearing.

"Any you like?" Bea asks.

"No," I say sulkily, folding my arms across my chest.

"You could ask the optician about contacts instead?"

"No," I say resolutely, "maybe we should leave it. He said my prescription wasn't that bad."

I take a step towards the door, but Bea catches my wrist.

"How about that pair?" she says, pointing to a pair I swear my old math teacher used to wear.

"I'll look like a giant nerd in those."

"A giant *sexy* nerd," she purrs, lifting them from the rack, balancing up on her toes and carefully sliding them onto my nose.

She has to lean in to me to do it, and her warmth and her scent would have me wearing anything she wanted, even a fucking thong and head dress.

"There," she says, leaning back to admire me, and resting her hands back on my chest.

I peek over her head towards the mirror.

"I look stupid."

She shakes her head. "You look incredibly yummy, Alpha."

Alpha.

My body reacts to that word. She's never called me it before.

I growl low in my throat.

"Careful, baby girl," I warn her. "You're playing with fire here."

She smiles at me like she knows exactly what she's doing. Then she removes the glasses and reaches for another pair. These are heavier set. They look just as ridiculous when she pushes them up my nose, but her eyes seem to heat with genuine attraction as she appraises me.

"I think you might need a few pairs," she whispers into my ear. "For different occasions. You look like Clark Kent in these."

"You like Clark Kent?" I ask her, my hands falling to her waist and dragging her in close.

"I may have had a Superman fantasy as a teenager," she confesses.

"And how did that fantasy go?" I whisper into her ear.

"Buy the glasses, Alpha," she says, "and maybe you'll get to find out."

I laugh. This girl is definitely playing me. Winding me around her little finger. But I love it. With any other omega it would have been 'buy the glasses', end of story.

"Okay, baby girl, you win."

I kiss the end of her nose. Then take both pairs of glasses to the optician who's pretending to be engrossed in work on his computer.

Unfortunately, or maybe it's fortunately, I can't walk away with the glasses today. They have to be made up.

But damn, I can't wait to wear them. I can't wait to play Superman and Lois Lane with my little Omega.

21

Bea

"So you're back already?" Courtney grins from the sofa as I walk through the door of the condo, my arms full of a box and Hardy right behind me carrying four more. "I knew you wouldn't be gone for long."

"Yeah." I grin. "I'm back. I think maybe I'm a city girl now. Or actually, a beach one."

"A beach babe," Hardy says.

"I thought you'd be back at your apartment already though," I say to my cousin.

"The cops are still fiddling with the place and besides I think you may have converted me into a beach babe too. You know I even went combing for garbage this afternoon."

"You did?" I place my box on the counter and go give my cousin a hug.

"Seriously, sweetie," Courtney murmurs into my shoulder, "I'm so pleased you're back."

"Me too."

"And with one of those alphas?" she whispers. I lean back and give her a look that reads I'll-tell-you-all-about-it later.

Hardy fetches more boxes from his truck and when he's done hovers by the door.

"I'd ... I'd better go," he says, scratching the back of his neck.

"Do you want a drink or anything first?" I ask.

He shakes his head. "No, the others will already be pacing the floors wondering what took me so long."

I peer at him quizzically, wondering what he can mean by that and he gulps.

"Better get going. Any problems, any–"

"I'll call you straight away," I say. "And you," I add, stalking towards him and balancing up on my toes to whisper in his ear, "call me as soon as those glasses come in."

His eyes flash but then he pries me from him and bolts for the door.

Courtney giggles from the sofa.

"What the hell was that?"

"To be honest, I don't really know. Before I couldn't get these guys to leave me alone. They were always trying to get me into bed. Now they're being all respectful and patient."

"Isn't that a good thing?"

"It is. It's also making me even more damn horny."

"Everything is always more tempting when you can't have it."

"Yeah, something like that." I flop onto the sofa beside

her, stealing the glass of wine from her hand and taking a much needed gulp. "But the thing is, I could have this."

"Sounds intriguing. Do tell." She rearranges the cushions behind her.

I chew on my lip. "I think, I really think, they're trying to make amends for what they did."

Courtney rolls her eyes. "Let me guess, they bought you some flowers."

"No, no. They've moved into Axel and Angel's family home. All of them. They're making amends. They've built a nest. They want to form one pack. All of them and ..."

"And?"

"And me."

Courtney's mouth makes a silent oh. She lifts her wine to her mouth, then lowers it without taking a sip.

Outside we hear the distant rumble of Hardy's truck.

"But they hate each other."

"I don't think they ever did. I think they hurt each other. And now they're trying to mend that hurt and love each other again."

"You think that will work? That it will last?"

I consider her question, thinking about what Axel told me in the car, remembering how they were with each other this evening.

"Yes, yes I think it will."

"And so, the question is, do you want to?" Courtney's eyes glide over my face. "Do you want to join their pack?"

I hesitate and then I nod. I nod with feeling.

"Does that make me a pushover though? Does that mean I'm always destined to be taken for a ride?"

"Why do you say that, Bea?"

"I want to forgive them. I want to forget about the hurt

they caused me and start over. But should I? Should I forgive them?"

"I think you should do whatever you believe is best. There's no right or wrong, Bea. There's only how you feel." She offers me her wine glass and I take another sip, the sharp white wine stinging my throat. "How do you feel?"

I hold out my hand and mime a bomb falling through the air and exploding on the ground. "Boom," I say.

"Still? With all of them?"

"Yep, I get these little explosions in my belly and in my chest every time I'm with one of them and, oh my gosh, it multiplies ten fold, when they're all together." I hand her back her glass. "It never felt that way with Karl. It's never felt that way with anyone before. They say we were destined to be a pack. That we're meant to be together, and I think they might be right. Is that crazy?"

Courtney sniffles, wiping at her face. "No, no it's not, Bea. If anyone deserves two hot packs, the two hottest packs in the city, it's you."

"I don't know about that ..."

"They seem to believe so and for what it's worth I don't think they'd be going to all this effort for you if they weren't serious."

I nod. They did seem serious. Deadly serious. And confident in their belief that the seven of us belonged together and that kind of belief, that kind of confidence, is damn infectious.

"So what happens next?"

"I said I'd think about things–"

"Good, good girl, let them stew a little longer."

"But I think I've made up my mind." I think I made it driving Axel's car. I think I made it sitting with all of them at dinner like we were already one happy family. I think I made it when Hardy handed me the key he'd carved. "I want to give this a try."

Courtney dives at me, spilling the rest of her wine all over our laps, and engulfs me in her hug. "I'm so happy for you." She squeezes me, then jolts her head back. "But, wait, does this mean I'm losing my roomie?"

"I don't know about that. I think moving in is a little too quick and besides I don't think I want to give up the beach." The engine noise has died away, leaving the noise of the waves pounding the beach. The waves and something else. "What's that?" I say, craning my head.

"Huh?" Courtney says.

"That noise."

We're both quiet, listening. Outside the window, we can hear the sounds of rustling.

"An animal?" Courtney suggests, then smiles. "Or perhaps your midnight chef."

It could be Nate, but he just fed me an entire banquet up at the house. It seems unlikely.

I place my finger to my lip, then creep to the window and peer out into the dark. I can't see anything. Dark clouds hang over the moon tonight and I can barely make out the sand dunes. Courtney tiptoes to the light switch and flicks on the outdoor light. There's no one there.

"Must have been an animal," Courtney says.

"I guess," I whisper, but I double check all the doors are locked just in case.

In the morning, I call the ecological association and check they've received my application. I expect to receive a curt yes or no, but instead the receptionist patches me through to the lady in charge of the training program.

"Bea Carsen ..." she says, and I can hear her tapping keys in the background. "Oh yes, we have received your application."

"Oh good," I say, wondering if I should just hang up, then reminding myself I want this job and here's my opportunity to make a good impression. "Did you have any questions about it?"

"Hmmm," I can hear her thumb rocking the wheel of her mouse, "we very much liked your personal statement. Not everyone's prepared to get their hands dirty when it comes to ecological work, but it sounds like you already have. You seem very passionate."

"I am. I love the beach and I want to help protect it," I say, hoping my words don't seem lame. I've never done the whole interview thing before.

The woman on the other end asks me a few questions about my school qualifications and any transferable skills I may have. I try my best to sound the confident and enthusiastic woman I really want to be.

"We'll be making our decision about whom to invite for an interview in the next few days. You should receive an email with the details if you've been successful." She pauses. "I think you've got a very good chance. Good luck."

"Thank you," I say.

I hang up with a lightness in my soul I'm not sure I've felt for years.

Are things finally falling into place? A job I might actually love. Six men I think I could fall in love with too. This is all too good to be true, right? I try to ignore the sudden gnawing idea that it can't possibly last, and focus on that lightness instead, changing into my running gear.

I'm tying up my sneakers when there's a knock at the door.

Courtney goes to answer it, peering through the spy-hole. "It's Angel. Should I open it?"

"Yes, you can open it."

She unbolts the door and swings it back revealing Angel leaning against the frame.

"Morning," he says with one of those dazzling smiles, "I know you are after space, but I had a feeling you might be out for a run this morning so I'm here to accompany you." He's dressed in running gear, although the gun strapped around his chest is hardly missable.

"Okay," I say. "Do you remember the rules?"

"Five paces behind and don't comment on your running style."

"Correct," I smile.

"Do you also have a water bottle you need me to carry?"

I hand mine over and, trying my best not to linger in order to check him out – the man has thighs the size of small countries and an ass so tight you could crack an egg on it – we set off down to the beach, sprinting over the sand dunes and down towards the shore. As my feet hit wet sand, I halt abruptly. The beach is swarming with people pacing up and down with markers and cones. Several more stand watching with clipboards and tablets. In the distance, three large trucks and a couple of diggers are parked up.

"What's going on?" I ask my running companion, shaking my head in despair.

Angel stops beside me and peers towards the crowd of workers.

I set off marching in their direction. Angel attempts to grab my arm.

"Bea, wait."

I shake him off and stride up to the nearest man and tap him on the shoulder.

"What's going on?"

The man, dressed in jeans, a workman's shirt and baseball cap, looks me up and down.

"You can't be here. This land is privately owned."

I glare at him and repeat my question. "What's going on?"

The man looks up at my minder and nods, then directs his answer to him. "We're doing some initial investigation on the ground, ready for architects to start designing the layout of the developments for this land."

"You can't do that." I land my fists on my hips.

"Why?" The man smirks. "Do you have some legal mandate prohibiting us?"

"No," I say with irritation. "But do *you* have the legal permission that allows you to do this?"

"Of course, you can look it up on the internet. Now if you don't mind." He spins around and walks towards another man who seems to be taking some kind of measurement in the sand.

"They can't get away with this," I mumble.

Angel watches the men with unease.

I glare at all the men busy working. Several poking at the sand. Others taking notes on tablets and two roping off areas of the beach. One man stands a little away from the others, with his arms crossed watching me. I bet he's security. Well they'll need more than one man once the eco-warriors get wind of their plans.

Maybe I'll be the one to give them a heads up.

"You want to run in the other direction?" Angel asks, pointing towards the undisturbed part of the beach.

I watch for a little longer, then nod. I might as well enjoy the beach while I can, before these assholes ruin it forever. Besides, irritation niggles all the way through my body and running will be the best way to dispel it.

That and possibly something else, I think, eyeing up the man beside me.

22

ngel

I'M A PERVERT.

A pervert and an asshole.

Because I'm meant to be accompanying Bea on her run for her benefit, to keep her safe, to make sure no one tries anything.

But, if I'm honest, I am enjoying this far too much. Enjoying it mostly for the view.

It doesn't help that the woman insists I run behind her which means I'm running with a perfect, unrestricted, undaunted, view of her ass.

And fuck, what an ass. Round and plump and, when she runs, jiggling.

Fuck, I could watch her ass jiggle like this for the rest of my days and be a very happy man.

I'd be an even happier man if I could land that ass in my hands. If I could give it a little slap. If I could bite it.

Bea peers over her shoulder at me with a smile, and I manage a pained smile back. It's tough running with a freaking hard-on.

I drag my eyes away from her ass and try to concentrate on our surroundings instead. That's why I'm here after all. To keep an eye on her, to watch for danger. I do what I'm meant to do and let my gaze float around, surveying the landscape. We're running back towards the condo now, which means that landscape includes the area where our men are working, surveying the land ready for the first works to take place.

I hadn't given it much thought. I certainly never considered the work might be a problem.

It's been a frigging problem for the last few years, competing with my brother and every other corporation in the city to land our hands on it. But now we've reconciled, now we're working and living together as one pack, our problems seemed solved.

We own the beach. We own the land surrounding the beach. No more problems. No more delays. At last we could start the development.

Now I see one very large problem.

And she's running right in front of me with a sweet, little jiggling ass.

She doesn't like that development. I can't see her ever liking it. And when she finds out we're behind it ...

Shit!

I need to talk to the others.

As we draw closer to the condo, she glances over her shoulder at me a second time and says, "Beat you there!"

Then she picks up her feet and sets off at speed.

"Hey," I yelp, "you had a head start."

The little thing is fast but not fast enough; if I drive my arms and legs fast enough, I could probably pass her. I decide, however, I'd rather let her win. I hold back and let her swat the front door first, bouncing up and down on her toes with squeals of excitement as I draw up behind her.

"I win," she says.

"You cheated," I tell her.

"You're twice my size, it was only fair."

I swipe the sweat from around my brow and hand over her water bottle. She unscrews the lid and takes several long gulps, some of it spilling over her lips and dribbling down her chin.

I never knew something like that could be so damn erotic, but everything she does seems to turn me on to some degree.

She wipes her mouth and offers me the bottle. I take a long swig and when I dip my head back she's watching me. More than watching, she's eyeing me up like I'm a dish she wants to eat.

Eat away, little Omega.

"I'm here on slightly false pretenses," I confess.

"If you've come to ask me, then–"

"I've come to ask you if you'd like to join us for lunch on our boat." I point to the cloudless sky. "It's a beautiful day."

"So you really do have a boat?"

"Between us we have several, but this one was my dad's. A bit like the house; he bought a wreck and did it up. It's pretty damn beautiful now, all sleek lines and curves." Just like the omega.

She screws her lid back on the bottle. "Hmmm. Sounds good."

"Is that a yes?"

"It is."

"Then go jump in the shower. My dad would turn in his grave at the thought of you dripping sweat all over his yacht."

Her eyes swim down my body, lingering where my shirt is stuck to my damp skin.

"How about you?"

"I'll grab one quickly when we swing by to pick up the others."

"Or ..." she says. Her scent deepens and my cock grows hard all over again.

"Or ..." I say cautiously, not altogether convinced I'm reading her signals correctly, and not wanting to fuck things up with her.

"You could use the shower here." A bead of sweat rolls down her throat and down to her cleavage. "Do you have clean clothes to change into?"

"Yeah," I manage to say, "in the trunk." I take a step towards her. "Is ... is there enough hot water for *two* showers, little Omega?"

She shakes her head. "No."

"Then maybe I should take my shower at home after all," I say, closing the space between us.

"Or ..." she says again.

"Or ..." I whisper, gripping the front of her top and pulling her towards me.

"We could share one?" she says.

I try to play it cool. Try to keep the fucking eagerness from my face. My mouth twitches into a smile and my cock jerks anyway.

I slide my hands to her hips.

"Will there be enough room for the both of us?"

"I doubt it. You are a very large person."

I laugh. Ahh, she has no fucking idea just how large I am. But I think she's about to find out.

"Come on, then," I say. "Let's get you into the shower, before you catch a chill."

There's no chance of that, but I'm eager to take her clothes off before she changes her mind.

Yeah, definitely a pervert.

The condo is empty. No cousin with a shotgun hanging about, so I lock the doors and let her guide us through to her bedroom.

The aroma of her heat-sweetened scent hits me so hard I see stars. It's a few days old and her bedding's obviously been changed, but, hell, it's still there lingering in the air.

If it was even possible for me to forget how good this one smelled in heat, then this is definitely a vivid reminder. My cock gets a million times harder and I'm done with any waiting, any playing of games.

I reach for the hem of her sports top and drag it right over her head.

Hardy spent yesterday evening bragging about how damn fine this girl's tits are, and shit, he wasn't lying.

Full and round with hard pink nipples. Cherries on the fucking icing. I groan.

But I don't get a chance to touch, because she's woman-handling my own top, struggling to tug it over my head.

Then we're both bare from the waist upwards.

"I'll show you mine if you show me yours," I say, with a wink.

She holds my gaze and her thumbs slide under the waistband of her running shorts. My breath hitches in my throat, my eyes lock on the waistband. I watch as slowly she lowers it, revealing more of her tanned belly, then her hip bones, and then the line of curls between her legs and then everything. Her shorts, along with her panties, land on the floor.

I reach for her and she shakes her head. "Your go."

I should take my time, teasing her like she teased me, but I'm too damn impatient. My shorts and my boxers hit the floor next to hers in a matter of seconds.

She takes a sharp intake of breath, her eyes wide as she takes in my cock, hard and standing to attention at my groin.

"Oh lord," she mutters.

"Come here," I say with a deep growl.

She glances over her shoulder to the darkened bathroom beyond. "I thought we were getting showered up."

"We are. But I want to taste you first, before you get covered in all that shampoo and shit, I want to taste you, little one."

For once, there's no hesitation. She steps in towards me and the sunlight through the window makes the sweat on her skin glisten.

I bend down, my nose hovering above her skin, basking in that caramel scent of hers, so sweet I think I'm going to end up with a sugar high. Her breath becomes needy by my ear and I can tell this is killing her. I lower my mouth to her shoulder and I sweep my tongue over her skin, my eyes drifting shut as I taste her. So concentrated, so sweet. Forget the high, my teeth are going to fucking rot.

"You taste so good," I groan.

She slides her hands around my waist and up my back, pressing herself into me so that I can feel those pebbled nipples of hers against my abs. Then she copies me, running her tongue up my chest, over my own nipple. And my skin turns to fire. She moans and sinks her nails into my flesh.

"Do I taste good, little one?" I ask.

"Like cinnamon," she mutters.

"You like it?"

"Hmmm," she mutters as she glides her tongue over more of me, chasing more of my flavor.

I find the crook of her neck and nibble at it, feeling how it makes her shake in my arms.

"We need to shower," I whisper and she whimpers in response like that's the worst idea I've ever had. I chuckle. "But I'm not sure you're dirty enough yet, little one. I think I need to get you a lot stickier."

She looks up at me with those amber eyes, lost in lust, and I pick her up and walk her to the bed, throwing her down onto the mattress and sinking to my knees. She squeals a little but then I have a grip of her thighs and I drag her pussy towards me, all the way until I'm breathing in the very source of her.

Fuck, she's even prettier down here. All pink and plump and gushing slick for me.

"Good girl," I tell her, sweeping my tongue through her folds. Her flavor dissolves on my tongue and it's like the sweetest, best fucking caramel candy I've ever tasted in my life. I'm never going to want to eat dessert again. Only her. Only her every night and every morning too. Shit, I'll wake her up every morning with my head between her legs.

"Angel," she moans as I suck on her, finding her sensitive bean and capturing it between my lips.

"Yes, sweetheart?"

But I'm making her feel too damn good for her to manage more coherent words than that. Instead, she starts moaning, her legs shaking around my ears and her hands locked around my head.

I flick her with my tongue, then rub my chin through her pussy, letting my beard tickle against her and making her squirm. Then I decide that's enough teasing. I press the heel of my hand down against her lower belly, plunge my fingers deep inside her pussy, massaging her spot and then I go to town on her. Licking and licking at her clit like it's a goddamn ice cream.

She goes wild in my grip, twisting and moaning, begging me for mercy and then her thighs tense, her belly stiffens. I kiss her sweetly one more time and she explodes against my mouth, gushing me with slick and screaming my name. Her back arches and she jolts about on the bed as the waves of pleasure I've stirred up crash through her body. And then finally she crashes limp on the bed and I flop down beside her, kissing her mouth as I squeeze at her tits.

"You sleepy now, little one?" I ask, as she lies there breathless, her eyes closed.

"No," she says rolling towards me, "needy."

"Needy?" I chuckle, "that wasn't enough for you?" It looked down right devastating from where I was kneeling.

"I need you inside me. I need you fucking me hard. I need your knot."

Fuck, I want all that too.

"I can't," I say carefully, not wanting to rock that omega heart of hers, not after I made her so vulnerable.

"W-what? Why not?"

"You're not ours yet, Bea. You haven't said you want to be. And if I fuck you, before you've decided. If I fuck you without the others, then ..."

"Then ..."

"That wouldn't be right."

"I don't understand."

"We're a pack, Bea. You don't just get to pick one or two of us. You want one of us, then you want us all."

I wonder if that idea will shock her, terrify her. She's a newly presented omega after all. The idea of being with six men might be enough to turn her away. But she needs to know what she's letting herself in for. If she wants to be in our pack, if she wants to be our omega like we want her to be, then that's how it will be.

However, I see no fear in her eyes, no alarm. No, only lust. She likes that idea.

Good girl.

Good fucking girl.

"Are they going to be mad about what you just did then?"

I lift a questioning eyebrow.

"You just went down on me."

"We're not having sex."

"It was oral sex."

"It's not the same."

"It is."

I lift her chin. "It's not the same as knotting you."

Her pupils explode at the thought of that idea and her hands trail down my body towards my cock. She glides her fingers from the tip of my cock and down my shaft.

"This is your knot?" she asks when she reaches the base.

"Yes, but it isn't inflated, little one. That only happens when I come," I nibble her ear, "when I'm pumping my seed in your pussy and locking myself inside you."

She shivers hard and rubs her fist up my cock.

Her hands are small but warm, and though it's nothing like fucking, watching her hold me like this, her eyes focused on her own movements, is a turn on like none other.

"Does that feel good?" she asks.

I growl. "What do you think?"

She smiles and grips me more firmly, picking up the pace, sliding her hand up and down my cock, up and down, squeezing and twisting at my head. I like the way she does this. With care. Not a rushed job like so many girls do. No, it's like she's enjoying holding me, enjoying pleasuring me, enjoying giving in return. I lean back on my elbows, giving her space. Watching her. I think I could get used to watching her. It doesn't even have to be me. Watching her with one of my packmates will be a turn on too. Watching her with all my packmates.

She peers up at me through those long eyelashes and then dips her head down, guiding my cock between her lips. Her hand felt good. Her mouth even better. All wet and warm. I close my eyes and imagine that's just how her pussy will feel.

"So good, little one," I murmur, knowing how much an omega thrives on these words of encouragement. "You look so good with my cock in your mouth. Look so good when you suck it hard."

She moans around my shaft and the vibrations feel insane.

I remain lying back, doing nothing more than encouraging her with my words, letting her dictate the pace and the depth, letting her pleasure me exactly as she wants to.

She swims her tongue up my length and around my head, licking up any trace of precome and she hums again in satisfaction. Just like the hand job, it's clear she's enjoying this and perhaps that's the biggest turn on of all.

"Going to come, little one," I tell her, "going to come in your pretty mouth. Are you going to swallow me down?" Her amber eyes find mine as I throb on her tongue and then I'm spilling into her, so much come that no matter how much she gulps some of it dribbles over those lips and down her chin. Just like the water did earlier. Fuck I knew that was erotic for a reason.

My cock still in her mouth, she wraps her hands around my shaft and reaches down, down towards my expanding knot. Her fingers explore me and then my cock leaves her mouth with a pop and she peers down to observe me further.

"Squeeze it, sweetheart," I tell her, taking her hands in mine and wrapping her fingers firmly around the base of my cock where my knot is now inflated, hot and hard.

She moans a little, rubbing her thighs together and I know we're both thinking the same thing: how good it will feel when finally I lock inside her.

We lie like that, with her hands squeezing my knot, until finally it deflates. My cock's still fucking hard for her though and I don't think, barring flipping her over and rutting her hard into the bed, that's going to change, so I scoop her up and carry her through to the shower.

"I think we're dirty enough now, little one," I say, glancing to the mirror and noticing how my beard is shiny with her slick. "We're going to be in trouble with my pack-mates if we're late."

"We could just stay here all day," she mumbles against my chest and as good as that sounds I'm trying to do right by my brother right now. I don't want to fuck things up when we're finally reconciled.

"You have five other men waiting on tenterhooks to see you, little one. Come on."

I lower her down and turn on the shower, fiddling with the water until it's just the right temperature. Then I lead her under the torrent and spend the next ten minutes massaging shampoo into her hair and gliding soap all over her beautiful body, washing away the sweat and slick and come, and spending far too long buffing her perfect ass.

"I'm so fucking sorry, Bea, for hurting you, for being

such a stupid fool. If I could turn back time ..." I say softly as I wash the suds from her long hair, letting the wet strands run through my fingers. "Do you think you're going to be able to forgive us, sweetheart?"

"I think I almost have," she says, her eyes closed, leaning into my touch.

I close my eyes too, and for a moment I have to reach out and rest my hand against the tiled wall to steady myself.

Could this happen? This dream I cradled all those years ago. That dream that was smashed to pieces on that hot summer's night.

Now the pieces are rearranging, reforming, binding together stronger than ever. A pack.

Me. Axel. The four men I love most in the world.

And Bea.

Beautiful Bea Carsen.

I can almost taste happiness on the end of my tongue, see it right there in the distance, ready for us to grab with both hands.

We can't afford to fuck things up. I need to talk to the others about that development.

23

Bea

I PERCH on the end of my bed wrapped in a giant fluffy towel and let Angel Stormgate rifle through my wardrobe and pick out my outfit.

It's not like when Karl used to do it, insisting I wear whatever he dragged out of the cardboard, not caring if I liked the clothes or not.

With Angel it's different.

I told him I had no idea what to wear to go sailing on a yacht, and he offered to help me find the perfect outfit. He's also keen to hear my opinion. When I frown at the first dress, he holds up, he notices immediately.

"You don't like it?"

"I like it, but the straps dig into my back and, I don't know, since I presented, I've found I'm way more sensitive to things like that."

"Omegas have sensitive skin – it's why you crave soft things." He slides the dress back onto the rail. "I'll take you out shopping if you want, find you things that would be more comfortable. We could bring Molly. She'll know all the best places."

I swing my legs and smile at him. "I'd like that."

Maybe the old Bea would have protested that she didn't need the charity, but I'm finding that actually it's rather nice to be spoiled. Especially when that spoiling comes in the form of mind-rearranging orgasms.

I also like the idea of getting to know his sister better.

My previous attempts to make friends with other omegas failed miserably, but I have a feeling Molly is someone I could actually get along with. And having a friend who knows more about this omega business than me, would be extremely helpful. I wonder if she'd also have some tips on how to keep her brothers in line.

I watch Angel, already dressed in chinos and a button-down, continue his perusal of my wardrobe. Even with his clothes on the man looks like some kind of Greek freaking god. I bite my lip.

I've had more amazing sex – which was not technically that kind of sex – in the last few days than I have my entire life.

My aunt Julia and cousin Courtney may actually be right. Being an omega – being a pack omega to these men – may be what I need. If every shower in my life was like the one I've just taken with the man in front of me, I'd be a very happy and satisfied woman.

And being in their pack, I'd get to keep all of them, all six.

Angel's words about the sex come floating back into my mind with that thought.

Could I handle sex with six men?

I close my eyes and try to imagine it. I half expect some monstrous and overwhelming vision to enter my mind; instead the vision that appears behind my closed eyelids is sizzling hot.

"Bea?" Angel says, and when I open my eyes I find him examining my face with a quizzical look. My cheeks sizzle and I'm grateful he can't read my mind. "What are you thinking about?" he asks, strolling over with a simple, white summer dress in his hand.

"Never you mind," I tell him, reaching for the dress.

"Now I'm intrigued."

I simply smile at him and pretend to be considering the dress.

"You know when we're bonded, our thoughts will be shared."

I look up at him. "What?"

He sits down beside me on the bed. "I'm guessing you haven't got to that bit in your Omega 101 literature."

"Bonding? No. It didn't seem to be one of the urgent things I needed to know."

"But you know about it? You know how it happens?"

I reach up and trace the teeth marks in his neck. "When your mate bites you."

He nods, taking my hand in his and encouraging me to stroke along the vivid white scar lines. He closes his eyes as if this simple touch feels divine.

"It creates a bond, unseverable, permanent."

I nod, that much I know.

"It also creates this ..." he struggles for the word, "portal between us. I can feel the emotions of my bonded mates, at times I can see what they're thinking too."

"You can read each other's minds?" I say incredulously.

I'm not sure I want anyone else in my head with all my crazy mixed up thoughts.

"It's not as simple as that. It's not like reading a book. People's thoughts are never neat and orderly, most of the time it's incoherent. God only knows what someone like Nate's mind would be like! But you learn to read it over time, like understanding that person's own personal language. And the emotions, they're clearer. I can read them innately, a bit like I can read people's scents."

I nod, understanding what he means about the scents. I'm finding it easier and easier to read these men. I know when they're tense, relaxed, happy, turned on. If I'd been more adept at reading scents in the first place, would I have spotted their stupid games sooner? Saved myself the heartache? Then again, I wouldn't have gotten to know them like I have. Maybe some heartache is worth it in the long run.

"I'm not sure I like the idea of my mind being read." I kiss the lines in his neck. "I do like some privacy."

"You don't get a whole lot of privacy in a pack, sweetheart. But that's what I like about it best. You're never alone. Never lonely."

I stare into his eyes, watching the whispers of silver float through his irises. Can he read my mind after all? Can he see how lonely I've been? All those years with Karl. I didn't realize it until I moved to the city and I wasn't alone anymore.

"Besides," he continues, "there are ways of shutting people out. You don't have to share every thought if you don't want to. I find most of the time I don't mind it, though." He smoothes his hands over the cotton-white dress. "So do we like this one or should I keep searching?"

"It's okay to wear on the boat?"

"You could wear a paper bag on the boat if you wanted to, sweetheart."

"Then yes, I like it."

THE HARBOR in Rockview jostles with yachts that range from Missy's size to ones the size of small palaces. They bob on the lilting water, sails flapping in the breeze and the water slapping against their sides.

Expensive restaurants and cafes line the shore and people in sunglasses, more expensive than all the clothes I own in my wardrobe, sit drinking overpriced coffees and glasses of champagne. Several more sit out on the decks of their boats, eating meals served by men in crisp white shirts, or lying out on sun-loungers.

The jetty under my feet shifts and I'm glad I took Angel's advice and wore sneakers, even if they look odd with my sundress. Everybody is watching as the six alphas accompany me along the rows of boats and I'd rather not face plant in front of all these rich and well-to-do people. Several call out hellos to the men, wave or slap them on the shoulders as they pass by. One or two try to engage them in conversation.

We don't stop to talk.

"It seems like every rich person in the city is here today," I whisper to Connor who holds my hand and leads me along.

"It's a good day for sailing. Tide's right, good amount of wind, sea's flat and the sun is shining."

"These people don't seem to be doing a lot of sailing."

"Yeah, but they know we will be," Connor says, frowning and I notice there are several groups of omegas lying out in teeny, tiny bikinis or hovering about in revealing outfits.

I growl a little under my breath and Connor squeezes my hand and drags me away from one table of omegas who I catch eyeing up my men. I scowl at them so hard, they drop their gazes. Good.

But I guess I'm not intimidating to every omega out here. One in particular. I should have known where there's a swarm of bees, there'd be their queen.

Melody steps right out into the middle of our path, a wide and fake smile plastered to her face. Her long, blonde hair is loose in perfect waves around her shoulders and on her head balances a wide straw hat that matches the oversized straw bag in her hand and the straw wedges on her feet. Her lipstick is a bright pink; a perfect match to her candy floss bikini.

"Bess," she squeals like we're best friends. "It's so good to see you!" She reaches for my hands with a feigned look of sympathy. "I heard what happened at the," she lowers her voice to a theatrical whisper that everyone within twenty feet must hear, "clinic. How awful! I can't imagine what you've been through."

I peer at Connor, wondering how the hell she knows all this, and he frowns back at me as if to say he doesn't have a clue.

"Hey Melody," Nate says, taking a step towards her that makes her hesitate a little. The smile on his lips is about as fake as the one on hers, although his is a hell of a lot more scary. A smile a lion would give a gazelle before ripping out its throat. "How'd you hear about that?"

"Oh," she says airily, "news gets around. Especially when it involves dangers to omegas. We have to be so careful." She flutters her eyelashes at him and I have the urge to pluck each one out. She turns her attention back to me. "But you know, sweetie, I think I did warn you to find a suitable pack for your heat. Checking yourself into a clinic," she tuts, "what a silly thing to do."

"Are you ... victim blaming her, Mel?" Nate asks, cocking his head to one side.

Melody holds her manicured hand to her chest. "Me? Oh no, of course not. It's just ... well ... we have to be careful." Ignoring Nate's deathly glare, she turns her attention to Axel. "Are you going out on your boat? It's such a perfect day for a sail, isn't it? But Daddy's boat is in the repair shop." She sighs, conveying her disappointment.

"What a shame," I say flatly. "Sounds like you'll be stuck on dry land."

"Oh no," she says, the fake smile back on her lips with triumph. "Don's taking me out on his." She turns her head, just as an older man comes to stand beside her, resting his hand on her elbow.

I recognize him from the Mackay dinner. The man who Connor said wanted Axel to back his campaign. He's dressed in a polo shirt and dark pants with a blue handkerchief tied around his neck. The color complimenting Melody's swimsuit. I wonder if they're dating. Perhaps I won't have to worry about Melody and her grabby hands anymore. Then again, the way she's eyeing up Silver, maybe I will.

"Axel, Angel," Don says, holding out his hand to shake theirs. "Together? I didn't think I'd ever see the day."

Melody seems to notice this for the first time too, swinging her gaze around the six alphas. She giggles. "I thought Pack Boston and Pack York couldn't stand to breathe the same air."

"And yet here they are about to take me sailing on their

yacht," I say in an overly cheerful voice that has Nate and Hardy smirking.

"And actually Pack York and Pack Boston are no more," Axel says.

Don and Melody both stare at him in disbelief. "What?"

"It's just Pack Stormgate now," Angel adds.

"What?!" Don chuckles. "How did this happen?"

"Bea Carsen happened," Connor says, pushing through the two of them and taking me with him.

When we're a few paces away, I lean in and ask him, "Do you think the two of them are together? He's old enough to be her father."

"Probably," he mutters, "bad smells attract bad smells."

I peer over my shoulder, the others are close behind us, leaving Melody and Don gaping at us.

"So," Connor says, recapturing my attention. "I want to see if you can guess which yacht is ours?"

"Angel said you have more than one," I point out.

Connor nods. "Well, yeah, technically that's true. But this one belonged to Axel and Angel's dad and she's a beaut. You must be special if Mrs. Stormgate is letting us take her out today. She doesn't often let us use it."

"Oh," I say, a little stunned.

"Yeah, she's had numerous offers to buy the yacht over the years and has always declined them."

"So I'm looking for something beautiful? Hmmmm."

A lot of the boats look like huge, ugly machines and I struggle to see any beauty in them. The sail boats are prettier, their lines sleeker and their sails bright white in the sun. I scan the rows of boats, breathing in Connor's scent and the scent of the others behind me. I'd assumed six scents mixed together would have my taste buds revolting;

instead they're in heaven. My tongue practically humming and my mouth salivating.

"I'm going to be disappointed if you can't spot her," Axel says behind me.

"I'm beginning to feel a little jealous here," I say, "it sounds like you all have a crush on this boat."

"She was my first love," Axel says.

I twist my head to smile at him and something catches my eye. I stop and turn that way, and then I spot her. Unlike the other boats, she's carved from brown wood, and she lies in the water like she was always meant to be there. Her mast stretches high up into the air and criss-crosses with beams and ropes, her sails resplendent in the wind.

"There," I say pointing to the boat and am awarded with six broad smiles.

"I knew you'd spot her," Nate says.

They lead me towards her and as I get closer, I read the name painted along her side in rosy pink letters. *Phoebe*.

I glance toward Connor.

"Did you change her name?" I ask.

"No," he says, "it's always been her name."

I tune into his scent, to the scents around me, looking for signs that they're playing me again. I find none. I find I trust them.

"You can ask our mom," Angel says, resting his hands on my shoulders. "It's always been her name."

"It means bright, radiant," Axel says looking at me. "Because she is."

"It's called fate, dumbass," Hardy says, jumping up onto the boat and holding out his hand for me to join him. "Phoebe Stormgate was our first love. Phoebe Carsen is our forever love."

I roll my eyes at him, although inside my heart is swelling. For such a big growly man, he really is a softie.

Then they're positioning me on the deck, while they busy themselves, untying ropes, lifting anchors and pulling on levers and gullies. They work together without a word to each other, instinctively knowing what the other is doing, working as a well-oiled team. Is it that the bond? Or a sign of how well these men know each other? Watching them now, it's hard to believe a rift ever existed between them. It's as if they've always been a pack of six alphas.

Fated.

Like Hardy said.

Fated to be together.

My heart tugs.

Is this my fate too?

I'm beginning to believe it is.

"We have to use the engine to leave the harbor," Axel tells me, "but once we're out on the open water, we'll use the sails."

I look up into the mast and excitement floods my belly.

"You don't get seasick do you, sweetheart?" Silver asks me, coming to sit beside me as we begin to chug out of the harbor, passing the other boats moored up and some on their way in or out.

"Bit late to ask me that now," I point out. "But honestly I don't know." I shuffle along on my seat until my body rests alongside his. He peers down at me, then hooks his arm around my shoulder and pulls me in even closer.

He breathes in my hair.

"Hmmmm I can smell Angel on you, sweetheart."

"Uh huh," I say. I'm not even going to deny that.

"You smell good."

The boat cuts through the water and soon we're out of

the harbor, and into the deeper water, the ocean turning the color of Connor's eyes beneath the belly of the boat. A little further and Axel and Angel are yelling instructions to the others.

"I gotta help the others," Silver whispers and I sigh, enjoying my snuggle with him. He chuckles. "It's all hands on deck running a ship like this." He jumps to his feet. "In fact," he holds out his hand, "I think you'd better help too."

"Me? This is my first time on a boat. Put me in charge of anything and we'll probably sink."

"In that case ..." he says, yanking me up and tugging me along behind him. We stop alongside Axel at the yacht's wheel.

Axel automatically steps aside, gesturing to the wheel. "You want a go?"

"I don't want to sink your dad's boat."

"I won't let you sink it," he says, coming to stand behind me and guiding my hands to the wheel.

Silver winks at me and then hurries off to help Hardy unwind a second sail. Soon, four large, crisp white sails are flapping in the wind above our heads, cracking like whips.

Angel yells more orders and ropes are pulled, booms swing and then the sails catch the air and billow out like the skirts of a wedding dress.

"It's beautiful," I say, gazing up into the yards of material. "I wouldn't have expected a boat to be beautiful."

"Told you she was," Axel says, nuzzling my ear. "But probably best to keep your eye on the water, Omega."

"Whoops," I say, dragging my eyes back to the crystal waves. I don't really know what I'm doing. In fact, I don't think I'm doing anything really. Axel is doing most of the steering. But it's still a thrill to stand here, with this alpha at my back, the sails billowing above me, the boat slicing through the ocean, the sun on my face and the sea breeze in my hair.

"Join us," Axel whispers, "join our pack, and you will always be the rudder to our ship."

I twist my head to look at him.

"The rudder? That doesn't sound very romantic. Shouldn't I be the sails, or the bow?"

"No, the rudder, Omega, because you'll always be in control, setting the course for our journey, dictating every direction that we take."

I twist around in his arms, the wheel at my back, the alpha at my front. I twine my arms around his neck and stand up onto my toes and kiss him.

"I don't need to be the rudder," I tell him when finally I pull away, sinking back down to the soles of my feet. "But I would like to be a part of this ship."

24

ate

The Bond shimmers.

All bright light and sparkling fucking crystals.

So deep so intense, I feel it right in the center of my gut, in the core of my being.

I spin around and he's kissing her, kissing her up against the wheel of the ship. Kissing her like I've never seen him kiss a girl before.

Like he's in fucking love.

Of course, it's love, asshole, he says through our bond.

And I drag my eyes from them to find all the others watching too.

Angel, Silver and Hardy, they aren't a part of our bond, but I know they feel this too. Or maybe they can read it in the way he holds her tight, like he'll never let anyone or anything steal her from him.

We stand there, stand there mesmerized like we're watching the fucking dawn of time.

Then something changes.

In the air.

My nose twitches.

My blood heats.

Before I even realize what it is.

Burned fucking caramel.

Deeper. Stronger. Sweeter.

Fuuuuccckkkk.

My eyes flick to Connor.

His spine stiffens. His eyes darken.

Axel's grip on the omega tightens, becomes more possessive, and his kiss grows hungry.

Fuck!

Angel signals to the rest of us and we all know what that means. We're anchoring up in fucking record time.

My hands shake as I lash down the sails, salt water spraying in my eyes.

"This can't be right," Connor mumbles under his breath.

But an omega's scent never lies.

And, shit, her scent. So sweet!

When the anchor's dropped and we're bobbing on the water, we turn our attention back to the omega. Axel's carried her over to the long bench of cushioned seats at the front of the boat. She's curled up beside him, mewing and pawing at him like a cat in heat.

It can't be. So close to the last.

But fuck I hope it is.

All I want is to show her how good this can be. How good it should be.

The shore's a distant strip of land, the sea a glimmering

mirror, the sky a never-ending expanse. It's just the seven of us and the big blue sea.

Axel looks up at us.

"This shouldn't be happening."

"Her hormones are a fucking mess," Silver says, "it could be."

Axel turns back to the omega, who's attempting to suck on his neck, her hands inside his shirt. He takes her chin in his hand and lifts her face to look up into his.

"Omega," he says. "Are you ... are you going into heat?"

Her eyes go in and out of focus.

"Heat?"

"Is this your heat?" Connor says gently, sitting on her other side.

She stares into Axel's pupils. "No," she says, "at least..."

Axel lays his palm on her forehead. "She's warm, not scorching."

"Pre-heat?" Angel suggests.

"The doctor said things might be unsettled for the first few months. That I'd experience false heats and ..." She shakes her head as if trying to rejumble her thoughts.

"It's okay, sweetheart," Silver says. "We got you."

"Does it hurt?" Axel asks her, laying his hand against her belly.

"No, I just ... I just need ..."

"What, little bird, what do you need?" I kneel down in front of her.

She whimpers. And we can all guess what she fucking needs. Especially when the aroma of slick hits the air.

"Words, little one," Axel says, still holding her chin in his hand. "Use your words and tell us exactly what you want."

"Knots!" she moans and I think I nearly come in my pants.

My sweet little bird needs a knot. No. That's not what she said. She needs more than one. She needs all our knots.

Well fuck me!

Hardy groans.

Connor's thoughts turn fucking explicit through the bond.

Me, I'm just staring at her thighs. Slick is trickling down them, glistening in the sunlight.

My mouth waters.

I know how good that tastes.

"You want our knots," Axel says, his voice low, feral.

"Uh huh," she murmurs.

"She doesn't know what she wants in this state," Silver mutters, his voice tight, his spine rigid.

The omega snaps her head around to look up at him, breaking Axel's grip on her chin. "I do know what I want, Silver. I've waited for a knot, I've been dreaming of a knot. And I need it now."

Her tone has Silver bristling, and he marches up to her and towers above. He scowls down at her. "Your mind is high on fucking hormones, little one. You think we're going to take advantage of you in this state?" I huff, taking advantage is exactly what I want to do. Take advantage until the fucking sun sets in the sky and rises again. "We're not going to risk fucking things up with you again."

My shoulders sag. The dude is right.

The omega, however, doesn't agree. And isn't this the reason this woman drives me crazy? She reaches up and takes a fistful of his shirt, dragging him down towards her. He doesn't fight her grip and soon she's caged under his arms.

"I know what I want." She threads the buttons of his

shirt through their holes. "I'm in my right mind. Test me, ask me anything."

He growls. "What's three hundred and forty-two multiplied by twenty?"

"Something she'll actually know," Hardy says.

"Six thousand, eight hundred and forty, Alpha," she says, her tongue flicking around the last few syllables.

Silver stares hard in her eyes. "The capital city of Peru?"

"Lima," she says, with only a hint of a slur.

"You really want this, little Omega? You really want to be fucked and knotted?"

She whimpers and opens her legs for him.

"Fuck," I mutter, making room for him. "Fuck, Silver, make her come before I toss your sorry ass in the ocean and do it myself."

He scowls at me, but before I can deliver on my threat, he's sliding her panties down her legs and hitching up her skirt, spreading her legs wide for all of us to see. She's even more swollen, even wetter than when I ate her out on the kitchen table.

Shit, that pussy. I've been fucking dreaming about it.

It's all I want to taste.

I've been sucking on fucking caramel candies like my life depended on it.

"Gonna get you ready for us, first, Omega. Open you up for us." He reaches for her, but she grips his wrist, meeting his eye before lifting her gaze to the rest of us.

"I want to give this a try," she says, her tone heavy with lust, "whatever this thing is between us. I want to try it. I want to see if it's real. I want to ..." She closes her eyes, her long eyelashes brushing against the peaks of her cheeks. "I want to give you my heart. But I need to know I can do this first."

"Do what, little bird?" I whisper.

"Be with all of you like this," she says, her cheeks pink, her eyes still closed.

Connor leans down to kiss her shoulder and I stroke my hand up her leg.

"There's only one way to find out," Silver says and, her hand still locked around his wrist, he glides his forefinger inside her. "Tight," he mutters, partly to himself, partly to the rest of us and Hardy curses under his breath.

He pumps slowly, using his other hand to find her clit and stroke at it. That has her falling back against the cushions, her hips rising, and her throat humming.

"That's it sweet girl," Axel says beside her, leaning over to press kisses to her throat.

"Good girl," Silver confirms.

I watch transfixed as he works his finger inside her and her pussy swallows up his digit again and again. He adds a second, stretching her wider and when she moans, I swear I feel it in my gut.

Axel nibbles the lobe of her ear, I run my fingertips up her calf and Connor strokes back her hair.

Slick gushes from her hole, coating Silver's hand and his wrist and I hear the wet squelch of his fingers inside her.

"So good," Silver purrs. "Such a good girl for us. Look at that pussy."

"So pretty," Angel says from behind us and I know he's as transfixed as the rest of us.

She murmurs and Connor kisses her, dragging that plump bottom lip of hers through his teeth.

"Can she take a third?" Hardy asks, voice deep and guttural.

"This girl can do any fucking thing," I say and Silver

must agree because gently he slides another of his thick fingers into her glistening pussy.

"Look at that," Hardy says in awe. "Fucking look at that."

"Is it too much, sweetheart?" Axel whispers into her ear.

She pulls away from Connor's kiss. "Not enough," she pants. "Not enough."

Silver growls and pumps her harder, fucking her with his fingers.

Hardy's hand lands on the man's shoulder and then he's kneeling on his other side, all three of us down on our knees before our omega.

He snatches Silver's other hand from her clit and lowers his mouth there instead.

She cries out, her hips lifting from the bench when he kisses her there, humming in satisfaction around her sensitive nub and driving her wild.

The two men work in unison, Hardy flicking at her clit with his powerful tongue and Silver massaging the spot inside her. I rest my palm on her lower belly, pressing down to give her that extra pressure and together we work her into a frenzy. Her hands are tight balls, one in Connor's hair, one gripping Axel's shirt. Her legs shake like leaves in a storm, and she tosses her head from side to side, tears tracing down her cheeks.

When she comes, it's fucking spectacular. Her entire body lights up, sings, and I practically see the bliss sparking through her body.

She tosses and turns, tumbling through the waves of it and then crashes down spent on the bench.

"Oh lordy," she mutters, all breathless and sweet as the caramel she tastes like.

"Good?" Axel asks her.

"Good is not the right word," she pants.

"And do you feel better now, sweetheart?" Silver asks, his fingers still deep inside her like he never wants to remove them.

She lifts her head to gaze at him and shakes her head resolutely.

"No?" Hardy growls, ducking his head down to go for round two.

"No," she says. "I need those knots."

25

Silver

Her eyes are darker than I've ever seen them and she holds my gaze with a fierceness I've never seen in an omega before. If she accepts us, if she agrees to joining our pack, this one is going to keep us on our toes. She's going to be demanding – not pearl necklaces and diamond rings – but orgasms, cocks and knots. The way it should be between alphas and their omegas.

This is what we were made for. This.

I rock back on my heels, feeling the warm bodies of Hardy and Nate beside me, and slowly, slowly, withdraw my fingers from her. She's so warm inside, so soft, so goddamn wet, and I'm having to fight the fucking need to sink all my fingers, my tongue, my cock, shit, even my fucking nose inside her.

My fingers are coated in slick when I pull them out,

ribbons of it trailing from my hand to her pussy and Nate dips down to capture the whole lot in his mouth, grinning at her and licking his lips.

I do the same because I have no fucking shame.

I've been dreaming of how good this woman tastes. Rock hard every time I imagine the flavor of her on my tongue.

I lift my finger to my mouth, close my eyes and suck.

Sugar explodes on my taste buds, explodes all around my mouth, sets off little explosions in my chest and in my gut, in my goddamn mind too.

Nothing, nothing in all the years I've lived has tasted as good as that.

We have to make her ours, because holy fuck, that taste is instantly addictive.

"Bea," I mutter, "Jesus Christ, Bea, do you know how good you taste?"

I open my eyes and find hers again.

"Knot," she says simply, with a little frown playing out between her brows. I chuckle and so do the other alphas on this boat.

Our omega is impatient.

"Whose knot do you want first, sweetheart?" I ask her softly.

She scrambles up so she's sitting, the skirt of her dress still bunched up by her waist. The entire freaking thing needs to be removed.

Her gaze hesitates around the six of us. "I don't want to hurt anyone," she says timidly.

"That's not how this works," Axel says, tucking a lock of hair behind her ear. "There's no room for jealousy, for feeling slighted, for silly grudges in a pack."

Bea turns her head and lifts her eyebrow at him as if to say, "What the fuck?"

And I have to agree with the woman. We've hardly been living by those rules.

Axel nods like he accepts the criticism. "I know," he says, "we haven't been doing things right. The six of us should have been a pack all those years ago, but we screwed up. We're older now. We know what's important. What matters. And we have more to lose." He strokes his fingertips over her lips. "Do you want us all, Omega?"

"Y-y-yes," she says, her voice faltering. "I don't know what's wrong with me. How I can possibly want all of you? But I do and I'm going to stop fighting what I want, going to stop denying what feels right, and I'm going to start embracing it. I want all of you."

"Then it doesn't matter who has you first," Axel says, then adds darkly, "We're all going to have you."

She shivers and I can see just how much she really does want that.

Fuck, this woman, this miracle of a woman.

"Then ..." she says, "then I want it to be Silver."

She turns her head back to me and I'm so stunned all I can do is gape at her. She smiles and my heart strains in my chest.

"Me?" I say, hardly believing that can be true.

She lifts her hand and strokes my cheek, her fingers soft as cobwebs. I lean into her touch.

"I'm so grateful it was you, Silver, that night. That night in the ballroom when this crazy, crazy journey began. I'm glad it was you that took me home. That made sure I was safe. I know now that I might not have been so lucky." Her fingers brush over my jaw and my cheeks, caressing my cheekbones and around my eye sockets. "You didn't hurt me. I know you won't hurt me now. I trust you Silver and I trust you with this."

I cover her hand with mine, twisting my head and kissing her palm.

I don't have the ability, the skill, to tell her how much that means to me, how my heart lights up so brightly I can feel the warmth of it in my chest. If I'd claimed her, if we were mated, she'd feel it through the bond. She'd know it.

But there's only one other way to show her.

I gather her up in my arms, and stumble to my feet. She snuggles up against my skin, just like she did that night I carried her up the stairs to her apartment. Then I stumble over the deck, towards the stairs and down into the cabin.

There are no protests from the others, no grumbles, not even any flash of dissatisfaction between the bond.

This is her first time.

"Just us this first time, sweetheart. There'll be plenty of time later for something more."

She hums her approval and I kick open the door to the giant bedroom below deck. It's practically one giant bed, covered in soft blankets and multiple pillows.

I drop her onto her feet and shrug off my shirt, losing my pants and my boxers as she watches me silently. Then I step towards her and find the hem of her dress, lifting it over her head. Beneath my hands, her body shakes.

"Are you frightened?"

"No," she says. She's shaking from desire, and fuck me, I think I am too.

I take a little step away. Allowing my eyes to feast on her. Bare for me at last.

"You're so fucking beautiful, Bea Carsen. So fucking precious. I'm going to spend the rest of my days ensuring you know it." I shake my head, mumbling, "So beautiful."

"You know you are too."

I huff and she closes the space between us, placing her

warm hands on my chest and then tracing her fingertips over me, over the muscles of my abs, the inks on my skin, the scar near my hip.

"What's this from?" she asks, eyes looking up at me in alarm.

"Sweetheart, I'd like to tell you it was some war injury but it's from having my appendix out."

"War injury?" she asks, tracing around the tattoo of my old military unit.

"Five years," I tell her.

"Did you..."

"See action ... yeah, some."

She sweeps her thumbs over the tattoo before kissing it. The taste of my flesh seems to send her wild, because in the next moment, she's kissing me everywhere, her mouth hungry, her tongue sweeping every groove and undulation of my body, her teeth grazing skin.

The smell of her slick becomes more potent and I can't wait for this any longer.

I've wanted to fuck this little omega since the moment I first laid eyes on her, since the first time her eager little hands tugged at me, since those big amber eyes heated my blood.

"Going to fuck you now, sweetheart."

She moans, and I back her up against the bed, resting my hand behind her back and laying her down gently.

She opens her legs immediately for me and I take one look at her pretty pussy before I lower down on top of her, caging her head with my arms.

My cock nudges between her fold, but I don't press on yet. I take a deep, steadying inhale, reminding myself I need to go slow, gentle, patient with this one.

Even if it's fucking agony.

"Ready, sweetheart?" She answers by lifting her head and nipping at my shoulder. "I'm going to take that as a yes."

"It is one," she says, twining her legs around my waist, and using the heels of her feet to push at my backside, pressing me towards her.

I growl a warning at her and then, I find her entrance. She gasps as I press into her, and I halt, kissing her mouth until I feel her relax, her pussy sucking at me as if it wants me all.

"More," she murmurs, and I give it to her, lowering my hips to thrust down further inside her.

Her skin smells like caramel, her eyes are bright watching my face and her pussy, her pussy, fuck her pussy, it's like heaven itself.

"Okay?" I ask her, all the taut control clear in my voice. I want to fuck her so badly. I'm hanging on by one straining thread.

"Hmmmm, yes, Alpha, it feels so ..."

Her eyes roll, her eyelids flutter, her legs shake as I give her more of me.

I know I'm big. I know all of us alphas are. Yet this little omega of mine is taking me, all of me, just like she was designed to do.

"You want more?" I ask her, growling in her ear.

"Y-y-yes, all of you, all of your cock, Alpha. Don't hold back."

Eyes locked on her face, I sink all the way inside her, feeling her writhe in pleasure beneath me as I brush against every sensitive spot along her channel.

"Feels so good," she mutters, "so, so good."

I lean down to suck at her hardened nipples, grinding into her and making her squirm some more, keep making her squirm until she can't take it anymore.

Her nails scrape at my back and she bites me harder this time.

"Fuck me," she says.

I've been waiting for those words. Waiting for that permission.

And I don't need to be asked a second time.

I fuck her. I fuck her hard into the mattress. I can't help myself. I have no self control left. Not when it comes to this one, not when it comes to this woman.

I thrust deep and unrelenting and our omega not only takes every pound, she loves it too. Crying out, writhing, lifting her hips to meet me, and squeezing and sucking around my cock.

"Good girl," I pant, "good fucking girl."

"Don't stop," she mutters, "don't stop." The convulsions of her pussy grow more frantic, her nails pierce right through my flesh, her legs lock tightly around my waist.

"Not going to, Omega. Going to pound this sweet pussy of yours until you're screaming my name."

"Silver," she gasps.

"Yes, like that, just like that. Say my name, Omega, Say my fucking name."

"Silver!!" she screams, clinging on to me and then she comes, her body exploding into ecstasy, thrashing about beneath me, her pussy milking me so hard, I come too. It's like lightning. It's like being struck by a fucking bolt. My nerves scream with pleasure, my vision whites and for a moment I'm lost, lost completely in her, in her touch, in her scent, in her voice, in her goddamn pussy.

Then I hold her down, meeting her eyes, as the pleasure courses through the both of us still. "Going to knot you now, sweetheart. Going to knot you so damn good."

Her eyes widen as I expand at my base, and she winces,

her brow wrinkling, as I stretch her wider and wider. She bites down on her lip and screws up her eyes. I kiss her neck, giving her words of encouragement.

It only lasts a few seconds, a few seconds of pain and then another wave of pleasure sweeps her away and she's coming in my arms all over again.

AFTERWARDS, I roll us onto our sides and gather her up in my arms, pulling her close to me, as I purr for her. She rests her head on my chest, and relaxes, sleepy and content, just how every alpha wants their omega. Well, that or screaming their name.

"How does it feel?" I murmur into her hair.

I know this moment won't last long. A pack is all about sharing and soon I'll have to make room for my packmates, but right now I'm going to enjoy the feel of my cock knotted into her pussy.

She pulses around me. "Divine."

"It didn't hurt?"

"A little at first but then ..." She smiles up at me. "I'm beginning to understand why omegas like that bit so much."

"It's even better in heat, little one," I growl. She screws up her nose. "What?"

She swallows. "I don't think I can go through another heat, Silver."

"Why not?"

She screws up her face and guilt and pain stab me deep in my gut. A wake-up call I rightly deserve.

"It's because you were alone, Bea. Next time ... next time we'll make it so damn good for you, I promise." She shudders. Not in the fucking good way. I hold her tighter. "I'm sorry, Bea. I'm so sorry we let you down. It's our fault you went through that alone. Our fault you suffered. You know we're going to spend every day of the rest of our lives making it up to you." I kiss the precious crown of her head. "I'll never let anything hurt you ever again."

"That's a big promise," she says.

"One I intend to keep."

She tilts her head back and peers into my face. "Is it really good? A heat, I mean. It's not just another deception. Good for alphas but not for omegas. You're not saying that just to ensure you'll be with me next time?"

"Bea, sweetheart, I'm not an omega. I can't tell you how they feel. But ..." I shift a little uneasily. "I've been with omegas through heat and–"

Her body stiffens. "How many?"

"How many what?" I say, feigning innocence.

"How many omegas have you helped through a heat?"

"Several."

"Several," she repeats unhappily.

"I'm thirty years old, Omega. You didn't expect me to be a virgin now, did you?"

"No ... it's just ... how about that girl?"

"What girl?" I ask, wondering if she's thinking of Melody or one of the other pushy omegas who like to make themselves known.

"The one that caused all the trouble between you all, between Axel and Angel."

"You know about that?"

"Axel told me."

"You know he was just as much to blame as–"

"Yes, he told me that too." My shoulders relax a little and I lie there silently. Have they really changed? Axel? Angel? I've been hoping they have but if I'm honest deep down in my heart I've been hesitant, unsure this can last. Nervous any moment it will revert to the way things were.

I don't want them to. And not only because I want the girl in my arms to be mine, to be ours permanently. But because I want Connor in my life too. And Axel. Heck, even that lunatic Nate.

I want this life. I want this pack.

I've been unsure if it can happen.

But Axel said that. To Bea. Told her he was as much to blame as Angel. I wouldn't have believed that was possible two weeks ago.

"No," I tell Bea. "No, we never saw her through a heat."

"Angel?"

"No, sweetheart. None of us. She never fell into one in the time we knew her."

Bea relaxes too. "Good," she says a little possessively and I smile.

"You're the only woman for us now, Bea Carsen, always and forever."

"Always and forever is a long time."

"Yeah, but I know you feel it too."

And for once, this little firecracker doesn't contradict me.

26

Connor

I'm impatient.

In fact for once I'm more impatient than freaking Nate who seems calm and relaxed given the circumstances.

No, it's me prowling the deck, ears alert for every agonizing scream of ecstasy the omega is making from the cabin. I'm hard as steel, my skin itching with irritation and all I want to do is fuck her.

I wish the six of us had already formalized the formation of this new pack. I wish I was already bonded to Silver, Hardy and Angel too. Then at least, I'd be there with him, experiencing the bliss of rutting our omega. The smug grins on Angel and Hardy's faces as they experience their bonded mate's pleasure second hand is almost unbearable.

"Is he still fucking her?" I mumble, stopping in front of

Hardy, who sits laid back on the lounger with his hands hooked behind his head, biceps bulging.

"Nah, lucky bastard's knotted her now."

"Jesus fucking Christ." I slink down beside him.

"What's wrong, man?"

I shake my head, dragging my finger through my hair. "I've never felt this way about a girl."

"None of us have."

"Yeah, I know." Then I shake my head, and chuckle. "But I don't think I've ever felt this impatient to have a woman before, so desperate to knot her, to make her feel good."

"You didn't make her feel good the other day?" Hardy says with a smirk.

"I made her feel good," I say, "but you know, knotting ..."

"Yeah," Hardy says, eyes darting to the cabin doorway.

"And ..." I say.

"And?"

"What if she changes her mind? What if it is just the hormones talking? What if it's a one-time only thing? What if she decides she doesn't want this pack?"

Hardy's quiet, he doesn't have an answer to that, but Angel leans forward on his other side, resting his forearms on his knees.

"We may have a problem when it comes to that."

"What's that?" Nate says, his eyes snapping open from where I thought he was dozing on the chair.

Axel glances at his brother too, his brow creasing.

"We may have a problem," Angel repeats.

"What do you mean?" Axel asks.

"The development," Angel replies. "I hadn't ... I hadn't appreciated that it's practically on the doorstop of her aunt's condo."

"Ahhh shit," Hardy says, scrunching up his eyes.

"Yeah, shit," Angel says. "She isn't happy about it. She was ranting and raving at one of the workmen there today."

"Little bird, loves the beach and the sea," Nate mutters.

Angel nods.

"Does she know it's ours?" Axel asks, his face deadly serious.

"No. Not yet."

"Only a matter of time," I say.

Angel is right, this isn't good. Just when we thought things were going our way, that we'd fixed things with Bea, that she might even be considering joining our pack. Now this. This could destroy everything. She'd never forgive us if she found out we were the dudes ripping up her piece of paradise.

"What are we going to do then?" Hardy asks the brothers.

We may not have a head of pack any more, but the two corporations have always been theirs. Axel is the CEO of Rock Developments. Angel, the head of Pack Estates.

It was their dad that taught them how to be the businessmen they are today. Their knowledge, their skills, their success that has brought us to where we are now. Floating out here on a multi-million dollar yacht.

I examine their faces. This development will take us to the next level. Our names will be known countrywide, fuck it worldwide. Everyone will want to do business with us. Doors will open. Opportunities will multiply.

It could make us billionaires.

This is our future.

But do we have a future without Bea?

I don't think we do.

Axel is quiet for a moment, then he says simply, "We'll cancel the development."

I stare at him, relief flooding my body. I glance to Angel who nods in agreement.

"He's right," Nate agrees, "our little bird doesn't want it, we won't do it."

"We can't just make that decision off the cuff," I say cautiously. "We'll have to discuss it with the boards and–"

"Fuck the boards," Nate snaps.

"Yeah," Axel agrees, "fuck the boards."

"You're serious?" I ask. Axel is a well-oiled businessman. Sure, he's had his fun over the years but most things he does, he does with calculation and consideration. 'Fuck the boards' is not something I'd ever thought I'd hear him say.

"You know me well enough by now to know that I am."

"If the development will make Bea unhappy," Angel says, "then we're canceling it."

"It will cost both businesses money," I remind them, "a lot of money."

"Doesn't matter," Angel says, stroking his hands through his beard.

The door to the cabin opens and we watch Silver emerge alone. His hair's all ruffled out of its usually neat arrangement and his shirt is creased too but the look on his face is one of a man who died and went to heaven.

"She's asleep," he tells us as he pads barefoot to join us. "But still fucking needy."

"Shit." Hardy whistles with a grin.

I shake that thought from my mind, focusing back in on the important matter we were discussing.

"We're killing the North Beach development," I tell Silver. "It's what Bea wants."

"Why would Bea want that?" Silver says confused, before the cogs turn in his head and it all makes sense. "The beach."

"Yeah," Axel says, "the beach."

"She wants the beach to stay as it is," Silver says and we all nod. "Does she know?"

"What do you think?" Hardy says.

"She won't want us to develop it, and that's fine. We'll sell it. We're not going to be responsible for making her unhappy ever again," Angel says.

"If we sell it," I say, "then there'll just be some other fucker who comes along and develops the land. Everybody has been trying to buy up that land for decades."

"They should never have given us permission to develop it in the first place," Nate says. "Did you know that turtles lay their eggs on that part of the beach? And it's a home to a rare kind of crab too?"

I assume Bea's been chewing his ear off. We really should have seen this coming.

Axel rubs his hand over his chin. Angel peers down at the ground.

The combined land our packs own down there by North Beach cost us millions. As did all the lawyers, architects and planners we've contracted over the years. Not to mention the team down there now doing preliminary works.

I glance towards the cabin, to where our omega is tucked up, safe and sound. The most valuable thing in the world.

I don't care about the money.

I'd sell my only pair of shoes and my last meal, if it meant I got to keep this girl. If it meant I got to make her ours.

Fuck, I think I'd do about anything for her.

"Then we won't sell it," I say.

Axel sucks in a breath, and Angel shuffles on his seat.

"And ... and lose all that money?" Silver says.

I go to answer him but Axel beats me to it. I hold my

breath, hoping against hope, he doesn't screw this all up for us.

"The money doesn't matter to us. Bea is the only thing that does."

I suppress the need to let out a second-long sigh of relief.

But there's still Angel. I look at him and he nods.

"Only thing that matters is this pack and I'm hoping that will include Bea soon. The land is all hers and she can do with it whatever she likes."

A LITTLE LATER, the wind changes direction and Angel decides it is safer if we head for shore.

"How about the omega?" I ask, eyes once again darting to the cabin door.

"Go check up on her," Axel says, squeezing my shoulder, "and take Nate with you. His calmness is creeping the hell out of me."

"Me too," I say as I motion to our packmate.

As the others work to turn the boat around, Nate and I tiptoe down into the cabin, being as quiet as it's possible for two men over six feet tall to be.

As I open the bedroom door, the smell hits me first. Sex. It smells of sex. Of her scent and Silver's. Of slick and come.

"Connor?" she says, in the fading afternoon's light, the cabin windows high above her head. "Nate?"

"Hey sweetheart, just coming to check how you're doing."

She's tangled in a sheet, her white summer dress discarded on the floor and her long caramel hair a tangle about her head.

"I was dozing," she murmurs, stretching her arms above

her head and arching her back, the sheet falling away so I'm rewarded with a flash of her beautiful tits.

Nate groans low beside me. I hold out my hand, signaling for him to wait.

"How are you feeling? Are you sore at all?"

She crooks her finger, beckoning us into the bed. Nate dives straight in, head fucking first, the omega squealing as she's sent bouncing on the mattress. I toe off my shoes and climb in with them.

"It was good," she says, as Nate showers her with kisses. "So good I want to do it again."

Nate freezes mid-kiss, then draws his head up slowly giving our girl a dark possessive look.

I close my eyes and count to ten slowly in my head, begging Nate to do the same through our bond. I have to keep reminding myself that she's a freshly presented omega. This is all new to her and her body is adapting, adapting to taking an alpha's knot. "You're not too sore?"

She doesn't answer. Instead, she crawls towards me, my heart pounding as she draws nearer, pushing me down onto my back and straddling my groin. The sheet's fallen away completely now and I can't help but let my eyes swim all over her naked body. Honey colored, smooth, curved lines fucking everywhere.

Nate flicks at his lip ring with his tongue, eyes darkening even more as he soaks her up.

"I'm assuming I don't have much say in this, Omega," I croak.

"You don't want to fuck me, Alpha?" she asks with a genuine pout that has me rolling up to suck that bottom lip of hers between mine. Then I'm flipping us over, pressing my weight down onto her so she can't squirm away.

"What do you think, Omega?"

She whimpers and I flip her over onto her stomach, dragging her up onto her hands and knees.

Her thighs are sticky with slick and Silver's come and all my alpha instincts thrum to life. I want to pump her full of my seed. Add mine to his.

She wriggles her rump impatiently and I yank off my shirt and pants as Nate watches us both.

The boat rocks beneath us, causing her tits to sway and I pull her up into my arms so she's kneeling, cradled in my arms. I kiss her neck as I squeeze those tits and she wriggles that ass even more, right against my erection.

Sweet little thing wants this so much. Silver was right about her being needy and I can't imagine what she's going to be like in heat. She'll have us working our asses off.

"It's going to be fucking amazing," Nate says, reading my thoughts with a grin.

Copying the omega's earlier movements, he crawls slowly towards us on the bed, his eyes full of menace and the omega whimpers, rubbing her ass up and down my length.

When he reaches us, Nate draws up on his knees too and, wrapping his hand around her throat, leans down to kiss her, his other hand stroking down her body and nudging her thighs open. She obeys automatically, and he begins to circle her clit, making her moan into his mouth. He kisses her harder like he can taste those syllables, like they're fucking delicious.

Then he breaks away.

"Fuck her, Connor, what the hell are you waiting for?"

"Yes," she mutters before he consumes her lips again, and I take a grip of her hips, lifting her up and then down onto my waiting cock.

I groan as she slides down my length, her pussy swallowing all of me.

"How does she feel?" Nate asks, a desperation in his tone.

"The best," I say because they're the only words I have. I'm too overtaken, too overwhelmed by the feel of her taking more and more of my cock.

"Gonna bounce for him, little bird? Gonna flutter up and down on his cock, like a good girl?"

I grip her waist harder, my fingers sinking into her soft flesh, and I help her to lift up on her knees again and then slam down on me, the both of us crying out as she lands on my lap.

"Fuck," I mutter, "fuck, Nate, she's ... Bea, you're so ..."

"Need you naked too," she says to Nate, all breathless.

The only person who can usually get Nate to do anything is Axel. He's never been one for following instructions or obeying orders. However, I'm getting the impression that Nate is happy to be at this woman's beck and call night and day because the words have only just left her mouth and he's stripped off his clothes, kneeling in front of her, with his cock stiff.

Her eyes light on the titanium ring pierced through his cock-head and she explores it with her fingertips as I continue to bounce her on my cock and Nate returns his attention to her clit.

Nate groans a little and with his free hand, guides her to take him in her fist.

"I don't want to hurt you," she pants, eyes still drawn to the ring.

"Little bird, it's not going to hurt me. It makes it feel even better." He bites at her neck. "It's going to make you feel even better too."

"Oh," she murmurs, head falling back onto my shoulder.

I catch Nate's eye.

"Let's make her come," he says, winking, and the two of us work together, me moving her up and down my cock, he flicking at her clit, the two of us pawing at her, sucking, and kissing, squeezing and tweaking, giving her no rest, no pause, stimulating every part of her beautiful body.

She turns wild, feral. Pumping at Nate's cock with one hand and reaching around her to grab at my hair with the other.

Delicious, unhindered noises come flying from her mouth and her skin turns scorching hot.

"Come on, Baby," I whisper into her ear, thrusting my tongue into her hole and making her gasp. "Come for us, come for us like a good girl. Come on my cock and come on his fingers."

She's so wet and when I'm done fucking and knotting her, I'm going to lick up every molecule of slick between her thighs.

"You can wait your turn," Nate growls.

"We can do it together," I tell him.

"Do what?" Bea gasps, "do what?"

"Eat you out, little phoenix. We're going to feast on you together."

His dirty words send her crashing over the edge. Her body stills, goes limp on a long-drawn-out sigh of pleasure, and then she convulses with the aftershocks, her pussy sucking and clenching around my cock. We don't give her any rest. I bounce her on my cock right through her orgasm and Nate's fingers never stop, and together we force another release crashing through her right on the tail of the previous. This time her pussy squeezes me so tight, it forces my own orgasm. I groan as the ecstasy explodes through my body, every part of me singing with pleasure.

Nate groans too, his eyes drifting shut as he spills all over her hands and her thighs. I feel his own pleasure reflected in our bond.

"Shit," I say, "shit."

"Knot me," Bea cries out, "knot me please, Alpha."

All so new to her and yet she already needs it, knows how good it will be.

"As if I could ever deny you anything, Beautiful," I whisper, my body still pulsating with pleasure as my knot expands and stretches her pussy wide open.

She winces and we both coo over her, stroking and kissing her skin until that pain subsides and another powerful orgasm rockets through her.

This time it's my knot her pussy grips and my head falls backwards as I moan with pleasure, my cock releasing more ribbons of seed inside her.

Nate grins, resting his hand on her belly.

"We're going to fill you so full of come, little bird, your belly will bulge with it."

Her eyes drift open and she gazes up into Nate's.

"Okay," she says. "That sounds fun."

"It does?" Nate asks, the side of his mouth lifting with a half smile.

"Uh huh," Bea says, her fingertips trailing down Nate's body.

Nate's eyes flick up to mine and I know it's time to move over.

27

Nate

COME dribbles down the golden thigh of my little bird. I scoop it up with my fingers and thrust it back up inside her.

Inside she's warm and soft. Like Heaven.

Her walls quiver around my fingers and her eyes roll around.

"Don't waste it, little bird."

She shakes her head, amber eyes dark and focused on me, waiting to see what I'll do next. I don't even know myself. There're so many ways I want to play with her, to make her fall apart.

I swivel my fingers around inside her until I find that spot that has her crying out.

I grin. That's where I'm aiming for.

"Right here, little bird." Her hips rise off the bed, begging for more, her tits thrusting into the air.

"Fuck," Connor mumbles beside me.

My little bird is a work of art.

I'm going to take pictures of her and hang them on every wall I own.

I'm shredding the fucking *Mona Lisa* and hanging her up in place.

I wink at my packmate.

I'm going to find all the special places on our little bird, all the spots and buttons. I'm going to fucking mesmerize each one. I'm going to draw a fucking map.

Maybe I'll hang that up too.

I stroke at the spot, making her writhe on the bed, making slick gush around my wrist.

Then I take a hold of her hips and I drag her across the mattress.

For a moment I just stare down at her pussy. Pink and plump. Wet and lush.

Then I flip her onto her belly.

She's lying out prone for me and I know this way I'm going to hit that spot.

Fucking bull's eye.

"Such an ass," I say, palming at it, while she wriggles eagerly, impatient for my cock.

I take a hold of those hips of hers a second time, and tilt them upwards, then I lower myself down onto her, listening as her breath hitches.

Connor's lying on his side, eyes wide, soaking in the spectacle.

It's been an age since we shared a woman like this. It's a million times better than I remember. Probably was never as good as this in the first place.

I nuzzle at her ear, rubbing my cock through her wet folds and making her even more frantic for me.

"Going to sing for me again, little bird?"

"Yes," she murmurs, rubbing her ass against me.

"Going to come around my cock and let me fill you up?"

She moans and I take that as an enthusiastic yes.

I gather the locks of her hair in my hand, twist it around my fist and jerk back her head, then I thrust into her, thrust deep into that all-consuming darkness. Darkness that will swallow me whole, drown me completely.

Except it doesn't.

As I slam down into her, it's not darkness that consumes me.

It's light.

Bright dazzling endless light.

And caramel, sweet fucking caramel.

I lick my lips, I lick her neck and her wet cheeks.

I hold her hips raised and her head forced back and I find that spot inside my little bird.

She cries out, her body limp one moment, taut the next.

Can't decide what she wants. What she feels. It's too damn much for her.

Bulls fucking eye.

"Right there," I gasp, ringing my tongue around her earhole, scraping the metal of my lip ring down her throat.

"There!" she pants. "There."

Fuck yeah.

I don't go easy on her.

I fucking should.

She's a new omega. Newly broken in.

But I'm not like Axel. I'm not like Silver or Connor.

I've always been half deranged. Trying to catch this little bird, grab her in my big bad paws, has driven me to the fucking brink.

Goodbye reason and self-control. I didn't have much of it to start with in the first place.

Yeah, fuck all that.

I pound my little bird hard into the mattress.

I rut her with the whole of my body.

I thrust into her with every ounce of strength I possess.

I fuck her with everything I have to give.

All of me.

My little bird can have all of it.

I rock back. Watch where she's swallowing up my cock. Watch sweat glide down her tanned back. Watch the cheeks of her ass wobble.

"So fucking goooood," I moan.

Connor hums his agreement.

"Oh God," she mutters. "Oh God, Oh God."

Her cunt pulses around me.

Wanting me so very much.

I close my eyes.

I concentrate on her.

Just her. Her. Her. Her.

So tight, so soft, so wild.

She squirms beneath me. She's so close, so fucking close.

"Nate!" she cries out, coming on my cock, coming spread out beneath me, coming for me like a good little omega ought to.

More of that white light envelopes me as her pussy sucks on me hard. Sucks and ripples and convulses.

Pleasure shoots from deep in my gut. Streaks through my body like a fucking shooting star.

I tip back my head and howl.

As I fill my little bird up with more seed, I howl.

Then I knot the little thing.

Knot her hard and good.

Knot her so she can't leave me.

Knot so she'll be close.

Here with me. My heart pressed against her warm skin.

The light dazzles around the periphery of my vision.

Fuck, it's never been like this.

I've never wanted anything so badly in my life.

But I want her.

For me. For us. For this pack.

Hope little bird wants it too.

28

Bea

I CAN'T BELIEVE my hormones are all over the place like this. I'd hoped after my first heat everything might calm down. But it seems the opposite is true.

One minute I'm perfectly fine. The next I'm begging six alphas to fuck me. Not that I'm complaining because, well, gee whizz, and oh my lord, I think the last few hours of my life may have been my best on this planet. Courtney warned me the sex would be hot, but I still didn't quite comprehend how hot. We're talking smoldering. We're talking volcanic. We're talking solar.

I think it may take me a week to recover. Which is fine because all those horny hormones have subsided now and all I want to do is snuggle with these two alphas in this giant floating bed.

I'm no longer knotted to Nate, but that doesn't mean I'm

letting them go. Anytime either one of them attempts to shift or move or creep towards the edge of the bed, an involuntary growl plays out in my throat and I pull them to me all the harder.

"It's okay," Nate says after this has happened a sixth time. "We're not going anywhere."

"Good," I murmur, my head resting on Connor's chest, Nate's body curled around mine. "It's so snuggly here. I never want to leave."

Connor hums his agreement.

"I didn't think it could be like this, you know?" I murmur.

"Like what, little bird?"

"A threesome."

Nate chuckles. "What exactly did you expect a threesome to be like?"

"Awkward, logistically difficult, uncomfortable." I close my eyes in bliss. "It's not, it's snuggly."

"Sometimes it is awkward or difficult," Connor says, stroking my cheek, "but with the right people it's always electrifying."

"It's never been that electrifying for me," Nate says.

I twist my head to look over my shoulder at him and determine if he's being earnest. He holds my gaze and for once those eyes aren't smoldering, they aren't dirty, they aren't puppy dog either. They're just his, staring back at me. Open, raw.

"Really?" I whisper.

"You're our omega, little bird. This was always going to be fucking mind-blowing with you."

"Are you going to be?" Connor asks me softly. "Are you going to be our omega, Bea?"

"Well," I say, smiling at Nate and then Connor, "that really does depend."

"On what?"

"The nest."

I haven't stopped thinking about it ever since they told me they'd built one. It must be another of those strange omega instincts because I've never felt so emotional or obsessive about home furnishings before, even when I was decorating my little house with Karl. I chose the colors, I painted the walls. Job done. Never thought about it again.

But this nest ... this nest has been on my mind constantly. Something deep in my chest wants to see it so badly. If I'm honest, wants me to claim it as mine.

"You wanna see your nest, little bird," Nate tells me, "we're going to take you right there."

It's late by the time we arrive at the Stormgate house, the sky dark, the air cooler and a distant owl hooting in the trees. The house lies in darkness too and I peer at Axel as he parks up the van.

"I don't want to disturb your mom and your sister–"

"It's our home now and they are expecting us to bring our omega here. If they didn't want us to, they wouldn't have let us build our pack nest. Besides, do you know how much my mom and sister like you? They haven't stopped talking about you. They keep asking me when you're coming round again."

"Oh," I say, pressing my cool palms to my hot cheeks.

"But if you don't want to go in, if you don't want to do this yet ..." Silver says.

"Oh God," I say, screwing up my eyes. "I'm scared."

"Of what, baby girl?" Hardy asks, purring softly for me.

"Of falling in love with a freaking nest and never wanting to leave it."

Hardy cocks his head like he has no idea if I'm serious or not. Then something occurs to him.

"You ever been in a nest before, baby girl?"

"No, I've never even seen one. But, oh shit, I haven't been able to stop dreaming about one ever since, well, you know, things changed."

Angel shakes his head in irritation. "I want to kick myself hard in the ass. Why the hell did none of us think of this? Why did it take Molly for us to even consider a nest?"

I blink at him, unable to understand his frustration. He takes my hand in his.

"Bea, if I'm honest, we've all been nursing wet dreams about ... erm ..." he smiles sheepishly, "having some fun with you in some soft nest, but had we ever thought to build you one?"

"Shit, we should have done this sooner, baby girl," Hardy says looking suitably ashamed. "I'm so fucking sorry."

"You didn't have to–"

"Build you a nest? Yes, yes we did," Connor says, kissing my forehead. "Come on, you need to see it."

"And I promise," Axel says, "as good as it is, you will be able to leave. I know these hormones are a mind-fuck but they're not a pair of handcuffs."

"Okay," I say, taking a steadying breath. "Okay, I'd like to see it."

The six alphas help me out of the car and gather around me like eager school boys, fussing and mollycoddling me as we walk through the house and up to the third floor.

"What if she doesn't like it?" I hear Nate whisper anxiously behind me.

"We tear it down and start from scratch," Axel tells him.

I giggle. "I'm sure I'm going to love it."

But Nate fiddles anxiously with his lip ring. I've never seen him nervous before.

Angel stops in front of a door at the far end of the hallway. The door handle is made from brass and shaped like a bee. I know I'm already going to love this room.

"Ready?" he asks me.

"Ready."

He reaches up and types in a code onto a pad by the side of the door.

"The handle's just for show," he explains. "The only way in and out of the nest is by keying in the code and only members of this pack have that code."

"It's extra security to keep you safe," Axel adds, "especially during a heat."

I nod, thankful for it.

"What's the code?"

Axel peers down at his shoes and rubs his chin. "The date we first met. 062722."

Angel hits the last number, a lock clicks and the door draws open.

Angel pushes it back, holding it open for me to enter.

I take a deep breath and step through.

Immediately all my omega senses buzz. It smells of this pack, of every one of these alphas, their scents combining to create an irresistible concoction.

I take a deep inhale, the aromas rushing down my throat and making my knees shake in that way they always seem to do when these men are nearby.

Then I take a good look around.

We're up in the roof and several large skylights spread across the ceiling. Each has a dark blind but these are drawn back, revealing the night sky above us, filled with twinkling stars.

The room is dark too, except for fairy lights strung around the walls and over the canopy of the giant bed that occupies one half of the room. It's built for more than one person; in fact, I'm sure it can fit seven easily and over its surface are scattered soft cushions and blankets of every size, shape and material.

In another corner hang several cozy-looking swing chairs, a bookcase and a small refrigerator, and opposite dangles another kind of contraption I'm pretty certain might be a sex swing. There's also a beautifully painted cabinet sitting beside its side that I intend to explore.

Positioned on the floor are more cushions, bean bags and several plants, the speakers from a built-in sound system are pinned into the corners, and one giant oversized teddy bear with a pink bow around its neck sits guard at the end of the bed.

I step into the room, touching and feeling all the soft materials, rubbing fur and velvet, silk and cotton between my fingers and against my cheek.

"What do you think?" Axel asks me gently and I turn to find the pack hovering behind me.

"It's beautiful," I choke out, tears swimming in my eyes.

Any omega would love this nest, it's like a dream. But this hasn't been designed with any old omega in mind. This has been designed for me, because everywhere I look there are little bees. On the sheets and the cushions, on the material covering the chairs, even on the mysterious cabinet.

It's my nest. Bea Carsen's. It's been designed for me.

"Look up," Hardy says and I do, finding the ceiling

painted with a meadow of wild flowers, bees of every size darting from petal to petal.

"Did you do that?"

He nods and a sob breaks free of my throat.

"She doesn't like it," Nate says tightly, his fingers twitching by his sides.

"No, I do. I love it." I bury my face in my hands. "I really love it."

"You haven't seen all of it yet," Silver says, taking me by the elbow and leading me to a door on the far side of the room. He pushes it and beyond lies a bathroom decked out in jewel-colored tiles.

"An en suite," I say, more tears tumbling from my eyes. "I've never had an en suite before." Inside there's a giant claw-footed bath, a walk-in shower large enough for a whole pack and a dressing table with a sink and gold taps. There's even the posh, odorless soap from the omega event I attended.

"Wow!" I say. "You said I'd be able to leave, but why would I ever want to?"

"You certainly have everything you'll ever need," Silver says, leading me back through into the main nest. "Food," he points to the refrigerator, "drinks," he points to a sophisticated machine, "clothes," he points to a wardrobe that Connor opens, revealing shelves of cashmere jumpers and cotton yoga pants. "Music," he picks up the remote that controls the sound system.

"Sex toys," Nate says, snapping open the cabinet and picking out a dildo the size of his arms.

My eyes widen and Hardy snatches it from him with an irritated look.

"There's even this," Angel says, attempting to distract me from the sex toy cabinet. He presses a panel in the wall and another cupboard is revealed this time with several men's sweaters and shirts hanging inside.

"What are those?" I ask.

"Our clothes," Angel explains. "If we're not here and you're in need of our scent."

"If there are any changes you want to make–" Connor starts, then halts as I stride towards the giant bed and perch down on the edge.

"Hmmm," I say.

Hardy bounces down beside me. "We spent a lot of time choosing this mattress. Soft but firm."

Nate bounces down on my other side.

"Perfect for fucking."

I give a little bounce of my own. "I guess we'll have to test it to find out."

"Little bird," Nate warns, but Hardy's already tossing me backwards onto the bed.

I squirm against the mattress, wriggling this way and that. Not a sharp spring or a saggy patch in sight.

"Amazing," I sigh, closing my eyes.

"Is there anything you'd like to change?" Axel asks, as I stare up into the canopy above the bed strung with more lights and a light gauze material.

"No, nothing, this is perfection," I sigh, meaning every word, my little omega heart content beyond belief.

Axel comes to sit on the bed, and Angel, and Connor do too, Silver leaning against one of the posts with his arms crossed casually across his body.

There's a serious tone to the air, and I scoot up onto my elbows to peer at them all.

I'm guessing they're hoping for a decision. They want to know if I'm willing to join this pack.

I could put them out of their misery but I decide I want to hear what they have to say first.

As usual, it's Axel who speaks first. He clears his throat and meets my eye, his face earnest.

"I'm sorry, Bea. Truly sorry for fucking things up between us so badly. For hurting you, for leaving you open to danger. I'm going to regret my decisions every day of my life and I only hope you can forgive me. I know it's a lot to ask, but if you will, I'll make sure I and every member of this pack spends every day making you happy. Fuck, I'd build you ten million nests if it makes you as happy as you looked when you first walked in."

I smile at him but before I can answer his brother speaks next.

"I'm sorry too, Bea. For being an asshole and a jerk. For not putting your feelings first. For worrying too much about my pride and not enough about the people around me. And," he says, glancing over to his brother, "whatever happens here, whatever you choose, I'll always be grateful that through meeting you, we've repaired this pack. That we've mended what was broken between us. I'll be grateful for that even if you choosing not to be with us rips the very heart out of my chest."

I roll my eyes at his hyperbole but he shakes his head.

"I'm not being fucking dramatic here, sweetheart. It's the truth. You're our omega, our mate–"

"Our fated mate," Hardy adds. "You know what that means, baby girl?"

I hesitate then shake my head. I've heard the term, of course I have, but I've never bothered to give it much thought before.

"It's fairytales," Silver mutters.

Hardy's jaw tightens as he stares at me. "It's not. It exists.

I know because I feel it here." He thumps his chest. "Bea was meant for us, and we were meant for her. It's fate. You can go against it if you want – there's always free will – you can choose not to be with this pack. But it'll hurt. It will gut us."

"No more than we fucking deserve," Connor adds.

"I don't want to hurt any of you," I say, rolling up to sit cross-legged on the bed. "I definitely don't want to gut you." I pull a face.

"But can you forgive us?" Silver asks quietly.

I stare up at him and then at the two brothers that caused all this pain and hurt, not only for me but for their packmates and their family too.

I think of all the other heartache I've carried, too. From Karl. From Serena.

Hardy's right; tearing myself away from these men, denying myself this pack will be a million, trillion times more painful than anything Karl or Serena did to me.

Because deep down I know they are good men. Kind, loving, protective. They've made their bad decisions and they've owned up to them. They've tried to make amends. Karl wouldn't know what amend meant if it slapped him round the face with a dead fish.

"Life appears to me too short to be spent in nursing animosity or registering wrongs," I say, peering at Connor. "You have my full and free forgiveness."

"*Jane Eyre*," he says and I nod.

"If Jane could forgive her Rochester, then I can forgive you."

For a moment, they simply stare at me as if they can't believe their own ears. Then Angel says, "Perhaps you had better hold off giving us your forgiveness just yet, little one."

"Oh?" I say, the blood in my veins running cold. I can

sense a confession coming and an unease overtakes me. Is there a mad wife lurking in this attic?

"There is something else we have to come clean about." My body stiffens in preparation for the next blow. I hope it won't be enough to destroy me completely, not when I've just handed them my heart. "The development on the beach. It's ours. We are behind it." I gasp, my hands flying to my mouth.

"You can't ... you mustn't–"

Angel lifts up his hand. "We've already decided to cancel it. We won't be proceeding."

"What?" I say.

"The development on the beach is not going ahead," Axel confirms.

All six alphas stare at me again, waiting for my reaction.

"You'd do that for me?" I say quietly.

"Yes," they all say, pretty much in unison.

I laugh, tears spilling down my cheeks all over again. I really need to get a grip on these hormones.

"We're going to sign the land over to you, Bea. It's going to be yours, to do with as you wish."

"Mine?" They nod. "I won't want to do anything with it – well maybe clean the beach up some more – but other than that I'd want to leave it exactly as it is."

"Entirely your decision."

"Won't it cost you money? Lots of money?" Axel and Angel both shrug like money is of no concern to them. "And your business reputations?"

"The only person we're interested in making a good impression on is you, sweetheart."

"You're doing a good job," I laugh, "a very good job," I add, glancing around at my heavenly nest. I wonder if they would build me a matching one down by the beach.

"About time we did," Silver says.

"And you ... you really want me for this pack?"

"Omega," Axel says, "we've faced bullets for you. We're gifting you land worth millions. I hear Hardy even got his eyes fucking tested for you and Nate gave you his knife. Is there any doubt how much we want you?"

I laugh harder, the tears running over my chin and splashing onto my dress.

"So what do you say?" Hardy asks from behind me. "We want you, baby girl, but do you want us?"

"Boom," I splutter through the tears.

"What does that mean, sweetheart?" Axel asks softly.

"It means yes, asshole," Nate says, lunging for me. "It means yes!"

"Does it?" Hardy asks, the rest of the pack, looking unsure.

"It does," I say, giggling, as Nate showers me with wet kisses. "It means, yes, please. Let's give this a try."

29

xel

IT TAKES me a moment to catch my breath. To catch my breath and realize my fucking eyes are wet and my freaking cheeks too.

I blink the tears away, staring transfixed at the girl none of us assholes deserve, but who has, somehow, chosen us.

I never cry. Not after the accident when they told me my football days were over. Not when dad died. Not even when the doctors said there was nothing more they could do for mom.

All those three things broke me in half and smashed a hammer through my life. But they didn't make me cry.

But this? This news. The best possible news. This makes me cry.

I swipe at my eyes, watching as she's sandwiched between Hardy and Nate in a crazy love-in.

I glance over at my little brother and he looks up at me too, a wide smile on his face. He has the best fucking smile in the world. Better even than our omega's. I spent most of my childhood trying to make him smile like that, trying to make him laugh.

I'm going to spend the rest of my adult days trying to make all of them smile like that.

No more asshole behavior. My priorities are with this pack now, this pack and my family.

I grab Nate by the scruff of the collar and drag him off the omega, leaning down to kiss her cheek.

"Thank you," I whisper to her, "thank you."

She wraps her arms around my neck and looks me hard in the eye. "Don't let me live to regret it."

"Yes, Ma'am," I say.

"If he does, I'll kill him," Nate says chirpily and I don't doubt it for a minute. We're going to have to keep Nate on a chain, because if anyone so much as looks at our omega the wrong way he's going to garrote them.

"I'll do it myself," she grins, "I'm good with a knife, remember?"

"Damn right."

She drags me in closer and I kiss her mouth, kiss those sweet lips of hers, and taste mint on her tongue. Then I pull back.

"Do you mind if I go tell my mom the news?"

A little wrinkle forms between her brows. "I said give it a try, I'm not agreeing to marry you or–"

"I know, sweetheart, but we're dating, right? You're dating this pack?" She nods her head eagerly. "Then let me go tell her that. She'll be pleased. I think she's shaping up to like you more than me!"

"She's met me once!"

I laugh, but I'm only half joking. My mom views the repair of our family as some kind of miracle, one Bea alone is responsible for. She'll probably be nominating the omega for sainthood.

I climb off the bed, making room for Silver, and walk to the door. There I pause and glance back to the massive group hug now taking place in the nest we built. My heart feels so full it might burst.

I don't deserve this. I don't deserve to make these people this happy. But somehow, somehow, despite my fuck ups, they are.

I pad down the stairs to the floor below and stop outside my mom's room. Light slips underneath the door and I suspect she's reading. She's finding it more and more difficult to sleep, the pain keeping her awake.

I tap lightly on the door and as if by magic Molly appears behind me.

"What's going on?" she asks eagerly, bouncing on her toes, and I bet she's been lying in wait for an update.

I raise my eyebrow at her in a way I know will infuriate her.

"Come in," my mom calls out weakly as Molly scowls at me and I turn the door handle and slip inside, Molly following me in.

My mom's dressed in a nightgown and sits up in her bed, a wall of cushions supporting her frame, a magazine open at her lap. She removes her reading glasses and peers up at me and my sister.

"Is anything wrong?"

"No," I say as Molly pinches the seat by my mom's bedside, curling her feet up under her, and I'm left standing. "Just thought you might want to hear how the date with Bea went today."

"Well, duh!" Molly says, rolling her eyes at me.

I really do not envy the pack that ends up with my sister.

My mom ignores her, folding closed her magazine. "I thought I heard Bea's voice earlier."

I nod unable to help a wide grin from spreading across my lips.

"She wanted to see the nest."

Molly claps her hands together and squeaks. "Did she love it? She did, didn't she? She must have, it's a work of genius. If my pack design me a nest half as good as that one–"

"Molly," my mom says, "let the man speak."

"Sorry," she says.

"She loves it," I say. I squeeze my sister's shoulder. "Thank you, Molly, for all your help with it."

"I didn't do much, it was all you guys really."

"So she likes the nest." My mom inspects the inane smile still pinned to my face. "And ..."

"She wants to give things a try ... with us ... with the pack ... with me."

"Of course, she does," my mom says. "That girl's crazy about the lot of you."

"She's definitely crazy," Molly mutters and I pinch her arm. "Hey, is that anyway to treat the future aunt of your children?"

"Woah, I said 'willing to give things a try'. No babies. No bonding. No wedding bells."

"Yet," Molly says. "Yet."

I can't help smiling even wider, my cheeks straining, because who am I kidding, that's where I'm hoping this is all headed. I want her for our pack. I want her as our bonded mate. I want to make our pack a family. Babies and puppies and all that shit too.

"I'm happy for you," my mom says, reaching out to take my hands in hers. "Happy for you, Angel and the others. I always knew you needed the right omega to bring you all together." She squeezes my hands and turns to my sister. "Now if we can just find a good pack for your sister ..."

My sister sticks out her tongue. "Who says I'm looking for good men, Mom?"

"Me," I say, "I am."

"She's incorrigible. Do you know what your sister arranged for her last heat?" my mom says with a frown.

I snatch my hands from hers and cover my ears. "No, no I don't and I do not want to know, thank you."

My mom harrumphs. "You can't be squeamish about these things, Axel, not when you're going to have an omega to look after. Especially one who's so inexperienced and won't know for a while what she needs and what she wants."

"Eww, I don't want to hear about that either." Molly mimes gagging.

I glance up to the ceiling, then back down to my sister and my mom. "Actually, that is something I could use your advice about."

"Yes?"

"Bea's hormones are still all over the show. She only had her heat a week or so ago, yet today, for a minute, we thought she was going into heat again. It doesn't seem right."

"My hormones were a mess for the first couple of months after presenting," Molly says. "I was up and down like a yoyo."

"True," my mom says, "but it would probably be best to get her checked out by the doctor."

I frown. "I'm not sure I'll be able to convince her to see another doctor again in her lifetime."

"She's going to have to for her blocker and suppressant prescription," Molly points out.

"Why don't you take her to see Dr. Clive?"

"Dr. Clive?" I say with a groan. The man must be in his eighties by now. He's been our family doctor since we were kids.

"He may not be a specialist but he can write out a prescription for Bea and check she's okay. Plus, more importantly, you can trust him."

"Yeah, maybe that's not such a bad idea." Dr. Clive went above and beyond to find my mom a diagnosis and then some kind of treatment. He was about the only doctor who actually seemed to care about doing so.

"Of course, it's not a bad idea," my mom says. "Call him tomorrow."

WHEN I CLIMB the stairs later and return to our nest, I expect to find the giant love-in has turned explicit. Instead, I find my pack curled up together on the bed, most of them still fully clothed, all of them sound asleep.

I walk to the edge of the bed and stare down at them my hands deep in my pockets. Bea's wedged between Hardy and Connor, Nate curled up by her feet. Angel's lying out by her head and Silver's asleep with his head resting on one of Hardy's giant thighs.

They all look content, and I think that makes this old heart of mine swell even more than the earlier happiness.

I could get used to this.

I unbuckle my belt and tug off my pants, then I climb into the bed, lying out beside my brother. He stirs as the mattress shifts and blinks open his eyes, turning his head to peer at me though the darkness.

"Mom okay?" he asks.

"Pretty thrilled."

"Yeah, thought she would be." He stares up at the stars framed in the sky lights. "She seems really taken with Bea. She never liked Celia, remember? She never said anything, but I could tell she didn't. I guess it should have been a sign."

I examine his face. There's the faintest of lines on his skin now. Lines that weren't there ten years ago. Ten years. It's a hell of a lot of time to lose. I'm never going to be that dumb again.

"Did you love her?" I ask.

I always assumed he did. That's why he was so angry with me. That's why it never occurred to him that she'd made the move on me.

"I thought I did. But now with Bea, I know I was wrong. This is love, right? This tug in my chest. This need to be with her. This need to make her happy. It's not just a sex thing, an attraction thing, although, fuck, she has me hard just thinking about her, but it's more than all that. Much more."

"Yeah," I say, "I never felt this way about anyone else before. I hope we can make this work."

We're quiet and after a while I hear his breath deepen and I know he's asleep. I roll onto my side, peering at my packmates a little longer and then sleep claims me too.

I WAKE the next morning to sunlight pouring in through the open blinds and the sound of someone tapping away on their phone. I lift my head and find the bed empty except for Bea curled up with her device.

"Hey sleepy head," she says with a smile that has my insides warming.

I rub at my face and yawn. "What time is it?"

"Nearly nine."

"Shit, really," I say, scooting up the mattress and coming to sit beside her. "I don't think I've slept past seven in years."

"You looked so peaceful, we didn't want to wake you."

"Where are the others?"

"Erm, making me pancakes apparently. Nate is giving them all a cookery lesson, although I'm hoping Molly might be in there too, helping."

I hook my arm around her and pull her in close, taking a large inhale of her sweet scent. Waking up to that every morning is going to be divine.

"What you doing?" I ask her.

"Checking my emails."

"Right."

"I got one from the ecological association."

"And?"

"I haven't opened it yet."

"Why not?"

She nibbles on her lip. "Nervous."

"You want me to open it for you?"

She takes a steadying inhale, bracing her shoulders. "Nope. I'm going to do it. Here goes..." She screws up her eyes and presses down hard with her thumb.

"Are you going to look at the message?"

She peeks open one eye. "Yes?" She glances down at the phone quickly. Then looks again, this time opening both eyes and reading the entire thing, as she does her face lights up and it makes me want to kiss her so badly.

"I got it!" she says in wonderment. Shaking her phone and looking up at me. "I got the interview!"

"Of course you did, sweetheart. You're perfect for it and I bet Mrs. Finch gave you a glowing reference. She keeps saying you're the best worker we've had."

Bea grins at me. "I can't believe it. I can't believe I have an interview for a job I actually want to do. I can't believe things are working out this way and–" She frowns.

"What?"

"My frigging hormones," she mutters.

"What about them?"

"You saw what happened yesterday. They're all over the place. How am I meant to give a half-decent interview when any minute I might be calling you up on the phone and begging for a knot?"

That idea has my cock jerking in my boxers, but I swallow back the rampant desire, and focus on her concerns.

"I may have a solution for you. I'm going to take you to the doctor and get you sorted."

Her face pales before my eyes. "I'm not sure I want to do that."

"He's our family doctor. He's been our family doctor since before I was born. In fact, I'm pretty sure he delivered me, Angel and Molly. We trust him and besides I'm going with you and we'll take Silver with us. Maybe Nate too."

She nibbles on her lip again but something about my confidence seems to reassure her and finally she nods her consent.

"Then come on," I say, "let's get dressed, eat some pancakes and go see the doctor."

"Don't we need to make an appointment?"

I sniff. “You’re Pack Stormgate now, Bea. You’ll never have to make another appointment in your life.”

“I’m not pack yet, remember?”

“We’ll see,” I say with a cocky smirk, pulling her in for a deep kiss that leaves her shivering.

30

Bea

Dr. Clive's office out in the city suburbs is a lot less intimidating than the clinic at the hospital. I can tell he's a family doctor by the cartoon characters he has pinned to the walls and the large collection of kids' toys stacked in the waiting room corner. Still, I'm glad Axel and Silver are with me for this, and I don't complain when both hold my hands, while we wait for the doctor.

"No need to be nervous," Axel reassures me, "Dr. Clive is a big softie."

When he opens the door to his office and calls us inside, I see 'big Softie' is exactly the right description. He's tall and squidgy with a big mop of hair on his head and some sprouting from his ears.

He greets Axel with a genuine smile and shakes his

hand, telling him how pleased he is to hear that he's mended the rift with his brother.

"We should have done it sooner," Axel says.

"And I assume this is the woman responsible?" the doctor says, holding his hand out to me. "Mrs. Stormgate has told me all about you."

"I'm Bea," I tell him, shaking his hand and then taking Silver's again immediately.

"Well, come in," Dr. Clive tells us, "and let's see how I can help you."

I guess the doctor's used to dealing with packs because there are a large number of chairs inside his office. I take the central one, Axel and Silver sitting either side of me, and the doctor perches on the edge of his desk.

I look to Axel.

"Bea's a newly presented omega, and she's having some difficulty regulating her emotions and feelings."

"Newly presented," the doctor says with a sympathetic smile. "How old are you, Bea?"

"Twenty six."

He rests his hands in his lap. "Ahhh, yes, of course, I've heard about you."

Axel frowns, glancing at Silver. "From my mom?"

"Yes, from your mom, but also from the medical community in the city. There's been quite a bit of chatter about you, young lady."

"There has?" I ask, alarm spiking in my gut, my scent peaking and Silver squeezing my hand. "Why?"

"You're a very unusual case and medical professionals are always fascinated by unusual cases. There's been lots of chatter about why you may have presented so late and what finally triggered you."

"He did," I say, turning to face Axel. "It was Axel."

"I triggered you?" he says.

"I think so, yes."

"Who was the doctor who first started the discussion of Bea's case?" Silver asks.

"I don't remember," the doctor says.

"It would be very helpful to us, if you could remember, perhaps you could go back through your messages."

Dr. Clive stares at Silver.

"Are you aware of what happened to Bea?" Axel asks quietly.

"Beyond her unusual presentation," the doctor says slowly, "no."

Axel glances at me and I nod at him. With Melody Grande knowing, I wouldn't be surprised if it's all over social media and in every newspaper anyway.

Axel explains about my abduction with Silver adding in a few details.

A frown forms on Dr. Clive's face that grows deeper and deeper as my story progresses.

When Axel's finally done, the doctor is quiet for a moment, then he says, "I'm very sorry to hear all this, Bea. Very sorry indeed. We take a Hippocratic oath to help people and do no harm. Unfortunately it seems there are always bad apples in this profession."

He stands up and walks to sit behind his desk.

"Any idea what their motive could have been?" Silver asks.

"Well, yes. Money, what else? There's a fortune to be made if someone discovers a drug or a treatment that could turn betas into omegas. Or even betas into alphas. I'm sure you are aware there are already some drugs circulating on the black market, although as far as I know they are pretty worthless. Nothing more than perfume capsules."

"But how am I connected to all that?" I ask.

The doctor straightens the papers on his desk. "Like I said, you're an unusual case. I presume they thought that understanding you might help them with their research. Or it could even be more complicated than that. I've heard talk of a theory that harvesting an omega's hormones while she's in heat might provide a successful treatment. And the hormones of a newly presented omega. A newly presented and older omega would be that much more potent."

Axel growls his disapproval beside me and Silver leans forward on his chair.

"Any idea who could have been behind Bea's abduction?"

"You said one of the doctors is already under arrest."

"Yes, but he was working for someone. Someone with money and muscle power."

"There are several pharmaceutical companies looking into this area of research but I doubt very much that any of them would stoop to such illegal activities."

Axel snorts like he doesn't believe that for a second.

"Anyway," the doctor says, "that's in the past, something I'm sure the young lady wants to forget."

"I do," I say.

"Well, let's get you sorted then." He opens the notepad in front of him and unscrews the lid from his pen. "Let's start with some of the details ..."

I tell him my date of birth, my height and weight and the date I first presented as well as the date of my first heat.

"Your heat came on very rapidly," the doctor says, "there is usually many weeks between presentation and a first heat. No wonder you've felt all in a muddle."

"Dr. Hannah seemed to think it was normal."

"Dr. Hannah who hasn't been seen since your abduction," Silver points out.

"You really think she was involved?" I ask.

"She told you that other doctor was her colleague."

"And we're pretty certain he was the one who broke into your apartment. Along with a woman."

I draw my hands up to my throat, the air in the room suddenly tasting sour. I shake my head; I can't believe she was in on it. I remember how frightened she seemed at that clinic.

"Did this Dr. Hannah have you on any particular medication?" Dr. Clive asks gently.

"Yes," I say, pulling my purse up onto my lap, and diving inside for the packets of pills she gave me. "Scent blockers," I say, passing them over to Dr. Clive, "and suppressants to help regulate my hormones."

Dr. Clive takes the second packet from my hand and examines the box, then opens them up and pops out a pill. He brings it to his nose and sniffs. Then he places them down on his desk and looks up at the three of us.

"I can't be certain. I'd need to send these pills to the lab. But I don't think they are suppressants, in fact I think they are fertility drugs."

My mouth drops open and the air not only turns sour, it turns suffocating. "What?" I choke out.

"These pills are designed for omegas struggling with fertility or who want to become pregnant quickly. They bring on a heat."

"What the fuck!" Axel says, jumping up from his seat and grabbing the pills. He sniffs them himself and coughs, then throws them back on the desk.

"But I'm still taking them," I say in alarm. "I thought they were suppressants."

"Have you been taking them regularly since your heat ended?" the doctor asks.

"Yes!" In fact, I'm pretty sure I took one as soon as I felt vaguely normal.

"How long has that been?"

"Just over two weeks."

The doctor meets my eye. "Then I expect you'll be due another heat very soon. Most probably in the next week."

"What?" I yelp, panic spiraling through me. "But ... if I stop taking them. If I stop now, won't that–"

He shakes his head. "I'm afraid it's too late."

"Isn't there some medication she can take to reverse it or at least slow down the approach of her heat?" Silver asks as Axel paces the room.

"I'm sorry, but I'd have to advise against that. Bea's hormones have already been tampered with. I think it could do her harm to tamper with them any further. We need to let things run their course."

Another heat? So soon. Panic switches to alarm. I can't breathe. I gasp for air.

"I ... I ... I can't," I say, desperately swinging my head from side to side. "I can't go through another heat. I can't do it again."

Silver drags me into his arms, holding me tight against his chest.

"Shush, sweetheart," he whispers, stroking my hair. "It's okay. If you don't want to go through another heat, you won't. We'll get the medication for you."

"It could do irreversible damage," the doctor says more sternly. "It could interfere with Bea's fertility for the future."

I sob harder. Babies are the last thing on my mind right now but I know I want them in the future. I want children. I want a family. I'm going to have to go through another fucking heat.

"It doesn't matter," Silver says, "if it's what our omega wants–"

"I don't want that," I say, my face buried in his shirt. "I don't want to ruin things for the future, but ..."

I close my eyes tight, trying not to think of that pain, that agony. I think I might throw up.

Axel comes to crouch down beside me, stroking his palm over my back and both alphas begin to purr, trying their best to calm me down.

"You underwent your last heat alone," the doctor says, "you'll have your mates for this one. It won't be the same."

"The doctor's right, sweetheart," Axel whispers into my ear. "We'll be with you this time. We'll make it good for you."

"So damn good," Silver adds.

I know that's what everyone says and I know the sex yesterday – with Silver, with Connor, with Nate – was incredible, but I'm finding it damn hard to imagine anything so painful could become as good as all these alphas and omegas make out.

"Trust us, Bea," Axel tells me. "It's going to be fine." And somehow his words soothe me. I take a deep breath. Then another and another. And then I retract my face from Silver's now creased and damp shirt and sit up straight.

The doctor holds out a box of tissues for me and I pluck out a handful and blow my nose.

"A heat with your pack might be just what the doctor ordered to calm your hormones and set you off on a more settled path."

"You really think so?" I ask him, my vision still blurry with tears.

"Absolutely. I've been practicing medicine for nearly fifty years. All this talk about omegas being calming influences on alphas, I can tell you now, it works just as well the other way around." He stands up and comes to pat my shoulder. "You'll be just fine, Bea. There are some tests I'd like to run," I flinch at the mention of tests, "but," he says quickly, registering my alarm, "those can wait until after your heat. Head back to your nest, snuggle up with your pack. Do you think you can do that for me?"

"Yes," I say, "my nest is pretty awesome." I glance at Axel. "But my interview?"

"We'll talk to them," Axel says. "They'll understand."

I'm not so sure they will. My experiences so far have taught me the opposite. But it seems like I have little choice.

I SPEND the drive home snuggled in Axel's lap, Silver driving with a look of thunder on his face.

"We need to find that woman," he says eventually through clenched teeth.

"Dr. Hannah?" Axel asks.

"Yes."

"Find her?"

"She's missing," Silver says, "has been since your abduction."

"Then maybe something's happened to her too. Maybe–"

"Bea, sweetheart, she was feeding you the wrong drugs. She was forcing your heat to come early. This woman is right in the center of whatever went down."

"She may not have a choice ..."

"There's always a choice," Silver says gruffly, his

knuckles white on the steering wheel.

I lean my head on Axel's shoulder.

"I don't want to think about it any more. It's in the past. I want to sort out this job and prepare for this heat."

Now I'm wrapped in Axel's arms, away from the doctor (however nice he was), I feel less wobbly. More resigned and determined. I didn't know what was coming last time. Plus, I was half in denial about the entire situation. This time I'm going to be prepared.

"Do you think we could swing by to pick up Courtney from the department store?" I ask, pulling out my phone to message my cousin.

"Sure thing," Silver answers, without so much as a query as to why.

We collect her from the side walk a half hour later and then drive her around to the Stormgate house.

She stands on the doorstep gaping, and I have to take her hand and drag her through the house as she mutters about the size of the place. In the kitchen, we find Molly baking what looks like macaroons.

"Molly," I say, "this is my cousin, Courtney. Courtney meet Molly."

The two exchange hellos and then look at me with curiosity.

"I need some advice," I tell them both. "Girlie advice."

"Oh goodie, This sounds fun," Courtney says jumping up on a stool.

"It does," Molly agrees, "let me make us some tea, though."

She wipes her hands on her apron, unties it from her waist and then boils the kettle. A few minutes later she hands around cups of some herbal concoction, and the two other women look to me again.

I blow across my drink, making the surface ripple.

"Bea," Courtney says, "out with it."

"I have another heat coming." They both nod. "Soon. Like, probably in a matter of days."

Courtney's face crumples and she drops her cup on the countertop and attempts to hug me. "Oh Bea, I'm so sorry."

"Sorry?" Molly scoffs. "Have you seen how hot her six alphas are?" She motions towards the door.

"*Your* six alphas?"

"Uh huh, we're giving it a try."

Courtney's gaze flits around my face. "Are you sure about this, sweetie? You don't have to plumb for the first group of men who show up on your door and–"

"I'm sure. Very, very sure. I believe they know they fucked up and I'm confident they aren't going to fuck up again."

"If they do ..." Courtney and Molly say together.

"Then I will personally be removing their ball sacks with the knife Nate gave me."

Courtney laughs. "She would, you know. She took a man's eye out."

"I think you're going to keep those douchebags in line," Molly says. "But what do you need our advice about?"

"The last heat was pretty awful," I say, and I'm sure the expression on my face matches the one on Courtney's. We're both traumatized by that experience.

"I'm sorry," Molly says, "I can't imagine going through one alone."

"If I'm honest, I'm scared this one will be bad too, even with my alphas."

"It won't be. Not if they're focused on you and everything they can to make you feel good."

"But how do I ensure they stay focused on me?" My

previous experience with Karl, has shown me I'm not entirely skilled at keeping a man's attention.

"Are you serious, Bea? Those assholes are crazy about you. Obsessed. You should have seen what they were like without you. When you went back home, they were like a pack of love-sick puppies. They were practically chewing up the furniture. I've never seen Hardy look so darn sad before. You are not going to have any trouble holding their attention."

"What you need to do, though, sweetie," Courtney says, her fingers creeping to the rows of neat macaroons Molly's baked, "is make sure you're vocal in bed."

My cheeks sizzle and I pick up my cup and take a big gulp. I'm pretty sure I was vocal with Silver, Connor and Nate yesterday on the boat.

My cousin appears to read my thoughts. "Not like that," she says, knocking her fist against my shoulder, "although good on you girl. What I mean is, don't be afraid to speak up for yourself. To ask for what you want. To tell those boys when they do something you don't like."

"That's half the problem," I confess, "I don't even really know what I do and don't like." I've never had the opportunity to explore my desires and fantasies before.

"Oh my gosh," Molly says, "you are going to have so much fun in this heat. And," she says, sliding the tray of macaroons our way and offering us both one, "I gave those boys specific instructions to fill that nest with sex toys. You're going to have a wild time Bea."

"I'm so jealous," Courtney sighs.

"The nest has a sex swing," Molly whispers.

"Bea, you're a lucky bitch!"

I laugh. Maybe I am. Maybe this is going to be fun after all.

31

Hardy

I'M in the gym in the basement of the Stormgate house with Nate and Angel when Silver and Axel return from their trip to the doctor's, Connor trailing behind them.

"Where's Bea?" I ask immediately. I thought we weren't letting her out of our sight from now on. Especially around damn doctors.

"Talking to Courtney and Molly about girlie shit," Axel says, dropping down onto one of the benches.

"Molly?" I say, "ahh fuck." Who knows what kind of ideas that girl will insert into our omega's head. Naughty fucking ideas, that's what.

I drop the weight I was using onto the mat with a thud and wait for the update.

"It seems," Silver says, anger flashing in his eyes, an

anger I can feel thrumming in his bond too, “that Hannah doctor was messing with our girl’s hormones.”

“Fuck,” Angel says, scrambling up from the floor where he was running through a circuit of sit-ups.

“Yeah, fuck,” Axel runs his hand through his hair. “It means she’s going to go into another heat.”

“So soon?” Connor says.

“Yeah, it was those tablets the doctor gave her. They’re designed to bring on a heat.”

“This is a good thing, though, isn’t it?” I say glancing around at my packmates. Our omega in heat is what we’ve all been dreaming of since we met her. Now we get a second shot at this with no long drawn-out wait.

“No,” Silver says, “little thing’s fucking petrified at the thought of it.”

“Because she did the last one alone?” Connor asks.

“Yeah.”

I pick up my towel and march out of the gym. Our omega should be on cloud nine thinking about spending her heat with us. Instead, she’s scared. And that’s our fault. The consequences of our fuck up, I realize, are going to be long-lasting. Making things up to her won’t end with a hand-carved keyring and a beautifully designed nest. No, making it up to her is going to be a long-lasting thing.

I storm out of the back doors and out onto the decking, tugging out my phone and calling the opticians we visited a few days ago. I give my name and details and after some strong arm twisting on my behalf, the dude agrees to have one of my pairs of glasses ready for me by the afternoon.

Yeah, making her happy is my new number one priority.

~

I FIND her in the garden when I return from the optician's later, rocking backwards and forwards on the tyre swing that hangs from the great oak tree. She budges along when she sees me and I drop down beside her.

"Silver and Axel told us about the heat business," I say. "I'm sorry, Bea."

She shakes her head. "Molly assures me there are worse ways to spend my time."

"Usually I'd say, don't listen to any of Molly's bullshit, but she's right."

She shifts closer to me, leaning her soft body against mine. Her caramel scent is clear even above the aroma of grass and pollen in the garden.

"How you feeling right now, though, baby girl?" Her skin feels warm, warmer than it did this morning, and perhaps her scent is already sweeter. How soon will this heat be arriving?

"I'm okay. Missing the beach."

"We'll get you back there soon enough."

"I was thinking, if my aunt says it's okay, we could redecorate the condo, maybe build a nest there too."

"More than one nest, huh? I never took you to be such a greedy little thing."

"I'm learning to speak up for what I want."

"Good girl." I reach into the pocket of my jacket. "Talking of things you want ..." I tug out the glasses case and balance it on my thigh.

"Oh," she says, one side of her mouth curling in a seductive smile. "Is this what I think it is?"

"Better open the box and see, Omega."

She shivers at that word and I make a note to use it over and over again. I bet it will make her all wet. Hell, I'm hoping these damn glasses will, too. I'm pretty certain I look like a frigging dork wearing them.

She strokes her finger over the box, teasing me, then snaps it open.

The glasses rest inside, folded up neatly. Carefully, she takes them out, unfolds the arms and examines them.

She glances from the glasses to me.

"Do we get to play Lois Lane and Clark Kent now, Omega?"

"Lois Lane and Clark Kent never got it on, you know."

"Yeah, but that's the good thing about fan-fiction, we can change the ending in our own little version of the story."

She takes my chin in her hands, brushing her fingers over my stubble and twists my face to face hers. Then she tilts my chin downwards and slides the glasses onto my nose.

I tip my head backwards and present the left side of my face to her and then the right.

"Meet to your approval, baby girl?"

"Oh yeah," she says, biting her lip, her voice turning all husky.

I chuckle at her. "You're serious? They really do turn you on?"

She nods slowly, then grabs a fistful of my t-shirt and tugs my mouth down to hers. I can't lie, kissing with glasses on is damn strange, but I'd wear a mask and flippers if she instructed me to, as long as I get to kiss the girl and hold all those curves of hers.

Her kiss grows needy quickly, little moaning noises escaping her throat and one of her hands capturing mine and leading it between her legs.

I pull away. "I think I'd better get you upstairs to the nest, baby girl, because as much as I'd love to fuck you up against the trunk of this tree, I'm pretty sure both Molly and Mrs. Stormgate are watching us."

"What?" she squeals, jumping up immediately.

I chuckle and swing my gaze towards the house, freezing as I do. "Well, fuck me," I mutter.

"What?" Bea says.

"The leaves," I murmur, pointing to trees in the distance, "and the grass! Fuck, the bricks on the house!"

"What do you mean?" Bea asks.

"I can see them. Clearly."

"That's what glasses are for."

"I never realized I was meant to be able to see that shit."

"And you look very handsome," Bea says with a smile.

I chuckle again, then bend down and scoop her up into my arms.

"Miss Lane, nest, now."

"Yes, please," she says, adjusting my glasses on my nose.

We keep it civil through the garden and the house, but as soon as we're on the stairs up to the third floor, we lose all restraint. Bea sucks on my neck like a starving thing, her hands roaming under my shirt, nails scraping at my skin.

"You want me, Omega?" I ask right by her ear, catching her earlobe between my teeth and tugging on it.

"Y-y-y-yes."

"Then ask for it, baby girl. Ask me for exactly what you need."

"I need you, all of you."

I key in the code at the door and kick my way inside, carrying the omega straight over to the bed and lowering her down with me.

She continues to suck on my neck like my skin is the best-tasting dish in the world, and scrabbles at my clothes.

"I want to see all of you," she tells me.

"Likewise, Omega."

And for a moment, we break apart, both stripping off jeans and t-shirts. When she reaches to undo the lacy bra she's wearing, I catch her wrist and tell her no. And when I go to remove my new pair of glasses, she does the same.

"Sex with glasses on," I moan, "is about as nerdy as wearing socks."

"I like them," she insists.

I relent and keep them on, although the damn things mist up pretty quickly as I get down to kissing my way along her neck, over her chest and down to her glorious tits.

"Fuck, these tits!" I say, taking both in my hands and squeezing them as I kiss the soft flesh there. Her spine arches and she presses herself firmly into my grip. Despite my ability to see fuck all, I'm ripping down the lacy cups of her bra, searching out her nipple next, ringing the soft pink skin and pinching the stiff peaks. "Fuck, I want to come all over these tits," I murmur as I bend down to capture a nipple between my teeth.

"Ohhhh," she moans.

"That feel good, baby girl?"

"Uh huh."

I love a pair of tits. It's always been the part of a woman I love the most. The way they feel in your hands, the way they move, the way they taste. The way if you play with them you can make a woman come.

But these tits? Fuck, I think they are the best I've ever seen, and, yeah, maybe I've seen a fair few pairs in my time.

Is it the tits themselves? Perfectly round, just enough weight in my hand, soft as fuck, nipples pointing up towards my mouth and begging me to suck on them.

Or is it that these tits belong to Bea? Is that what makes them so fucking special?

"You ever come from someone playing with your tits, baby girl?" I ask, as I drag my tongue slowly round her nipple, making her shiver deliciously underneath me.

"N-n-no," she says, "I don't think it's possible. For me anyway. I mean it feels good but– OH!"

I flick her nipple hard with the tip of my tongue and she loses the ability to speak.

I like a challenge. I like to win a challenge even more.

She says she can't come from a bit of nipple play. Yeah, we'll see about that!

I move to the other tit. "Is this one feeling neglected, baby? Does it need my attention too?"

"Yes," she gasps, her hands tight in my hair, my topknot coming loose.

"Well, that's no good, is it? Let's see what I can do."

I squeeze at the tit I've just been teasing, pinching her nipple between my finger and my thumb while I take the other in my mouth, sucking on it hard, then lathering it with my tongue.

She squeals and I smell the aroma of her slick. I know I can make her come this way. Fuck, the little thing is so sensitive to my touch, I bet I could make her come in just about anyway I wanted.

I continue this little game, flicking and nibbling at one nipple, while I pinch and pull on the other. Then I swap, pausing as I do, to bury my face in her cleavage, to breathe her in and feel the softness of her skin against my cheeks.

"Fuck, fuck, I love these tits, love them so fucking much!" I growl as I nip at her nipple with my teeth.

She moans, her legs beginning to shake and her body tensing, taut as a stretched elastic band. I smile to myself, smile with a mouthful of tit, and then I flick at her nipple with my tongue, over and over again until the tension in her body snaps. She sighs, her body goes limp, her skin flushes pink and her nipple vibrates against my tongue.

So fucking good!

I flick her some more as she jolts through the aftershocks, murmuring my name as she does.

When she's done, I lift my head and look up into her face. I can hardly see her through the fog on the glasses that are now sitting on my nose in some fucked up angle.

"Oh lord," she says, reaching up to slide the glasses from my face. "That was ..."

"I love these tits," I tell her one more time, squeezing them both in my hands.

"Uh huh," she says, "but do you think you could love another part of my body now too?"

"And what part is that, baby?"

I'm going to make her say it. I bet she's not used to saying it. But, damn, I want to hear those words on her sweet lips.

Her already pink cheeks blush a shade deeper.

"Your toe?" I ask her, capturing her foot in my hand and tickling her sole.

"No," she says, giggling.

"No?" I say innocently. "Your elbow?" I lift her right arm and kiss the crease in her arm.

"Not there either."

"Then perhaps, your thumb?" I take her hand and suck her digit into my mouth.

She squeals. "No, not there either, Alpha." She takes a handful of my hair and tugs me in closer to her. "I think you know exactly where I'm talking about."

"Yeah, baby, I do, but I want to hear you say it."

She hesitates, her tongue moving behind her teeth like she wants to say it. "I don't think I can."

"Of course, you can. It's just a word. But a word that

really fucking turns me on, especially when you say it, Omega."

Ha, the power of fucking words! Because saying that name again – Omega – my body pressed down on hers, my hard cock digging into her belly, has her pupils blowing wide.

"Come on, Omega, say it for me. Where do you want my attention now?"

She holds my gaze, her eyes as dark as midnight. "My pussy."

"Yeah," I smirk, "your pussy."

She yelps in embarrassment and goes to try to whack me on the shoulder, but I'm already scooting down her body and diving between her legs. I open her thighs.

"Here, baby girl?"

"There," she says with a squeal.

I hum my approval. "This pussy is so fucking pretty too, Omega. Do you know every goddamn part of you is freaking beautiful?" I kiss between her plump folds. "Actually, I stand corrected. I think I was wrong. I think I like this part even more than your tits." I glance up at her. "You got a favorite part of my body, baby? And don't say my smile," I warn her.

She combs her finger through my loosened hair. "I do love your smile, Hardy. And I especially love your mouth and your fingers."

"Oh yeah?"

"Yeah, but I have a feeling I'm going to love your cock most of all."

I chuckle. "Damn sure you are, Omega. But shall we find out?" She nods and I roll over onto my back, taking her with me. "Come ride it then, baby girl, and give me a view of those glorious tits while you do."

She stares down at my stiff cock, then traces her hands

over my abdomen, over the inks that mark that part of my body, following the happy trail of jet fuzz. She pauses at my cock, dribbling fucking precome at the sight of her. She takes it in her hands.

"You're very big," she whispers, with a lot of desire and a hint of trepidation.

"We all are. But you managed Silver, you managed Nate and Connor too." I reach between her thighs, where she's dripping slick. "And you're so fucking wet. Such a good little Omega." I flick at her clit and she moans, shuffling up my body, until she's hovering above my cock.

I hold my breath, and watch in awe as she lowers herself down, lowers herself down onto my waiting cock.

"God, that looks so fucking good," I tell her, my hands tight on her waist, pushing her down further, guiding her to take more and more of me. She's wet and warm and so very tight. "How does it feel, Omega? Tell me."

Her chin tips backward and she shakes her head unable to find her words.

"It hurts?" I ask her.

"N-n-n-n-nooooo."

"It feels good?" She bites her lip and swivels her hips and now it's me who can't find my words anymore, because that feels good and it looks good too. Our little Omega grinding on my cock, her tits jiggling as she does.

She teases me and herself like this for several drawn-out minutes, grinding and grinding me, using my cock to hit every sensitive part inside her. It's obvious that it drives her mad because she starts to chase the feeling, grinding harder, rotating her hips faster and then lifting up on her knees so my cock slides through her pussy, before slamming back down on me.

"Shit!" I groan. "Shit!"

She does it again, and then again and again. Building speed until the little thing is bouncing up and down on my cock, her tits bouncing too, her back arched and her hands tight on my thighs behind her. Pushing her pussy and her chest forward, giving me a view of everything I want to see.

"Fuck, baby, you're good, so fucking good. Look at you, like some kind of Goddess, sitting on my cock like it's your throne."

"I wanna come," she wails.

"Then come, baby. Come on, come on my cock." I grip her more tightly, taking control of her motions, bouncing her up and down and thrusting up into her from below. Meeting her pussy with a wet thwack every time she lands slap on my lap.

Soon she's falling apart again. Just like before. I'm learning the signs. Animalistic little noises bubble in her throat, her legs shake, her stomach tenses and then she falls apart. My grip is the only thing keeping her upright as her sweet little pussy milks me. Milks my fucking cock like it's desperate for my spunk.

How can I deny her that? I'm coming with her, flooding her with my seed, rubbing her up and down my cock as we both sail through our orgasms.

"Knot me," she cries, as the after-waves jolt through our bodies.

Yeah, no fucking way I'm denying her that either. Not when I've been dreaming of – yeah and fucking jerking off to – the idea of this, for weeks.

I hold her down firmly on my cock as my knot expands, feeling her pussy clench around me, squeezing me tight, forcing another fucking orgasm from my core. I watch her face, watch as she winces at the pain, then comes again, pleasure washing over her features.

I pull her in close, dragging her down to lie flat on my body. I nuzzle her forehead, purring despite myself. I can't help it. I'm so fucking blissed out.

I knew she was the one. I fucking knew it. And this heat of hers, it's going to be insane.

32

B ea

THE NEXT FEW days pass in some kind of crazy dream. I don't venture from the house because the alphas are too concerned about my security this close to my next heat. But, to be honest, I'm perfectly happy where I am.

I hang out with Molly in the kitchen learning a thing or two about baking to rival Nate's skills, I read gossip magazines with Mrs. Stormgate in her bedroom, I explore the acres of garden and in between I have a lot of fun in my new nest, in my new nest with my six alphas.

I take Molly and Courtney's advice and get busy exploring what I do and don't like. I'm surprised to find there is an awful lot of stuff I do – letting my alphas tie me up, tying up my alphas, threesomes and foursomes, even fivesomes, being watched, lots and lots of dirty talk, and to my surprise, having my backside eaten out. I also discover one or two things that are a hard no – my gag reflex is way too sensitive to ever get on board with deep throating and the idea of fisting scares the living daylights out of me. I'm pleased to find, though, that my alphas are perfectly happy with my tastes and preferences. There's no pressure to try something I don't want to and tons of enthusiasm to undertake the things I do.

I speak to the ecological foundation and find them surprisingly understanding about my situation and happy to push back my interview until my hormones have settled. Hormones that don't seem so bad in the run up to this heat. In fact everything seems manageable – scrap that, pretty darn enjoyable.

Especially when I'm snuggled up on the deck with my alphas watching the sun fall behind the distant ocean.

It feels like things might be stabilizing. It feels like I'm beginning to get a handle on this being-an-omega thing. I'm beginning to think I even like it.

It feels like nothing could pop our perfect bubble of bliss.

Which means, of course, that something does.

A piercing scream.

Immediately my six alphas are up on their feet, Silver reaching for a gun I didn't even know he was wearing in his jacket, Hardy dragging me to my feet and clutching me to his chest.

"What the fuck?" Nate says, thundering towards the garden doors.

We hear footsteps racing through the house and then Molly calling her brothers' names, her scent so tense it's bitter in my mouth.

Axel and Angel are sprinting into the house, everyone

else but Hardy behind them. I try to follow, but Hardy blocks my path.

"No," he says sternly, "stay here."

I glare at him. "It's Molly," I say, trying to shake off his hold. "Hardy!"

He relents, letting me go, and together we run through the house, following the sounds of the others' footfall and voices. We find them in Mrs. Stormgate's bedroom. Molly and Axel are on their knees, next to the still body of their mom.

I gasp, rushing forward to help.

"Is she breathing?" I ask.

"I don't know," Molly cries, tears cascading down her face, her body shaking.

Axel gathers his mom up into his arms.

"Mom?" he says. "Mom, can you hear me?"

Her eyes flicker open for the briefest of seconds and we all take a collective sigh of relief.

"We need an ambulance," Axel says. Angel already has his phone to his ear, barking instructions at someone down the line. I sink down next to Molly and wrap my arms around her as Angel's words grow angrier.

Finally, he tosses the device to the ground.

"Twenty minutes! Twenty fucking minutes until an ambulance."

"A doctor?" I ask. "Is there a doctor nearby?"

Angel shakes his head.

"Then, you need to take her in yourselves," I tell them.

"No," Angel says, "we'll wait for the ambulance."

Molly sobs and crumples in my arms. Her mom gasps for breath in Axel's arms.

"You can't!" I cry. "You have to go now!"

"You're about to start your heat, Bea. We're not leaving you alone."

"I won't be alone. I'll have the others with me." Angel scrubs his fingers through his beard, indecision and pain clear on his face. "You have to take her, Angel. You and Axel. Now. She's your mom."

He screws up his eyes. "We're not letting you down again, Bea. We made a promise to you–"

"Don't be ridiculous. This isn't letting me down. You have to go. You're her sons."

He shakes his head and I turn to Axel, gripping onto his arm.

"Axel, my heat hasn't even started properly yet. You'll be back before it does. I'm sure of that."

"Bea ..." he groans.

"Please," I say, "please take her."

"We'll be here for Bea," Silver reassures them. "She wants you to go."

Axel gazes down at his mom, his face drained of all blood. He hesitates, then he nods.

The next few moments are a blur.

The brothers carry their mom to the car port, Nate helps Molly to her feet and I race through the house, grabbing blankets and cushions and bottles of water. I thrust it all at Angel who stores them in the trunk, before kissing me and climbing into the passenger seat beside his mom, his sister on her other side.

Nate places his hand on my shoulder and I turn away from this family I love so much, and peer up at his face. It's riddled with pain too.

"Go," I tell him. "They need you."

He hugs me, squeezing me tight against his muscular frame, and then he's jumping into the passenger seat beside Axel as the car speeds out of the garage and down the drive.

I follow them out, racing down the driveway until the car turns a bend and disappears from sight.

When they're gone, it hits me. My body shakes like Molly's had. Tears roll down my face and my other three alphas surround me, pulling me close, enveloping me in their scents. We hold each other as the sun slinks behind the horizon and the world turns so much darker than it was just a few minutes before.

WE DON'T KNOW what to do with ourselves after that. We're all tense, waiting for confirmation they've arrived, anxious to hear some news. Finally, Connor finds a movie for us to watch and Silver orders us a takeaway.

I don't know if it's the shock of what's happened or if it's just one of those damn annoying consequences, but my body decides now is the time to go a little berserk. We're barely through the credits of the movie when a pain spikes deep in my gut. I double over and grunt and Connor looks at me with alarm.

"Bea, are you okay?"

I squeeze my eyes shut, waiting for the pain to pass, trying not to panic. This pain is familiar, all too familiar, and I can't help shaking with the knowledge of what's to come.

Slowly, the pain subsides. I rub at my lower belly and roll up.

"A cramp?" he asks.

"Yes, a bad one."

"Your heat's getting closer," he says, nostrils flaring as he glances at Hardy.

I nod and chew on my lip.

I don't want it to come yet. Not with half my pack away. Not with Mrs. Stormgate sick in the hospital.

Why can't my freaking body behave for once?

I try to concentrate on the images on the screen, on the words the actors are saying. But it's scrambled nonsense and my temperature creeps upwards. Sweat trickles down my neck, making my hair damp.

I take a deep breath in. Then out. As if I can blow the feelings away. As if I can cool this heat if I blow hard enough.

It's no use.

I double over a second time, the agony even more intense. I groan.

"Shit, Bea your scent!"

I can taste it in my mouth; burned sugar. My stomach cramps harder, slick flooding between my thighs, soaking through the shorts I'm wearing.

"Oh no!" I cry out in horror.

"It's all right," Hardy says, "you're okay."

"But Mrs. Stormgate's sofa!" I try to stand up and inspect the damage but when I try, I'm way too light-headed and end up swaying on my feet, Hardy catching me in his strong arms. "I think this is happening."

"Let's get you to the nest," he says. But as he does the gong of the front door vibrates through the house.

"It's our pizzas," Connor says, "I'll go get them."

He sprints out of the room as Hardy scoops me up in his arms.

"You're going to be just fine," Silver reassures me, placing his cool palm against my now scorching forehead.

"But Nate," I sob, "and Axel and Angel."

Silver opens his mouth to reply, always ready to reassure me.

The words don't leave his mouth. Instead, a loud bang rocks the floor. Hardy stumbles with me in his arms, his gaze flicking immediately to Silver's. Someone shouts out in the hallway, the noise followed by a gunshot.

I scream, wincing as a second gunshot rings out.

"Get her to the nest," Silver yells at Hardy. Hardy nods.

Silver reaches into his jacket to grab his gun for the second time today, but it's not there. In all the confusion with Mrs. Stormgate he must have left it in her room. His eyes widen with alarm for the briefest of seconds but then he's running towards the door.

"Get her to the nest, Hardy, and lock the fucking door!"

Hardy tightens his hold on my body and sprints, running towards a small door in the lounge I've never seen used before. He slams it open with one firm kick of his foot and carries me through to a small back stairway.

"Hardy!" I yell, "he hasn't got a gun." I struggle in his arms. "We have to help him. We have to help Connor."

I don't know what the hell is going on, but whatever it is, I know it's not good.

"Omega," Hardy says so sternly my spine stiffens, "we're under attack. Silver knows how to take care of himself. There is nothing you can do to help. Just hold on tight."

He races up the stairs three at a time, my weight not hindering him at all. His feet clatter loudly on the old wooden steps that groan and creak under us. But despite the noise, I can hear more gunshots, more shouting and more yelling.

I cling to Hardy's neck, closing my eyes tight. My alpha smashes through another doorway and races out onto the landing of the third floor. Below us the sounds of men fighting are even louder now and I whimper in alarm.

Hardy drops me to my feet and taking a hold of my wrist drags me quickly along the hallway to the nest door.

"What's the number?" he curses under his breath. "Damn it!"

I push him out of the way and start to type numbers in. Behind us, many pairs of heavy boots thunder on the main staircase.

I press the last digit. The panel lights up, beeping positively. The locks click, the door opens.

"Get inside and shut the door," Hardy orders, turning his back to me. "And don't you dare open it unless you're damn sure it's–"

An object crashes on the floor in front of us. It spins on the spot, then hisses, rolling toward us.

"Bea!" Hardy yells.

A second loud bang.

A cloud of smoke consumes us.

I can't see.

I can't breathe.

I cough.

Thick soup-like fog envelops me.

My eyes stream.

I try to shout Hardy's name.

I try to find the door.

I reach for the knife in my pocket.

My head spins.

My legs falter.

The world goes black.

33

Bea

WAVES CRASHING. Bright sunlight against my closed eyelids.

Where am I?

My skin is hot.

My body stiff.

I wiggle my toes.

I feel soft cushions beneath me.

What happened?

Something bad. I know something bad happened. There's a panicked sensation bubbling in my chest.

Remember, Bea, remember.

"Are you awake?"

A voice. Familiar. I know it from somewhere.

Feminine.

"Would you like some water?"

I force open my eyes. Sunshine floods my view, golden and piercing, reflecting off a glistening surface.

I squint, lifting my heavy arm to shield my eyes.

The ocean.

"Beautiful, isn't it?"

I turn my head towards the voice.

A woman lies out on a sun-lounger beside me. Behind her, stretches endless white sand, palms trees and colorful cactuses.

I squint harder, her face slowly coming into view.

She's wearing skin-tight denim shorts and a skimpy bikini top, her long hair is plaited loosely over one shoulder, and her lips painted a blood red to match her nails.

Oversized sunglasses cover most of her face but as I stare at her, she lifts her hand and snatches them off her face, resting them down on her tanned thigh.

My head thumps.

My throat burns.

I close my eyes and open them again.

"Dr. Hannah?" I croak. Is it really her? She looks so different. No conservative turtle neck top, no knee-length skirt. And around her neck is a chain of bite marks. Ringing her neck like a collar. Old scars not new. I thought she wasn't bonded.

"Bea Carsen," she smiles, returning her glasses to her face and peering out at the ocean again.

I shake my head this time, so confused.

What happened?

I force myself to remember. Gunshots. Voices. Smoke.

"Where are my alphas?" I sit bolt upright on my sun-lounger, the movement making my stomach lurch, and swing my head around. To my left is more beach, in front of me the ocean, but behind is a huge mansion, several stories high, a pool shimmering on an upper terrace, the entire building formed of glass.

"*Your* alphas? They're not yours, you're unbonded, darling."

"Where are they?" I demand, not caring about the semantics.

"Somewhere safe and sound."

"What's going on?" I growl.

"Hmmm, you must have worked out by now, darling, that you are a woman in demand. And not just with the alphas of this city but with us scientists too. You're a fascinating specimen, Bea, one my pack is hoping will make us very rich." She laughs, gesturing to the house behind us. "Not that we're not rich already, but we're hoping to diversify into more legal forms of pharmaceuticals."

I frown, struggling to understand a word this woman is saying to me.

Specimen? Pharmaceuticals?

I glance down at my body. I'm still wearing the t-shirt and shorts I was earlier, dried slick all over my legs. I shift my arm, attempting to feel for Nate's knife.

"If you're looking for your weapon," the doctor says, stretching out her legs and tipping her head back towards the sky, "we took it away. Wouldn't want another accident with an eye, would we? Talking of which, my brother was rather insistent we chop you into lots of little pieces and feed you to the sharks. He's still pretty unhappy about losing his right eye." She giggles girlishly. "But luckily for you, my pack is more interested in money than revenge."

"Your brother?"

"Yes, my brother. I'd lie and say this was all his idea. But it wasn't, it was mine." She sighs dramatically. "I'm rather sick of hiding who I am, who my pack are. I've been looking for a way to make everything respectable. To join in with all the fussy little omegas I've been treating all these years."

I rub at my head. None of this makes sense. I don't understand what she's telling me.

"Who are your pack?" I ask, stumbling for something that I might be able to comprehend.

She doesn't answer me, instead, leaning forward and twisting her body away from me. Immediately I see it, the tattoo winding down her spine, from the bite mark at the base of her neck all the way down her back, disappearing inside her shorts. A snake. Its angry eyes red like her lips, its tongue coiled.

I still don't understand. She sits back against the lounger, reading the confusion on my face.

"You really are a little hillbilly, aren't you, darling?" She reaches down to the ground, picking up a water bottle and unscrewing the lid. "Surely you've heard of them. The Snakebites?"

"Your pack is part of the Snakebites? But they're a criminal gang."

"My gang *is* the Snakebites, darling. They run the operation."

I swallow. Dr. Hannah. Beautiful, intelligent, bonded to a criminal gang?

"How?" I blurt out. Maybe I was right, maybe her involvement in whatever the hell this is has never been consensual. I remember what she told me, about being careful who I shared my first heat with, careful not to become attached.

"How?" She takes a long mouthful of water, screwing back the lid. "Micko, head of my pack, has a little omega sister. He brought her to my clinic. It was one of those things. Instantaneous. He wanted to make me his."

"He forced you?"

Dr. Hannah lifts her glasses to look at me, amusement dancing in her eyes. "Oh no, I wanted him too. You wait until you see him." Her eyes flick towards the house. "He'll be here soon enough, with Antonio and Leo." She laughs. "And my brother. They'd like a word before we proceed."

"Proceed with what?"

"You still haven't figured that out? And yet my brother says you've had your pack sniffing about for answers. Two of them even broke into my old house, did you know that?"

"I don't know anything," I say, swinging my legs down to the floor, ignoring the building pain in my gut, the burning of my skin, the spinning of my vision.

"The blood we collected last time you were in heat contained some unique alterations to normal omega hormones. Seems they had quite an effect on our little beta guinea pigs. Not that I think they'll actually change them into omegas but they'll be enough to convince our customers. Enough to convince our investors."

"You've already got my blood. What do you need me for?"

"For more, of course. Eventually we'll work out how to synthesize those hormones ourselves, but until then we're going to need a supply." She places her bottle on the ground. "In case you haven't worked it out, that's you. You're the supply."

"I want to go home."

"I don't think that's going to be possible. Wouldn't want you blabbing everywhere now, would we?"

"People are going to come looking for me."

"Omegas go missing every day, darling. No one goes looking for them. Trust me."

"My pack will. My pack will come looking."

"Isn't their mother sick? Such a shame. But I think they have more important things to worry about than a girl like you. I don't think anyone's even going to notice that you're gone."

"My pack will," I snort in disbelief. "My mom and my dad. My cousin and my aunt."

"Another girl who turns up in the city, gets mixed up in some bad business, and, poof, is never seen of again. Happens all the time. So common the cops don't even care."

"My pack will. You know they'll kill every single one of you for this." I don't doubt that for a minute. I've never asked any questions but I'm pretty certain my alphas are not the types to have kept their hands entirely clean over the years. If there's dirty business to be done, they'll do it.

Grinding metal sounds out behind our heads, and when I look towards the house, I see the huge glass doors sliding back and three men stepping out into the sunshine. They are all dressed in dark suits with dark shirts, tattoos crawling up their necks. On one man the ink spills from his neck up his jaw and onto his cheek. Another owns a scar that slices his face in two. The third, the oldest and the biggest, wears a thick gold chain around his neck and his fingers are covered in heavy rings.

They stride towards the two of us, their eyes locked on me with curiosity. A fourth man steps outside as they do; he's dressed more casually: jeans and a corduroy shirt. Over his right eye he wears a plain black patch. His other dark eye finds me, and hatred burns in it.

As the first three alphas draw closer, I catch a hint of their scents. Acidic, rancid, making me want to gag. I've never tasted anything so rotten in my life.

When they reach the sun-loungers, the man with the chain bends down to kiss Dr. Hannah on the mouth, his hand curling around her throat as he does. He keeps it there, as he pulls away.

"Your delivery worked out this time then, sugar?"

"Yes, Daddy. Thank you."

His eyes dart to me. "When are you going to start work? She smells pretty ripe to me."

His nostrils flare and the tip of his tongue darts out of his mouth, tasting the air.

I cower away but out of the corner of my eye, I look desperately for some way to escape. A weapon? A cell-phone? Something? Anything?

There's nothing.

"Just waiting for you to help me move her inside. I wanted a little chat with her first."

"And are you done now, sugar?"

She nods, and the man with the scar sneers at me. "Peter, she's all yours."

The man with the eyepatch prowls closer and I try not to scream.

34

ngel

Yet another doctor is talking to us; this one assuring us that Mom was simply dehydrated. He's confident that they've returned her fluid levels to normal and for now she is perfectly stable and comfortable.

I nod along, a million questions bustling in my head, my eyes straying anxiously over my mom's face, when alarm strikes out through my bond.

I wobble on my feet, grabbing to hold on to the nearest wall.

Something's not right.

The thoughts scrabbling through the bond are desperate, angry, confused. I can't make sense of them. I can't understand what the hell is going on. One thing I know though, my pack is in trouble. That knowledge sucker punches me right in the gut.

"Axel!" I yelp. But I can see it in his eyes too. And when I turn to Nate, he's already pacing towards the door.

"Fuck," Axel mumbles, grabbing Molly by the shoulders. "Something's going down. We've got to get back to the house."

"What?" she says, the alarm spreading to her features too.

But there's no time to stand around and explain, the three of us sprint through the hospital, knocking into trolleys and barging through waiting visitors as we do.

We dive into the car and screech out of the parking lot, breaking every damn speed limit in the city.

"What's going on?" Axel asks me as he swerves the car around a bend, all three of us lurching sideways in our seats.

"Don't know. It's chaos. I can't make sense of what's happening. You?"

"Connor's out cold," Nate says.

"Fuck," I mutter. Out cold? That is not fucking good.

As soon as we hit the driveway to the house, we can see just how 'not good' the situation really is. The gate is hanging off its hinges as if someone drove straight through it, the gravel's all torn up to shit and the front door has been knocked in.

Before Axel's parked up, me and Nate are out of the car and running towards the house, both of us reaching for weapons in our jackets.

As we fly through the open doorway, smoke billows into our faces, making us choke, our eyes streaming.

"Silver!" I yell. "Hardy!"

There's no answer and holding an arm to my face I run down the hallway. There are bullet holes in the plaster, a man with his skull cracked-in dead at the bottom of the stairs and the lounge is ripped to shreds, furniture knocked over and glass everywhere.

I reach through the bond, searching for my packmates.

"This way!" I yell to Nate, motioning with my elbow and then sprinting further down the hallway to the kitchen.

I hesitate at the closed door, listening. I can hear muffled voices from within. Axel races up to join us and I raise my finger to my lips, my gun ready in the air. The other two copy, and then I swing back the door and storm inside.

I come face to face with the barrels of two guns.

"Fucking Hell!" Hardy yells. "Are you trying to get yourselves killed?!"

Hardy and Silver lower their guns and we lower ours. Connor's slumped by the table, groaning, but at least he's fucking conscious and there's another man, tied to a kitchen chair. He's dressed in black jeans and a black t-shirt and on his neck is the tattoo of a hissing snake.

"Where the fuck is Bea?!" I yell.

"They've taken her," Silver says, his bond flooding with pain and his voice quivering ever so slightly.

His right arm hangs from his shoulder at an odd angle and I can tell he's dislocated it. A fat bruise blooms across Hardy's cheekbone and dried blood is matted in Connor's fair hair.

"What the fuck!!" Nate says, stepping into the room.

"It was an ambush. They took us by surprise. Hardy tried to get her to the nest but ..."

Hardy's eyes drop to the floor, and more agonizing pain spirals through the bond.

"We were outnumbered," Silver says, more to Hardy than to the rest of us.

I brace myself, expecting Nate to go for Silver's throat, to blame him for letting Bea go.

But to my surprise he doesn't, instead he walks up to Silver, cradles his arm in his hands and wrenches his shoulder back into place.

Silver grunts and even more pain flashes over his face.

"Thanks," he groans with a grimace.

Axel points to the man in the chair, who much to my pleasure looks scared shitless. These weasels always are little hard men when they're in their gang, but as soon as you get one on their own you discover they're gutless, spineless creeps. There's nothing hard about them at all.

"Is he one of them?" Nate asks, not waiting for an answer as he thumps the man in the gut.

"Yeah," Hardy says. "Snakebites."

I shake my head. "What the fuck do Snakebites want with Bea?"

"Same thing these scumbags always want with omegas," Silver says through gritted teeth.

"They wouldn't risk starting a war with us for that," Axel says, glaring at the man quivering in the chair. "Not when they could easily groom omegas who don't have a pack to protect them."

"Drugs," Connor mutters from the table, rubbing at his head, his eyes swimming about.

"What?" I say in irritation. We can deal with his fucking headache later.

"It's like Dr. Clive said."

I frown but Axel nods. He crouches down in front of the Snakebite. "Is that what it is? They're hoping to use our omega in their bid to find a way to turn betas into omegas."

"I don't know anything."

Axel grabs the man by the throat and squeezes until the man is choking, his feet scraping along the floor. Then Axel releases him. He gasps for air.

"Did that help loosen your memory?" Axel asks.

"All I know is our mission was to grab the girl and take out as many of you as we could," the man wheezes.

"Failed there, didn't you?" Nate says, opening a kitchen drawer and taking out a kitchen knife. He holds it up to his face admiring it, the light glinting off the metal. He shakes his head, returns the knife to the drawer and selects another. When he examines this one, a sinister smile spreads across his face which has the man in the chair leaning away.

Nate walks towards him.

"I like cooking," he tells the gang member. "But if you want to be a good chef, you have to be good at chopping. Did you know that?"

That man stares at him, stunned. Nate lifts an eyebrow.

"No," he mutters.

"It's the first thing they teach you at cooking school apparently – how to chop real fast. I wonder how quickly I could chop up your little finger?"

The man's eyes widen and he swings his gaze around the rest of us, trying to determine whether to take Nate's threat seriously.

He's obviously dumb as fuck. Everyone knows to take Nate's threats seriously.

"I'm thinking the bone might be quite hard to saw through but–"

"I don't know anything!" the man yells.

"You do," Silver says. "And you're going to tell us, or I'm going to let my packmate here use your fingers for vegetable-chopping practice."

"I told you everything I know. The plan was to storm in, take the girl unharmed and take out anyone else inside."

"On whose orders? Micko's?"

The man nods rapidly.

"And where were they taking her?" Hardy asks.

"To Micko's place."

"Micko's place," Silver mumbles, and I feel his concern through the bond. Micko Sondrio is head of the Snakebite Clan. No one knows where the hell his hideout is. But wherever it is, it will be guarded and fortified like Fort fucking Knox. "And where is Micko's place?"

"I don't know. I've never been there and we're never allowed to know."

"Bullshit," I say, stepping forward to untie his right hand. He struggles when it's freed, but I slam it down hard on the surface of the kitchen table. "All yours Nate."

Nate grins and spins the large knife in his fingers.

"Okay, okay," the man says, struggling to pull back his hand as I hold it down flat with his fingers splayed. "I don't know the exact location. But I know it's somewhere on the coast, over the Rockview hills."

"In the south?" I ask, pressing down even harder on his hand as Nate steps closer.

"Yes, yes. In the south. Rumor is it's some fuck-off big villa."

"Huh," I say, thinking that sounds exactly like the obnoxious dickwad. "Were they planning to keep her there or move her on?"

"I don't know for sure, but I overheard them saying, she'd be more secure there than if they moved her anywhere else."

"Makes sense," Silver says, clutching his injured arms. "It's his fucking fort. He thinks he's impregnable there."

"How's it guarded?" Axel asks the man.

"I've never been there!"

Nate slams the blade of the knife down hard on the table, mere centimeters from the man's trembling hands.

"Fucking hell!"

"Whoops, missed." Nate grins, yanking the blade from where it's wedged in the wood and swinging it up over his head.

"Okay, okay," the man screams. "I'll tell you."

Nate swivels the knife in his hand, smile twitching.

"Nate," Axel says. "The man says he'll talk."

"Just one little finger ..." Nate whines.

"There's a high perimeter fence and guards stationed inside and outside patrolling, plus sensors on the road down to the villa and cameras everywhere. That's all I know. I've never been inside so I don't know what the security is like in the villa."

"Probably a safe room," Silver muses.

The man nods his head violently up and down. "Probably."

"Let's go then," Hardy says. "Let's go fuck these dudes up and get our girl back."

"We can't show up all guns blazing," Silver says.

"Why the fuck not?" I ask.

"We'll be outnumbered."

Axel scoffs. "Being outnumbered has never hampered us before."

"We're attacking their stronghold. They'll be expecting us. We won't stand a chance."

"Then bring your men with us, Silver."

"And have them butchered like cannon fodder?"

"Then what do you suggest?" Axel asks tersely.

Silver massages his shoulder, gaze swimming over the Snakebite's face.

Nate flips the knife through the air and it lands tip down

on the table, twanging loudly, the gang member nearly pisses his pants.

"The beach," Nate says.

Silver's gaze flicks to him, then back to the gang member.

"Is it guarded?" he asks.

The man frowns. "A few guys patrolling, but not as heavily."

"It's a weak spot?"

"Possibly, but the only way on to the beach is from the road and like I said that's monitored."

"It's not the only way," Hardy says, catching on.

"No, it isn't," I agree, twisting the man's arm back behind him and tying it up. "There's the water."

Then I smash my fist against his skull and watch him flop forward unconscious.

35

Bea

THE MAN with the eyepatch takes a firm grip of my arm, his fingers digging hard into my skin, his nutmeg scent sour in my nose.

Perhaps it would be better to go along with this. Perhaps I should comply. But I'm sick and tired of being a woman who bends to everyone else's whims and needs. If I'm going down, I'm going down with a fight.

So I scream. I scream and cling to the sun-lounger, refusing to stand when he attempts to force me to my feet.

"Get up, you little bitch," he sneers.

I growl up at him, hanging on to the sun-lounger with all my might. He yanks me forward and the sun-lounger scrapes along the smooth tiles, then topples over. I don't let go. Not even when I tumble down on my knees and he drags both me and the sun-lounger together. Not even when I skin my knees.

No, I grit my teeth against the pain.

I'm going to make this as damn hard for him as I can.

I know they're coming. I know my pack will come for me. I just have to buy myself some time.

"Stupid bitch," the man says, kicking me hard in the ribs.

I grunt, but I don't flinch, staring up hard into his disfigured face.

"Careful Peter," Dr. Hannah says, stretching her arms above her head, before sliding off her lounger and sidling up to the man with the chain. "We need her in one piece." She wraps her arms around the man's waist. "Although it probably doesn't matter if the piece is a little bruised here and there."

Her brother smirks at me, then slaps me hard across the face. So hard I tumble backwards, stars twinkling in front of my eyes, my fingers finally loosening.

He gives me no time to find my balance or regain my grip on the sun-lounger. He yanks me up onto my feet and brings his face right down to mine.

"I don't think she needs both her eyes either, does she?"

"Not really," Hannah purrs. "In fact, she probably doesn't need any eyes at all."

Her brother grins and lifts one hand, bringing his forefinger up to my face, hovering it in front of my right eye. I squirm in his grip, trying to break free, trying to remember what Silver had told me.

But I don't have Nate's knife. I'm not even wearing a pair of shoes. However, I do have my nails. My stupid fucking fake nails from the wedding. Most of them anyway.

"Hold still, little bitch," he spits, "and let me pop your

fucking eye right out of its socket." I do exactly as he says, stilling in his grip. He sneers, his remaining eye flickering with darkness. "Such a shame to lose it, isn't it? It's such a damn pretty eye. Half the fucking city's been talking about how pretty your eyes are. That and your fucking ass." His gaze flicks down my body and I take my opportunity.

I strike at him, swiping my nails right across his cheek, cutting deep into his flesh.

"Fuck," he cries out, letting me go and clutching at his cheek. Blood pours through his fingers. I guess he's going to look like a proper pirate now with an eyepatch and scar. All he needs is a parrot.

I don't wait for the counterattack, I turn and run. I run just like Silver told me to do. I run down onto the beach.

I'm fast. And with my regular practice I'm able to run far. To outrun even an alpha. Even three alphas. If I can run to the mass of trees on the horizon, I can lose them. I know I can.

Fuck, I'll run all along the coast if I have to.

But I'm also on the brink of a heat. My legs won't move like they should. I drive them as hard as I can, but it's like running through treacle, every movement an effort, every muscle screaming.

I run. My heels kicking up sand, my lungs burning, my heart pounding. I run over the sand, the trees drawing closer, closer.

It's no good. But my legs won't move as fast as they should.

An arm swings out from behind me and wraps around my waist.

I scream again, kicking and pummeling the arm, turning to try to bite the shoulder of the alpha that grips me.

But his grip is his vise-like. His body rock hard. I don't think he feels a single one of my blows.

It's the man with the chain. The head of the pack. The leader of the Snakebites. His hand is covered in a tattoo of a skull, another snake twisted through the eye socket. The word hate scrawled above his knuckles.

He chuckles right by my ear, his breath warm, his scent stinging my nose and my throat.

"There, there little pussy cat. That's enough. Put your claws away." He yanks me in closer to his body, his other hand coming up to squeeze at my breast through my shirt. "Look at you, all riled up, all hot and bothered. You know what I think would calm you right down, little pussy cat? A good rutting. How about you get down on your hands and knees for me? How about I have you purring on the end of my cock? How does that sound, little pussy cat?"

My vision swoops in and out, my legs shake. My body's responding to the alpha pawing at my body, pouring honey in my ear. But I don't want him. I don't want him.

I screw up my eyes and clench my teeth, hanging onto my reason harder than I clung to that sun-lounger. This is one thing that won't be wrenched from my fingers.

I don't care that I'm an omega now. I don't care that my body isn't always under my control. My mind is and it always fucking will be.

No more gas lighting. No more clever words. No more trickery. No more falling for the tongues that twist words around and morph my reality.

I know what I want.

I want my pack. My alphas.

"You have an omega," I say with disgust, twisting in his arms.

"So what, little pussy cat? You think that stops me having my fun elsewhere?" For a brief second, I feel sorry for Dr. Hannah. I can't imagine how agonizing that must be. Not only knowing her alpha is with someone else but feeling every moment of it through their bond. The man is sick. But then so is Dr. Hannah. And frankly, she deserves all the torture she gets.

His free hand strokes up from my breasts. It wraps around my throat, his fingers curling over my chin, forcing their way into my mouth.

"I bet those hormones we plan to collect are even more potent when you're coming. Maybe we'll rut you through your heat as my omega collects all that priceless blood of ours. You're going to make me a very rich man, Omega." He scoffs. "Well, even richer. And happy too. I like the idea of two omegas now I come to think of it."

His fingers are calloused against my tongue. I bite down hard on them but once again he doesn't even flinch. Doesn't even register when I sink my incisors deep into his skin.

"Ahh, I do like a pussy cat who puts up a fight. It makes this all the more entertaining. Do you want to run again, little cat? See how quickly I catch you this time? Catch you and drag you to the ground."

I bite as hard as I can, jamming my teeth together, screaming with the effort.

I won't let this happen. I will not let this happen.

My alphas are coming. I know they're coming.

I close my eyes tight and will it. When I open them, I'm staring out at the ocean, flat as a pancake, calm and glittering in the setting sun.

Then I see it, cutting through the water like a knife. A speed boat.

My heart leaps in my chest. But I don't show it. I don't think this man has seen the boat yet. If it's them – and it has to be, doesn't it? – then I need to keep him distracted for as long as possible, so he doesn't have a chance to call for backup.

Out here on the beach, it's just us. His two alpha pack-mates, his omega and the psycho brother are somewhere behind us. I can smell them on the breeze, but they're keeping their distance. Like they know not to interfere when this man is toying with his prey.

I can't smell anyone else, no other guards, and I can't see any either.

I make up my mind.

I swallow the vomit bubbling in my throat, and I suck on the man's fingers. I suck and slurp on them like they're lollipops and I've never tasted candy in my life.

He groans. "Ahhh, little pussy cat's growing needy."

"Hmmm," I say, wiggling in his arms, grinding my ass against his cock.

"You want that, do you?" he says, his voice thick with desire. Good, if my heat drags him into a rut, he'll make poor decisions. He'll be too focused on me to even realize he's being attacked from the sea. "You omegas are all the same. Claim you only want your forever pack, but you're grinding against another alpha's cock as soon as that heat strikes. You'd take any fucker's cock, right now, wouldn't you? Even fucking Peter's."

"No, Alpha," I purr, watching as the boat drives across the ocean, coming closer and closer. "No, not any alpha. You."

"Me, little pussy cat?" He draws his wet fingers out of my mouth and I feign a whimper. He drags them back down my throat and paws at my breast, squeezing them hard. It's painful, not erotic, and I bet the scumbag has no idea how to please a woman. I bet he doesn't even care if he does. "All this talk about your ass, but I think your tits are pretty fine too."

"Micko!" a voice shouts out behind us. "Micko!!"

He ignores whoever's calling to him, bending down to suck at my neck. The sensation makes me shudder with horror. "You taste good too."

The boat skids into the shallows, the roar of the engine audible. Micko doesn't seem to hear. He moans as he nibbles on my skin, his hands trying to find their way under my shirt.

But then a gunshot sounds out and another.

He jerks upright, his head snaps to the shoreline. My alphas crash through the water, firing at Micko's packmates as they race to meet them.

"What the fuck?" he mutters, releasing me momentarily.

I pull away, trying to creep from him. But he grabs my arm and the next thing I feel is the cold metal of a gun, pressed to my temple.

My alphas come to a stumbling stop. The gunshots cease.

"Drop your weapons," Micko shouts out over the lapping of the waves. "Drop your weapons or I shoot the girl."

I try to tell them. I try to tell them no, with my eyes, but all six of them drop their guns slowly into the water by their feet. The waves swallow them up and they sink below the surface.

I suppress a moan of distress.

Micko marches forward, dragging me along before him, stopping where the water meets the sand.

"Down on your knees," he tells my alphas, pressing the gun harder against my skin, his forefinger poised on the trigger.

Six pairs of eyes don't leave mine, as each one of my alphas fall to their knees, the water lapping around their thighs. Six pairs of eyes I've come to know intimately, come to depend on, come to love. Sea blue. Emerald Green. Golden. Mahogany brown and silver gray.

"What a fucking bonus," Micko says, his packmates coming to stand either side of us. "I get the girl and I also get to take out the fucking nuisances that are Pack Boston and Pack York." He laughs. "Fucking brilliant."

"What do you want, Micko?" Axel growls. "Money? We have money. You can take it fucking all. Our properties? You can have those too. Just let her go."

"No," he says, "with you gone, I'll take it all anyway. There won't be anyone to stop me. And as for this one?" He strokes the gun along my forehead. "I was thinking of adding her to my pack."

"No," Dr. Hannah murmurs from behind us.

"Why not? Two omegas, twice the fun, hey boys?" He winks at them. "The question is, do I kill you now, or do I make you watch as I fuck her first? It would be fucking awesome, wouldn't it?"

"Let's just kill them, Micko," the one with the tattoo on his face mutters in irritation.

"No," I mutter, "please, don't hurt them, I'll do anything you want. Anything at all."

Dr. Hannah stumbles forward twining her hands around her alpha's neck. "But I'm your omega. I'm this pack's omega."

"'Course you are, Sugar," the one with the scar says scowling at the head of his pack.

"She's going to have to learn to share," Micko tells him gruffly. "She's had her own way for too long. She's grown greedy."

"I haven't Micko. I've done everything you've ever asked of me and–"

He shoves her away, and she tumbles down onto the sand. The other two alphas immediately go to her aid, turning away from the ocean to help her to her feet.

My pack takes its chance. Before I know what's happening, Silver crashes under the water, darting through the waves to grab Micko's ankle.

He pulls his legs from under him and the man crashes down onto the sand, firing into the air as he does.

I dive towards the sand, away from him and a large familiar body lands on top of me, covering and shielding me completely.

"Get off me, Hardy. Get off me. We need to help them."

But he refuses to budge and I'm left to watch helplessly through Hardy's arms as the battle unfolds.

Sand flies into the air, feet thunder in front of our faces, more gunfire rockets. I flinch with each bang.

I watch as Micko clambers upwards, scrambling for his gun in the sand beside him.

I watch as Nate slides a kitchen knife from the back of his pants, grips the handle and slings his arm forward.

The knife spins in the air as Micko finds the handle of his gun, wrapping his fingers around it, and lifting it up towards the water. The knife twists again and again, the blade flashing red in the setting sun. Micko pulls the trigger just as the knife slams right between his eyes. He falls backwards.

"Angel!" Axel cries out. I turn my head in time to see him lunging for his little brother, pushing him out of the way as a bullet slams through the air. They both smack into the water, the liquid turning red around them.

A scream fills the air.

It takes me a moment to realize it's mine, to realize it's Dr. Hannah's too.

She's slumped over the dead body of her alpha, his eyes staring lifelessly up at the sky. Her hands scrabble over him in desperation as she screams and screams, her every movement frantic. Her other alphas try to comfort her, grappling at her, trying to pull her away but she's hysterical.

"Come on, baby," Hardy says, "we need to go before backup arrives."

He drags me to my feet. I can't tell if I'm still screaming or if it's Dr. Hannah, but I wrench free of Hardy's grip and race to the water, crashing through the waves. Silver and Connor have an arm hooked under Axel's shoulders, Angel has his hands pressed to his brother's chest. There's blood everywhere.

"Axel!" I scream. "Axel!"

I try to reach him but before I can, Hardy bundles me up into his arms again and races through the water, throwing me into the speed boat and jumping in after me. Nate's already at the wheel, revving the engine and Hardy helps lift Axel into the boat as the others climb in.

I peer back at the beach. The Snakebite pack don't even seem to have noticed us gone, they're too distraught at the loss of their pack leader. But then I hear shouting, and I know there are more people coming. People with guns.

"Nate!" Silver shouts, and Nate swings the boat around and heads for the horizon.

I clamber over to Axel. His shirt's red with blood, his brother's hand still attempting to stem the bleeding.

His eyes find mine, those beautiful gray eyes that started

this whole change in my life. They're bright as ever but his eyelids are drooping, he's struggling to keep them open.

I reach for his hand, squeezing it tight between mine.

"Don't leave me, Alpha!" I beg. "Please don't leave me!"

36

ngel

I don't leave my brother's side. Not in the boat as Silver delivers first aid, not in the ambulance when we make it to dry land, and not at the hospital.

I only just got my brother back. Goddamn it, I'm not losing him now. I'm making damn sure the doctors do everything they can. *Every. Thing.*

They try to usher me out of the way, nurses asking me nicely in soothing voices and when that fails, doctors marching up to me with stern orders. I tell them all the same thing.

"I'm not leaving him."

Because, to my shame, that's what I did the night of the accident. The night of his fall. I thought I'd killed him. I thought I'd killed the brother I loved more than I loved myself. And what did I do? Did I stay to help? No, I fled like a fucking coward. It wasn't the consequences or the punishment. It was the fear of seeing my brother, always so alive and full of life, cold and soulless.

Like that alpha on the beach.

This time I'll be here. Here with him.

My brother is not going to die. Not on my watch. Not when he took that Goddamn bullet for me. A bullet that should have been mine.

When they wheel him through for surgery, I bark at the medical staff until someone hands me a gown and helps me scrub up.

I stand in that clinical operating theater and watch as they cut him open, as they slice a sharp scalpel through his skin, as they sink tweezers into the bloody wound, as they remove that bullet, as they toss it into a tray. It's the same color as our eyes. Gray.

I stare at it for several minutes, wanting to crush the useless thing in my hand, then turn back to watch as they stitch him back up.

"What are his chances?" I ask gruffly, my voice seeming to come from somewhere other than my own mouth. He's lost a lot of blood, although by some miracle of the gods, that bullet missed his heart and his lungs.

"He's going to be all right," the doctor says, as he strips off his rubber gloves, leaving his junior to finish the stitching. "He's an alpha after all. It takes a lot to kill you." A knife to the head will do it. "Your brother will be on the mend soon enough. We're going to transfer him to recovery now. Why don't you go grab a coffee?" he says, patting my shoulder as he passes me.

I shake my head.

I ought to check in with the rest of my pack. They are somewhere in the hospital too. Silver insisted they get Bea checked out. I know they'll be desperate for an update on Axel, but I can't leave him, not yet.

They wheel him out to the recovery bays, where other patients lie lined up, their faces obscured by oxygen masks, various machines beeping and blinking around them.

I take a seat by his side, and like Bea did earlier in the boat, I take his hand in my own.

Even our hands are alike. Same thick long fingers. On his middle finger he wears my dad's ring. Plain gold. He liked fine things, our dad, but he was never flashy. I trace my fingers over the metal, smooth to the touch.

"I love you, Axel," I say.

I've never said those words to him before, although I've always felt them, deep in my heart.

"I love you so fucking much."

His eyelids flutter and slowly open. His pupils swoop in and out of focus and I can see pain drawn out across his face. His brow creases and he squeezes my hand.

I know what it means. I know what he's telling me.

He loves me too.

It only takes a few hours for the doctors to decide that Axel's stable enough to transfer to the ward. He's still sleeping so I kiss the motherfucker on his forehead and head off in search of my pack.

When I check, I have about five thousand missed calls and text messages on my phone. I feel bad. I also hope the emotions I've been projecting through our bond is enough to reassure them.

I find the elevator and follow the signs through hallways

until I find room 3b on the third floor. It's not in the omega clinic. I hear that's been temporarily closed down.

When I open the door, Bea's sitting up in a hospital bed, looking as beautiful as ever, even dressed in the hideous hospital gown which looks like it might have been fashioned out of paper towels. The others are gathered around her on chairs. All except Nate, who's balanced on the window sill.

"Angel!" Bea says, scrabbling to jump down from the bed. Three pairs of arms hold her down.

"Resting, remember?" Silver tells her sternly.

"I was only going to give him a hug," she pouts.

"He can come to you."

And I do, only realizing I'm still covered in blood and sand and seawater when I've wrapped my arms around her lithe body and held her so tightly I can feel her heart beating against my chest.

"Omega," I murmur.

I can't believe I came so close to losing her. To losing him. To losing them both.

"How is he?" she whispers to me, her body shaking slightly in my arms.

"He's doing just fine, sweetheart. That old bastard's made of stern stuff and he is going to be okay." I release her, kissing her cheeks, her nose and her lips. "Well, actually, maybe even more goddamn grumpy than usual."

Hardy groans until Nate swings his leg and kicks the back of his chair.

"Hey, man, Axel's grumpiness is his most endearing feature."

Bea strokes her fingers over my cheek. There's blood and sand under her nails and I think I love her all the more for it. "It's not, Nate," she says to him while looking at me.

"Axel's most endearing feature is his love for this pack." I nod, blinking away the Goddamn water that swims in my eyes,

"He took that bullet for me," I whisper.

"Of course, he did," she says, resting her forehead against mine.

I close my eyes and breathe in her scent. Like the thickest, stickiest caramel on Earth.

"I'm so glad you're okay, Bea," I tell her, "okay and ..." I flick my eyes open, only just registering the change in her scent, "no longer in heat."

"Yes, no longer in heat."

"The doctor thinks the shock of what just happened has kicked her heat into the long grass," Connor says.

I heave a sigh of relief. Don't get me wrong, having our omega in heat is all I've been wishing for since I met this woman, but right now, with both Mom and Axel in hospital, this is a blessed relief.

"How do you feel?"

"I'm ay okay, Alpha. Don't you worry about me." The side of my mouth tugs up in a smile.

"Sweetheart, I'm going to be worrying about you for the rest of my days. That's my job. That's all our jobs. We want to keep you safe." I shake my head. "Shit, we've been doing a fucking awful job of that so far."

"I'm here now, aren't I?" she says. "I think you've done a good job. Personally."

Nate scoffs, kicking his boots against the wall beneath the window sill and scuffing the paint work.

"Now, we know who was behind Bea's abduction," Silver says with confidence. "Now Micko's dead, keeping you safe is going to be a hell of a lot easier."

Bea's gaze flicks to him. "Won't they come after you for

revenge?" Her gaze floats over Silver's head to Nate at the window.

"You don't need to worry about me," Nate says casually.

"But I will," she says. "Just like you will worry about me, I will worry about you. That's what it's like being part of a family. That's what it's like," she hesitates, "being in love. You give your heart away, even though there are risks involved. Despite them. You know you might be left with heartbreak or devastation, but when you meet the people who were meant for you, you risk it all anyway, because, well, the rewards are worth it."

She's right. I'd happily endure the last decade of heartache all over again just for this shot of happiness with her.

"You love us?" Nate says with a big fuck off grin on his face and mischief in his eyes.

Bea's cheeks sizzle but she grins right back at him.

"Yes, I love you."

I tug her in close again. She's so precious, every bone in her body, every thought in her mind, every beat of her heart and every breath in her lungs.

"Fuck, I love you so much too, sweetheart," I murmur. I feel the surprise resonate through the bond with my pack-mates. I'm not always the most vocal when it comes to my emotions. But maybe that's something else I might change. "I love all you assholes too," I tell the others.

When I finally let Bea go, Silver rests his hand on her thigh. "You're right, sweetheart. There'll always be risks, obstacles, problems, in life. I don't think the Snakebites or Dr. Hannah are going to be one."

"Really?" she says skeptically.

"Yes, the whole clan is going to be in disarray with Micko dead."

"But that won't be forever. And when they're back up and running ..."

Silver shakes his head. "I may have tipped off my friends in the police that now might be the perfect time to escalate any live investigation they have going on the Snakebites. I wouldn't be surprised if they're all behind bars by tomorrow morning."

Bea sinks back against the cushions, obviously relieved at that piece of news.

Then her brow crinkles. "How about my blood?"

"Your blood?" Connor asks.

"That's why they were after me. For the hormones in my blood. They said they were special."

"That's why you smell so Goddamn good." Hardy leans forward and nibbles her shoulder.

"It's also why they were after me. They think it can be used in their research to convert betas to omegas."

"Fucking stupid," I mumble.

"Yes, but what if they're not the only people who want my blood?" The color in her cheeks drains.

"What do you mean, sweetheart?" Silver asks.

"Dr. Hannah mentioned an investor."

I glance at Silver who glances at Connor.

"I'll get on it," he tells us both.

"Sweetheart, I don't want you worrying about that. We'll get it sorted."

Her eyes flick between Silver and Connor and she giggles. "Yeah, I know you will." She shuffles deeper into the cushions, leaning back her head and closing her eyes. "I have the best pack," she sighs.

"Too damn right," Hardy says, licking his tongue around the shell of her ear and making her giggle.

I lean back myself, watching as our tiny omega attempts

to wrestle the largest of us alphas, trying her best to lick him back.

All the adrenaline, all the panic and heartache from earlier, seeps easily away, and all that's left is this humming sensation of contentment in my veins.

This is the way it should always have been.

37

Bea

One week later

I CAN'T SIT STILL. Every time I try, I end up fidgeting so much, I have to admit defeat, jump to my feet, and start pacing again.

It's partly this coming heat. It seems the shock that had it retreating was only a temporary reprieve and now it's returning with full force.

My skin is hot and sensitive to touch, my belly's cramping and there's an ache between my thighs which is becoming harder and harder to ignore.

But my heat isn't the only reason I'm feeling impatient. It's also the fact that today is the day that at long last they're releasing Axel from hospital.

My sixth alpha is coming home.

The separation has felt gut-wrenching and raw. Another clear signal to me – if I needed any more – that this pack is where I belong.

I wanted to go with Angel to pick him up from the hospital, but with my coming heat, my pack is taking no chances. Silver has had numerous new security features built into my aunt's condo as well as the new nest – this time one I helped design. Plus he also has half an army guarding the house.

The other half are escorting Angel to the hospital and back. No more pack abductions. Silver's not risking it, even if Angel insists he can handle things alone.

"You sure I can't eat you out?" Hardy says, eyeing me up from the other side of the room like I'm a freshly baked apple pie.

"No, we're waiting for Axel," I tell him, keeping my gaze firmly locked on the window, because I know if I peer his way, I'll be relenting quicker than you can say 'sit on my face'.

I shiver thinking about that. Turns out perching on top of one of my alpha's faces is one of my favorite places to hang out.

"Little bird," Nate purrs, and I shiver even harder, fresh slick gushing into the panties I'm wearing. Panties that are already thoroughly ruined.

"How much longer is it going to be?" I whine.

Angel's been communicating with Hardy and Silver through the bond but I'm still impatient. I want all of my pack. Every single member. Here. Now. With me. In my nest. Rutting and fucking and knotting me and ...

Another gush of slick.

I huff in irritation and snatch off my panties, throwing them to the ground.

Immediately, Hardy and Nate dive for the discarded pair like dogs fighting for a bone. Usually, I'd find the sight of them rolling around on the floor dumb – but in my current state I find it darn hot.

I sigh. Who am I kidding? I always find it hot. Especially when Hardy's dressed in a pair of gray sweater pants and nothing else, and Nate's growling in that panty-melting way he does.

"Can you please stop that?" I plead.

I rub my hands up and down my arms, my legs shaking. I think I'm going to combust.

Nate and Hardy freeze, both peering up at me from the floor.

"Whatever you want, baby girl," Hardy says, releasing his grip on Nate.

Nate sees his opportunity and snatches the panties from Hardy's hands, dragging his tongue through the gusset and then handing my underwear over to Hardy.

"We can share," he says.

That's one of the things that surprised me most about living with this pack for the last week.

I never really believed this many men could share this nicely. I thought there'd be sulking and quarrels, bickering and temper tantrums. But there's been none of that. It helps that all of them seem just as keen to watch me with their packmates as they do in actually taking part.

"They're here," Silver announces, scowling at Hardy and Nate as he strolls to the door, but swiping my panties from Hardy's grasp nonetheless, and pocketing them.

I rush to the door too, my alphas stepping to one side to let me pass.

Outside there's the crashing of waves, the ocean fierce

and violent today, and the ring of Silver's men. There's also Angel.

Angel and Axel.

His left arm rests in a sling and he winces slightly as he climbs out of the car. But when he sees me running towards him, all that vanishes from his face, replaced by a smile so wide so genuine, that ... *boom*.

"Alpha!" I cry, flinging my arms around his neck and pressing myself against his good side.

"Bea!" he says, wrapping that good arm around my waist and burying his face in my hair. "It's so good to be home."

"Home?" I say.

"Anywhere you are, is home, sweetheart." He takes a deep breath in and groans, his eyelids fluttering shut. "Fuck, you smell ..." His eyes snap open. "You're going into heat?"

"Pretty much already there," I say, whimpering a little as I lower back down onto the soles of my feet. The man smells pretty damn delicious himself. I want to lick him like Nate was just licking my underwear.

"Then what are you doing out here?" he asks, then lowers his voice to a growl, "dressed?"

"I've been making them wait. It's been driving them all mad. Them and me. But I wanted you here too."

"I'm not sure how much use I'm going to be to you, sweetheart." He lifts his bent arm, wincing a second time.

I shake my head. "I don't care about that. I just want you all here."

Finally, a heat with all my alphas. With all my mates.

"Then let's get you into that nest. Angel's been telling me all about it."

"It's not as fancy as the one at your family house."

"Does it have a bed?"

"Yes." I giggle.

"Can it fit all seven of us in?"

"Yes."

"Then it's going to do just fine."

He wraps his arm around my waist and I wrap mine around his and together we walk back inside the condo.

"Good to see you back, man," Connor says, slapping Axel on the shoulder.

Hardy and Silver do the same, but Nate comes in for a full hug, squeezing Axel so tight, I have to bat him away in case he damages my newly healed alpha.

"Missed you, man," he mutters before turning and bolting towards the nest.

"He's been unbearable without you around," Connor whispers.

"He has not!" I tell Axel, "I've been teaching him new recipes."

"Thank God," Axel says, "I'm bored to death of the same five meals."

I pinch him. "For that, Axel Stormgate, you're on washing up duty for a week."

"I can't, I only have one functioning arm." He smirks.

"Hmmm, don't worry I'll think of something else."

The door to the nest hangs open and we walk through.

It's not as fancy as the other nest. Somehow, though, I think I love this one even more. It's snug and ours, and through the windows I can see the ocean and hear the waves. The bed is big enough for our whole pack and takes up most of the space, leaving enough for a few armchairs, and a couch. Blankets and cushions are scattered throughout and strings of fairy lights hang about the ceiling.

What I like best about the place, though, is the way it smells. Of all my mates. Of me too. Intermingled, tangled together, complementing and enhancing. And now at last Axel's here too.

"It's beautiful, sweetheart," Axel says, kissing my temple.

And maybe it's all these heat hormones, but my little omega heart swells with pride.

"It'll look even more beautiful with our mate naked and spread out on the bed for us," Silver says gruffly.

I think I've been torturing my alphas long enough and now they've reached a breaking point.

They descend on me, tugging down zippers, ripping open buttons and pulling off clothes until I'm standing butt-naked in front of them.

The six of them stare at me, their gazes traveling achingly slowly down my body, eating up every inch of my skin with a hunger that burns in their eyes.

I shake, more slick sliding down my thighs and before I know what's happening someone is tossing me onto the bed and someone else has their head jammed between my thighs.

"Not fair," I screech, "you're all wearing clothes!"

"What's not fair," Connor says with a mouthful of my pussy, "is smelling this ripe and keeping us waiting this long."

"That was Axel's fault not mine," I whimper feebly but I can't argue any more because Nate claims my mouth and Hardy is tugging at my nipples. I guess it should feel overwhelming, being pleasured in so many places, by so many men, all at once. But overwhelming is just what I need right now. I want to be overtaken, consumed, and devoured by my alphas. I want to feel and pulse, slick and come. I don't want to think. I want to ride waves of sensation and emotion. I want to float in their scents, hang suspended by their ministrations.

I want to be completely and utterly undone.

"Drag her up onto her knees," Angel commands from somewhere in the dim room.

I'm pulled up and held in place.

For a moment, the hands, the mouths, the fingers, the tongues stop, as they readjust themselves on the bed, stripping off their clothes and positioning themselves around me.

"Alphas," I stutter, swaying, needing their touch to ground me, to stop me from floating away.

A cramp spikes in my gut and I close my eyes, waiting for the pain I know is coming. It doesn't. It's swept away, molded into pleasure instead, as Connor sucks on my clit, Hardy nibbles on my nipples and Nate ravishes my mouth. Angel grabs at my ass cheeks, holding them apart and lowering his mouth to my backside. He laps at my hole there and soon I'm moaning with pleasure. Moaning straight into Nate's waiting mouth, hearing my noises vibrate in his chest.

"Such a good girl," Angel says, sliding a slick-covered finger into my tight hole. Massaging me there, so that when Connor begins to flick his tongue at my sensitive nub I know I'm done for.

"Can you take me there?" Angel whispers in my ear, as he slides in another finger. We've been doing this all week. Stretching me here, gently, carefully adding one finger, then another and another. It's not an intrusion like it felt at first, not when I relax around his fingers and he whispers sweet nothings into my ear.

"Yes," I say. "Y-y-yes."

I want to take him. I want to be able to take two of my alphas at once. And this, this is the first step.

He glides his cock through my wet folds, until he's

coated in my slick, and then he's whispering in my ear. "Good girl, such a good girl."

I relax into his words, relax as Connor's flickering against my nub whips me away, and my alpha's cock pushes into my hole, deeper and deeper. I feel the pressure against my pussy too as it clenches and convulses, and soon my entire body does the same, Nate and Hardy's hands the only things keeping me from crumpling onto the bed.

When I float back down to earth, I find Nate cradling my chin, examining my face.

"Okay, little bird?"

"Hmmm," I say.

"Okay for Angel to move?"

"Yes," I say and kissing my neck, Angel slides carefully from me before pushing his way inside. I expect the friction to be too much, to be too strong. It isn't. It's anything but. Soon I'm begging him for more and his thrusts become harder, stronger, his hips pumping into mine.

The others are too busy watching us both now to be able to concentrate on me, instead their eyes are locked onto where I'm taking everything my alpha has to give me.

"Going to come now, little one," Angel grunts in my ear.

"Knot me," I tell him.

I feel him shake his head against my shoulder. "You're not ready for that, sweetness."

"Yes, I am. I'm ready for anything you can give me. All of you."

Axel and Silver groan from where they are watching from the sofa and I look over at them, capturing their gazes.

"Knot me, Angel," I tell him. "Knot me in the ass."

"Jesus fucking Christ!" Nate murmurs.

Angel's fingers sink into the flesh at my hip.

"Whatever you want, Omega. Whatever you want I'm

going to give to you. Every damn piece of me. Including my fucking knot and my fucking seed." He hisses the last word through his teeth, pumping into me once, twice, three times, the final time, pushing deep inside me with a groan so loud it shakes the bed.

I gasp as I feel that oh so familiar stretch. That stretch I go gaga for every time. That stretch I'll never ever stop wanting or needing.

I expect it to hurt, to sting. But I'm in heat now. The thing my body was designed to do. And I wasn't lying, I can take anything these men give me.

His knot expands, stretching me, but all I feel is bliss, floating, gliding, swooping through my body, my mind blanking, my vision dissolving away, those two pairs of eyes blurring into darkness.

When I come back to myself, I find I'm curled up in the bed, Angel locked behind me, the others stroking and petting my body.

"Fuck, baby girl," Hardy says, when he notices I'm awake. "Never expected you to ... fuck, you're amazing. Do you know that?"

I smile up at him, too sleepy and content to answer him.

Deep inside, though, I think that maybe, finally – after all those years of having my confidence, my self-belief, the love for myself eroded away – I'm beginning to truly believe it.

Bea Carsen, yeah, maybe she is, just a little, amazing.

I DON'T KNOW how long I sleep, but I'm woken by that aching need in my pussy. I blink awake and find five alphas passed out in the bed around me.

Five?

One's missing.

Pulling my arms and body out from under the heavy bodies that encase me, I sit up in the bed, peering around as my head spins and my pussy throbs.

"Axel?" I whisper.

"Right here sweetheart," he says from the couch. He's the only one of us clothed, still dressed in the pants and shirt he wore home from the hospital.

"What are you doing all the way over there?"

"You know over there is where I want to be but ..." he glances down sheepishly at his side.

"We can be gentle," I whisper, crawling on wobbly knees towards the end of the bed.

"The others are in rut, sweetheart, and I don't want to bust open these stitches. They're very nearly healed."

"You're not in rut?" I ask.

He closes his eyes and groans and I take it that he's damn well close, hanging onto any sanity by the skin of his teeth.

I drop down onto the floor and I hobble towards him, having to stop once to close my eyes and catch my breath as my head spins so fiercely, I'm sure I'm going to fall.

"Omega," Axel says right by my ear, catching my elbow, and steadying me.

I lean into him, burying my head beneath his chin, rubbing my body against his solid one and inhaling his scent.

"Alpha," I murmur.

"Come on, sweetheart, back into bed."

I growl, absolutely refusing to be separated from him.

"You're no good on your feet." He peers at me with obvious distress, caught in indecision about what to do.

I push him gently towards the sofa with a look I hope tells him how determined I am.

"Want you," I pant, and his eyes darken as he sinks back down onto the sofa and I crawl onto his lap, straddling his thighs.

We're back here again, just like we were in his car. Only now I'm not fighting anything, I'm no longer hesitating, I'm not harboring any doubts. I've never been so sure about anything in my life.

"Have me," he growls, "have every piece of me, Omega. Take it all."

I lock my gaze with his as I thread the buttons of his shirt through their holes and gently tug his arms out of the sleeves. His wound is covered in a bandage, taped to his skin and I bend down and kiss it, lingering there for a fraction of time.

"Thank you," I say.

"For what, sweetheart?" he says, his voice low and gruff now. He's losing his grip. He's falling into rut.

"For saving him. For saving Angel."

He hesitates. "I didn't do it for you, sweetheart." He strokes the pad of his thumb along my collar bone. "I didn't even do it for this pack, or Molly or my Mom." His eyes flick up to meet mine. "I did it for me."

"I know," I say, my hands stroking down his chest and over his abs to the waist of his pants. He shivers against my touch, his breathing becoming heavy as I undo his belt, lower the zipper and reach inside to free his cock.

It's warm in my hand, warm and velvety and hard as steel.

"I've waited so long for this," he whispers almost to himself, as I rise up on my knees and slam down hard on his cock.

We both groan and I fall forward onto him, biting his shoulder.

It feels too good, so good.

"I ... I ... I can't," I say, my body shuddering.

"You can, little Omega," he says as he wraps his good arm around my waist. "You can do anything you want."

He lifts my body and I slide up along his stiff cock, the friction lighting me up inside, forcing wild noises from my throat. Then he slams me back down. It's just as good the second time and I wail, definitely waking the other alphas in the room, probably waking our nearest neighbors several miles away.

"So beautiful," he moans as he finds a rhythm for us, lifting me up, and slamming me down.

There're murmurs of agreement from behind us, but I hardly notice. I'm locked in this moment with Axel. The rest of the world disappearing completely.

"I love you," he whispers, as we both become more and more frantic for the feeling of each other's bodies. "I've never felt this way about anyone before."

I come.

Loud and noisy, and he follows straight after, telling me over and over again how much he loves me, wants me, needs me.

I cling to him, his cock seated deep inside me, as his knot expands and he locks me in place. Then he's kissing me everywhere, my ear, my cheek, my mouth, my jaw, my neck, my shoulder.

"I love you too, Axel," I sigh, melting into a world of Axel Stormgate, his spring-rain scent and his endless kisses.

"Alex," he whispers, "my name is Alex." I rock back peering into his gray eyes.

"What?"

He strokes my cheek. "My name is Alex," he smiles, "but it was a name Angel couldn't pronounce as a kid. He mangled it all up. Used to call me Axel instead, and, well, the name kind of stuck."

I smile back at him. "Alex," I say, resting my forehead against his. "Alex."

38

Nate

I TANGLE my fingers in her hair and watch as our omega suckles on my cock.

I knew her heat would be fucking insane. But I never imagined it would be this good.

All she wants, all she begs for, is our cocks and our knots, our touch and our kisses.

There's none of the usual whinging and whining. None of the silly sulks or pissy attitude. She wants us as much as we want her, and together we're like something electric, sparking, fizzing, frenetic. So scorching hot we could burn the fucking world down if we chose.

"That's it, little bird," I croon, as she flicks her tongue against the ring in my cock, making me jerk on her tongue.

She moans, her eyes fluttering shut, as Angel fucks her from behind and Hardy licks at her clit from below.

It's filthy. Depraved. Probably illegal in some fucking parts of the world.

Fucking incredible.

I smile so wide my cheeks ache and the little phoenix can't help but smile back.

"Hey," I say in a mock stern tone, "back to sucking, little bird. I want to pump my seed straight down your throat and into your belly."

She harrumphs a little, but she loves the taste and the feel of me between her lips too much to argue. Soon enough, she's back to humming around my cock.

I tug her hair and she resumes her sucking.

Good fucking Omega.

I want to bite her.

Want to bite her so bad.

Sink my teeth in her neck and make her mine.

I fling back my head and howl at the ceiling, my grip in her hair growing tighter.

She moans loudly and this time I know she's coming. Her spine arching like a cat's, her skin blushing hot, her eyes rolling around in their sockets.

Fuck, I want to bite her even more.

I growl and bare my teeth and from somewhere in this warm room, I hear Axel's low voice.

"Nate," he warns.

"Fucking ... need ... to ... mate ... her," I hiss out through my teeth.

Hardy mutters a string of curse words from under her.

The omega sucks me hard, like my words are winding her higher.

It's so fucking good! It blows my fucking mind.

Ecstasy crackles from my balls all the way to the tip of

my nose and the ends of my toes. Shit, even my fucking earlobes hum.

I pump come into her mouth, watch as she gulps it all down.

Good little Omega. Good little bird. Good little pet.

"I want it too," she whimpers, as she wriggles her ass against Angel's expanding knot. "I want you to claim me, Alpha. All of you. I want all of you to claim me. Make me yours."

I cradle her face and drop down to kiss her hard on the mouth, tasting my seed on her tongue. Salty. Dense.

Erotic as hell.

I want her mouth to always taste of me.

I want to breed her. I want my seed in her cunt. Not wasted in her fucking mouth.

Shit!

My fingers stroke at her throat, over the place where her pulse jumps against my fingertips.

Going to do it.

Going to bite her.

Going to make this one mine.

"Nate!" Axel growls with such menace, my spine stiffens. "No!"

No?

I falter.

No?

I blink.

Can't do it.

Can't do it to her.

I stumble away. Shuffle backwards even as she mewls for me.

It isn't right.

She's in heat.

We need to talk about this first.

She needs to be sure.

I drag my hands through my hair, scraping my blunt nails against my scalp.

Try to drag myself back to some sort of sanity.

It's different. A different type of darkness that's struggling to bury me.

It's like being under water. But I can see the surface, see the sun above, can taste the air.

"Nate," Connor says, resting his hand on my shoulder. "All right?"

"She's just so ..."

"I know," he replies and I can see the restraint tested in his eyes.

As soon as this heat is over, we need a serious fucking conversation.

I peer back at the omega.

She's turning sleepy and floppy, just like she always does after we rock her world. Angel gathers her up in his arms and rolls the two of them down on the bed, Hardy lying down next to her, still licking his lips after feasting on her slick.

I watch, fucking captivated like I always am by my little bird, observing as sleep claims her. Her lips parting softly, her face mellowing.

Like a princess from some fairytale. Waiting for a prince – or six – to kiss her.

The red-hot need deep in my soul dampens.

It's not extinguished.

It never will be until she's ours.

"*Give it time,*" Axel whispers through the bond and I lay down on the bed too, reliving the way her lips curled around my cock as sleep engulfs me.

I FUCK her more times than I can count.

I watch the others fuck her too.

I lick her out.

She sucks me off.

I eat her ass.

She scrapes me with her nails.

I feast on her tits.

She bites my shoulder.

I lose track of time.

Light fades.

Light brightens.

The waves pound angrily against the shore one moment.

The next they whisper softly.

Somewhere among the piles of discarded clothes a wristwatch ticks.

Tick tock. Tick fucking tock.

I should be dog-tired. I should be exhausted.

I'm not. I've never felt more alive.

All the freaking rotten stuff I've done just to make myself feel? It's never come close to this.

Because afterwards, when the fire burned out and the darkness melted away, it left me drained. Beaten. Angry.

Rutting our omega through her heat makes me feel.

It makes me feel … elated.

Good.

Worthy.

I don't want it to end. I don't want it to ever end.

But time's a bitch.

And good things always do.

Soon her need fades, her temperature wanes and she can finally string a sentence together.

Angel fetches bottles of water and chocolate ice cream from the kitchen and we sprawl out over the bed and sofa, eating and drinking.

Our omega balances in Hardy's lap as he insists on spooning lumps of ice cream into her mouth and my own spoon rests untouched on my thigh as I watch her.

Could watch this one forever.

My bird.

My girl.

"What was your dress like, little bird?"

"My dress?" she asks, forehead crinkling as she licks her lips.

"Your wedding dress. The one that made you sad."

She looks at me, cocking her head to the side. "Why?"

I shrug. She wriggles closer to Hardy.

"Beautiful, I guess. It was a big puffy princess dress." She smiles and I nod. Then the smile falters. "But now that I come to think about it, I wanted something even more puffy, even bigger, but Karl didn't want me to wear one like that."

"I'll buy you all the puffy dresses you want," I tell her. "And slinky ones," I add. "And short ones." I pause. "And those ones with the slit right down the front." I lick my lips. "And those ones with no fucking back."

She laughs. "I'm going to own a lot of dresses."

"You are," Hardy says. "We're going to spoil you rotten, Bea."

"I think you've already done a very good job of spoiling me these last few days," she says, sighing with contentment. "You don't need to spoil me."

"We don't *need* to," Silver says. "But we *want* to. There's a difference."

"Fair enough," she rests her head on Hardy's shoulder, "just as long as you let me spoil you too."

"You can suck my cock anytime you want to, little bird."

She sighs a second time, like that is a very appealing idea.

I love this girl.

Shit, I love her.

"Love you, little bird," I say.

Her eyelids flutter as she gazes at me.

"I love you too," Hardy says, murmuring into her temple.

"Do you think you'd ever want to get married again?" Connor asks softly.

"Are you fucking proposing?" Hardy asks. "Because that is not the way to do it, man."

The tips of Connor's ears burn bright red. Something I haven't seen since high school.

"No, I'm not ... I mean I'd want to if ... but I was just ..."

Bea puts the dude out of his misery.

"I don't know. After what happened, I didn't think I'd ever want to date another man, let alone ever consider marriage again. But here I am living with not one, but six men," she laughs, "so maybe one day, yes, I'd like to get married. But," she says, and I sit forward on my seat sensing something important is coming, "I'd want to get bonded first. I mean, that's more important to me than marriage and weddings and all that stuff."

My heart pounds and even though I'm no longer in rut, I have that urgency again, that need to sink my teeth into her throat.

As I glance around my packmates, I can see that need shining in their eyes too, can hear the way Axel and Connor's hearts pound through the bond.

"When?" Axel asks, his voice a croak. "When would you want to do that, sweetheart?"

"Not now," she says, smiling at us all, "we've only been

dating officially for a couple of weeks. But soon, I want to do it soon."

Soon.

I flop back in my chair.

She wants to bond with this pack soon.

I grin.

That's good enough for me.

39

Silver

One month later

I squeeze Bea's hand as she hooks her arm through mine. I still can't believe I'm this fucking lucky. So fucking lucky, I get the most beautiful woman in the city, probably in the whole country, hanging on my arm. Sweetest, funniest and cleverest too. Her new employers are already talking about sponsoring her through a college degree. I'm hoping she'll accept. We've been offering to pay for her to go, but the little thing is just as stubborn as she is beautiful – she wants to do things her own way.

"I really don't want to do this," she mutters.

"It won't be for very long," I promise her for the tenth time this morning.

She pulls a face, but then I nudge her and she plasters on a pleasant smile. It's not particularly convincing. But then I can't blame her. It's going to take all my best powers of control to keep the look of disgust from my face.

"I can't believe they're actually agreeing to have lunch with us," she mutters, watching as Melody and the head of her new pack, Don Cleaver, walk side by side along the promenade and stop in front of the restaurant.

Melody's dressed in some designer outfit, so skin tight, I'm surprised she can breathe. Her purposely curled locks tumble around her shoulders and giant sunglasses block out most of her face.

It reeks of fakery. Pretending she doesn't want to be seen, when really it's all she wants. To be looked at and admired. To be honest, most people are looking her way, except her alpha. He hardly seems to register her presence. Maybe he's already discovered just how shallow his new omega is.

Good. The two deserve each other.

I'm really looking forward to ruining their day.

"And miss the chance to scoop some gossip she can spread like muck among her minion friends?" I whisper and Bea giggles.

Fuck, I love that noise. I'm not the best at making her laugh. I'm not Hardy with his easy jokes, or Connor with his quick wit, I'm definitely not Nate with his chaotic ways. But, fuck, I'm trying, because every time this woman smiles it lights me up like a furnace inside.

"I doubt she'll be spreading the details of this lunch," Bea says, with a sneaky look.

Melody reaches us first, greeting Bea with a squeal, gripping her shoulders and kissing the air by her cheek.

"So good to see you, Bess. I'm so sorry we couldn't stretch to have you at the wedding ceremony. But you know," she giggles, "it was all such a whirlwind and ended up being quite an intimate thing."

I hear she had three hundred guests at the wedding as well as photographers from each of the gossip magazines.

Next she turns her attention to me, locking her hands on my bicep and squeezing as she plants a wet and lingering kiss on my cheek, sucking in my scent. I catch Bea's eye over the omega's head and she's suppressing another of those giggles. Probably at the bewilderment dancing across my face. Isn't this woman meant to be newly bonded?

If my omega was fawning all over some other man, I'd be flinging her over my shoulder and taking her home for a spanking. Once again, Don barely notices. Instead his eyes are all over *my* omega. I shake off Melody's grip and step in front of Bea, holding out my hand for Don to shake. Then I wrap my arm firmly around my omega's waist and lead her to our table, making sure I secure the seat next to hers before Don can.

"So nice of you to invite us to lunch," Melody says, unfolding the napkin from the table and spreading it across her knees. "Although, I'd have loved an invitation to the place you're building on the beach, I hear it's quite spectacular."

"We're not building anything," Bea corrects her. There's no way Bea would allow that. "We're just remodeling a property we own there already." The condo her aunt has sold to us.

Melody ignores her, directing all her attention to me. "And still not bonded, huh? Yet rumor has it you're virtually living together."

"Not virtually. We are."

"Then what on earth are you waiting for?" she laughs.

She leans across the table, pretending to whisper to Bea. "Cold feet? Unsure?" She laughs again and leans back in her chair, placing her hand over Don's. "Because when you find the ones, you really have no cause to wait. The connection, you know," she holds her hand over her heart, like the woman actually owns one, "it's so strong, you just have to bond."

"Oh, it's strong," I say, resting my hand on Bea's shoulder and stroking over her throat with my thumb, the place I'm going to bite her one of these days, bite her and make her mine. "But there's no need to rush. I love this woman and we have all the time in the world."

Don frowns. There's about as many sparks between these two as there are between a damp match and a used flint box.

"You're really not proceeding with the development down on North Beach?" Don asks, opening a bottle of sparkling water and pouring himself a glass.

"No, we're not," I say, reaching for the bottle myself. "And we're not going to be selling it either, before you ask." We've had plenty of offers. We've said no to them all. I pour Bea a glass of water and then one for Melody too.

"Ahhh no," Don chuckles, "I've no interest in property."

"Don's focus is purely political," Melody chimes in. "Have you seen the polling data? He's definitely going to make Senator."

"Too damn right the amount of money my pack has spent on this campaign."

"And did you see the *Rockview Times*? They're dubbing him as a potential presidential candidate." Melody flicks her hair. I'm pretty certain her alpha paid for that article but I don't bother to correct her. "Can you imagine? Me as First

Lady." She smiles smugly at Bea like she just won a point in some game.

"I can't," Bea says.

Melody frowns, not quite following Bea's logic.

I pick up my menu and scan my eye down the list of options.

"I had an understanding that your focus on politics hadn't completely overtaken your focus on pharmaceuticals."

"Of course not," Don huffs, "we still have a business to run."

"Still researching new treatments?"

"Yes."

Melody flutters her eyelashes. "Cleaver Pharmaceuticals is investing in future cures for some of the world's most deadly diseases." She spiels off like she's memorized that little line of PR.

"Deadly diseases like being a beta?" I say casually.

"Being a beta?" Melody says, eyes flicking to her alpha who frowns at me.

"Is that some kind of joke, Silver?"

"No, not at all. I hear all kinds of organizations," I lean in on that last word, "are looking at ways to turn betas into omegas."

"Ridiculous," Don mutters, straightening his knife and fork.

"Really?" Bea says all innocently. "Melody, you've heard of such things, haven't you? I remember you telling me about it."

"Well," Melody shuffles on her seat, aware there's tension in the air but unclear why. Melody's always been wowed by the glamor and the money. She's never bothered to do her research. To look at what lies behind the facade.

"I've definitely heard rumors about drugs on the black market ... but that's probably rumors."

"It's not. I had a father hire me recently because some sick bastard was selling his daughter medication he promised would turn her into an omega."

"Gosh," Melody says with feigned astonishment, "how awful."

"It's just low-lifes," Don says, "low-lifes selling gullible young men and women magic beans. That's all."

"No, it's not," Bea says. "It's far more serious than that. Some people seem convinced those magic beans exist and they'll do anything to land their hands on them."

I reach for her leg under the table, squeezing her thigh.

"I'm sure you're right. People are always searching for ways to make themselves rich," Don turns in his seat, "now where's the waiter?"

"People like you," I say lowly, a threat in my voice.

Melody's mouth falls open a little. Her alpha, however, turns back around to me slowly.

"Are you accusing me of something here, Silver? Is this why you invited us to lunch because I won't stand for you flinging–"

"Yes, I'm accusing you. I'm accusing you of working with Micko Sondrio and his omega. I think you see big potential in this, but you knew making any legitimate progress would take years and years of slow, costly research. So, you went for the cheaper, quicker and morally repugnant route instead."

"This is nonsense! Can you hear yourself, Silver? Me, my pack, work with a man like Micko Sondrio? Head of the Snakebites. Are you insane? Has the presence of your omega scrambled your brains?"

"No, her presence has made me a very determined man."

It's made both me and Connor very determined. We've worked day and night to track down the Snakebite's investor. Neither of us were surprised when we discovered who it was.

I turn to Connor, sitting inconspicuously behind us, and nod. He swivels his chair and joins us at the table, removing the baseball cap he was wearing low over his face, and slamming a file down in front of Don.

"We have evidence. Evidence that links the two of you." Connor glances to Bea. "Evidence that shows you were aware of the plan to abduct our omega."

"Not just aware," I say, "you fucking well approved it, you piece of shit."

"You're lucky," Connor says quietly, "Nate hasn't found his way to you yet."

Don's eyes examine me and then Connor.

"What do you want?"

"Who says we want anything?" Connor says.

"If you didn't, you'd already have handed in your so-called evidence to the cops, and I'd be under arrest."

"Oh, you will be," Bea says, jerking her chin towards the entrance of the restaurant where a police detective flanked by several officers comes striding through, walking in our direction.

Don leaps to his feet, his chair toppling to the ground behind him. He swings his gaze desperately around the restaurant, then makes a sprint in the direction of the kitchen.

He doesn't make it two strides before Hardy and Nate, hiding at a table at the back of the restaurant, leap into his path and block his escape.

"Hi Don," Nate says cheerfully, spinning a butter knife in his hand.

Don gulps and obviously decides he'd be better off taking his chances with the cops. He backs away, hands in the air.

"I'm happy to come with you officers and help you with your investigation," he says loudly so all the restaurant can hear. "I'm sure I will be able to provide invaluable info–"

The officer nearest him doesn't wait for him to say more, he jerks Don's arms behind his back and cuffs him.

"Don Cleaver, you're under arrest."

Melody stumbles to her feet. "What? No? You can't do this? Do you know who we are?" she screeches, then noticing the many pairs of eyes on her, pats down her hair and perfects a concerned-wife look.

As the cops lead her husband from the restaurant, she spins around to retrieve her purse from the table.

"You will pay for this," she hisses at us.

"So lovely to see you, *Melanie*," Bea says with sarcasm, waving her fingers at her. "Such a shame we won't get to see each other so much from now on." Melody scowls at our omega like she's talking gobbledygook. "Oh," Bea says, blinking, "you'll be moving over to Hanobury, won't you? To be closer to the county jail and your pack."

Melody screeches, stamping her foot on the floor, then hurries after her alpha, holding her purse up to her face as people take photos on their phones.

Yeah, now she really doesn't want to be noticed.

We watch from the table as they're both ushered into police cars, and a feeling of satisfaction and relief radiates through my gut. I'm going to sleep a hell of a lot easier knowing that man and his pack are locked behind bars. I'd sleep even easier if Micko Sondrio's packmates – the two alphas and that omega – were there too. Unfortunately, while the cops did a good job of rounding up most of the Snakebite gang and smashing apart their criminal empire, those three got away. They've fled the city. With warrants out for their arrest and a sizable reward for their capture (courtesy of our pack), I'm guessing they've fled the country too. Most likely to Mexico. And though I don't think they'll ever return, we'll be keeping a very close watch just in case.

I wrap my arm around Bea's shoulders. I've made a vow to protect this woman and I intend to keep it.

Nate, Hardy, Axel and Angel join us at the table.

Axel still has his arm in a sling, but I think it's to encourage the omega to fuss over him, rather than needing the damn thing.

He's healed remarkably quickly. Something Hardy is convinced is to do with the presence of our fated mate.

I used to think all that guff was bullshit.

These days I'm finding I pay more and more attention to Hardy's fairytales.

"Well, that was fun." Bea grins. "I just wish Aunt Julia and Courtney had been here to see the look on Melody's face."

"It's all right, sweetheart," Angel tells her. "I took photos. Nearly cracked the lens of my phone!"

Bea tucks a piece of hair behind her ear and looks up at us all with mischief. "Would it be really crappy of me if I posted those photos on social media?"

"If you don't," Axel says, "I'm giving them to Molly, because I know she will."

Bea's smile grows wider. "You know, I always thought revenge would make me feel worse. Like when you try to treat a tummy ache with more food. But actually, I have to admit, that felt really, really good."

"Want to plan some revenge on that ex next, little bird?" Nate asks, still fidgeting with that butter knife. I shake my head and take a sip of my water.

"No, I already got my revenge on him," Bea says.

"You did?" Nate says, his face falling with disappointment.

"Yes, of course. I'm happy, aren't I? With six insanely hot men. That is all the revenge I need."

Angel adjusts his shirt collar. "Hot, huh? I'm feeling objectified here, sweetheart. Are you only with us for Hardy's abs and Axel's broody looks?"

"No," she says, "Nate's cock ring too."

I spit my water all over the tablecloth. This woman could hardly say the word pussy when we first met her. One month of living with us in our nest and her mouth has turned a hell of a lot more dirty.

I pat my mouth, staring at hers.

Oh, yeah, that mouth of hers has been up to all sorts of dirty things.

"Sweetheart," Axel says, "you're breaking my heart here."

"Poor baby," she says, laying her palms gently above his healed wound. "You know I love you for your other qualities too, right?"

"Like ..." I prompt.

Hey, we're only human, and maybe hearing our omega talking us up is a massive ego boost we can't resist.

"Hmmm," she teases. "Brave, smart, kind and ..."

"And?"

"And ... all mine."

"You bet, sweetheart," Axel says, nuzzling her neck, "all yours. You want us to show you just how much we're all yours?"

"I thought we were going to eat?" Hardy says, drooling over the menu.

"You can eat me," the omega purrs.

Hardy looks up from his menu. "Let's go," he says, and the seven of us jump up as one, striding out of the restaurant and back out into the sunshine, heading for my favorite place in the whole damn world. The beach, our nest, our own little piece of heaven.

EPILOGUE

Bea

One year later

"Ready?" Courtney asks me.

I peer out of the nest window towards the lawn. It's been cut, rolled and flowers planted all along the beds. Plus, Courtney and Molly spent yesterday hanging ivory and lilac ribbons in the branches of the great oak tree and the smaller beech. It looks like a bouquet exploded out there in the garden, but I love it. It's over the top and crazy. Just like our pack.

Want to find out just how crazy we can get? Nate whispers through the bond.

Out! I screech back. *You're not allowed to see the bride on the wedding day! It's bad luck!*

We can't see you, sweetheart, Axel chimes in. *But we're getting mighty impatient down here. Hurry up and come get hitched.*

It's been three months since we took the step to bond, since we made this pack of ours official that way.

It had been the first truly warm day since the winter, the heat lingering as the sun sunk and the full moon rose, and somehow Nate had convinced us all to go swimming in the ocean, the water glistening around us as silver as Axel and Angel's eyes. As we'd stumbled from the waves, wet, our skin tasting of salt, I'd known this was the moment. That there would never be a more perfect moment. So I'd told them "claim me" and in the moonlight, with sand between our toes and the sea crashing around our ankles, six alphas had held me, kissed me, caressed me, stroked my skin and whispered to me; and then each one had bitten at my neck, sinking strong alpha teeth through my skin and binding us together forever.

The connection had been instantaneous, like a light igniting in my mind. I could feel them with me. I could hear their voices. All of us connected in an infinite glittering circle of trust and love.

I thought the intrusion of six other people into my mind would take some getting used to. I thought the connection with six alphas would be overwhelming at first. It's been none of that. It's as if they were always meant to be in my head and I was meant to be in theirs.

My fingers stray to the scar marks where my shoulder meets my neck, and trace over the indents my alphas' teeth have left in my skin. I smile and Courtney rolls her eyes.

"You're doing it again, aren't you?"

"What?" I say innocently, turning to the mirror,

admiring the white lines of my scar proudly like they are the most dazzling diamond necklace.

"Talking to your alphas through the bond."

"Maybe," I say.

Courtney bumps her hip against mine. She's wearing a lilac dress that matches the flowers in the yard and brings out her eyes. Molly's wearing an identical one. I'm pretty certain both dresses were meant to be below the knee but somehow have miraculously shrunk to mid-thigh. Molly's been filling Courtney in about all the eligible bachelors invited here today. I suspect they conspired to hitch up their dresses together.

"You're so in love!" Courtney laughs. "If it was anyone else, I'd be green with jealousy and puking in the corner, but instead I'm so deliriously happy for you."

I grin back at her. "I am in love. Head over heels in love."

"And happy?" Courtney asks, resting her hands on my bare shoulders.

"I've never been this happy."

Everything has been falling into place. The trial of Don Cleaver and the alpha members of his pack finished several months back and all of them received lengthy sentences. Dr. Hannah and her two alphas were last seen in Columbia with no sign of ever returning and I'm now officially a college student, studying what I love the most. Then there are my six alphas ... My days are filled with more love and laughter than it seems fair for one person to possess.

"You deserve it, Bea. Not just because you've been through some seriously ugly shit, but because you are the loveliest person I know. I was beginning to believe that only the mean girls got their guys. But the fact that someone as lovely as you can find their happily-ever-after gives me hope."

"And me!" Molly pipes up from the corner where she's fiddling with the long blonde locks of her hair.

"Neither of you two need hope," I point out. "Both of you are gorgeous and amazing. Both of you have men swarming around you. Both of you are going to find your happily-ever-afters, too."

Molly snorts, adjusting the flower pinned above her ear. "I thought it was hard enough dating when I was stuck at home all the time, now my big brothers are around it's even harder. The last dates I had didn't make it past the front door. Axel scared them away."

"If they're that easily scared, they're not the pack for you." I'm pretty certain about that. My very-soon-to-be sister-in-law is going to need a pack as strong willed as she is, not a bunch of men she can run rings around. "Besides, no one's buying the whole dating act, Molly."

"What do you mean?" she asks innocently.

"I mean we all know it's a ruse for what's really going on in your love life."

Molly twists her head and peers at us over her shoulder. "Do two certain alphas know what's really going on in my love life?"

I shake my head. "Your secret's safe with me."

"They can see inside your head!" Molly says.

"I think they've learned to stay well-clear of the box marked 'Molly' after they stumbled upon your dildo advice stored away in my brain."

Molly smiles wickedly. "Serves them right."

"What *is* going on in Molly's love life?" Courtney asks.

Molly's smile grows smugger, and she twists back to the mirror without another word.

"Now I really want to know," Courtney whispers in my ear.

"Let's just say that the fact Axel and Angel would disapprove of what's going on in Molly's love life is half the appeal," I whisper back.

"I can hear you," Molly says, coming to join us, "and yes, it is."

I laugh as my two bridesmaids fiddle with my veil.

"So, are you ready?" Courtney asks me a second time.

I stand up straight in front of the mirror and stare at myself. Here I am all dressed up in yet another white dress, the sweetheart bodice smothered in crystals and the silky tulle skirt flaring out from my pinched waist and flowing out wide around my feet.

I didn't expect to be here again. I didn't think I'd ever want to stand at another altar. And barely a year since the last time I did this? No way.

But the illness that's been slowly claiming Mrs. Stormgate is whipping her away from us, and though she would never say, although she'd never want to put that kind of pressure on us, I know she would give anything to be here today, to witness her boys happy and tying the knot.

"Is this dress too much?" I ask, burying my hands in layers of skirt, a smile hovering on my lips.

"Yes!" Courtney and Molly say together.

"It's the most over-the-top wedding dress I've ever seen, and you look amazing in it!" Courtney says.

I wanted a dress that would blow that other one out of the water. This certainly does the job. No holding back. No expense spared. I love this dress nearly as much as I do my six alphas.

"Let's go then," I say.

Courtney hurries to the door and opens it wide. On the other side my mom and dad stand waiting. My dad's wearing a suit for the first time since the failed wedding and looks like he's hating every minute of it, but any trace of discomfort vanishes from his features as he takes me in.

He whistles and smiles wide. "I hope those men know just how lucky they are, Cupcake, because you are a damn knockout."

My mom rushes forward, grabbing my cheeks in her hands.

"Beautiful, you look beautiful."

"So do you, Mom."

"You both do," my dad says, carefully maneuvering around my dress to engulf us both into a hug. "And I'm very glad we're doing this again," he says, "not only because this time Bea's getting it right, but also because I get to see my girls all dressed up and looking fine for a second time."

"Second time lucky," Courtney jokes.

I'm too happy to give her the stink eye.

"It's just a shame we're not doing this in St Luke's," my mum sighs, pulling away, and adjusting the purse on her shoulder.

Mom wanted me to host the wedding back in Naw Creek – I suspect to show me and my seriously wealthy pack off to the town – but I vetoed that with a hard no. Angel suggested the beach and, though I was tempted, I wanted to do it here. I'm a Stormgate now and holding the wedding here, at their home, where their mom could be with us was the most important thing to me.

You're late! Silver says through the bond. *Everything okay up there?*

A bride is expected to be late. And I'm coming.

Relief, excitement and a jubilation so strong it whips my breath away floods the bond and my feet can't move fast enough.

I take my dad's arm on one side and my mom's on the

other and we set off. Down the staircase, through the house, out into the garden.

It's a beautiful day. A crispness hangs in the air and the distant sea is a dark emerald. Above the sun is milky white and there's not a cloud in the wide blue sky.

I inhale, blossom and grass flooding my senses plus the faintest hint of salt.

And them.

All six of them.

I'll never get enough of their scents, of the way my pulse quickens, and my blood warms every time I'm near them. Nor the way their scents blend together like they were never meant to be apart, like they were designed to be together. Designed perfectly for me. My alphas. My pack.

They stand in front of an arch of flowers, blooms twining and trailing in all directions above their heads, all looking more handsome than I've ever seen them. Even Nate, just as uncomfortable as my dad in his suit.

I smile at them. Six very large, very hot and very eager alphas smile back.

"Jeez," my dad whispers in my ear, "these men scare the bejeezus out of me, Cupcake. I think my chances are pretty slim if I ever needed to take them on, but if you have any doubts, any misgivings at all, I'm prepared to cause a distraction while you run for it."

I pinch his arm. "You know I have no doubts at all, Dad."

He squeezes my hand back. "*You* know I wouldn't let you do this again if I thought you did."

No doubts? Angel asks, his silver eyes more dazzling than ever.

None. Not one. None at all.

And, oh, I'm familiar with doubts. My head and my heart were brimming with them that day I waited for Karl at the altar. My heart and my head never stopped brimming with them when I made my escape to the city and all those new, crazy omega hormones only added about twenty billion new ones.

But not anymore. This feels more right than anything else I've done in my life.

Every day, I feel more certain, more positive, more secure in my knowledge that this is where I belong. With them. With my pack. Right here.

Damn sure you do, Hardy says. *Right here.*

Once upon a time, the love and belief I had for myself had been eroded away. I didn't believe I could have happiness like this. I didn't believe I deserved it.

Not anymore.

Smiling at the six men who have stolen my heart, surrounded by all the people I love most in the world, I step forward and grab my happily-ever-after with both my hands.

~

Molly's story is coming next!
Preorder *Pack Choices* now

Want to read more Bea and her pack?
Download their bonus scene from my website www.hannahhaze.com

Thank you so much for reading. If you enjoyed this book, please consider leaving a review or rating — it's a great help to indie authors like me!

ALSO BY HANNAH HAZE

More Soft and Steamy Omegaverse...

All available on Amazon and Kindle Unlimited.

Contemporary RH omegaverse

In With The Pack

In Deep - Rosie's story

In Trouble - Connie's story

In Knots - Alexa's story

In Doubt - Giorgie's story

In Control - Sophia's story

The Rockview Omegaverse

Pack Rivals Part I

Pack Rivals Part II

Pack Choices

Contemporary MF omegaverse series

The Alpha Rock Stars

The Rockstar's Omega

Rocked by the Alpha

Fourth Base with the Alpha

Contemporary MF omegaverse standalones

Oxford Heat

The Alpha Escort Agency

Omega's Forbidden Heat

Contemporary MF omegaverse novellas

The Omega Chase

Online Heat

Christmas Heat

Alien omegaverse MF romance series

The Alpha Prince of Astia

Alien Desire

Alien Passion

ABOUT THE AUTHOR

I'm a British romance author who loves writing soft and steamy omegaverse romances, sure to get your pulse racing and your heart fluttering. My couples are destined to find each other - and when they do, oh boy!

My other loves include long romantic walks in the countryside, undisturbed soaks in a hot bath and even hotter stories. I have one husband, three children and a very naughty cat. When I'm not writing stories, I'm thinking about stories, listening to stories, reading stories or dreaming about them. Come follow me!

Sign up to my newsletter:
www.hannahhaze.com/about

Join my readers' group:
www.facebook.com/groups/375024943829423/

Visit my website:
www.hannahhaze.com

Catch me on TikTok:
www.tiktok.com/@hannahhaze_author

ACKNOWLEDGMENTS

Firstly, a big thank you to my readers for trusting me with this story after that rather naughty cliff hanger (sorry, not sorry - I love a cliff hanger!). All your awesome comments, reviews and messages keep my creative pot well and truly filled and inspire me to keep at this old writing business.

Another big thank you to my team of beta readers: Alexis, Melissa, Lily and Sara. Your ideas for book two were super helpful and I'm so grateful that you tagged along with me on this journey.

Also a thank you to all the wonderful omegaverse and paranormal romance writers out there. I am so lucky to be part of such a supportive community. Long live the omegaverse!

As always, I cannot express how grateful I am to my Mr D and Stephy. Always cheering me on from the side lines and listening to me whitter on about my books. Thank you xx

Finally, lots of love to Deanna. So pleased you are feeling better.

ABOUT HANNAH'S OMEGAVERSE

I write soft and steamy omegaverse romances — stories that are on the sweeter side — mixing the sauciness of omegaverse dynamics with contemporary plots.

My omegaverse stories are set in a modern world just like ours, except people can be one of three kinds — Alphas, Betas and Omegas. Betas are just like you and I, but Alphas and Omegas are slightly different biologically. In my stories, the characters are often battling with their biological urges, needs and instincts, and trying to fit into a modern world which can be judgemental and sometimes prejudiced.

Alphas

Alphas are generally larger, stronger and more aggressive. Their instincts can make them domineering and controlling. Alpha males are also a little anatomically different where it counts the most. Yep, I'm talking the peen — at the base there is a knot which expands when an Alpha comes, locking him into his partner where they remain stuck together for a period of time. Biologically, this increases the chance of pregnancy. Some Alphas can control the expansion of their knot, others can't.

Omegas

Omegas are smaller and their instincts can make them more submissive — especially towards an Alpha. Only an Omega can 'take' an Alpha's knot. An Omega has regular heat cycles where they are especially fertile. During this period they become hot and horny and very uncomfortable unless they are fucked and knotted frequently by an Alpha.

Heats, ruts and bites

Similarly to menstrual cycles, the Omegas in my world have differing heat cycles. Some have very regular heats, some have them less often, and others control or suppress them with medication. A heat typically lasts three or four days. When an Omega falls into a heat, their scent alters and they become especially alluring to any Alpha close by.

An Omega in heat can drive an Alpha into rut. An Alpha in rut isn't hindered by the usual biological restraints that your average guy is. I'm talking about permanent erections, no recovery, and the ability to come multiple times! (Sounds like fun, huh?)

Both Omegas and Alphas have glands at the back of their necks, the source of their scents. These glands are especially sensitive when the Omega or Alpha is turned on. Biting this gland is known as claiming and binds the pair together, often irreversibly. It also leaves a scar and changes the Alpha or Omega's scent which signals to others that they are 'taken'. During a heat, when an Omega is at the mercy of their biological urges, an Omega can often beg for an Alpha to 'claim' or bite them.

Scents, blockers and suppressants

Both Omegas and Alphas have heightened senses of smells and distinctive scents. An Alpha and Omega can recognise another Alpha or Omega by their scent alone, often over great distances. Their scents can also signal how they're feeling — especially when they are aroused or aggravated. Omegas and Alphas can mask their scents using blockers. They can also try to quell their Alpha and Omega instincts with the use of suppressants — for example an Alpha might take an emergency suppressant to stop themselves responding to an Omega in heat.

Soft and steamy Omegaverse

In my world, Alphas and Omegas are rare and viewed as a source of fascination by Betas. Alphas are often struggling to fit into a society where aggression and violence isn't tolerated, and Omegas are torn between their desire to be independent and their instinct to be controlled. It is often true love and the perfect partner that allows them to find the balance, acceptance and happiness they need and deserve. Happily ever afters guaranteed!

Printed in Great Britain
by Amazon